SO
IT IS

LIAM MURRAY BELL

Myriad Editions

Published in 2012 by
Myriad Editions
59 Lansdowne Place
Brighton BN3 1FL

www.MyriadEditions.com

1 3 5 7 9 10 8 6 4 2

A CIP catalogue record for this book is available from the
British Library.

ISBN: 978-1-908434-14-2

Printed on FSC-accredited paper by
CPI Group (UK) Ltd, Croydon, CR0 4YY

In memory of A.M.

Book One

1

I wait for Whitey in the Regal Bar, sipping at a tonic water. Typical Loyalist hole, the Regal is, with portraits of the Queen and Norman Whiteside side by side on the walls. Usual crowd in too: stubbled heads, rolled necks, beer guts, tattoos. It takes two hours for Whitey to arrive, with his friends, and take the corner table. They're all nudges and winks, seeing the ride at the bar with the short skirt. He's not sure whether to take it serious or treat it all as a great geg.

'Can I buy you your next one?' he asks, as he approaches the bar.

'Would you be having one with me?' turning to him then so as my knees brush against him. He nods and we go to a table. Around the corner, out of sight. I play with his hair and pluck his shirt away from the nape of his neck. He has a tattoo there: a single screw. Inked so as you can see the detail of the thread. I ask him about it, even though I know rightly. His dad was a prison guard, died three years ago, in '93. I ask him about his job, even though I know that too. He's an RUC recruit, fresh out of school. I've done my homework. He can tell me nothing that I haven't already found out. I've scouted out the whole area. A man walking about around here with a sports bag over his shoulder would be pulled to the side. Not me, though. A woman's inconspicuous. Even months after, when someone lands up in hospital, they never suspect the ginger-haired girl who sells jewellery door to door. Why would they? For five

3

months I've been calling at Whitey's house, selling his mother earrings and necklaces. His photo sits on her mantel beside a cracked Charles and Diana wedding plate. I listen to her proud stories of her son. Over tea. Terrible thing, a mother's love.

'Get that pint down you and we'll get you a real drink, eh?' I says to him. Then I swallow the rest of my own. Leaning over I press my lips against his. Count the seconds – one, two, three. He'll be my third. Only two I've done before this one. Two in just under two years. Plenty of time between. Healing time.

Whitey's perfect. Eager enough that he'll not think twice before, green enough that he'll think twice about telling anyone after. As I stand up, I lift my handbag and the empty miniature tonic bottle.

'Wait there a minute,' I say, and make my way to the ladies'.

Aoife's mammy started to have problems with her mouth in the weeks after Eamonn Kelly was shot by the Brits. It started as a tingle, she told the doctor, like a cold sore forming at the corner of her lip, then it began to scour at her gums as though she was teething. It was when it started to burn, though, like taking a gulp of scalding tea and swilling it around... when it began to feel like the inside of her mouth and throat were nothing more than a raw and bleeding flesh wound... it was only then that Cathy Brennan phoned for the doctor.

In those weeks, as the pain intensified, she'd call Aoife or Damien over to her with a wee wave of the hand and reach into her apron pocket for a five-pence piece. Tucking it into Aoife's school pinafore or into the torn remnants of Damien's shirt pocket, she'd send one or the other scampering down the street to McGrath's on the corner to buy an ice-pop. All different colours, they were. Aoife liked the purple ones best, while Damien liked the green. Neither of them would ever even think to buy the orange ones. They would race home and give it to their mammy, who would clamp it unopened between her thin lips. Lengthways, like the flutes played during the

Twelfth parades. She would keep it there, between closed lips and beneath closed eyes, until all the white frost had melted and the inside of it had turned to brightly coloured juice. Then, opening her eyes and letting out a wee sigh, Aoife's mammy would lift it away from her mouth, snip the end of the plastic with the kitchen scissors and hand it to whichever of her children had run the message. Give it to them so as they could squeeze at the sugary slush with their fingers and suck on the end of it like a babby.

'How come Mammy needs ice?' Aoife asked her daddy.

'Her mouth burns her, love.'

'Why?'

'It's psychoso… ' Shay Brennan lifted his daughter onto his knee, clearing his throat as he did so. 'It's all in her mind.'

'So her mind's burning her, then?' Aoife paused, waiting for her daddy's nod. 'Why?'

'It's what happens, wee girl,' he whispered, 'when you go touting to the peelers.'

'Is that right?' Aoife asked.

'Not a word of a lie. It's what happens when you feel guilty about turning on your friends and neighbours.'

Eamonn Kelly had been a neighbour of the Brennans for as long as Aoife, with all of her eleven years and ten months on this earth, could remember, but as far as she knew he'd never been a friend to either her mammy or her daddy. In fact, she'd have sworn by all that was good and holy that she'd heard her daddy talking of Eamonn as 'nothing more than Provo scum' at Mass one Sunday when he was having the craic with Gerry from down the way.

Still, it had fair shook her mammy when the Army raided the house, two doors down, where Eamonn was living. Aoife had seen it as well, even though Cathy had pulled her daughter's head in against her chest and kept it there with a firm hand. By twisting her neck a wee bit, Aoife had managed to squint out and see the whole thing. She'd seen the soldiers shouldering in the door without so much as a knock, even though Sister Beatrice at school said it was rude not to. She'd seen Eamonn squeezing out of the upstairs window then, as the soldiers crashed and shouted inside, and jumping from the sill – feet-first like Hong Kong Phooey – onto the lawn below. She'd seen him landing, with his right leg part-buckled beneath him, and then springing up and hobbling out the garden gate. She'd seen the Saracen then, from further down the street, speeding down towards Eamonn and she'd heard the shout of 'Get your hands up, you bastard!' She'd seen him limp on for a pace with his gacky half-run, and then heard the shot. Then she'd felt her mammy flinch as Eamonn crumpled to the ground.

'Did you like Eamonn, then, Daddy?' Aoife asked.

'Ach – ' he bounced his knee beneath her, so that she felt as though she were on a juddering bus ' – it's not that I liked him, love, but he was a member of this community, is all.'

Aoife paused at that, her arm up around his shoulder and her hand nestled in at his neck. She didn't look him in the eye, as unsure of her footing now as Eamonn had been when he'd left those two footprints – one deep and straight, the other shallow and slanted – in the tiny square lawn, two doors down.

'Joanne from school said...' she started. 'I tell a lie – Joanne's brother said to her, and she says to me, that Eamonn was making bombs in that house.'

Her daddy shrugged. Aoife felt it up the length of her arm.

'If he was making bombs, though,' she continued, her thoughts stumbling on ahead of her, 'is it not right for Mammy to be telling on him?'

Another shrug and a settling of the bouncing knee. 'There were other people she could've talked to, Aoife,' her daddy said, 'if she had worries.'

'What if the bombs had blown up, but?'

'Eamonn was being careful, love.'

'What if – '

'I'll tell you this.' Her daddy lifted her down. 'These houses we've got, all in a row, they're near enough bomb-proof, so they are. Remember what your mammy told you, when you

6

were wee, about them windows – triple-glazed. As long as you're under this roof, you'll be protected rightly, OK?'

Aoife nodded.

'Besides, a wee girl like you shouldn't be concerning herself with bombs or any of that there.' He smiled. 'You and your mammy both, you're too fond of the gossip.'

Aoife's mammy hadn't even said that much. It wasn't like she'd come out and gone, 'That Kelly lad on the other side of Sinead is making bombs for the IRA.' If she'd said that, then there'd have been cause for all the ructions that had taken place since. Instead, all she'd said was that there was a powerful smell coming out of Eamonn's house sometimes and that the windows, from time to time, did steam up like the wee window in the kitchen did when the dishes were getting washed after dinner. That was all she said, Aoife's mammy, and every word of it the truth. Out on the doorstep, as the woman from the social came out from seeing young Sinead O'Brien and her two fatherless children. Aoife had been there, with her shoulder against the door-jamb, watching Damien as he plucked the black and orange striped caterpillars from the bush near the gate and set them down on the windowsill. He collected a brave amount of them, all slithering slowly across the sill and clambering over one another as though they'd a notion to make it to the other side before Damien's grubby fingers could scoop them up again.

Still, nine days later Eamonn Kelly was spread out across the concrete with his arms splayed out to the sides, as though he was trying to make a snow-angel and hadn't realised that it was springtime.

'She works for the Brits,' Aoife's daddy had said to her mammy. 'She's a Prod and she works for the Brits and she's from East Belfast. Come on to fuck, Cathy, you know that if you tell them the time of day they're liable to take the watch from your wrist.'

Aoife wasn't meant to hear this. She'd been sent upstairs to mind Damien after all the commotion had died down. She'd crept back down the stairs, though, because Damien's room faced the road. As she sat on his bed and read to him from his Roald Dahl book – about George stirring in a quart of brown gloss paint to change the medicine to the right colour – her eye kept being drawn to the bloodstain, out in the middle of the pavement outside. Further down the road, beside the peelers' meat wagon, was another patch of liquid. It was as slick as the blood, but darker and with a swirl of colour at its centre.

'That's it over and done with, though,' her daddy continued. 'Enough with the waterworks. You're not to be blamed for what that scumbag was up to, Cathy, so don't be beating yourself up over it.'

He'd looked up then, Aoife's daddy, and seen her standing in the doorway, staring beyond him at her mammy, who lurched to her feet and felt her way across to the sink, using the worktop as a handrail. Then she set the tap running and twisted her neck in beneath it, making a bucket of her mouth. As the water passed her lips, Aoife could have sworn she heard a sizzle, like the first rasher of bacon hitting a hot frying pan.

Whitey is stocious by the time we leave the Regal. Absolutely full. That's how I need them, though, so I've no complaints. I lead him down Conway Street. Past the UVF mural with two sub-machine-gun-wielding paramilitaries guarding plundered poetry written in black and gold:

Sneak home and pray you'll never know
The hell where youth and laughter go.

He follows me on down Fifth Street, not noticing that we've turned right and right again, not noticing that the flags on the tops of the lampposts are changing. Out onto the Falls Road. We've skirted right around the peaceline. Whitey seems happy enough, though. Like a dog following a scent, his eyes on me, his hands grabbing for me and, for the most part, missing. Leading him on, past the garden of remembrance. More words in black and gold, but no poetry to them. Lists of the Republican dead.

Whitey stops under the first mural of the Hunger Strikers and mumbles to himself. As though he's trying to memorise the quote painted on it. Unlikely he'll remember much of anything from the walk home. He'll remember the rest of the night, mind. Pain sobers you up quickly. I steer him to the right before the second mural, the one of Bobby Sands MP. Down Sevastopol Street, then Odessa. Doubling back on myself. It was Baldy who set me up with the place. A safe house. Number forty-eight. The house beside has woodchip across the windows, fly-posters plastered on the woodchip and weeds sprouting from the posters. I check the other side, Number fifty. All the lights are out. I don't want there to be kids in next door when Whitey sets to squealing. That sort of thing can leave a kid shook for life.

'Whitey, love –' I step in close, searching his acne-scarred face ' – are you going to be of any use to me?' I reach a hand down to check. Something stirs. I smile. 'Good lad.'

Aoife and Damien were about equal with the ice-pop runs, purple versus green, when the steady supply of five-pence pieces stopped. Aoife made it home first that day, near clattering into her mammy as she slid around the lino-corner into the kitchen. Her mammy was on her knees in front of the fridge. The butter and milk and all were spread out across the floor, giving her enough space to get her head right in. Aoife caught on to what was happening. Rushing forward, she clawed at her mammy's cardigan until her head came out of the fridge.

'What are you at, Aoife?' her mammy asked, a frown on her as though she'd caught Aoife at the biscuits before dinner.

'You're looking for a goose!' Aoife shouted.

'A goose?' The frown deepened. 'What're you on about?'

'It was how Big Gerry's sister committed sue-side.'

'Suicide.' The frown disappeared. 'She'd her head in the oven, love.'

'And she died, Mammy.'

'That she did, Aoife.' She was smiling now. 'But a fridge wouldn't do that to you, now.'

'Well, why did you have your head in there, then?'

'Because I'm burning up.'

'You wanting me to run for an ice-pop, then?'

'No, love.' Her mammy shook her head. 'I'll call for the doctor, maybe.'

Aoife's daddy had told her about Caoimhe McGreevy – Big Gerry's sister – one Saturday afternoon when he had the smell of drink on him. She'd had to wrinkle her nose against the whiskey breath. Caoimhe's husband had been put in Long Kesh prison for planting a bomb down near Newry somewhere, then Caoimhe got herself blocked on the gin and put her head in the oven so as she didn't have to live the life of a prisoner's wife.

'Why'd she put her head in the oven, though, Daddy?' Aoife had asked.

'Why?' Her daddy had thought for a moment, then chuckled. 'She needed to see if her goose was cooked.'

'Really?'

'Really.'

'And was it?'

'It was, and she passed on up to Heaven, love.'

'Can a goose do that to you, but?'

'If it's cooked, love, then it can. Only if it's cooked.'

The doctor came during the day when Aoife and Damien were out at school and gave Cathy Brennan a wee white tub of pills that had her name neatly typed across the side. Their daddy warned them not to be touching them, said they were only for mammies and that if Aoife or Damien ate one then they'd find themselves frozen stiff and still, unable to move even their arms and legs.

'Is that why Mammy takes them?' Aoife asked. 'Because she likes ice?'

'What d'you mean, Aoife?'

'Like, she says her mouth burns her, so are these pills to cool her down?'

'Aye, that's exactly it, so it is. Exactly.'

The pills certainly seemed to work for their mammy, anyway. In the late afternoon, Aoife and Damien would come home from school and run into the kitchen to find her by the sink, with her back to them and her hands plunged up to the wrist in the soapy water. For hours she'd stand, staring out of the wee steamed-up window, moving only to top up the basin from the hot tap every now and then. Aoife reached up to dip her finger in the water once, after it had just been drained and refilled, and it was scaldingly hot. Her mammy's hands stayed in there, though, getting all folded and wrinkly like her granny's skin. It seemed to Aoife that her mammy had real problems getting herself to the right temperature: before the pills she'd been roasted and was always trying to cool herself down, and after the pills she was baltic and was constantly trying to warm herself up.

The benefit of having their mammy spending the majority of her time at the sink was that Aoife and Damien found they had free rein. They'd sprint from room to room of the terraced house, playing at chases or hide-and-seek. Damien took to carrying the bow-and-quiver set that he'd been given for his seventh birthday wherever he went and firing the plastic arrows at anything that moved, whether that be the neighbourhood cats in the garden outside or Aoife as she made her way from her bedroom to the bathroom. After her mammy had been taking the pills for a few days, Aoife realised that she could reach up and take the biscuits from the cupboard beside the stove without being noticed. Their daddy was working on a garden out near Hillsborough and wasn't back at night until darkness had taken control of the streets outside. By the time he trudged in, Aoife and Damien were both tired out and would be sprawled out on the sofa in the living room, watching the telly and nibbling on biscuits. Their mammy would be in the kitchen, her hands deep in the warm water, until her husband put his dirt-stained hands on her hips and walked her, dripping, across to the dining table for dinner. She'd feed herself, and smile vacantly, but there was no conversation from her, and Aoife's daddy had to steer her away from the kitchen and up the stairs to the bathroom after they'd eaten to make sure that she filled the bath, rather than the sink, for her nightly wash.

The days slid by and the dishes piled up by the side of her mammy's misused dishwater. The mountain of clothes began to spill over the top of the laundry basket like a saucepan boiling over, and the floor around the telly became littered with biscuit wrappers and mugs of half-finished tea with floating islands of congealing milk in the centre of the brown liquid. Damien came in from school with a mucky blazer and it fell to Aoife to scrub at it with the nailbrush. The newspaper boy came knocking and she had to root through her mammy's pockets for enough change to pay him with. Her daddy dandered in with the smell of whiskey on him and asked her to wet the tea leaves and put the chip pan on for their dinner. It took all this, and more, for Aoife to grow scunnered of the new way of things.

On the second weekend, after putting on the wash, running out to McGrath's for the messages, taking the dirty dishes up the stairs to the bathroom sink and scrubbing at the tomato ketchup stain her daddy had left on the sofa after he came in blocked, Aoife stood in the doorway of the kitchen and picked up Damien's bow-and-quiver from where it lay on the worktop. Stretching out the string, she imagined aiming one of the plastic arrows at her mammy's back. She imagined pulling it back as far as it would go and then calling out in a loud voice, with an unfamiliar accent, 'Get your hands up, you bastard!' She could see her mammy's head twisting, then, to look over her shoulder as Eamonn had; could hear the *twang* from the taut string as it was released, a second noise coming just moments after the shout of warning; could see the arms lifting up, raising themselves as Eamonn's had, suds flying up and around, splattering the lino like blood against concrete.

Instead, she soundlessly set the bow down on the side and leant against the door-jamb to stare at her mammy's back. The shoulders of Cathy Brennan, either because the water had gone cold or because she had caught the arrow of her daughter's hatred, shuddered and then were still.

The place is a dive. They always are. Streaks of damp down the walls, single mattress by the radiator in the upstairs bedroom. Bare. With a bottle of whiskey beside it. Like I asked for. I lead Whitey over to the mattress, ease him down, tie his wrists to the radiator, and then clamber on top of him. Lifting the whiskey, I keep him drinking whilst I straddle him. The smell of the alcohol rises like antiseptic.

'You think I'm a ride, don't you?' I breathe, into his ear.

'Aw, Cass,' he mumbles, from between thickened lips. 'Aw, Cassie.'

'You ever killed a man, Whitey?' I ask. 'Or hurt him so as he'll never recover?'

He looks confused by that, shakes his head. I reach in underneath my skirt and tug my underwear to one side. I can feel the thing inside, shifting as I shift, moving as I move. Waiting, it is, impatiently. As I pull his fly down, he murmurs something about having a packet of rubbers in the pocket of his jeans. He tries to point with his bound hands.

'I've plenty of protection,' I say. Then I ease my body up, seeking the angle. There's a whistle and a wheeze coming from him now, he's fair fit to burst. Like a kettle near boiling point. With a blissful smile spread across his face. He's drunk as a lord, getting his hole. All is right in the world of Whitey. For now. Just a final movement of my hips, a final positioning, and then I'm ready. I grit my teeth and wait for his thrust. Always wait for the man, just for those few seconds of deadly anticipation.

A sudden, high-pitched screech of pain. He's squirming and twisting beneath me. I'm not for letting him go, though, not yet. Clamping my thighs, keeping him in. My own teeth set together with the agony of it. I close my eyes, grind down, and listen as the screams grow louder and sharper. I listen as the hurt and sorrow of it all penetrates through his whiskey-addled confusion. I'm for waiting until his cries crack, until the tears stream, until he's ready to plead.

2

Aoife wasn't worried when her daddy didn't come home. At least, not at first. She waited patiently for the bookie's shop at the far end of the street to pull its graffiti-scrawled shutters down. No sign of Shay Brennan. Then she watched the clock for closing time at the curry house, nine pm, and at the chip shop, ten pm. She sighed and watched the telly, right through until the wee hours of the morning when even the pubs that stuck a middle finger up to licensing laws and to security concerns would be kicking their staggering regulars out onto the streets of Belfast.

The telly had finished for the night, the national anthem at the close, then a screen of flickering grey static. With the worst swear that her twelve years of experience could come up with, Aoife rose from the sofa and made her way through to the kitchen. Her mammy stood staring out of the window, looking every inch the anxious wife awaiting her husband's return. Problem was, the window only looked out onto the back garden and the brick wall at the end of it. Nothing more than empty flowerbeds and a golden-yellow crisp packet caught on one of the spikes of the gate.

With a hand on the small of her mammy's back, Aoife guided her up the stairs to her bedroom, manoeuvred her fully dressed into the bed and tucked the sheets up and over the water-wrinkled hands. Even as she flicked off the light, leaving her mammy lying in the double bed, silent, still, wide-eyed and alone, Aoife wasn't worried. It wasn't unheard of, after all, for her daddy to spend the whole night out and about. Unwise perhaps, what with the boys in balaclavas tending to work the night shift, but not unheard of. It was just the first time that he'd done it since her mammy became chained to the sink. Chained to the sink and tuned to the moon.

The next morning, having been up half the night, Aoife found her eyelids leaden and her thoughts hazy. She couldn't concentrate in the English lesson, and chemistry ended with her nodding head coming perilously close to the blue flame of a Bunsen burner. It was only Joanne that kept her awake.

'What's with you?' Joanne gave her a sharp nudge with the point of her elbow during morning break. 'Hi, what's with you, Aoife? You've been away in your own wee world all day.'

Aoife shrugged. 'I'm just tired.'

'Why? What were you up to last night?' Joanne's eyes gleamed in anticipation of some scandal. 'Did you go round and see that neighbour of yours, that Ciáran Gilday one?'

Aoife shook her head.

'What, then?'

'My daddy pulled an all-nighter. Never came home.'

'So?'

'I waited up for him. I waited up for him and he never came back.'

'Why's that your problem?'

'He's my daddy.'

'Aye, but it's your mammy who should be up worrying, not you.'

Aoife shook her head, but kept silent. She'd not told anyone, not even Joanne, about the length of time her mammy took with the washing-up. She'd certainly not be telling anyone that her mammy hadn't noticed the absence of her dinner, much less her husband, the night before.

'Has he not done it before, Aoife?' Joanne asked. 'My daddy has.'

Aoife nodded. 'This time it's different, but.'

'Why's that? Are the peelers after him or something?'

'Wise up.'

It was different because her daddy had been supposed to bring the dinner along to them after a swift pint and a fiver bet on the four-fifty at Newmarket. The size of the dinner he brought back to them depended on the fortunes of the horse. If he was lucky then he'd either get them a curry each – with naan bread and poppadoms and all that there – or four cod suppers with a side of peas for those that wanted. If he was unlucky, it was just a portion of curry chip or a plain chip between two with no side orders. Aoife had been confident that they would end up eating a feast.

The gardening work had dried up for Shay in recent months. He still set off in the mornings to look for lawns to mow or flowerbeds to tend, but he was back at lunchtime to see that his wife took a bite to eat and, given that he'd be reminding her of the need to eat dinner in a few hours' time in any case, he tended to take the afternoon off and sit himself down at the kitchen table with the racing pages so as he could study the odds. As he said, that much research was bound to pay off eventually. It was a sure thing.

Aoife had given Damien two slices of bread with the contents of a bag of crisps between – cheese and onion ones from a yellow bag – to tide him over until their daddy got back. Just a wee snack, like her mammy used to give them, so as he wouldn't be hungry while he was running around outside with his friends. When Damien had come back in at around seven o'clock, though, and dinner still hadn't arrived, Aoife had been forced to give her brother a second crisp sandwich. She kept the two heels of the loaf for herself, but didn't eat them straight away because she could still sniff the promise of vinegar and taste the spice of the coming curry. Her daddy would be back, she decided, but it might be well after Damien's bedtime by the time he got in.

A couple of hours later, when she went in to kiss Damien goodnight, she heard his stomach rumbling beneath the covers.

Her own stomach answered in kind. Neither of them said a word, but as soon as Aoife got downstairs she ate away at the heels of the loaf.

I make my way down the fire escape and out the back lane. The runback. You don't want to allow time for the shock to flicker into rage. Like with Nigel, my second. I've no such problems with Whitey, though. He's a lamb. I've time to ease myself off and straighten my clothes. Time enough, even, to kiss him on the forehead, through the furrows and the sweat, and look him square in the eyes. So as he understands. He just sits there, though, looking down at the ruins of it all.

Baldy is waiting in his black taxi, meter off. Just a nod he gives me, no more, then we speed off. He knows that I'm not for talking. Bog roll on the back seat to soak up the blood. I wedge a fistful into my knickers, but it's a stopgap. By this stage, I'm needing to get the thing out of me. Baldy takes the long route round to the wash house, avoiding the city centre and Sandy Row. Force of habit, avoiding checkpoints and roadblocks that are no longer there.

There's a routine to this now, to what I do when I'm safe. No need for thinking, just go through the motions. First it's closing the door behind me and making sure it's locked tight. Then it's stripping down to bare skin. Next, scalding hot water into the bath, and disinfectant. Not much, mind, just a wee slug. I stand there, naked, waiting for the bath to fill. The thing inside shifts and stabs, stings and slits, scrapes and scours. As soon as the water is deep enough to cover my hips when I lie down, I climb in. It needs to be hot enough to near-blister the skin. Lowering myself in, I wait for the familiar agony of disinfectant against torn flesh.

Screwing my eyes shut, I wait for the pain to dull to a throbbing ache. Panting, short gasping breaths. Then I reach down. There's always some amount of swelling. It's tender as hell. If I go slowly, though, then I'll get it out. I always have before. The first time was a nightmare, worse than the deed itself, stabbing around like a surgeon with the shakes. I've gotten better at it, though. Nice and slow, so the edges don't snag. The water gets a faint red tint. Then one final pull and it bobs up, loose, to the surface of the water. The broken and jagged neck of a miniature tonic bottle.

'Listen,' Joanne said, wrapping an arm around her friend's shoulders, 'whenever my mammy's shattered after a night shift or that, she just has a cup of coffee. You can flavour it with milk and sugar and all so it doesn't taste stinking.'

Aoife wrinkled her nose. She'd never tasted coffee before; she'd always been given cups of tea or cocoa at home. Still, the prospect of something warm filling her belly until lunchtime was welcome. The only thing she'd been able to find for their breakfast had been a bag of out-of-date currants. A handful of them in the morning hadn't even made a dent in her hunger.

'Where would we get coffee from, but?' Aoife asked.

'Follow me,' Joanne replied, lifting her arm and taking Aoife by the hand instead. They made their way, on tiptoe, up the stairs at the back of the Convent. It was morning break and they weren't meant to be inside the building unless they had some special educational or spiritual reason for being there. Stealing coffee probably wouldn't count.

For a brief, sickening moment Aoife thought that Joanne was leading her to the staff room on the first floor. There would certainly be coffee, but there would also be more Fathers and Sisters than at Lourdes, and a fair few lay teachers too. If they tried to take the coffee from in there, and they were caught, they'd be put in detention for months. Either that or they'd be excommunicated. Aoife was on the verge of protesting, but then Joanne rounded the stairwell and went on skipping up the steps towards the second floor.

'Where are we going?' Aoife asked Joanne's back. There was no reply. 'I'm not sure I really need coffee, anyway – I'm quite awake now.' This was true. The adrenalin had wakened her up rightly.

'Be quiet, will you? And keep up,' Joanne hissed.

They crept through a fire door and into the quiet and dusty corridors of the science department. More than any other part of the school, besides the chapel itself, this wing of the building was cluttered with religious iconography. The priests had advised the nuns to place a few relics where they were most needed. There was a crucifix in the wall hollow by the first physics classroom, with the map of the solar system tacked at an angle beside it, and on the windowsill between the two biology classrooms was a statuette of the Virgin Mary, slightly chipped around the base. Pinned above the door of the second chemistry classroom was an image of St Jude. He had an expression of patiently borne pain on his face that the nuns attributed to his position as the patron saint of lost causes but which the girls thought was constipation.

Joanne and Aoife finally stopped beside the photograph of Pope John Paul II. Beside the door to the school's laboratory.

'The laboratory's off-limits, Joanne,' Aoife whispered.

'Is it?' Joanne feigned an expression of shock for a moment, all dropped jaw and widened eyes, and then stuck her tongue out of the side of her mouth. 'Just keep a lookout, will you?' she said.

'What if we get caught, but?'

'Who's going to catch us?' Joanne replied. 'All of them are down there in the staff room and, even if Extra Anchovies were to walk in on us, he'd not know what to do. He'd probably wind up apologising and leaving us to it.'

Without waiting for Aoife's answer, Joanne reached forward and turned the handle. Aoife shook her head, but didn't attempt to stop Joanne as she slipped into the room and pulled the door shut behind her.

Extra Anchovies was one of the few young men who worked in the Convent and one of very few who weren't celibate. He had a permanently haunted look about him, as his gaze flitted about the clusters of schoolgirls that surrounded him. Aoife had heard it told, by the older girls, that you could get near enough anything you wanted out of him if you just stepped in close and maybe brushed your hand up against his chest. That was what she'd heard, anyway.

His nickname had evolved naturally enough. First, he'd been branded with the simple if unoriginal Pizza Face, as a result of his acne. Then this had been changed to Anchovy because of the odd fishy smell that came off his lab coat. The stench was probably due to the chemicals he worked with. In any case, it had become such a strong smell that the girls had felt the need to upgrade his nickname from Anchovy to Extra Anchovies. It was only a matter of time before he became Extra Anchovies with Cheese.

'Here.' Joanne reappeared, holding a teaspoon heaped with a mound of instant coffee granules and a light dusting of sugar. 'This'll perk you right up.'

'I'm not eating it raw,' Aoife protested. 'What about the water?'

'You're the one that doesn't want to be caught.' Joanne spilt some of the coffee in her indignation. It scattered across the floor. 'I'm hardly going to stand there like a muppet waiting for the kettle to boil, am I?'

'I can't eat it raw, though.'

'It's a delicacy, so it is. Chocolate-covered coffee beans.'

'There's no chocolate, but.'

'Sugar-covered, then.' Joanne rolled her eyes and sighed. 'We'll go down to the bogs after and you can swirl it down with some water from the tap. Honest to God, I never had you down as Lady Muck, Aoife.'

Stung by this, Aoife took the spoon and gulped the granules down in one swallow, like medicine. Her face contorted itself into a grimace. 'Bloody hell,' she spat. 'That's rotten.'

'My mammy says only grown-ups like the taste.' Joanne took the spoon and tucked it into the pocket of her blazer. 'I've a fondness for it myself.'

The rest of that morning passed in a bit of a blur for Aoife. Her right leg set to jiggling uncontrollably beneath the desk and her left arm to twitching out across her workbook. Her fingers folded and refolded the corner of the page until its dog-ear became a concertina. At one point, during double maths, as the girls all sat quietly doing their sums, her leg became so energetic that her knee began to lift the table from the tiled floor. *Tap-tap-tap*. She didn't notice at first. *Tap-tap*. Then she felt the eyes of the entire class on her. *Tap*-silence.

Mrs Agnew advanced on her, with one eyebrow raised. Aoife had not been doing her maths – that much was obvious from the blank page in front of her. Instead, she'd been sitting there worrying. Not about her daddy, but about Damien. Her wee brother was quiet at the best of times, but he'd barely spoken a word the previous night. Just nods and shakes of the head. Even when she'd given him his two crisp sandwiches, he'd managed to eat away at them without making a single crunching noise. It was miraculous really, a freak of nature. Aoife's fear was that he'd react to his daddy's disappearance in the same way as her mammy had reacted to the death of Eamonn Kelly. True, wee Damien wasn't tall enough to reach the sink, but he could easily stand right there in the kitchen beside his mammy and stare, straight ahead, at the pipes whilst she stared out the window. Then where would Aoife be? A mute for a mammy, a mini-mute for a brother and a daddy who'd not been seen or heard of since he'd left to go and place a bet on the four-fifty at Newmarket.

After a stern telling-off, Aoife made her way towards the canteen for the long-anticipated lunch. She was looking forward to the dinner ladies' mince and potatoes, with the mince that formed itself into rock-hard balls like raw potatoes and the flaky potatoes that broke apart like mincemeat against your fork. The thought of it made her mouth water.

It seemed like the thought of it had made her nose run too. She wiped it away with the back of her hand and hurried on down the corridor. It was coming thick and fast, though. She looked down at the back of her hand and swore. The word that came out was worse than the one she'd used the night before. It was one of the words Ciáran and the other boys from the estate used loudly and often, but Aoife herself had never dared make use of it until that moment. Swerving across the streams of pupils in the hallway, she pushed her way into the toilet and hung her head over the sink. Two drops of blood fell and began to spread through the rivulets of water that the steadily dripping tap formed on the grey enamel of the basin. A second later another drop followed, then another and another, until her nose began dripping blood faster than the leaky tap dripped water.

With one hand holding her hair back in a ponytail and the other grasping at the smoke-thick air of the bathroom in a vain attempt to reach the paper towels, Aoife began worrying about her daddy. Maybe it was the sight of the blood that did it, or the hunger that gnawed at her stomach. It could even have been the sickening smell of cigarettes coming from the cubicles, or the frustration of knowing that she wasn't going to be getting any lunch because of the nosebleed. For whatever reason, Aoife began picturing her daddy lying in a ditch somewhere near the border, with a canvas bag over his head. Her daddy with his arm twisted behind him and his eyes glassy after an explosion on a country road. Her daddy lying unconscious in some back alley with his legs broken, bones jutting and blood pooling. Aoife had grown up with the news reports. She knew what happened. Normally it happened far away; normally it was something you heard about and wondered about late at night whenever you heard a dog barking or the distant popping of gunshots or the *thud-thud* of golf balls driven against the triple-glazed windows from the Loyalist estate on the other side of the train tracks. But who was to say that it hadn't happened to her daddy? The way it had happened to Eamonn Kelly.

A final image of her daddy limping on for a pace before crumpling to the pavement flashed across the bloodied basin.

Aoife blinked it away and then made a desperate lunge for the paper towels. She decided that she might as well try her hand at mitching: she'd stay off school just for that afternoon. After all, it was unlikely that her mammy would answer the phone if the Sisters did decide to call home.

They say you always remember your first time. For me, though, it all passed in a bit of a blur. Too much adrenalin. Too much vodka, maybe. I near enough blacked out by the time we got to the act itself.

Looking back, it was a poorly planned job carried out by a wee girl with more anger than sense. If something had gone wrong, that first time, I'd have been on my own. This was in the days before Baldy. It was just me and the broken glass back then. It wasn't until after Nigel, my second, that I felt the call for anything more. After Nigel I knew I needed protection.

Anyway, I forget the name of my first now. It's not important. I'll call him Billy for handiness' sake. They're all Billy at heart. I've met him in the city centre, as if by accident, outside the gates to the city hall, and I've struck up a conversation. The usual chat: good to be out shopping on a Saturday, shame about the weather, and would you look at them, your tattoos are gorgeous, so they are, Billy. A Loyalist man and proud of it: a Union Jack inked there on his forearm beside a limp-looking leopard and some faded writing that I might have taken offence at if I could have made it out. Being my first, I've not given it much thought beyond that. It's all about appearance at this stage. True, I have a dander around the streets where he lives, sell a bangle here and a pair of earrings there. It's the search through the computer at the library that seals it though. It's the article from back in '92, two years before, in the Newsletter, *that names our Billy as one of three Loyalists put away on six-month sentences for 'crimes of a sectarian nature'. That's enough for me. I'm ready to afford him the honour of being my first.*

They say you remember the wee things – the small details. For me, it's the shiver of revulsion that creeps through me as he touches my hand. It's the feeling of being watched, from all corners of the bluenose bar. It's the dread expectation that at any fucking moment I'll hear a cry of 'Taig!' and find myself being torn to shreds by many pairs of willing hands. It's the rush of excitement I get as I stand up, slide the glass tonic bottle into my handbag, and make my way to the ladies'. Most of all, though, it's locking the cubicle door, pulling the flush and bringing the edge of the bottle down against the cistern. It's the shattering glass showering onto the grimy floor like confetti, leaving the neck of the miniature bottle in my hand, with its newly angled edges glinting. Glinting the way a weapon should.

'Go you to the shop,' Aoife told Damien, once he got home, 'and get a tin of corned beef for our dinner and a couple of bars of chocolate for after.'

'Ciáran and them boys are waiting outside, but,' Damien protested.

'They'll have to do without you for a while.'

'That's not fair.' His fingers worked at the straps of his schoolbag. 'Where's my daddy?'

'He's away.'

'Away where?'

'Just away.'

'Can he not get the corned beef and that on his way back?'

Aoife stared her eight-year-old brother down. It was a hard enough task, because there were tears filling the corners of his eyes. She was in no mood to be questioned, though. Having made her way back from the Convent at lunchtime, she had spent the majority of the afternoon peeling spuds. As an Irishwoman, she felt peeling should have been second nature to her, but she seemed to have taken more skin from her knuckles than she had from the potatoes. With every fresh scrape and graze she cursed her daddy all the more bitterly.

25

'When's he coming back, Aoife?' Damien asked. She was on the verge of scolding him for that, but something stopped her. Wee Damien was a sensitive soul, beneath the bowl-cut and the layers of dirt he seemed to acquire throughout the course of the day. Besides, he still thought of his daddy as this giant of a man: Georgie Best and Elvis Presley rolled into one.

'Soon,' Aoife said, eventually, reaching down and smoothing Damien's hair. He squirmed away from her. 'Now you go and do as you're told, OK?'

Damien nodded. Aoife folded the loose change into his hand. She had found it by rooting through her mammy's purse, her fingers searching right down into the lining and coming up with lint and brown coins. She'd been wanting to get them a decent dinner, maybe a chicken pie from the butcher or something like that there. Even with the twenty-pence piece she'd found down the back of the sofa, though, it had been a mission to scrape up enough for the tin of corned beef and the chocolate bars.

'Aoife?' Damien looked back before opening the front door.

'What?'

'Why does my mammy never make our dinner any more?'

Aoife's mouth opened as if to speak, but she could think of nothing to say, nothing that she could tell her wee brother that wouldn't lead to another question – an unanswerable question. So, instead, she just lifted her hand and impatiently waved him on through the door, then she turned back to the patchily peeled potatoes. The door quietly clicked closed behind him.

Damien was into his fourth year of primary school by that stage. He'd never been the biggest child, but it was beginning to become all the more noticeable. All the boys that lived near them were either older or had taken growth spurts, and he was dwarfed by them. On the football field you'd think the sides were uneven, maybe eight on one team and seven on the other, then you'd see wee Damien emerging from the ruck of legs with the ball and realise that there were eight on each side. Or they'd be playing hurling and the ball would go flying right over his head, only to land perfectly in the hand of some taller boy standing just behind him.

The saving grace, as far as Aoife could tell, was that Damien was often in the company of Ciáran. Her wee brother's classmates would all happily take the mickey out of him for a bit of craic, but it was never going to go further because Ciáran was older and stronger than them all. True, Ciáran had to be seen to rip it out of wee Damien from time to time, but it was just to keep up appearances.

In any case, Damien seemed to take it all in his stride. In fact, Aoife had never known him to refuse when Ciáran called on him for a game of hurling or a kick of the football. He never refused and he always came in with his white teeth gleaming into a grin through the top-to-toe filth. No, it seemed to Aoife that he was as happy and healthy as an eight-year-old boy should be.

Although, she did worry about the way he chewed on his nails. It seemed like something that a lot of folk did – you even saw adults out and about on the streets of Belfast biting away at their nails as if they too had eaten only a handful of currants for their breakfast – but Damien took nail-biting to a whole new level. At all hours of the day, he'd have one finger or another in at his teeth and he'd be tearing strips off it until it was bare down to the quick. Often he'd contort his head this way and that, to near impossible angles, so as he could get at a loose shard.

Aoife didn't look in on him while he was sleeping, at night, but she was fairly certain that there'd be sleep-shredding going on, that he'd have his fingers in his mouth like a babby sooking on the thumb. Even whenever he came in from playing outside, when his hands were caked in a second skin of muck and God knew what else besides, he'd still set to eating away at his fingernails. Aoife's daddy, before he went missing, didn't pay it a blind bit of notice, maybe because his own fingers were that tobacco-stained that Damien's looked near-manicured by comparison. Whatever the reason, Aoife had to take it upon herself to, time after time, march wee Damien up the stairs and scrub away at his hands. It was a matter of hygiene, after all.

After a while, though, she became wile annoyed by the constant trudging up and down the stairs and she began just leading her wee brother into the kitchen, lifting him by the waist and letting him plunge his hands into the sink beside his mammy's hands. The water was there, after all, so it was as well to make use of it. It only took a brief dip in the scalding-hot water and his hands would come out clean enough that he could set to work on what remained of his nails.

'You didn't give me enough, Aoife,' Damien said accusingly, coming into the kitchen with a plastic bag swinging from his wrist. 'I was short.'

'I gave you the correct change.' Aoife frowned. 'Besides, there wasn't any more to give you – that was all I could get.'

'Twenty pence short.' Damien raised his right middle finger to his mouth and set his teeth to work. The plastic bag went up with his arm, rustling through the silence.

'Give it,' Aoife said, after a puzzled pause, snatching the bag from her brother and emptying the contents out onto the kitchen counter. There was one tin of corned beef and three Mars bars. She looked around at Damien. 'You bought three chocolate bars.'

Damien nodded. By taking the bag from him, Aoife had removed the finger from his mouth, but he had lost no time in replacing it with the thumb.

'What do we need three for?' Aoife said. 'Mammy won't want a bite of chocolate for her dinner, will you, Mammy?' Their mammy didn't turn from the sink, or give any indication that she'd even heard. Aoife sighed. There were times when she would answer a direct question and times when she wouldn't. She had her good days and bad days. 'She'll barely eat any of her dinner as it is, never mind a chocolate bar.'

'It's not for my mammy,' Damien replied.

'Who's it for, then?' Aoife asked, although she already knew the answer.

'It's for my daddy.'

'Daddy's not here, but.'

Damien shrugged.

'How did you get the money for the extra bar, then?'

'It was only twenty pence,' Damien whispered.

'Did you steal it?'

He shook his head.

'How did you pay for it, then, Damien?'

'Mary-Jo McBride from down the street lent it to me.'

'Are you serious?' Aoife was sore tempted to shake her wee brother then, to pick him up and rattle him from side to side as if he was a piggy-bank she was trying to get the last coin from, the last twenty-pence piece. If Mary-Jo McBride knew that the Brennans were scrounging money then soon enough everyone on the island of Ireland would know about it. 'What did you tell her, Damien Brennan?'

'I just says I was short.'

'Fuck sake,' Aoife hissed, then clamped a hand up and over her mouth. She looked down at Damien, who didn't seem put out one way or the other by the profanity, then she turned to see if her mammy had heard and was going to give her into trouble. No danger of that, though. 'Away into the living room, then,' Aoife said to her brother, 'and I'll get your dinner made.'

It took Aoife a long time to cook the dinner that night. Over the previous months she'd grown used to having a hand in the feeding of the family, but it was normally just setting the forks and plates out for the takeaway food, or opening a bag of lettuce so as they could have a salad along with the mince and onion pie that her daddy brought home, steaming hot, from the butcher. She'd never had to prepare a dinner from scratch.

There were the practical considerations, of course, like figuring out how to get the gas lit without using the lighter that her daddy carried in his pocket and working out how long to boil the potatoes for. In the end, after a search that included all the pockets of her mammy's assorted aprons, Aoife found a box of matches high on a shelf to the side of the cooker. She needed to climb up onto a stool to reach. It wasn't the only thing up on the shelf; there was also a ten-glass of gin, half-empty and lying on its side. Aoife left that where it was and set the large pan of water on to boil. Then she turned her mind to the timings. An hour seemed like a reasonable length of time to cook the potatoes for. If they were still hard after that, then she could always put them back on for another half-hour or so.

As the pan bubbled away, Aoife seated herself on the kitchen counter and slipped two pills in under her mammy's tongue. Back in the day, Cathy Brennan would have shouted at her daughter for sitting up on the counter and probably would have given Aoife a swift slap for trying to hold onto her nose and wait for her mouth to open so as the pills could be popped in.

By the time the three of them sat down at the table with a plate of grey-looking corned beef hash in front of them, it was already well past Damien's bedtime. At first Aoife and Damien both crammed the food into their mouths, slopping it upwards with their forks as quickly as they could. Aoife's appetite soon drained away, though. The potatoes sat in an ever-growing puddle of water and, even with a piled forkful of meat added, they tasted of nothing and slumped off the fork like the collapse of a soggy sandcastle. Cathy hadn't eaten more than a mouthful of it. Aoife looked across at Damien, but he was more interested in his nails than the half-filled plate in front of him. Standing up, and tucking two of the Mars bars into the pocket of her wee brother's trousers, Aoife sent him off to bed.

Damien wanted her to come up the stairs to tuck him in and share the extra chocolate bar, but she point-blank refused. At that moment, with the disappointment of the failed dinner producing tears that burned their way down her cheeks, she just wanted to be rid of him, so as she could actually do something about the situation they found themselves in. As her wee brother climbed the stairs, Aoife made her way out into the hallway, lifted the phone from its hook and listened to the dialling tone. She hesitated. Upstairs, the cold tap was turned on as Damien began brushing his teeth. Downstairs, the hot tap was turned on as her mammy refilled the sink. Aoife dialled.

I have my doubts. That first night, I have my doubts. All tooled up and with somewhere to go, but I've the butterflies. Maybe butterflies is wrong. The wee bastards zipping about in my stomach definitely have stingers on the end of them, so they do. Maybe it's wasps I have inside me. I've tried to drown them with vodka, but the drink just makes them more vicious. I'm near enough doubled over with the cramps and cringes of it.

We step outside the Rangers Supporters' Club and wait for the private taxi that Billy called for. He's gripping at my arse with one hand and whispering thickly in my ear.

When the taxi comes, I give the driver the address in Damascus Street and settle back into the seat. I found the deserted house the week before. The door swings loose on its hinges and there's a fierce smell of cat's piss, but it has four walls and a roof. I need nothing more. As the car speeds along Great Victoria Street, Billy sets to fumbling. He clasps and claws at the hem of my skirt. I'm ready to stop him if he reaches the knickers, if he gets close to discovering the surprise ahead of time, but he seems to have a fair amount of trouble getting the skirt to ride up. Not to worry, he'll get his dues soon enough. The bottle waits, carefully placed, its edges sharp and uneven.

If I'm not meant to do this, then there'll be a sign. Something will pull me up short of actually going through with it. Not that I'm expecting a blinding light or anything like that there. No, Jesus doesn't live in Belfast any more. He's much talked of, but never present. I'm just hoping for a minor car crash, a freak snowstorm, maybe a gentlemanly action from Billy. Come on to fuck, now. None of those is going to happen and I know it.

'You know what they should do?' I hiss, leaning in close as we pull up outside the house in Damascus Street. I'm wanting

to have one final check, just to make sure. 'They should let the army come down here, right into the Holylands, and allow them to just open up on the Fenian student scum that live here.'

Billy is quiet for a moment, then his eyes light up. He laughs and I smile. That's enough of a sign for me. The rough edges stab and sting at my inner thighs as I clamber out of the taxi, but the wasps have gone. In their place are butterflies. Proper flutters of excitement and anticipation. I slam the car door behind me and beckon him on.

To be fair to Auntie Eileen, it was gone nine o'clock when Aoife phoned and she did live ten minutes' walk away in the Short Strand. If she went out and about in those streets after dark, she said, then she'd be taking her life in her hands. She asked if Aoife had heard tell of the Shankill Butchers that operated back in the Seventies, a decade before, lifting people from the street if they thought the person was a Catholic. Aoife said she hadn't. That led to a pause and a lot of dark muttering, then her Auntie Eileen sighed down the phone. The force of it produced a static noise so loud and sustained that Aoife was forced to hold the phone at arm's length.

'I'm sorry, Auntie Eileen,' Aoife whispered, once she'd brought the phone back to her ear. 'I just don't know what else to do.'

'There are boys in this city, Aoife, who will lift anyone off the street. It doesn't matter if I'm on my way to help youse or not, love, they'll still lift me and you'll be seeing what they do to me on the news for years to come…' Auntie Eileen went silent at that, as though considering her new-found fame.

'I know,' Aoife said, though she couldn't help feeling that her auntie was being a wee bit dramatic. After all, Aoife had been out and about this late with her mammy or her daddy, on occasion, and had seen nothing more than deserted streets and overflowing pubs. 'Could you not get a taxi over?' she suggested, timidly.

'A taxi?' The words, spat at her, caused Aoife to hold the phone away from her ear again. By the time she felt confident enough to bring it back, her auntie was off on some other rant. '...what with your mammy being a vegetable and your daddy never feeding you vegetables, I won't be surprised if you do end up that way, you know.'

Aoife didn't know, but she didn't want to say. She wasn't wanting to find out what way her auntie was meaning, particularly. Besides, her auntie sounded so pleased with her point that Aoife didn't want to puncture the pride of it by admitting that she hadn't been listening.

'What age are you now, love?' Auntie Eileen asked.

'Twelve.'

'See?' Eileen paused, letting her point sink in. 'You're old enough to look after your brother for a night or two, just until your daddy gets back. Besides, your mammy is still there, isn't she? You'd be surprised, Aoife, how much of mothering is just instinct. With or without her pills, your mammy'll look after you both.'

'She's not even caught on to the fact that my daddy's gone, but.'

'If you just get a good night's sleep tonight and then – '

'It's OK,' Aoife said, wearily. 'I can go to the police tomorrow, maybe.'

'What?' This time the word was screeched and, as quickly as Aoife wrenched the phone away from her ear, it still echoed in her eardrum. She only heard snippets of what came next. Firstly a garbled 'What would the neighbours say?' then an indistinct combination of the words 'Republican', 'tradition' and 'turn in the grave'. Finally, she clearly heard, 'I'll be right over,' followed by a click and then silence.

Aoife frowned to herself as she put the phone back in its cradle and made her way back through to the kitchen. People were always saying that the peelers were a useless shower. Even Sister Assumpta up at the Convent had told the girls that if you wanted something sorted you were better approaching the 'community leaders' than the police, yet Aoife had only had to mention getting them involved and her auntie had been spurred into action.

Aoife decided that she'd spend the time before her auntie arrived productively, getting her mammy undressed and into bed. That way, when Eileen did arrive, she could just give Aoife enough money to be getting on with and then leave them to it. That was the plan, at least.

Putting an unresponsive adult to bed wasn't easy, though. The night before, Aoife had just folded her mammy in between the sheets, fully clothed, and flicked off the light switch. After all, it did no harm to sleep a night in the clothes you wore that day, no harm at all. Something told Aoife, though, that to put her mammy down to sleep for the second night in a row in the same woollen jumper and tartan-patterned skirt would be crossing some sort of line. It would be as neglectful as sending her wee brother off to bed with two chocolate bars and then not even going up to tuck him in.

Aoife was shy about undressing her mammy at first, politely asking her to lift one foot and then the other so as she could roll off the tights. Quickly, though, she lost patience with the lack of response and set to heaving limbs up and tugging this way and that at the fabric until it worked itself loose. The tights came off with only one tear and a couple of ladders, and the jumper slipped off without even a single hitch, but Aoife found it fair difficult to squeeze the skirt out from beneath the weight of her mammy. She could get it down as far as the hips, but then found that it wouldn't go any further. Her mammy just sat there. Aoife went round in front of her and tried to pull her up by the arm, but she didn't have the strength for it. When that failed, she knelt on the bed behind and tried to push her mammy upright with her shoulder. Cathy Brennan rocked forward. With a couple more of these pushes, and a hand quickly darting out to tug at the fabric of the skirt, Aoife managed to get it down to the knees, and then down to the ankles. She paused to survey her work: the tights lay on the carpet and the skirt was crumpled into a heap down around them. Aoife looked at the yellow T-shirt, tight enough to show the outline of the bra straps beneath, and the white knickers, waistband pulled high, that remained. She shrank away from the idea of removing the knickers. Not just because of the effort of it, either. It was partly the difficulty of it, and partly a fear that it would be at that moment, as Aoife pushed and clawed the underwear out from underneath her, that Cathy would choose to speak directly to Aoife for the first time in weeks. 'Aoife, love,' she'd say, with clear, unclouded eyes, as her daughter reddened and sprang upright from her task, 'what *are* you up to?'

So, Aoife set to work removing the yellow T-shirt instead. The neck of it caught beneath her mammy's chin. It stretched but didn't rip. Aoife left it where it was for the time being, a yellow balaclava with no eye- or mouth-holes, and tackled the bra instead. It took her quite a while. Bra clasps were fiddly things. Her mammy's breath sucked the yellow fabric of the T-shirt inwards as Aoife worked. Eventually the bra came free and Aoife looked down at her mammy's breasts, lying heavily against her ribs. The paleness of the skin seemed almost transparent in the half-light of the room, the nipples swollen shadows against the twin moons. Aoife hadn't seen her mammy's breasts since the regular glimpses of them back when Damien was breast-feeding. They were linked, in Aoife's mind, with her wee brother's puckered lips and tiny, grasping hands. In that darkened room, with her mammy hooded and her daddy gone, Aoife wanted nothing more than to bury her head against those breasts. She wanted to feel her mammy's hand come up, then, to caress her hair, to keep her steady and nestle her in closer.

The doorbell rang.

'What have you done to her?' her Auntie Eileen shrieked as she came into the bedroom and flicked on the light switch.

'I couldn't get her shirt off,' Aoife said, trailing behind her auntie into the room. She didn't look at her mammy, seated on the bed like a hostage, with her head covered and her feet bound. 'And then you rang the doorbell.'

'You're right, that was inconsiderate of me.' The loaded sarcasm of her auntie's voice at least pulled the whine of it down to a lower register. 'I should have waited outside, maybe,' she continued, 'until you were ready for me.'

'I'm only saying – ' Aoife began.

'So, the doorbell rang,' her auntie interrupted, 'and you just left her with her skirt round her ankles and her shirt up and over her face, did you? She looks like she's had a fight with the wardrobe and lost.'

Aoife felt a tear trickle down her cheek. She'd done her best.

'Don't be giving me the waterworks, either,' Eileen said, shaking her head and tugging the yellow T-shirt roughly up and over her sister's head. Cathy's eyes, blinking into the light, peered straight past her. 'I've had to come out at this hour because of your waster of a father, only to find a scene that should by rights be reported to Amnesty International. It should be me that's crying, love.'

'We've no food, or money to buy food – ' Aoife sniffed.

'One thing at a time. Your mammy's sitting here shivering and half-naked and all you can think of is your own stomach. Aoife, honest to God, you need to take care of others before you take care of yourself, you hear me?'

Aoife nodded.

'That father of yours – ' Eileen began.

'What's going on?' Damien's sleepy voice came from the doorway, interrupting the tirade before it could get started. He looked first at Aoife, then at his Auntie Eileen, then at the slumped pile of clothes, then at his mammy. His eyes, in stages, widened into wakefulness. 'What's going on?' he repeated.

'For God's sake!' Eileen sprang into action, trying to cover her sister's nakedness with her waving hands. Cathy chose this moment, though, to focus for the first time in weeks. Peering round the bulk of Auntie Eileen, she smiled down at Damien.

'Your pyjama top is on inside-out, love,' she said softly.

Aoife looked down at her brother. Right enough, having been left to his own devices at bedtime, he'd pulled his top on so as the stitching showed on the outside. Reaching across, Aoife flicked at the label with her index finger and grinned at her mammy. Cathy Brennan only had eyes for Damien, though.

'Aoife,' Eileen snapped. 'Take your wee brother in next door and get him to sleep.'

'But, my mammy – ' Aoife began.

'Do as you're told,' Eileen took her sister by the shoulders, pinned her to the mattress and reached down to tug her pants off her. 'Where are your mammy's pills?'

'Down by the kitchen sink,' Aoife replied. 'But she's already had her dosage for this evening.'

'A couple more'll do her no harm.'

'But – '

'Do as you're told,' Eileen repeated. 'And I'll get your mammy washed and to bed.'

Aoife nodded and steered Damien out of the bedroom with one hand resting on his shoulder and the other covering his eyes. She had to promise to stay with Damien until he fell asleep in order to get him to lie still and pull the sheets up over himself. So, she seated herself on the bed and began stroking his brow gently with her hand. It took him that long to fall asleep, it was a wonder her caressing hand hadn't worn a dent into his forehead in the meantime.

After a long while, though, his breathing grew shallow and his head lolled back on the pillow, away from her hand. Aoife stayed where she was for a few more minutes, partly wanting to make sure he was sound asleep and partly wanting to see if her theory about him gnawing on his nails in his sleep was true. It wasn't. At least, he didn't raise his hands from the mattress in the time she sat there watching. A couple of times his arm twitched upwards, as though his dreaming self was considering the possibility, but he always settled back down soon enough. Satisfied, Aoife quietly crept out of the room and out onto the landing. Closing the door behind her, she heard the low sound of conversation coming from downstairs. For a brief second, with a flicker of a smile, Aoife thought that the sound might be her mammy and her Auntie Eileen talking away to each other as they used to. There was only one voice, though. Leaning over the banister, Aoife strained to hear.

'As if I've nothing better to be doing,' the voice said. 'Place hasn't been cleaned in forever and there's a pan here looks like it's been used to boil up wallpaper paste. That sister of mine standing with her hands in dishwater the whole day and she's not even the sense to make use of it once in a while. Give me patience.' A pause, a clatter of pans. 'Oh, for fuck sake, what in God's name is this, now?'

Aoife drew back from the banister and made her way, on tiptoe, down the stairs. In the hallway, as softly as she could, she clicked the connecting door closed. She needn't have bothered being quiet, though, because her auntie had discovered some fresh hell in the kitchen and was complaining loudly about it. If she went on like that to an empty room, then it was as well for Aoife to make herself scarce for a while. Seating herself, cross-legged, on the ground, Aoife lifted the telephone from its hook and dialled.

'Hello?' Joanne's voice was thick with tiredness.

'Joanne,' Aoife whispered. 'It's me.'

'Aoife? Why are you calling? It's wile late, is it not?'

'I needed to speak to someone,' Aoife replied. 'My daddy's still missing.'

'Why call me, then? Should you not phone the police?' She paused to yawn. It slurred its way into her next question. 'Come to that, should your mammy not be calling the police?'

'My mammy's not well.' Aoife felt the tears welling in her eyes. 'She doesn't even know what day of the week it is. My Auntie Eileen's here, but she's just... she's just...' Her eyes brimmed and then overflowed.

'Calm yourself now,' Joanne sounded brighter now, the unexpected scandal wakening her. 'What are you thinking has happened to your daddy?'

'I'm not sure, Jo.'

'Is he…' Joanne's voice dropped. 'Is he connected?'

'Connected?'

'Is he one of the boys?'

Aoife frowned at the empty hallway.

Joanne sighed. 'Is he in the IRA?'

'My daddy?' Aoife smiled, just a wee curl at the corner of her mouth. It soon faded away. 'He's not involved in anything like that. Catch yourself on, Joanne, you've met my daddy.'

'OK, well,' Joanne considered. 'Could he have been lifted by accident?'

'What d'you mean?'

'Could he have been targeted by our boys in a case of mistaken identity, or could the peelers have thought he was involved and scooped him?' She paused. 'That can happen, you know.'

'Can it?'

'Of course.' Joanne stifled another yawn. 'What you really need to be worried about is him just getting caught in crossfire or something like that. There was one of my daddy's friends, a roofer out near Crossmaglen, who was up on a Church roof fixing some loose tiles when a bomb went off nearby. He lost his footing and fell to his death, so he did.'

'What would my daddy be doing on a roof, but?'

'I'm only saying, it's not only paramilitaries that – '

'My daddy'll be fine,' Aoife interrupted. 'Just fine.'

'That's what I'm saying,' Joanne replied. 'Even if the IRA were to pull him off the street, they'd soon realise their mistake. My mammy says they don't harm innocent folk, so long as they know ahead of time that the folk are innocent.'

'It's the other side I'm worried about,' Aoife brought her hand up to her mouth and began biting at a ragged edge of nail. 'Have you ever heard tell of the Shankill Butchers?'

'Course I have,' Joanne said. 'They're all either in jail or dead, but.'

'Aye, but what if – '

'Nothing like that will have happened, Aoife, I promise.'

'How can you know?'

Silence on the line. Aoife looked at her hands through tear-hazed eyes. She could hear the rumble of her Auntie Eileen's voice from the kitchen.

'I've got to go,' she whispered into the receiver. 'I'll see you tomorrow.'

Aoife sat upright on her bed, with her knees hugged up to her chest. Her eyes itched. There was no chance of sleep, but in the absence of it she had no idea what to do with herself. She silently wished that the city would distract her: a golf-ball to the window, a siren speeding along the street, the distant tutting of gunfire. All was quiet, though. All was quiet, that was, until her Auntie Eileen got on the phone.

Surprisingly, eavesdropping on Auntie Eileen wasn't that easy. Not because she was softly spoken, far from it, but because the speed of her gossiping rushed each and every word into the next. It sounded like a tin can being kicked along the pavement: the constant ringing-rattle of her voice, then a pause as she redialled, before the ringing-rattle started up again. Aoife crept out onto the landing and listened intently. She was only able to catch every second or third word, though.

First of all, Eileen called somebody called Martin. That conversation held a lot of questions about Aoife's daddy and laughter that seemed to be about something else. On the back of that call, her Auntie Eileen phoned Mary-Jo (presumably the same Mary-Jo as had given Damien twenty pence for a third chocolate bar earlier in the day) and told her how Shay Brennan had won over a hundred pounds the evening before on a long-shot in the four-fifty at Newmarket. It only took a moment to relay this information, but Auntie Eileen then seemed to feel the need to repeat it a good few times before finally hanging up on Mary-Jo and ringing through to someone whose name Aoife didn't quite catch. Maybe Aidan or Aaron. The information gleaned from that call warranted another call to Mary-Jo.

It took Aoife until the fourth retelling to gather all the details: Shay Brennan had taken his winnings and paid a local taxi-man to drive him up to Buncrana in County Donegal. He'd been singing 'The Hills of Donegal' fit to burst his lungs as he left the pub.

There were a couple of calls, after that, in which Auntie Eileen tried to find out the taxi-man's number. Eventually, she rang through to someone called Feargal who, as Eileen told Mary-Jo afterwards, had taken half the winnings as payment for the fare and left Aoife's daddy at a bed and breakfast on the outskirts of Buncrana the night before.

The third call that Eileen made to Mary-Jo that night was her second-to-last overall. All in all, she'd spent the best part of two hours on the phone. Aoife had spent the best part of two hours listening. Before she made the last call, Auntie Eileen paused to catch her breath. Aoife could hear the inhale-exhale from all the way up on the landing. It was as though her auntie was building herself up for the big finish, for the final swiping kick at the can.

After a minute or so, Aoife heard the phone being lifted again. There was a brief question asked by her auntie, then a tense silence. Aoife waited, breathlessly, until her auntie said, 'Shay Brennan, you bastard, is that you?'

Then she settled down comfortably on the rough carpet of the landing and drifted in and out of sleep through a ringing-rattle torrent of abuse from downstairs.

3

Ciáran's younger sister, wee Becky Gilday, was an awkward child. The growth spurt she took when she turned eleven gave her gawky long arms that hung down by her sides and shoulders that hunched over in a permanent shrug. Acne and a slight cast to her right eye soon followed. As soon as her body rid her of one reason for being self-conscious, another would appear, then another, then another. By the time she moved up to the Convent, a year behind Aoife, she was a shy and over-tall girl who chewed on the raw ends of her plaited hair with cold-sore-laden lips. Whenever the nuns spoke to the class of pestilence and plague they must have found it wile hard not to point Becky out as an example.

A group of young ones from the estate would congregate after school by the concrete playground at the end of the road and hang around until their tea was ready. Only up until it got dark, mind. If it was getting dark you got called inside, whether your food was ready or not. The boys would get the hurley sticks or the football out and try not to let on that they were showing off for the girls' benefit. The girls, for their part, would stand by the swings and natter away, trying not to let on that they were watching the boys. Becky, though, didn't speak. She'd just stand there staring down at the buckles on her shoes, chewing on her hair all the while. If you spoke directly at her, she'd murmur something, without looking up, and then carry right on with her chewing.

One day Aoife found herself in possession of a pack of chewing gum, which was contraband at the Convent and therefore highly sought-after. Ciárán had given it to her with a casual grin, having been off on a shoplifting operation with the rest of the boys. All the girls clamoured round Aoife for a stick, but she ignored them and slipped one into Becky's hand instead. Not from friendship, but from a wish to see if it might stop the wee girl from eating at her hair like a cow at the cud. All it achieved, though, was a mangled lump of the stuff working itself between the strands of Becky's hair as she absent-mindedly did what she was used to doing. They'd had to cut it out with a pair of kitchen scissors and Becky had walked around the Convent for a couple of days with the right plait an inch or two shorter than the left, until her mother noticed and took her to have it levelled off.

If truth be told, having Becky at the school was a nuisance for Aoife. As often as not, the younger girl was close enough at her heel, during break and lunchtime, to trip her up. She'd be dandering to the canteen with Joanne and Becky would suddenly appear at her side, offering up her tinfoiled package of sandwiches. Or a clutch of girls would be sneaking a fag out the back of the gym hall, where the overhanging roof sheltered them, and they'd spot Becky a few feet away, placing the end of her plait in her mouth and chewing on it as though it were a Cuban cigar. The wee girl was a second shadow, so she was.

Then the friendship bracelet phase began. A few weeks after Becky started at the school, she began to wordlessly hand a series of friendship bracelets to Aoife. Never less than three in a week, but sometimes as many as two or three in the one day. They weren't just made out of woven thread either, she was creative with the materials. On a certain Monday she'd offer a simple daisy chain, delicately pieced together while the rest of her class were playing camogie. She wouldn't sit at the side of the field to make it, either, but instead she'd sit herself down in the middle of the grass and fiddle with it as sticks flew over her head and the ball grazed her shoulder. Then on the Tuesday she'd slip a piece of elastic with multicoloured beads threaded onto it into the pocket of Aoife's coat. The elastic would be taken from the top of one of her socks, so that the sock kept on slipping down and landing her in trouble with a bare-ankle-spotting nun. Aoife would have a quiet word with her on the Tuesday after school, getting no more than a murmur and a nod in response, and the jewellery obsession would take the Wednesday off, but then Becky would be back on the Thursday with a simple woven offering, formed from strands frayed from the stage curtain in the assembly hall, followed on the Friday by neatly twisted shoelaces, pulled from the shoes of the Gaelic football girls as they played a match against another school.

'If she gave the bracelets to people other than you,' Joanne said to Aoife one lunchtime, through a haze of forbidden cigarette smoke and a mouthful of banned chewing gum, 'then she might have more hope of actually having a friend or two, you know.'

'Don't speak so loud,' Aoife hissed. Becky was at the corner of the gym hall, hopefully out of earshot. 'She'll hear you.'

'So? It's true, isn't it?' Joanne turned her back to Becky. 'How many of them d'you think you have, all in all?'

'The bracelets? Fifty or sixty, maybe.' Aoife tried to picture the drawer in her bedside table where they lay scattered, one on top of the other. 'Maybe more.'

'Jesus.' Joanne laughed and shook her head. 'Listen, you know what we could do?'

She waited for an answer, dragging on her cigarette.

'What?'

'We could sell them on to the younger girls. Ten or twenty pence a bracelet.'

'No, I couldn't do that to the wee girl.'

'It would keep us in fag money, but.'

Aoife shook her head.

'Listen – which is worse?' Joanne stubbed her cigarette out on the brick wall and put her arm across Aoife's shoulders.

'Stealing a coin here and there from your mammy's handbag so as you can buy fags, or setting up a wee business to turn a profit?'

'Becky made them to give to me, though, not to be sold.'

'They're yours to do what you like with, then,' Joanne said. 'Besides, you don't have enough wrist for the half of them.'

'I'll ask her.'

'Think of it like this. Every time we take a coin from our parents we need to go to confession, but if we're just selling friendship bracelets to get money then we're golden. No sin, so no confession.'

'I said I'd ask her.' Aoife shrugged Joanne's hand from her shoulder.

It took Aoife a couple of nights to work up the courage to ask Becky about the bracelets. Not because she thought the younger girl would say no – far from it – but because of the guilt of it. It felt like a betrayal to be thinking of selling them on. Still, they'd agreed that Becky should be properly compensated for her work. Out of every ten pack of fags, she'd be given one as payment. Ten per cent. On the face of it her cut seemed a touch useless, since she didn't even smoke, but they reasoned that she could exchange the cigarettes for chewing gum or chocolate or something like that there. Or she could always just take up smoking like the rest of them.

The question was asked and the answer was yes: a nodded yes. Aoife had known rightly that it would be. Still, she couldn't shift the uneasy feeling she had about the whole thing. Becky hadn't looked down at the buckles on her shoes when asked, but had instead stared straight at Aoife with eyes widened to the size of shiny ten-pence pieces. There was hurt in those brown eyes, Aoife was sure of it, but Becky didn't say a word. She just nodded, up and down.

The business took off. Soon enough every girl in the playground had a bracelet of some sort on their wrist. Jewellery was one of the items on the nuns' list of prohibited items, but it was only really to stop the girls wearing earrings and necklaces;

they weren't going to extend the rule to a wee strap of fabric that was hidden under the cuff of the blouse in any case. Aoife and Joanne split the profits straight down the middle and this half-gate arrangement meant that they both had more cigarettes than they could reasonably smoke during those times of the day when they were out of both sight and smell of adults. Even after they'd given Becky her cut – the cigarettes folded into a sheet of notepaper so the nuns didn't catch on – they still had enough left over to sell single cigarettes on to the younger girls. They began to sell more than they smoked, making a sizeable second profit. Racketeering was wee buns, really.

It only took a week or so, though, for Aoife to notice that Becky wasn't for smoking her share. Since the start of trading, Aoife had been making an effort to be a fair bit nicer to her, sitting with her for a minute or two at lunchtimes before the other girls arrived, or dropping behind the rest on the way home to walk along with her. For all the time they spent together, Aoife had never seen Becky light up. Worse still, she wasn't even using the cigarettes to barter with the other girls for something she really wanted. Cigarettes were currency in the school corridors – as they were in Long Kesh – but Becky seemed oblivious to the fact that she was turning into one of the richest girls at the Convent. Instead of selling on her share, she tucked the unopened folds of notepaper into her satchel and took them home with her, as if she'd a wish to save them up. If that were the case, then Aoife had no doubt that she'd soon have more cigarettes than the Marlboro man.

It came to be obvious, though, that Becky's cigarettes were not being stashed away but were instead going straight into the pocket of her fourteen-year-old brother. Ciarán had taken to tucking a fag in behind his ear as he stepped outside the house and then carelessly lifting it down and lighting it whenever he met one of the boys. Acting the big man. It stung Aoife to see him taking a drag or two from one of Becky's cigarettes and then flicking it down into the gutter to smoke itself, as if he were so landed that he didn't need to annoy himself with smoking it down to the filter. So Aoife took to paying the wee girl with the money she got from selling the cigarettes on instead. Drip-feeding her fifty pence here or twenty pence there, like whenever Aoife's daddy gave her pocket money from his winnings after a successful afternoon in the bookie's.

Whether she was paid in cigarettes or cold, hard cash, the supply chain from Becky never let up. Even at the weekends, even when it was sunny outside, or when a crowd gathered at the Ormeau Bridge to shout abuse at the passing Orangemen, Becky would stay inside and graft away. The money that Aoife gave her from the sale of the cigarettes all went into a washed-out jam jar and was saved until it added up to enough to buy a supply of thread or beads or tiny plastic jewels. She reinvested every penny she earned. Tanned leather bands with engraved patterns and bracelets formed of delicately twisted wire began to emerge as Becky's repertoire expanded to make use of the soldering iron, its glowing end no bigger than a pinprick, that had cost her near enough a full jam jar's worth of coins.

Becky had a corner of the table by the window in the Gildays' kitchen spread with thread, wire, beads and assorted scraps. In the evenings, Aoife took to dropping by and standing there with a cup of tea to watch. As she stepped up to the table, her footfall would softly crunch against stray beads, like treading on grit-salt on a frosty morning. Not a sound came from Becky. There was no hair-chewing or buckle-watching either, just pure concentration.

Aoife had other reasons for calling round, though. As often as not, her visits were made in the hope of seeing Ciáran rather than his wee sister. Ciáran went to St Joseph's School, over towards West Belfast, so they rarely saw each other during the course of the day, and the evenings were dark now winter had set in, so the time spent in the concrete playground after school was brief. Even when they all braved the cold and the wet, Ciáran would more often than not be kicking a football about with Damien while Aoife could only watch quietly from the sidelines, shivering into her coat and bleakly wondering when it was that a chill turned into frostbite. As much as she liked Ciáran, he didn't seem worth losing a toe over, especially since he barely acknowledged her. In the warm kitchen, though, she had him all to herself, save for the silent presence of Becky at the table.

''Bout you?' he'd say, coming in and opening the fridge.

'Hiya.'

'What're you at?' straightening up and taking a drink from a pint bottle of milk. He'd lean against the counter and fix Aoife with that cheeky grin, all crooked teeth and wrinkled nose. 'You here watching over your slave labour, is that it?'

'Not at all.' There wasn't a thing Aoife would change about Ciáran. 'I'm just keeping your sister company, is all.'

'You weren't out at the playground after school, were you?'

'No.' Maybe he could do with a wee touch less gel in his hair. 'It's baltic out there, sure.' And his tracksuit trousers were too short in the legs. 'I'd rather stay inside and not risk hypothermia.'

'Is that right?'

'It is.'

'Well, the craic's ninety in here.' He'd pull a face. 'I'm off.'

Every evening that Aoife was over at the Gilday house they'd have an encounter like this, sometimes three or four in the one night. Ciáran got through a brave amount of milk. In fact, his mammy complained to Aoife that she'd had to increase the order with the milkman to cover the pints and pints of it that Ciáran drank over the course of the week. Aoife had reddened at that, though she didn't know why. It wasn't her fault, after all. She was only there to help Becky with the friendship bracelets; it made no odds to her whether there was milk in the fridge or not.

I haven't thought it through. Beyond the act itself, I mean. I haven't thought about how I'll be getting clear, about whether I'll be able to get myself home and hosed. Besides, I'm so shook

48

that I'm stumbling about that wee terraced house like a drunk at closing time, bouncing off the walls and thinking I'm at the back door whilst I'm still up on the first-floor landing. My situation isn't helped by the cloying blood, both his and now mine, that inches its way down my thighs, or the acid tears, all mine, that leak from my eyes.

Still, I make it out of there. Out the back, I go, down the alley and then around a corner, or two, or three. My ears ring with the echo of screams, both mine and his. I totter along, on my high heels, gradually wakening up enough to realise that there's an ever-growing glistening slick at my crotch. Not the primary-colour red of my dress, but something darker. I must look like a high-class hooker with an incontinence problem. Not the look you want if you're trying to play it low-key.

Darting into another lane, then, I press my back against the brick wall. I'm a few streets away, maybe up near Jerusalem or Palestine Street. Further into the Holylands. I take a deep breath and I focus. The object that catches my glare is a wooden door. An ordinary enough pine door, with broken hinges. Discarded, left up against the opposite wall. Bloody typical. Every time you open a door in Belfast, you walk smack-bang into a brick wall. Fucking symbolism, that. Peeling off my shoe, I step across to it. Square-up.

Images flood my mind: the curl to his lip as I lift off his shirt, the tremble to him as I hook off his boxer shorts. The ripple of his bicep, beneath his tattoo, as he claws at his bound wrists, as he bucks his hips to try to lift me up and off him. That's the thing that surprised me the most: his surprise. Afterwards, when I back away, he looks up at me as if waiting on an explanation. He thinks it has all been an accident. There's a question amongst the thin whistle-wheeze of his pain.

Lifting my heel, I drive the point of it into the wooden door, hammering again and again until splinters begin to litter the ground around my bare foot. I'm lopsided, unbalanced. The rain begins to fall, patterning my black jacket with tiny unburst beads. Still, I hammer away, again and again, not caring that

I might be drawing attention to myself, not caring that the varicose vein of blood is trickling down to my ankle and is now on the cusp of being soaked into the sawdust-strewn concrete. Not caring if I'm found, either now or later. Just hammering and hammering, knowing that it hasn't been enough. It will never be enough.

Joanne was the first one at school to get her ears pierced, but the rest of the girls weren't slow to follow suit, Aoife included. The whole thing was a bit of a head-melter: waiting until you were out of the house in the mornings before hooking in the earrings, then wearing them for the ten-minute walk to school, unhooking them and hiding them in your schoolbag, then reattaching them at the end of the day for the walk home, only to take them off before you went in for your tea. Still, it meant that Becky could diversify into making earrings and they could all profit from the continual earlobe fiddling that went on by the school gates.

Aoife used the new income to buy herself all the necessaries for to catch Ciáran's eye as he drank his nightly milk. She bought eyeshadow and lipstick, concealer and mascara, hairspray and perfume. It was her Auntie Eileen that took her shopping for them, in place of her sink-staring mammy. It was Aoife and her auntie who littered the bathroom with cosmetics and stood in front of the mirror chattering away and plastering their faces with make-up, while Cathy Brennan stood in the kitchen below, staring at her unchanging reflection in the window. Every once in a while the hot taps in both kitchen and bathroom would be turned on at the same time and the water would run cold.

The hairspray was vital. It was only with half a can of the stuff that Aoife's ginger curls began to calm down so as they hung down around her ears as ringlets. Her frizzy hair had never seemed like much of an issue before, but she'd spent so much time tidying her face that leaving the hair unchecked would have been like keeping a tangled thicket of weeds beside a neat patio garden. At least, that was how her Auntie Eileen put it. Problem was, even once they'd succeeded in making Aoife look like Madonna from the neck up, she still looked like a schoolgirl from there down. The green and brown uniform she wore day to day was as unflattering and shapeless as a binbag (Auntie Eileen's words) and the colours were those of vomit and shit, all mixed together (again, Eileen). Aoife would need a whole new wardrobe if she was to catch Ciáran's eye: skirts and tops that were more glamorous than the T-shirts and jeans she had for the weekends. A shopping spree like that, though, would cost more than the pocketfuls of change Aoife got from the selling of jewellery and cigarettes, and her daddy point-blank refused to give her more than a crumpled ten-pound note. So Aoife took it upon herself to get a Saturday job in Cliona's salon at the end of the next road along, sweeping up the hair from the floor and making endless cups of tea. It wasn't as easy as hawking earrings or friendship bracelets, but it filled her pockets that wee bit quicker.

There was to be no gradual change to her appearance. One evening Aoife was standing in the Gildays' kitchen in her ankle-length green and brown checked skirt with brown blazer and white shirt; the next she was posing in a short denim skirt and sequinned top. A miraculous transformation, so it was. It took her near enough half an hour to get over the shivering from the short walk between the two houses, but she knew the sound of Ciáran's jaw hitting the floor would make it worthwhile.

It wasn't only Ciáran who noticed, though. Becky's daddy, Declan Gilday, collected the bins for the council. It was a job for early in the day, but he still managed to drag his working hours on until late into the evening. He never made it in until after the sun had gone down and he never made it in without the smell of rubbish that lingered about him being joined by the smell of whiskey. Whenever Aoife had stood there in her uniform, he'd only nodded in her direction and then gone over to the oven, where his dinner was being kept warm for him. On the first day after Aoife's makeover, though, he paused mid-nod. 'Alright, love,' he said. He had a smoker's voice, with a croaky sound to it, and a smoker's smile, with yellowed teeth. 'You one of our Becky's friends?'

'Hi.' She nodded. 'Aoife.'

'The same age as her?'

'Year and a half older. Thirteen.'

'Right.' Declan wiped at his moustache, in the same way as Ciáran always wiped at his milk-moustache, with the back of his hand. Aoife was slower to smile at the father, though. 'You're a fine-looking girl, Aoife,' he said.

'Thank you,' Aoife replied, looking away. Her eyes fell on Becky's hands, which held a shaking soldering iron. The wee girl didn't look up.

'Leave the girls be, Declan.' The voice of Teresa, Becky's mammy, carried through from the living room. 'And get your dinner out of that oven before it gets a crust on it.'

'I'm just passing the time of day,' Declan replied. 'No harm in that.'

Teresa made a noise in her throat. Even after travelling down the hallway, it was still loud enough to cause Aoife to flinch slightly.

'Aye, you're pure-bred Irish, so you are,' Declan said softly to Aoife, lifting his plate from the oven and giving her a final look. 'Well, feel free to visit any time,' he said. Then he left the room.

Aoife's visits to the Gilday household tailed off after that. The joy at seeing Ciáran loitering about the kitchen, gulping at his milk, was lessened by the fact that for every one time she saw the son she would see the father twice. Declan Gilday would come in to clink a bottle of stout free from the others in the fridge or run himself a glass of water from the tap. There would be a lot of moustache-wiping and questions that felt more like interrogation than small talk, then the sound of a throat being cleared in the living room would lead him to wink and make his way slowly out of the room.

More than that, though, Aoife noticed that the atmosphere around the kitchen table had changed. Whereas before Becky had been content to work away quietly whilst Aoife watched on, occasionally with a smile or a whispering laugh passing between them, there now seemed to be a strain to the silence. The younger girl would look up at Aoife every so often, as though checking on her, and stop her work for long spells to frown out of the window. Becky began to remind Aoife of her own mammy. There was a tension to all of her movements. A miniature scrap-heap of broken and spoiled jewellery began to build up in the centre of the table.

The event that stopped Aoife's evening visits to the Gilday house for good came three weeks after the makeover. She had taken to going over a wee bit earlier and ducking out before Declan Gilday appeared, but he still always managed to catch her either as she drained her cup of tea or as she made her way out the door.

Aoife went round to see Becky directly after her dinner and near scalded her tongue with trying to swallow her tea down before it had cooled. It was a flying visit, no longer than twenty minutes, and Aoife was in plenty of time to get away before Becky's father came home. Ciáran had even been in for two drinks of milk in the short time she'd been there. It had been a successful evening, so far as Aoife was concerned.

Before she left, though, Aoife went to the toilet. Up the stairs, first left, just like in her own house. She was gone for only a couple of minutes, but when she walked back into the kitchen she screamed. Wee Becky, her eyes streaming with silent tears, had the soldering iron up at her right cheek and was pressing the point of it into her skin. On her left cheek there were already three tiny perfect circles, each beginning to blister into a pimple of whitened flesh raised from the spreading, inflamed red around them. Becky was looking at the table, down at the pool of tears forming on the worn wood.

Aoife's scream brought Becky's mammy running, and Ciáran too. With one swing of her hand, Teresa knocked the soldering iron out of Becky's hand. With the next, she slapped her daughter across the pock-marked left cheek. Then she hurried over to the sink and ran the cold tap. She cupped her hands together and filled them with water, as best she could, which she then ladled over Becky's swelling face. She spilt more than she carried and the pool of water on the table began to grow into a lake, until it dripped down in a steady waterfall to the tiled floor.

'You stupid wee girl,' she scolded. 'Why the fuck would you do something like that?'

Becky snivelled, her tears coming faster now.

'I only left her for a second, Mrs Gilday,' Aoife said.

'Why, Becky?' Teresa asked again.

There was still no answer. With a hand firmly gripping each shoulder, Becky's mammy shook her until the wee girl gave a gasping cry. 'I wanted freckles,' she said. 'Like Aoife's, like all Irish girls.'

'No, Becky, no.' Teresa's shaking slowed and collapsed into a rocking hug.

'Freckles are what pure-bred Irish girls have,' Becky sniffed. 'They're wholesome.' She stumbled over the last word, saying it as two separate words.

'I never said anything, Mrs – ' Aoife began.

Teresa looked back over her shoulder. 'I think it's best if you go home, Aoife,' she said, quietly. 'I think that would be best.'

Aoife didn't need to be told twice; she turned and made her way out of the Gilday house without another word. She didn't look up at Ciáran as she pushed past him, but she was fairly certain he was looking at her, and she was fairly certain that there would be no cheeky smile and no milk-moustache.

I still have the gilt edge on me from my first time out when I set about preparing for the second. The swagger of it leads me right into the heart of the Loyalist Shankill. This is back in the days before Baldy, back when I thought I'd no need for planning or the check once-twice-three times and once more for luck. Fuck it, I was invincible, I was invulnerable. I was the avenging fucking angel.

The shop is on the corner of a typical Belfast terraced street, Orkney Street you call it: wee red-brick houses all crammed together in a row with cheerful-looking lintels, in different shades of brick, above the windows. Houseproud folk down this way: flower-boxes on the sills, smoke out the chimneys, bunting draped from windows, flags above the doors. Houseproud and Ulster-proud. Most of the flags and that there will have come from the shop itself, I'm guessing. The red, white and blue paint that still flecks the kerbstones from the Twelfth will have come from there too. A narrow shop, painted in a royal blue, with the words 'British Souveniers' painted in white above the door. Spelling mistake and all. Anyone who noticed the error would probably be too feared to point it out, though. Petty gripes get sorted the same way as deep-rooted grievances, so they do, in Belfast.

No tourists up this end of town, so the portraits of King Billy and Queen Lizzy are for the locals, for the descendants of those that lie stretched and stiff in the Shankill Rest Garden. A corner shop for bigots. I know rightly that whoever I find inside is my second target. If you're looking for sweets, you may as well go to the sweet shop.

The door chime plays 'Rule Britannia'. I set my teeth. The aisle is fringed with Norn Iron flags, marking out a triumphal promenade down to the counter. Behind it, staring at me, with a look caught between a sneer and a leer, is a muscle-bound man in his thirties with a shaven head that has a tuft of brown hair at the very front. He wears a twisting vine shirt, in blue and white, with the sleeves cut shorter than they should be. Shorter so as he can display the Red Hand tattoo on his bicep. A blood-coloured hand, framed in black, that bulges as he leans on the counter. He's perfect, so he is. He's going to be my second.

Having grown used to being out of the house of an evening, even if only for a spell, Aoife didn't know what to do with herself now. A couple of times Joanne came around and they flicked through magazines and pretended to do their homework, but Joanne lived away up in the Ardoyne so her mammy had to drive down and collect her early enough. Aoife spent more time with Damien, playing board games and teasing him because he didn't know even half the swear words that she did. No teenage girl wants to spend her evenings with her wee brother, though. Besides, Damien was even quieter than Becky, so he was, a right book-worm. They'd be in the middle of a game of Monopoly or Guess Who and he'd suddenly up-sticks and make his way over to the sofa to curl up with some book or other. As though she'd nothing better to do than sit there waiting for him while he finished his chapter.

It took a couple of weeks before the front doorbell rang and Aoife swung open the door to see Becky standing there examining the buckles of her shoes. The tiny round scars on her cheeks were glistening with new skin. Behind Becky, down by the gate, was Ciáran.

'Would you and Damien like to come out and play?' Becky whispered.

'Where?'

Becky shrugged. 'Playground?'

Aoife thought about it. They hung around in the playground before their tea, not after. It was different after. Out on the Ormeau Road the continual sound of passing traffic would be interrupted by a screeching set of tyres and then a siren, or a series of shouts and whistles would drift across the train tracks from the Prod estate on the other side. Then there was always the threat of flying golf balls. Belfast at night was quiet, but not relaxed. It was like Becky sitting hunched at the kitchen table those last weeks: strained and tetchy, waiting for something to happen.

Aoife didn't want to go round to the Gildays' house, though, what with their daddy always being about, and she also didn't really want them in her house, on account of her mammy's condition. She didn't want the embarrassment of it.

'She misses you,' Ciáran called, grinning through the glow from the street-lights. That settled it. They could play up the stairs, in her bedroom. It'd be fine, as long as Becky and Ciáran didn't stray into the kitchen or notice the gurgling of the hot water every half-hour as her mammy refilled the sink.

'Sure, it's you that misses me, Ciáran Gilday,' Aoife shouted back, with a surge of confidence.

'Wise up,' he replied, looking away.

'Give me a wee minute, Becky,' Aoife said, 'and I'll see if you can play here.'

Aoife's daddy was used to her calling in for the Gildays in the evenings, so he only grunted when she asked. It was Damien who was the problem. He sat there, beside his daddy, with some book in his hands, not even looking up when she said to him that he was to put it down and come to play with Becky and Ciáran.

'You hearing me, Damien Brennan?' she asked, hands on hips.

He nodded.

'Well?'

'I'm reading.'

'Stop reading, then, and come upstairs.'

He shook his head.

'Daddy?' Aoife said.

'What, love?'

'Tell Damien he needs to stop reading and come to play.'

'Leave him be, Aoife,' her daddy replied.

'I'm asking Mammy, then.'

Making her way through to the kitchen, Aoife tapped her mammy on the shoulder. It was like knocking on wood. No response, not even a flinch or a shudder of surprise. Craning her neck round, Aoife looked directly into her mammy's blank stare. Her mammy was having a real tuned-to-the-moon day. Every couple of weeks she'd waken up a bit and start talking to them all, maybe even wash a plate or two, just for a day or so. This was not one of those times.

'Can I tell Damien that he has to play with us?' Aoife asked.

Nothing.

'Speak now or forever hold your peace,' Aoife said. Her mammy still kept her wheest. 'Thanks, Mammy.'

Aoife made her way back through to the living room and told Damien that he'd been ordered to be sociable by their mammy. He just quietly smiled and went on with his reading. This led to a wrestling match, with the book in the middle of it. Eventually it was broken up by their daddy. 'Listen, Damien,' he hissed, 'go and play with them all for an hour or two and give my head peace, OK? You'll learn rightly when you get older that it's always best to just do as the wee woman says.'

'See,' Aoife said.

So Damien reluctantly put his book down on the arm of the chair. Aoife went back to the front door with a flutter of panic that Becky and Ciáran would have just got bored and gone home. They were still there, though, waiting for her return. The four of them trooped up the stairs and set up camp in Aoife's bedroom.

'Let's do something different,' Aoife said, after five or six abortive attempts at playing board games. The problem was that nobody actually said they wanted to play anything; they would just pick a box, unpack it and then sit with the makings of the game in front of them, waiting for someone else to join in. Ciáran was playing Monopoly with Scrabble tiles, while Aoife and Becky shuffled the Chance and Community Chest cards and played a half-hearted game of Guess Who. Damien rolled a pair of dice, over and over again. 'These are just wee kids' games anyway.'

'What do you want to do, then?' Ciáran asked.

'A proper game of something.' She paused, as though she needed time to think up something suitable. 'Truth or dare,' she said, finally.

'No way.' Damien threw the dice he was holding down onto the carpet. He shook his head, as though disappointed at the double-six he'd rolled. 'Girls always use that game to try and kiss you, so they do; it's always that and nothing else.'

'Don't be soft,' Aoife replied. She was surprised by her brother's answer, and not only because of the force of it. Also because there she was at thirteen, still waiting for her first kiss, and her nine-year-old brother was acting as if he'd hordes of girls chasing after him with puckered lips. 'Besides,' she said, 'you're my brother so I'm hardly going to try to kiss you, and Becky and Ciáran are brother and sister so they're not going to kiss either.'

'But that just means that you and Ciáran – ' Damien began.

'Do as you're told, Damo,' Ciáran interrupted, snatching the dice up from the carpet and rolling them off towards the far wall. They landed on a three and a four. If they'd been playing a proper game, Damien would have been well ahead of him.

'Good.' Aoife smiled. 'Ciáran, you can start. Truth or dare?'

It took them several rounds to get to the inevitable. In the meantime they'd all told a fair few lies and Ciáran had shown his bare arse at the window. In theory he was mooning the Orangies across the way, but it was doubtful they could see the Brennans' windows from that distance. As he was doing it though, just to be safe, Aoife offered up a silent prayer that the Prods couldn't see him, because, truth be told, she'd no wish to provoke that lot. After all, it might lead to a volley of golf balls. Or worse.

Then, finally, it came to Becky's turn. She sat there, on the edge of Aoife's bed, chewing at her plaited hair. It was the first time she'd been called upon and she seemed to have no clue as to what was expected of her. To help her out, Aoife leant across and whispered a suggestion. Just a suggestion, mind.

'Ciáran,' Becky said, looking up. 'Truth or dare?'

'Dare.'

'I dare you to kiss Aoife.' Becky hesitated. 'On the lips.'

'I told youse,' Damien shouted. 'Here's me: girls can't play truth or dare without bringing kissing into it. That's what I said.'

'It's nothing I've not done before,' Ciáran said then, pulling Damien down into a playful headlock. 'Plenty of times.'

Aoife took a breath. She didn't know whether she should shuffle forward now, lips pursed, or wait for Ciáran to come to her. Always let the boy make the first move, Joanne had said; it was one of the rules.

'Maybe the two of you should kiss and all,' Ciáran said, knuckling Damien's head with his free hand and turning to Becky. 'Otherwise you'd only be spying on us.'

'I won't look,' Damien said.

'Give Becky a kiss,' Aoife replied quickly.

'No.'

'Is there something wrong with my sister?' Ciáran asked, his headlock becoming less playful. 'Eh?'

'No.'

'Well, then,' Ciáran said. 'You'll do it, won't you?'

Damien tried to shake his head, but he was being throttled now by the crook of Ciáran's arm.

'Won't you?' Ciáran repeated.

Damien squealed. 'Alright, I'll do it!'

They stood on either side of the bed, two by two, waiting in silence for someone to take the lead. Aoife broke the tension by placing her hands on either side of Ciáran's waist. Becky, watching intently, followed suit. Then Aoife leant in and closed her eyes. She paused there for a moment, for a stretched second of dread anticipation. Always wait for the boy. Then she felt Ciáran lunge forward. It was different from what she'd been expecting. His lips were dry and she was more aware of his thudding heartbeat than she was of the kiss itself. It lasted only a few seconds. As they pulled away, Aoife looked over at Becky and Damien. Their lips were still together but both sets of eyes were wide open. When they saw Aoife looking they broke apart.

'Damo,' Ciáran called over. 'Truth or dare?'

Damien shrugged.

'You'll take a truth.' Ciáran grinned. 'Did you enjoy that?'

'No.' The word hung bluntly in the air. Damien shrugged again, not bothered by the sight of Becky, still beside him, welling up with tears. He made no effort to lessen the impact of what he'd said.

Aoife turned to Ciáran. 'What did you go and do that for?' she hissed.

'Do what?'

'You've hurt Becky's feelings, so you have.'

'It wasn't me that done it.'

Aoife shook her head and stepped around the bed towards Becky. She was closer to the door though, and she darted out before Aoife could reach her. Shaking with sobs from head to toe, she sped down the stairs.

'Leave her be,' Ciáran called to Aoife.

'I will not,' Aoife replied. She was raging with Ciáran more than she was with Damien, because she knew rightly that Damien wouldn't have said anything unless he'd been asked.

'She's just a wee girl,' Ciáran said. 'She doesn't understand.'

'She does too, Ciáran Gilday, and she's a right to be upset.'

'Wise up.'

'Fuck off.'

With that, Aoife stalked away. Anger took over from the excitement she'd felt in the moments before the kiss. She skipped down the stairs as fast as she could, although she was more than aware that Ciáran could have caught up with her if he wanted to.

She found Becky in the kitchen, beneath the table. She was sat there with her knees hugged up to her chest and with tear marks snaking down around the soldering-iron scars. Aoife's mammy was still at the sink, with the hot water running.

Aoife clambered in underneath the table and cuddled the younger girl.

'Don't listen to them, Becky,' she said, softly. 'They're only boys.'

They sat like that for a long while, then, until Becky's trembling began to steady and her sniffs became less regular.

'Aoife?' Becky whispered.

'Yes?'

'Truth or dare?'

Aoife smiled. 'Truth,' she said.

'Do you think I'm a hoor?'

The smile froze, then vanished.

'Do you?' Becky asked again.

Aoife couldn't really see in the dim light underneath the table, but she knew that Becky's head was turned up to look at her. The trembling had started again. Aoife took Becky's hand in her own.

'What you just did,' she said, 'was normal. All the girls in our school do it and it certainly doesn't make you a hoor, I promise you.'

'It's not just that, but.'

'How d'you mean?'

Becky looked down, at the friendship bracelet that Aoife wore. It was the first one Becky had ever given her. The one made out of a weave of blonde Barbie hair. Between finger and thumb, Becky began to pluck at it.

'He says…' Becky swallowed, then spoke in a whisper. 'He says that I'm not *wholesome* like you. He says I'll stray before long and that he needs to check up on me regularly to make sure.'

'Who does? Ciáran? Your daddy?'

Becky was silent.

'Check up? What does that mean?' Aoife leant in close, so that she could see Becky's eyes, so that she could see the silent tears dripping down. In the half-light the burns from the soldering iron did look like freckles, a neat triangle of them on one cheek and then a single one at the top of the other.

'Truth or dare, Becky?' Aoife asked. There was no answer.

'Truth or dare?' Aoife squeezed at her hand.

'Dare.' Becky bit at her bottom lip and looked up at Aoife.

'I dare you to tell me what you mean.'

'That's not a proper dare, but.'

'It is.'

'It isn't,' Becky shook her head. 'Besides, it must be near enough my bedtime, I should head on.'

'Tell me what you mean first.'

'No,' Becky let go of Aoife's hand and began to crawl out from underneath the table. 'It doesn't matter,' she said, over her shoulder.

He backhands me as soon as we're in the door. No time to scream. No time to soften him up with whiskey, or to tie him down. No time, even, to raise my hands to protect my face. He lamps me, I fall, and then he stands over me. Nigel. For a minute, I think it might be tears that cause his eyes to gleam in the dim hallway. It isn't – it's something else. Something I've not come across before.

'You like it rough, you wee hoor,' he hisses.

'You hit me,' I say. There's a whimper to it.

'Don't be a prick-tease, love,' he smiles. Showing his teeth.

'Fuck you,' I reply, scrabbling to my feet and making for the stairs. It's in my mind that he'll get his dues when he gets to the deed itself, but I'm not for letting him get that far. I don't want him on top of me, pinning me down. There's nothing so dangerous as a wounded animal.

His footsteps follow me up the stairs. Slow, creaking footfalls. Up the stairs of the same house I used for the first one, the abandoned two-up, two-down in the Holylands: Damascus Street. Tripping on the top step, I think of the bloodstains on the carpet in the front bedroom: the blood of Billy. I've no wish to be adding my own blood, for the two to be mixing together amongst the twist-pile.

'Fuck me?' Nigel calls out, chuckling. 'Fuck you, more like.'

I dart into the bedroom. Wrong room. It's the one I used before. It's bare, save for the stains and the half-empty whiskey bottle in the corner. I dart back out and into the next room. I've set it up earlier with a single mattress and a bottle of Jameson. I've even gone to the lengths of putting a beige sheet on the bed, tucked in at the corners. Hospital corners. Quickly, I lift the full whiskey bottle and position myself. My heartbeat quickens to the sound of his breathing on the other side of the door. As it opens, I swing. You'd expect the bottle to shatter against his skull. It doesn't. It thuds against his forehead and collapses him to his knees. Skipping past him, as he makes a grab for my ankles, I'm back down the stairs and making for the back door. I hear him clattering after me. He's either upright and ready for the chase, or he's taken a tumble down the stairs in trying to get after me. I don't hang about to find out which. I just want to get the fuck out of there. I just want out.

4

'You're not getting right in underneath.' Cliona snipped.
'I'm not wanting to get in your way.'

'You're not wanting to do the work, is all it is.'

Aoife sighed and moved forward to clank the wooden broom in at the base of the swivel chair. The stray strands were dragged out to the centre of the cracked tiles. It was Muireann Sloan who was having her hair cut, so the clumped gatherings were both blonde and brown: fringe and roots. Aoife hadn't wanted to step right in and sweep in and around Cliona's stiletto shoes because Mary-Jo, to the other side of Muireann, was wearing the tin hat of a hooded hairdryer and the blasts of hot air from it settled on Aoife as sweat.

'You'll have heard about the young girl, then?' Muireann asked.

'Which one is that, now?' Cliona sniffed, lifting the water-sprayer and sending a fine mist over the head of her customer to drift on towards Aoife. Closing her eyes and raising her face, Aoife waited for it.

'The one out on that rock – what's it called?'

'Gibraltar,' Mary-Jo piped up, from beneath her helmet. 'It's a British colony.'

'Sure, we know all about those, Mary-Jo.'

'You'll be needing to get your roots done soon, love,' Cliona said, trailing the damp hair through her fingers, 'if you're wanting to keep it blonde.'

'I'd have had them done today,' Muireann replied, quickly, 'if he hadn't been out on the rip last night, spending the housekeeping and coming in blocked with the drink. Blocked, he was. Wait till I tell you, as well, the excuse he had. He says he met an uncle or something of your girl who died out on that rock-colony there and that he needed to pay his respects. Here's me: how's that paying respect? And here's him: it's the done thing. Drinking to her memory, they were, as though that'd bring the wee girl back.'

'Mairéad Farrell, you call her,' Mary-Jo murmured. 'She was three days after her thirty-first birthday when she was shot. Not so much a girl as a full-grown woman.'

Aoife rested the broom against her hip and grimaced, her insides clenching again. The pain had been coming and going all morning, the worst of it causing her to dig her nails into the handle of the broom fit to raise splinters. It was like a stomach cramp, but deeper somehow, as though her innards were being slowly twisted around the broken curling tongs from the back-shop, the ones that fizzled with surges of searing heat when they were plugged into the socket.

A waft of cool air billowed the apron around Aoife's waist. She knew without looking that the opening and closing of the front door signalled the arrival of auld Mrs McGrath, because there was suddenly a fearful smell of piss throughout the tiny salon. Every day she stopped in at the salon on her way into town, even though the mangled mullet on top of her head hadn't felt the scrape of a brush or the suds of shampoo for many a year. It wasn't for quelling the plughole-clumps and wisped webs of her hair that Mrs McGrath called in at Cliona's salon, it was for use of the bog. The shop was just one of many designated toilet stops on her daily journey in to Royal Avenue.

'It wasn't just her that was shot, though, was it?' Cliona asked, her voice made nasal by the effort of not breathing in. 'There were two men, as well.'

Muireann nodded her head forcefully, pulling a collected bundle of hair from Cliona's fingers and out of the reach of the scissors. 'One of them went to school with our Patsy, so he did,' she said. 'And with the company our Patsy keeps, I tell you, it could have easily been him who landed up dead instead of that other poor boy.'

'It's Farrell they're talking about, though,' Cliona stilled Muireann's bobbing head with a gentle hand. 'She's the one that all the papers are on about.'

'She's well thought of.'

'It was her that led the hunger strike in Armagh Prison,' Mary-Jo added, some aspect of her hairdressing apparatus sounding out with a *ding* against the hairdryer as though marking her re-entry into the conversation. 'The one in 1980, at the same time as the first of the H-Block strikes.'

'Like I said,' Muireann looked across at Mary-Jo, 'she's well thought of.' She paused. 'Although what a wee girl like that is doing trying to get herself in with the Provos is beyond me.'

The lingering grip of discomfort passed and Aoife felt something stir within her. It was a loosening, like stretching away the stiffness after sleep. And then a flush up her neck and across her cheeks, a half-remembered shame and a frozen horror as she realised that the loosening was accompanied by a dribble down the inside of her leg. Sweat turned cold; the fading smell of stale urine turned sharp. It had been how long since she'd last wet herself: eight years, more? Just a seepage, no more, now trickling and tickling at each and every sensitive inch of skin as it travelled slowly towards her knee. With a clatter, the broom toppled from her hip and fell to the floor.

'Sweet Jesus!' Mary-Jo exclaimed from within her heated cocoon, her panic *ding-ding*-ing at the sides as she looked blindly about herself.

'What're you at, Aoife?' Cliona asked, her lips pursed and her scissors hovering above Muireann's head.

It took Aoife a moment to answer, during which she bent over to lift the broom from the hair-strewn floor. She went down in stages, bending her knees and squatting down onto her haunches as she had seen pregnant women do, taking care to keep the fabric away from the growing moist patch. The last thing she wanted was for the dribble down her leg to soak into the denim of her jeans. If it did she'd end up reeking like the incontinent Mrs McGrath. She sent a silent prayer of thanks heavenwards for the black apron that covered her crotch from the staring eyes of Cliona and Muireann.

'Nothing,' she finally answered. 'I just need to run to the toilet.'

'Well you'll have to wait.' Cliona started snipping again. 'The living and breathing urinal is in there now and you don't want to be messing with that woman's routines, love.'

'You'd come away smelling of *eau de* piss,' Mary-Jo chimed in.

'God forgive you, Mary-Josephine.' Muireann drew in her breath.

'I'll go on in back and wait,' Aoife said, quietly. She set the broom upright against the third, unused chair and walked, straight-legged and self-conscious, towards the back of the shop. Despite her best efforts she could feel the denim sticking to the inside of her leg, the wetness tacky and ever-spreading.

'*...as of yet there is no word as to when the three bodies will be returned to the families for burial. British authorities state that the IRA volunteers involved posed a significant risk to both the public and military personnel...*' The radio was on softly in the narrow corridor that led to the bathroom, its words spoken in a Belfast accent that had long-ago been retuned to BBC English. '*...it is unclear, at this stage, whether Seán Savage, Daniel McCann and Mairéad Farrell were armed...*'

Aoife reached in underneath the apron and plucked at the sticky patch on her jeans until the denim pulled away from the skin. Even the radio was on about the SAS shootings out in Gibraltar; it was all anyone could bloody talk about. Standing outside the bathroom door, Aoife listened to the drip-drip of Mrs McGrath beneath the steady murmur of the news announcer – it sounded like the uncertain pittering of a leaky roof against the backdrop of insistent rain.

Mrs McGrath had lost her husband seven years before, in 1981, back when her plumbing was in order and her hair was regularly tended to. Back when all the talk was of hunger strikes and dirty protests, when those who died had fallen among their own people in their own streets and not on some Godforsaken rock off the coast of Spain. His was one of the names on the wall out at the end of the next street but one to the salon. Another volunteer, another death.

As Aoife waited, she leant over to inspect her jeans. Lifting the apron, she found the growing stain to be more than urine, more than some part-memory of the shame of wetting herself way back when she was a wee girl. The crotch of her jeans was slick with the brown-red of blood: the blood that Aoife had spied once amongst the assorted white of rubbish in the bin at the swimming pool; the blood that meant that she'd finally caught up with Joanne, that she finally knew what Joanne was on about when she'd whispered about her *period*.

I just want it out. That's all I can think – I just want it out. My shoes are off. Not like the first time. Bare feet so as I can get to the Ormeau Road quicker. Down to the Hatfield Bar. I'll be safe there. Nigel wouldn't be daft enough to follow me – the boys in there would rip the tattoo off his arm for free, save him the price of laser surgery later in life.

Staggering into the toilets at the bar – my shoes in my hand and my cheek starting to swell – I'm just another slapper who's walked into a fist. They'll all think nothing of it, those boys at the bar. Even if they knew what I was doing, they'd never tout. They'd probably stand up and cheer, if truth be told. Anyway, I'm not thinking about all that. I just want it out.

I've put medicated wipes and all in my handbag, so as I could clean the mess from me after the deed was done. Only there's no blood – we never got that far. There's bruising but no blood. Into the cubicle, then, and slamming the door. Breathing hard and shallow. Knickers pulled down to my ankles, fingers fumbling. The pain of catching the uneven rim of it on my inner thigh dulling the sting of my cheek. The warmth of blood. Then it's out. Falling to the floor – ding, ding – like when someone's wanting to make a speech at a wedding. Silence afterwards, though. Then the blood falls – one drop, another, spotting the grey tiles. I'm not for caring. It's out.

She opened her legs and craned her neck to get a look at the grey toilet paper – spots and blotches of blood, as pure red as child's paint, seeping towards dryness. Aoife thought of the time during the Christmas holidays the year before when Ciáran was hit by a snowball thrown from the other side of the train tracks. A slushy snowball with a stone hidden inside, one harmful thing inside a harmless one, like the car bomb the Provos had parked outside the peelers' barracks down at Donegall Pass. They'd never worked out whether the stone had been pushed inside, as intentionally as the planted bomb, or gathered up with an innocent handful of half-melted snow, but given that it had been thrown from the Loyalist estate there was a fair chance that it had been assembled carefully by the Protestant kids. Either way, it had left Ciáran flattened on the icy pavement with a hot stream of blood flowing from a gash above his eye.

'She was an educated woman.' Mary-Jo's voice travelled faintly from the main room of the salon. Then she repeated herself, loudly, for the benefit of Mrs McGrath's wax-encrusted ears. 'She was an educated woman.'

'Indeed she was,' Muireann agreed.

'Educated?' screeched Mrs McGrath; her voice sounded as though there was a layer of rust to be scraped off before it would be in working order. 'Away on with you, Mary-Jo – what would a volunteer need an education for?'

'Up at the university there,' Muireann said.

'A volunteer needs an education like the rest of us,' Mary-Jo shouted. 'Sure they need to understand the history of it all and the culture of it all. Without an education they'd be fighting over nothing.'

'Is that so?' Mrs McGrath replied. 'Well, she'd more need of a mother's education or at least a bit of religious training, if you ask me. In my day, it was the man that went off at night on the jobs.'

'Changed days, Mrs McGrath; a modern woman, she was.'

'A hallion, is all,' Mrs McGrath answered quickly. 'Youse all saw the way that her and them other women carried on back seven or eight years past, smearing their cells with each and every excretion that came out of them. Disgusting, it was.'

'It did turn my stomach, now, I'll admit,' Muireann said.

'They were on a dirty protest,' Mary-Jo replied. 'You should remember rightly what it was they were protesting as well; after all, wasn't it yourself that was strip-searched time and again as you went in to visit your man.'

'Appalling, it was,' Mrs McGrath said. 'Every visit.'

'And those women prisoners had to put up with that and more, a brave amount more from what I hear, each and every day.'

'And I'd to carry out the comms and support not just my own, but all of them blanket men. That was my role, as a woman in the community, but I'd never have lived knee-deep in my own filth, with even my monthly blood mixed in – '

'They were on a protest,' Mary-Jo repeated, interrupting.

'It's unclean, is my last word on it.'

Aoife smiled softly to herself, a smile as sour as the settling smell of urine that clung to the walls of the airless bathroom. She reached up and pulled the flush, drowning out the voices of the women in the next room, then raised herself from the cold toilet seat. Unfurling a long ribbon of bog-roll, she folded the paper over and over again before tucking the neat square of it in at the crotch of her once-white knickers. They were stiff now with the tie-dye of blood. Easing them on, and the jeans after, Aoife turned to the sink and set the tap running. At first she only turned the dirt-veined block of soap over in her hands to draw enough suds for the washing of her hands but, as the slimy-white of it gathered, she found herself rubbing at her cheeks, over the bridge of her nose and up onto her forehead. The skin on her face stung as she scrubbed at it with her nails and rinsed it with the icy cold water from the tap.

I sit there trembling for the next hour, so shook that I can't move. My skirt is hitched up to the waist, the blood trickling from my white skin to the whiter toilet bowl. I know rightly that I need to clean myself up. I know that. But not yet. Outside the cubicle, in the bathroom, groups of girls come and go, chattering on about all manner of things. I need help, I know that too. Not from the likes of them, though. I need help from the boys.

Months later, in a bar just down the street, I'll explain to Baldy how I've gone about those first two. I'll go step-by-step through how I've set about getting Billy and Nigel. Modus operandi, they call it – MO. Once I've finished, though, Baldy will just shake his head. The flick of it will set his thick brown hair to rippling, like in a shampoo advert. I'll think, at first, that he's shaking his head because of the dangers of it, the risks I've taken. Not a bit of it. He's doing it because I've not done my homework. I've selected targets based on their appearance, where they lived, the big-man boasts they'd come out with – I've been operating a system of tells. Like the Loyalist death squads who lifted Catholics, any Catholic, off the street back in the Seventies. Like the Shankill Butchers. Nothing political about my choices, no research. It's amateur hour, so it is: random targets chosen without even knowing the first thing about them. It's sectarian.

Seated on the toilet after Nigel, though, I'm not thinking that my choosing him has been a mistake because he might have been an innocent. I'm not thinking that singling him out on the basis of a tattoo was ropey reasoning, or that he might not have been the best fit for the slit-and-wrench of the thing inside me.

All of that comes later, with Baldy. All I'm thinking, in the toilets of that bar, is that I've chosen poorly because the brick shithouse of a man I picked out could've laid me out. I could've been properly hurt. That's my only regret in the aftermath of my second time out. That, and the fact that I didn't properly hurt him. The knowledge that Nigel is still fully functional.

Shivering as much from the chill now as from the fright, I decide that I need help in case things go arse-about-tit again. I need a safety net. Back-up. I don't know it there and then, with blood cooling and crusting on my inner thigh and hot tears dribbling down my cheeks, but I also need help to make sure that it's the right men that are being forced to take their oil. The men who get this treatment shouldn't just be wrong place, wrong time. They should be marked. Eye-for-an-eye.

5

Through the rest of 1988, Aoife and Ciáran began to meet near enough every evening in the concrete playground at the end of the street. More personal trainer than girlfriend, she would spend the evening cycling alongside as Ciáran ran along the Ormeau Road, up the Embankment and out onto the Lagan towpath, before cutting through at the bottom of Stranmillis and circling back via the university. He was training for the trials for the St Malachy's Gaelic Athletic Club hurling team in the new year and he needed to be fit and strong so that there'd be a hope of them overlooking his age and including him in the first-team squad.

Aoife was happy enough to take the tour of the leafy streets of South Belfast during the spring and warmer weeks of summer, but it began to feel like a chore as the nights drew in and the tyres of the bicycle began crunching and then sliding off the frosty pavements so that she fell behind the steady pace of Ciáran and had to swerve out onto the road to catch up with him. There were only two things that kept her going. The first was the look of grim satisfaction on Ciáran's face as they turned off Botanic Avenue and rounded the corner towards home. He'd give her a wink then, as they slowed to a stop – like a famous sportsman acknowledging an adoring fan – and she'd clamber off her bike to reward him with a kiss that tasted of the salt of his sweat. The second was the promise of the end-of-season dance at St Malachy's at the end of September.

It was taken for granted that Aoife would go to the dance with Ciáran. He never asked her and she never asked him to ask her, but he got his mammy to take the trouser legs up on his daddy's suit trousers so as they would fit him and she went to the shops on Royal Avenue with her Auntie Eileen to find a dress. Still no mention of being boyfriend and girlfriend, right enough, but surely it was only a matter of time once they'd been on their first proper date.

Aoife's excitement seemed to stir some dying ember in her mammy too. All of a sudden, Cathy took to humming softly to herself as the sink refilled and turning to Aoife every time she entered the kitchen so that she could fix her with a smile that was half admiration and half envy.

'You like my dress, Mammy?' Aoife asked, two days before the dance, little expecting an answer. She held the dress up against herself, admiring the way it fell down past her knees, brushing imaginary lint off the black trim and smoothing non-existent wrinkles out of the purple and white flowery pattern.

'It's gorgeous, love,' her mammy answered.

Aoife was silent and still, until she realised that her hand had dropped and that the dress was trailing on the kitchen floor. She lifted it quickly, and set to brushing at the hem again.

The days that followed saw Cathy Brennan take more of an interest in events going on around her than she had in many a month. There was even the occasion – when Aoife came in to show her the hairstyle that Cliona had spent all afternoon pinning and spraying into place – that she stepped away from the sink and placed soap-sudded hands onto Aoife's cheeks.

'You'll be the prettiest girl there, I'm sure of it,' she said.

On the day itself there was even some talk, between Aoife's mammy and daddy, of Damien and Becky forming a second couple and going to the fundraiser as well, but it was decided – mainly because of Damien's scowl at the suggestion – that it was maybe only teenagers who should be going to a dance where alcohol would be served.

At the dance, the hurling players gathered around the bar of the streamer-strewn hall and were cheered to the low-slung rafters by the rest of the room. Then everyone sat down to dinner and the craic was such that the spluttering laughter sent mouthfuls of sausage roll flying across the table and pints of stout were toppled by enthusiastic supporters who were wanting to shake hands with the local boy – from just down the street, you know – who'd played in the all-Ireland down at Croke Park. The dancing itself saw the wives and girlfriends of the GAA players hanging onto the muscled arms of their partners and spinning round the hall until they were so dizzy that they had to sit themselves down for a spell.

And all Aoife could think, all through the night, was that the frozen fingers fumbling with the bicycle chain and the grazed knee that had wept into a bandage for a full week after she came off the bike by the King's Bridge had been worth it. It would be a sacrifice worth making if only Ciáran would actually dance with her, if only she could have all eyes on her as she was whirled, light-headed, across the dance floor. He showed no sign, though, of rising from his seat, holding out his hand to her and leading her out to join the gathered couples. Instead he spent his time twisting his head this way and that to try to catch sight of the coach or the club secretary, with his leg jiggling underneath the table until it rattled the cutlery, and his fingers flaking the label from the bottle of beer that had been bought for him by one of the older boys. Aoife tried to drop a hint or two, tried to stay his leg by setting her hand on his knee, but he quietened her with a frown and reached down to remove her hand with fingers that were damp from the condensation of the beer bottle.

There was a hush at the end of the dancing and a rush of cold air as the doors to the hall opened, and then three men in top-to-toe camouflage, with balaclavas over their faces, sauntered through the tables towards the stage at the front. They passed collection tins down into the willing hands of the crowd and the band struck up to play 'The Soldier's Song' while someone busied themselves with setting up the slide projector. As the coins rattled the sides of the collection tins, the slides showed men similar to the ones up on the stage, crouching down in ditches as if waiting for a passing foot patrol, lying on their fronts in a sniping position with their gun focused on a distant target. *This is where your money's going*, the slides said; *this is what it's being used for.*

It was the silence that came over him, the sidelong glance at Aoife, that made her question the real reason for Ciáran wanting to get himself fit for the St Malachy's trials. There was no distraction to him now, no fidgeting. Aoife sat back in her seat, took a gulp from the untouched glass of Coke that had been set in front of her at the start of the night, and examined him more closely. It was the way he leant forward, the concentration to his stare as he listened to the speeches, that let on that he was thinking of the glory of walking in at the end of the GAA fundraiser rather than at the beginning. The curl to the corner of his lips as the slides changed told that he was imagining carrying an armalite rather than a hurley, and of being met by reverent silence rather than drunken cheering. With a wave of nausea, Aoife realised that Ciáran had his sights set on becoming a gunman rather than a hurler.

The memory of the two funerals sharpened for her then, took on an added significance. They had taken place in March of that year, back when she'd been blinded as to what Ciáran's ambitions might be.

True, she'd seen the anger that had contorted Ciáran's face when he got back from the first funeral up at Milltown. He was raging, there was no doubt. Deep breathing fit to burst a lung and with a vein bulging from his head that was near pushing his hair into a side-parting. He'd been on the edges of the crowd when Michael Stone ran up the slope. There'd been that first explosion from the lobbed grenade, those seconds of confusion, and then he'd seen the IRA men at the front telling everyone to get down, telling everyone to crawl to graves that were not their own and hide behind the headstones.

The way that Ciáran told it, he'd been one of the first to give chase. He'd been at the head of a group of young men who sped down towards the Loyalist gunman, weaving in and out of the headstones as they ran. A fourteen-year-old leading the charge, a boy leading the men. Bullets from Stone's gun had skimmed his shoulder, he said, had embedded themselves in the granite of the headstones as he passed. He wasn't for caring, though, he wasn't for hiding behind a grave; he'd no notion that one of those bullets might catch him and leave him back in Milltown three days later, to take up permanent residence there.

Aoife hadn't thought that there was anything other than anger to him after that first funeral. He'd been shook. His face had drained of colour and he was trembling so badly that he couldn't even hold his cigarette steady. When she saw him after the second funeral, though, after the two British soldiers had been murdered in broad daylight by the IRA, he was flushed. His eyes were sparking with that much excitement that Aoife reckoned he could have lit up his cigarette just by looking down at the tip of it.

'You OK?' Aoife had asked.

'I'm grand.'

'You saw what happened?'

'I heard.'

'You didn't have anything to do with it, though?'

'Wise up,' he'd replied, making his way over to the bench.

It was only all those months later, at the end-of-season dance at St Malachy's, that Aoife saw that those two-word answers had hidden a decision. That was the folded corner in the history books that showed the point at which Ciáran Gilday decided to volunteer for the Provos. It was his experiences that day that had seen him begin his training regime, taking to the streets to get himself ready for active service.

Watching him at the dance, seeing that the excitement in his eyes came not from the anticipation of stepping out onto the dance floor and showing off his pretty young girlfriend

78

in her new purple and white dress with the black lace trim but from the opportunity to rub shoulders with the great and good of the Republican movement, Aoife realised the part he'd probably played in that second funeral back in March.

It wasn't that she thought he'd have been one of those who pulled the two soldiers, in their civilian clothes, from the unmarked car, or that she thought him capable of dragging them to Casement Park, stripping them to their underwear and beating them. He wouldn't have been the one who, finally, pulled the trigger and left the two men lying there to receive their last rites. But Aoife was certain now that he'd have been one of the ones in the crowd. She had her doubts about his bragging that he'd been the first one to chase Stone; but she had precious few doubts that he'd have been one of the first to shout, and maybe even let out a small cheer, as the windows to the car were smashed and the soldiers were pulled out through a shower of broken glass. It wasn't the anger of being the hunted that tipped the scales and led to his wanting to be a gunman, but the thrill of being the hunter.

It's Ciáran who first introduces us, at the Rose and Crown on the Ormeau Road. A packed bar, all cigarette smoke and gilt mirrors. The horse racing is on the telly, muted, and there's a spread of sandwiches, sausage rolls and the like, up the back, by the bogs. A grey-haired man with crutches is running an amateur bookie's, handing out slips of paper and stuffing the money down into an overflowing pint glass. Ciáran looks beyond him, though, to a man at the table behind. Baldy. It's obviously an ironic nickname, judging by the long, flowing hair and the thick, brown beard on him. Like Jesus. Like the blanket men.

"Bout you,' I say, nodding to him.

He nods back and peers at me from behind tinted specs. Sepia-tinted. You can't see his eyes for them. To the side of me, Ciáran shifts from foot to foot.

'What can I get you?' Ciáran whispers, leaning towards me.

'Tonic water, just.'

'I'll leave youse to it, then.'

As Ciáran leaves for the bar, Baldy motions to the empty chair opposite. I sit myself down. He offers a cigarette. When I wave them away, he lights one up for himself. Through the fresh haze of smoke, he stares at me. The rest of the bar is all movement and noise. A popular horse has won and the pint glass is being emptied into dozens of hands. The entire place is in uproar. Yet it's silence and stillness I feel.

'I'm led to understand that you want to serve the cause,' Baldy finally says, flatly. It's neither a question nor a statement. He speaks as though to himself.

'Yes.' I nod. 'And no.'

'Oh?' This time it's a question, but his tone of voice doesn't change. Instead, an eyebrow lifts itself above the wire rim of his glasses.

'I have something in mind, you see,' I say. 'It's help I'm after. Assistance.'

The other eyebrow lifts and he looks at me over the top of the glasses, so as I can see an upper edge of his green eyes. Bloodshot.

'I'm not wanting to be doing errands,' I continue, swallowing. 'Or to move arms in a pram, or make cups of tea for the Army Council. I have something specific in mind. Something that would inflict real damage.'

'I see,' he says. And smiles, gently.

Acting as Ciáran's personal trainer lost some of its appeal for Aoife after the night of the fundraiser. It had all been a brave disappointment, particularly since he hadn't passed even a single comment about her dress. Without washing it, or even smoothing out the wrinkles, Aoife placed it on its hanger in the wardrobe and left it there for the moths. Her bike, kept in the hall for handiness' sake for the past six months, was left out by the back gate to be eaten at by rust. She resolved that she'd not be needing either of them again in a hurry. There was more to discourage her than the weather now; more to it than the fact that, as they moved into winter, the bite to the night air stopped them from lingering on their parting kiss; more than the feel of his chapped lips – rough as sandpaper – against her own. There was more to it, even, than her sudden sharp dislike for the taste of his sweat – vinegar rather than salt now – or the clammy moisture that transferred itself, in a thin film, from his cheek to hers.

So Aoife had no complaints when Ciáran drafted wee Damien in as a like-for-like replacement in the weeks before the hurling trials. The younger Brennan didn't need to be asked twice. He also didn't need a bike. At a trot, he followed close at the heel of Ciáran, keeping pace but never pulling out in front.

For her part, Aoife reverted to helping Becky with her jewellery-making in the evenings. After dinner, she would make her way round to the Gildays' house and stand by the table with a cup of tea cradled in her hands whilst Becky worked away. If Declan came into the room at any stage, then Aoife just fixed him with a glare and answered all of his questions with one word or less – a grunt, a shake of the head – until he was drawn away from the kitchen, either by boredom or by the noise from his wife's throat carrying through from the living room.

There was no fear to Aoife now. She'd learnt rightly that there was no one looking out for her other than herself. She wasn't feared to meet Declan's appraising gaze, or to place a staying hand on Ciáran's chest whenever he came in from his run and leant in towards her, expecting a kiss.

'What's wrong with you?' he said to her, the first time.

'You're all sweat, so you are. Away and have a wash.'

'Will you kiss me after, then?'

Aoife shrugged as if she couldn't care less, but she kissed him when he came down the stairs tasting of soap and toothpaste.

Quickly enough, they settled into a new routine: Aoife waiting for Ciáran to come in from his run and then the two of them standing by the kitchen counter while Becky worked silently away at the kitchen table. Ciáran even stopped drinking milk from the bottle and took to staying in the room long enough for the kettle to boil and the tea to draw.

'When are the hurling trials?' Aoife asked him, one night, over the rim of her mug.

She was trying to make conversation, so as to glide over the fact that Ciáran had come down from his wash bare-chested, with only a pair of shorts on.

'Next week,' he replied, reaching an arm past her to click on the kettle.

'Is that right?' Aoife caught her lip between her teeth. 'Are you going to them, then?'

'I would say so, aye.' He grinned. 'Wouldn't want it all to go to waste, would we?'

As he spoke, he stepped in to Aoife and she tilted her face up towards him. He pressed against her, angling his hips. Aoife pulled away.

'Becky,' she hissed, as a warning to Ciáran.

'Yes?' The wee girl looked up, innocently, from her work.

'Nothing, love, I was just reminding your brother that we need to include you in the conversation.' She stepped away from Ciáran, over towards the table. 'What are you working on, anyway?'

Ciáran sniffed and shrugged and wet the tea in his mug, as if he didn't mind, but the next night – when he came down the stairs after his wash – he was wearing a T-shirt and trousers.

On the night of the hurling trials, Aoife spent a fair bit of time on her appearance. She didn't wear a purple and white dress or brave the cold in a miniskirt, but she did spend a long while taming the ginger frizz of her hair, carefully applying make-up, and choosing the right jeans and top combination for to catch the eye of the Gilday son without drawing the eye of the father.

There was precious little work done at the kitchen table that night. Becky was near shaking with anticipation, and smiling shyly up at Aoife every few seconds as though they'd a secret between them. Aoife, for her part, found herself drinking the kettle dry – time and again – as she made cup after cup of tea. The caffeine set her to fiddling with her hair until the tightly coiled curls of it began to trail messily down across her cheeks.

When Ciáran came in, though, he didn't so much as glance at her. He'd a face on him that would send you running for an exorcism kit and the holy water. Aoife didn't step forward to kiss him, but instead busied herself with refilling the kettle and getting the milk from the fridge.

Ciáran wasn't for waiting for a cup of tea, though. Instead, he reached in past Aoife and lifted one of his daddy's bottles of stout.

'What's the matter with you?' Aoife finally asked, after the kettle had built up a head of steam and Ciáran had swallowed away half the bottle of stout.

'Nothing.'

'There is too.'

There was no answer, but the stout bottle clinked against his teeth as he took another gulp. Aoife stepped in close, placing a hand on his chest. She'd have reached up to give him a kiss, maybe, if he hadn't eased her aside.

'Ciáran?' she tried again.

'What?'

'What's the matter? Did you not get in?'

'They said I could come along to training on the odd occasion, if I'd a mind to, but that I wasn't ready for the firsts,' he said it sourly.

'Is that not good, but?'

He shrugged, and took another pull on his bottle of stout.

'Well?'

'It was your wee brother they were mad on.' Ciáran lifted his eyes to her, then looked away. 'Said he was one of the best they'd ever seen for his age. They had a hard time believing it, so they did, that he was only ten years old.'

'Is that right?' Aoife placed a teabag in a mug and poured in the milk and then the boiling water. She was stalling for time, trying to process what Ciáran was saying and work out why he was so annoyed by it. 'How come Damien was even there?'

'He was waiting for me outside, so I saw no harm in bringing him along.'

'And he was that good?'

'For his age, aye.'

'Right.' Aoife nodded, as if she understood, and lifted the teabag out with a spoon. She tried to hand the cup to Ciáran, but he ignored it and slammed his empty bottle down on the counter. The glass wobbled and rang for a moment before settling. 'Is that not just because he plays with you older boys, though?' she asked.

'I'd say it is, yeah.' Ciáran began peeling off his sweat-stained T-shirt. 'But, whatever the reason, they'd precious little interest in me once they saw him flying around.'

'Ach, Ciáran, I'm sorry. There'll be other chances, though; other – '

'It's no bother to me,' he replied. 'None at all.'

'You can still go up to training with them, they said?'

'Will I fuck.' Ciáran wiped at his mouth with the back of his hand. 'I've better things to be doing, in any case, than hanging about with armchair Republicans. I'm not wanting to be wasting my energy chasing a ball round a pitch – '

'What would you rather be doing?' Aoife asked, softly.

Ciáran didn't reply.

'Ciáran?'

'You know rightly,' he answered, in a whisper.

Aoife looked up at him, knowing full well what he was meaning. There were better ways to serve the cause, he was thinking – to get himself noticed. Ways to get his name in the mouths of the youngsters running about the estate. Or in the newspaper. Or on the gable wall.

'Ciarán – ' Aoife began.

'I'm away for a wash,' he said, turning from her and striding towards the door.

'The most important thing, then,' Baldy says, after I've finished telling him, 'is that you don't leave anything behind. That's vital.'

Bloodstains on the carpet. 'Like what?' I ask.

'Anything that can be linked back to you.'

High-heeled shoe, down a lane. 'Anything else?'

'Well, no witnesses, if you can help it.'

'I'm always going to be leaving one witness, but.'

'True. There's not many men would come forward to tell that story, though. Particularly not if they've a wife or a girlfriend.' Baldy smiles, briefly. I look away. The rest of the pub is paying us no mind. The pint glass of money is beginning to fill up again and the next race is about to begin. 'Another thing,' Baldy says. 'Make sure never to use the same house twice.'

Damascus Street. I nod, but don't meet his stare.

'You've already done that, haven't you?' Baldy clicks at the top of a pen, tears a square of card from his cigarette packet, and slides the two of them across the table to me. 'Write down the address,' he says. 'I'll sort it.'

As I scribble it down, Baldy motions to the grey-haired bookmaker at the next table. Lifting himself upright and walking across to us, without use of his crutches, he seats himself down beside Baldy and starts to pick at his teeth with his thumbnail.

'We took a hit in that last race,' he says. 'But we should make it back soon enough.'

Baldy nods. 'Meet Cassie,' he says.

'Benny,' the bookmaker stretches out the toothpick hand. 'Benny Fits.'

'Is that your real name?' I ask as I shake it. I clack my teeth together at the end so as to try and swallow it back in before he

hears it. No use, though – it's out. I should know that this isn't
the time or the place to be asking questions.

'Is Cassie your real name?' Benny replies, winking at me.
There's that much of his face involved in the wink that I think
he might be having a seizure or something, but he recovers
from it with a grunting laugh. 'My friends call me Benny Fits,'
he says. 'But there are different names on the social security
cheques, I suppose, so – '

'Listen,' Baldy cuts in. We listen. 'Benny can sort you out
with whatever you need, OK? Properties, fixtures and fittings,
whatever. Just remember one thing.' He pauses to grind his
half-smoked cigarette out against the side of the ashtray. Then
he licks his index finger and thumb, snuffs the smoking tip, and
tucks it away in his shirt pocket. 'At some point, you'll either get
caught or killed.'

I nod, and then swallow.

'Are you prepared for that?' he asks.

I swallow, and then nod.

'Good girl,' he says.

Getting into the Provos wasn't as easy as Ciáran first thought.
There was no dotted line to sign on, no recruiting officer for
to discuss pension options. It was a closed club. Especially to a
teenager whose only claim to Republican credentials was that
he'd once learnt – and subsequently forgotten – how to recite
the alphabet in Irish. Maybe that would have been enough
back in the late Sixties or early Seventies, when the Nationalist
areas were burning and the letters 'IRA' were said to stand for
'Irish Ran Away'. Back then, when anyone with two hands
and half a brain would be called on to defend their community
from the Loyalist mobs, they would have overlooked his
age. Maybe. Not in this day and age, though, what with
supergrasses bringing down entire Active Service Units with
their testimonies. The Provos weren't for just taking on any
hallion who took a notion to join. There was a screening

process, designed to make sure you weren't a Brit spy and that you had enough conviction to stop you becoming a tout if you were lifted, taken to Castlereagh and subjected to threats against you and yours. Truth be told, you needed to know one of the boys if you wanted in. You needed to be connected.

The good thing was that Ciáran knew more or less all of the boys. The bad thing was, they knew him too. They knew him rightly.

Big Gerry from down the way suggested that Ciáran join Sinn Féin, so as he could learn a bit about the history of the Republican struggle and maybe get involved in community organising or something like that there, turning to politics rather than to the paramilitaries. Problem was, that was all a wee bit too much like school for Ciáran. He didn't like attending school at the best of times, so volunteering himself for more lessons was never really an option, especially since it was as likely to see him ending up in a suit as in a balaclava. What he really wanted, Aoife reckoned, was to daub 'Brits out' on the gable wall, or to throw stones at the meat wagons when the peelers came calling, or even to carry out punishment beatings on the drug dealers or touts in the Nationalist community. He had no interest in marching against Army brutality or raising his voice in protest at police collusion with Loyalist paramilitaries. He wanted to be where the action was. He wanted to be a Che Guevara, a self-styled freedom fighter, the poster-boy for those fighting for a united Ireland.

That was how Aoife saw it, at least. As far as she could tell, Ciáran wanted to hold a gun and take pot-shots at Brit soldiers and then swagger back to the bar to a cheer and a waiting pint. It wasn't like that, though, this war. It couldn't be like that, with one of the best-equipped armies in the world breathing right down the back of your neck. You needed to have more than Ciáran had, Aoife was certain of that; you needed to be more than a teenage header with a death wish. She'd seen IRA men. Focused, they were. Ciáran Gilday didn't have that. And the boys knew it.

Still, Ciáran mitched off school and made his way down to the bars on the Ormeau Road every day to hover behind the high-stools of the connected men. That wasn't to say that he was playing butler to Army Council men, or even to active volunteers. Instead, he was running errands for the cousin of an IRA man or the brother-in-law of a Sinn Féin spokesman. He would take their crumpled pound notes – often the last of their dole money – and run to the shop to the right of the pub, to get them cigarettes, or to the bookmaker's on the left, to place a bet on the horses. It was all done in the hopes of getting a foot in the door with the Provos. And it was pointless, as Aoife knew full well. Truth be told, Ciáran probably knew it too. The boys that Ciáran actually wanted to be licking the arse of were mostly either on the run or in jail. Those of them that were free to come and go would dander into the pub only on the odd occasion, and they wouldn't let anyone they didn't know and trust within a hundred yards of them.

'Here I am,' Ciáran complained to Aoife, on the night of their Valentine's Day dinner. 'Here I am fucking busting my balls to try to serve the cause and no one's bloody taking me up on it. If I walked in there with a Union Jack draped over me, whistling the Sash, they'd still not pay a blind bit of notice.'

'Maybe, then, it's time to try – ' Aoife began.

'Aye, you're right,' Ciáran interrupted her. 'Maybe it's time to do something on my own. A spectacular, to get their attention.'

'Catch yourself on.' Aoife pulled away from him. 'If you went out on your own then those boys would be after you, them and the peelers. There'd either be a kneecapping or you'd be lifted.'

'Not if I did it right.'

'Don't even start.' Aoife looked him in the eye, then rose from the sofa to go and get the dinner from the kitchen. 'What I was going to say was,' she said as she walked away, 'maybe it's time to start thinking about school or that. Maybe a weekend job, like I've got down at the salon – '

'Away on.'

'Why not?' she called from the kitchen.

'I've chosen to fight for my community.'

'Your community doesn't want you, but.' Aoife winced as she said this. She'd been concentrating on carrying the heated plates of chicken and vegetables, not on choosing her words carefully. 'Listen, Ciáran,' she continued, as she handed him his plate, 'I'm not wanting to argue about it, anyway.'

Not tonight, she wanted to add. This was the night she'd set aside for clear-the-air talks with Ciáran: it was during the dinner that she would make him see that he'd no need for anything other than her in his life. He'd finally look her in the eye, declare that he'd no interest in becoming a gunman, and ask her to be his girlfriend.

Ciáran nodded, but the way he stabbed at his chicken made Aoife think that he'd not been best pleased with what she'd said. Not to worry, though – as long as they moved on and spoke about something else. As long as their Valentine's Day wasn't ruined. She'd put a fair amount of effort into the evening. Her daddy was working the evening shift, driving a taxi for the company that worked out of a wee shack off Botanic Avenue. He'd packed in the gardening and was instead nursing his bad back by driving people about, day and night, for a pittance. Getting rid of Damien had been more difficult, what with him tending to follow Ciáran about like a bad smell. Aoife had been forced to bargain with him. The final cost of getting him to stay upstairs for the night had been ten packets of football stickers and a tin whistle.

After concluding negotiations with Damien, Aoife had set to work on the food itself. The cooking was made wile fiddly by the need to duck and dive past her mammy at the kitchen sink. It was astonishing to Aoife how much her mammy, despite standing stationary for the duration, got in the way. Aoife would turn from the oven and near scald her mammy's arm with the baking tray, or she would dash from the hob to the sink with the steaming potatoes, and trip over her mammy's feet so that she had to stumble halfway across the room just to stop herself from landing flat on her face. At one stage – as Aoife moved from fridge to cooker whilst peeling the raw bacon rashers apart – she was sure that her mammy even took a step backwards so as to knock her off course. Cathy Brennan never said a word though, even when Aoife challenged her about it. With a shake of the head, Aoife just got on with her preparations.

The chicken wrapped in bacon with sides of mashed potato and sweetcorn had been carefully chosen, because Ciáran was the kind of fussy eater who wouldn't eat anything that a child couldn't draw with a handful of crayons. Aoife had been interrogating him for days about what he did and didn't like to eat, and she'd ended up with only one possibility: chicken, bacon, potato and sweetcorn. Then there had been the issue of actually getting Ciáran to come over. She wasn't wanting to tell him that it was a Valentine's date, wasn't wanting to force him into anything official. It was better, Joanne said to her, to get him to the stage where he couldn't deny he was her boyfriend and then to ask him out. A relationship by stealth. That evening was all about tempting Ciáran over and then easing him into a date-like situation. The problem with that was, by the time Aoife had got all her cooking done, Ciáran had already had his own dinner at home. So Aoife and Ciáran's (unofficial) Valentine's date consisted of Ciáran eating a surprise second dinner, whilst a wheezy off-key whistling noise serenaded them from up the stairs in Damien's room.

'Maybe your da could have a word,' Ciáran said, spearing a kernel of sweetcorn. It was the first time either of them had spoken since they'd started eating and both of their plates were now half-empty. Aoife was glad of the conversation, but was also puzzled by it.

'Mine?' she said. 'My dad?'

'Yours, aye.' Ciáran sniffed and laid down his fork. 'I was actually meaning to come over and have a chat with him, so I was. Are you expecting him back?'

'My daddy?' Aoife repeated.

'Jesus Christ, wee girl,' Ciáran sighed. 'How many times?'

'What would you want to speak to him about, but?'

'I wanted to see if he could pull a few strings, maybe, arrange a meet for me.'

'But my daddy's no more connected than you are,' Aoife said. Her bewilderment was that intense, and Ciáran was looking at her with that much scorn, she felt tears at her eyes. 'Is he?' she asked.

She was doubting herself now. Maybe she'd just never noticed. Maybe her daddy was out on jobs each and every night and he was just acting drunk whenever he staggered through the door in the small hours of the morning. Maybe his taxi had a balaclava helmet in the glove box and a stack of armalites in the boot. Maybe there was Semtex behind the plasterboard in their house, or maybe her mammy was standing guard over a box of grenades hidden beneath the kitchen sink. Right enough, there were rumours that the cab company that he worked for was a front for the Irish National Liberation Army, but Aoife had thought nothing of it. After all, every taxi company in Northern Ireland was a front for one paramilitary organisation or another. If that was the only thing that made him connected, then every businessman who hailed a cab to get to a meeting and every housewife who phoned a taxi to get the shopping home was connected.

'He works for Baldy Carroll, doesn't he?' Ciáran spoke slowly, obviously thinking that he'd need to spell it out at eejit pace if she was to understand. 'Baldy's high up in the INLA, Aoife.'

'I thought you wanted to join the Provos, but?' It was all Aoife could think of to say. She knew she wasn't being daft. It was Ciáran himself who was, in presuming that, because her daddy drove a cab for that shower, then he must be one of the boys. He couldn't possibly be more than a taxi meter to them.

'The INLA is close enough,' Ciáran replied, wiping first at his nose and then at his face. A slug's trail of mucus smeared itself across his cheek, but Aoife didn't think it was a good time to be pointing things like that out to him. 'Besides,' he continued, 'the IRA obviously aren't wanting me, so this is just another option.'

'But – ' Aoife began.

'It's the same struggle, Aoife. The INLA had hunger strikers who died too, you know. Two of them.' He paused. 'At least, I think it was two.'

Aoife stood and angrily began clattering the plates together. Neither of them had finished their food, but as far as she was concerned the meal was over. Forks and clumps of mashed potato went flying.

'What the fuck's the matter with you?' he asked.

'Are you serious?' She sat down. 'You are serious, aren't you?' Her voice had dropped. She set the plates down on the cushions and cradled her forehead in her hands.

'I'm deadly serious, certainly.'

'My daddy couldn't pass on your name to Baldy Caldwell, even if he wanted to, Ciáran. Those boys wouldn't have an earthly notion as to who he was.'

'Carroll. His name is Baldy Carroll.'

'I'm guessing his name isn't Baldy Carroll, actually,' Aoife snapped. 'No mother in her right mind would christen a wee babby with the name of Baldy.'

'It's a nickname, you daft wee girl.'

'I know it's a fucking nickname – ' Aoife clamped a hand over her mouth and waited for her breathing to return to normal. The night wasn't going to script. She didn't know what annoyed her more: the idea that her daddy might have links to men like that, or that Ciáran actually wanted such links. Thieves and murderers, they were. She knew all the arguments, she'd heard the spiel, but they were still just thieves and murderers.

'Are you expecting him back, then?' Ciáran asked, again. 'Your daddy, I mean.'

'He's working,' Aoife replied. 'That's why I invited you over. I thought it'd be nice to have the place to ourselves on Valentine's night.'

This time, as she picked up the plates, her hands were steady. She'd worked out why she was so upset. It wasn't just that the romantic evening was done for, or that he'd not noticed the new black skirt with gold trim that she'd picked up that afternoon in the city centre, or the wave to her hair that Cliona had spent over an hour on. She was raging about those things as well, right enough, but it was more than that – more than him trying to turn their Valentine's Day into a recruitment drive for the paramilitaries. It was the realisation that Ciáran's plan might actually come off. He had no earthly hope of getting himself into the Provos, but he might have a fair chance of slipping under the radar and getting himself involved in another Republican grouping. Her daddy might even be able to help him with it. After all, he ferried those men around Belfast at all hours. He might have only been a taxi meter, but Aoife was yet to meet a person who didn't pay close attention to the meter from the very moment the taxi journey began. All it would take would be a word or two. It might just happen the way Ciáran hoped it would. He might get the folded corner in the history book yet. Aoife worried what that book would say about him, though. She had a wile sickening feeling that it wouldn't be complimentary. He was more than likely to end up as a footnote to an atrocity. Or worse.

'Ciáran,' she said, over her shoulder, as she made her way back through to the kitchen. 'If you do ask my daddy about this then it's over between us, OK?'

The Regal job is the first that Baldy has a hand in. My first official job as a volunteer. Not that I've been green-booked – truth be told, I don't have a notion if the INLA even have a handbook in the same way as the Provos do – and not that I've been paid. It isn't about the money. This is casual work.

Meticulous, Baldy is. Every detail covered. We meet in his spare bedroom and he hands me a brown manila envelope. There's a sheaf of papers inside with a photograph attached by a paperclip. It shows a young man: fair hair, with a rash of acne across his chin.

'Take a good look,' Baldy says to me. Then he stands behind, waiting, until I nod and hold the photo out to him. He takes it, holds a lighter to the corner until the flames begin to curl, then drops it into the wastepaper basket.

'How did you get all this?' I ask, flicking through the official papers – DWP, DVLA – that tell more or less everything about this Charles White except for his dick size. That's the one piece of information that might have been useful, but it isn't on his application to join the Royal Ulster Constabulary.

Baldy ignores the question. 'Whitey, you call him.'

'Whitey,' I repeat, like an amen.

Then Baldy spreads a map of the city out on the mattress and points a nicotine-tipped finger at the right-hand corner. 'Lives with his mother out in East Belfast,' he says. 'Father was a prison guard. Deceased.'

'Why him?' I ask, wanting to know if it's for his sins he's been identified or for the sins of his father.

Silence. Baldy looks at me. Green eyes beneath thick brown hair that's beginning to get the odd streak of silver through it. A cold stare, but not one to give you the shivers. Cold like granite rather than ice.

'You asked for legitimate targets,' he says, evenly. 'This is one.'

I look away, back down at the map, and swallow the other questions. He talks about how I'll scout it out, how I'll turn up on the doorstep and sell jewellery in return for information, over a course of months. We talk about Baldy waiting around the corner in his idling taxi. He'll be there, he says, as back-up. Take no chances, leave no loose ends. Standing there in his spare bedroom, with the floral wallpaper and curtains neatly tied back from the window, he takes out a gun – a handgun – that looks too heavy for his slender wrist and he gestures with it in a way that's meant to reassure but which serves only to scratch at my doubts.

'*Any questions?*' Baldy asks.

I shake my head.

'*This time will be different from the last,*' he says. '*No mistakes.*'

I nod.

6

As the Easter holidays came and went, Aoife focused on the jewellery business. Sales had been steady, but the school holidays had highlighted a problem with her business model. It was all well and good selling to wee girls when they were captive in the school playground, but what about over the long months of summer when the customers would be scattered off to the four corners of Belfast? Well, not the four corners, maybe. She didn't know any girls from East Belfast, and precious few were from the south of the city. Two corners, then, three at most.

Aoife's solution was simple enough. The two weeks or so that they had off for Easter had allowed Becky to build up a fair stockpile of earrings, bracelets and necklaces. There was a small mound of jewellery at the corner of her kitchen table, a few fistfuls, enough to expand the business to other nearby schools. If they couldn't sell any over the summer, Aoife reasoned, then they should sell their excess stock now and get some savings in place so as they could keep the whole enterprise lit over the holidays.

So, with an attaché case belonging to Declan Gilday tucked under Becky's arm, they started on a mini-tour of the schools of Belfast. They would have to skip the last class of the day so as they could get to the other schools before the bell, but they were learning more out on the streets than they would have in the classroom anyway. At least, that was what

Aoife told Becky. Becky just nodded and hoisted the case of jewellery up under her arm. Aoife had been sore tempted to ask what a binman needed an attaché case for, but she hadn't really spoken to Becky about the younger girl's daddy since the day that had ended with her hidden underneath the kitchen table.

The first school they visited was Methodist College. Methody, as it was known, was right across the street from Queen's University, and had the same vaulted-window grandeur and leaf-lined space. Aoife had formed a fanciful notion, over the years, that she would have gone to school there if her family had lived up the Malone Road. She could have walked up Malone to Methody every day and then, when the time came, made her way to the university on the opposite side of the road to begin her degree studies. It would have been a simple and sheltered existence, with no need to stray from that one road that cut right down through South Belfast. Never mind the issue of the fees for her schooling or the even bigger issue of her grades being nowhere near good enough for university admission. Never worry about all of that there – it was a fantasy after all. She took the time to air it freely as they sneaked in at the wrought-iron gates and set up a makeshift stall on an uneven tree stump by the chapel door.

Business was slow at first. The younger Methody girls, filing out in their royal blue uniforms, were nervous of the two girls who stood by the tree stump in brown and green with a gold trim. They twittered and flitted towards Aoife and Becky, but darted away as soon as Aoife opened her mouth to speak to them. Wee flighty things, they were, like the tiny birds that used to nest in the hedges at the edge of the estate. It wasn't until the older girls began streaming out – with the boys just behind them, hooked on their every word and in quite a few cases hooked onto an arm as well – that the sales started. Aoife didn't even need to pitch to these girls. They clustered around the case like magpies, plucking up one shiny thing after another with squeals of delight.

They weren't short of a bit of confidence, these older girls, and Aoife found that she felt shy in the face of their brashness. It was an odd sensation for her. After a while, she just stood back and let it happen. Boys bought for the girls, girls bought for other girls, girls bought for themselves. The younger girls, seeing the older ones buying and bartering, stepped forward as well. Becky's cupped hands filled with a pile of clinking coins.

Aoife watched on, carefully checking to see that no one took advantage of the scrum and tucked an unpaid-for necklace or set of earrings into their blazer pocket. It wasn't like that, though. The sun was angling through the trees, glinting on blonde hair and gleaming on brown. Laughter trickled through the conversation. Jewellery was hung from every available earlobe, around every neck, and fastened to every wrist. The gathered schoolgirls began to look like so many mannequins in a store window. Most of the girls were Protestant, all of them from the south of Belfast or the suburbs. They all had money. None of them had a mother who stood with her hands plunged in the sink day in, day out, or a daddy who was rarely seen or heard from unless he had the stink and slur of drink on him. None of them had to do a wash that night if they wanted their wee brother to wear a clean pair of trousers to school the next day. None of them had a boyfriend – an almost boyfriend – who would have chopped off his left hand if it meant he was given a gun for his right.

Aoife took a single stride forward and snapped the attaché case closed. The lid of it almost took the fingertips off a girl with ginger hair. Aoife stared her down and then turned to Becky, who wordlessly held out her pile of coins. Aoife poured the majority of them into her blazer pockets and then drip-fed the remainder back into Becky's hand. That would do for the younger girl's share, Aoife reckoned. It might not be an even split, but the whole thing had been Aoife's idea and there would be a fair amount of materials needed if they were to keep producing over the summer months. She patted at her pockets to make sure that the fabric would hold. The coins rustled against one another.

'Is that youse off?' a girl with curly brown hair and dimpled cheeks asked, sauntering forward. She seemed to have stilts for legs, but she was accomplished enough on them. 'Will you be back, at all?'

'Maybe,' Aoife replied. She'd been stung by the experience, but she knew rightly that they'd turned a sizeable profit.

'Who makes the jewellery anyway?' Stilts asked.

Becky tentatively raised her hand but, before all eyes could turn to her, a reedy voice interrupted. It came from behind Aoife. Close behind.

'What's all this?' it said. 'These uniforms don't look like ours.'

Aoife turned to face a man who was an inch taller than her, but a good two or three inches shorter than Stilts. In spite of his lack of height, he was obviously in charge. His own uniform was the tweed jacket and corduroy trousers of a teacher. He re-set his glasses on his nose and waited for an answer.

'I'm from the Convent,' Aoife replied. 'Both of us are. We're here visiting some friends.'

'Is that so?' He raised an eyebrow.

Aoife nodded.

'They were here to see me,' Stilts spoke up.

'You know these two girls, then, Bethany?'

'Yes, they're friends of mine.'

The teacher smirked at this, and then nodded. His eyes lingered on Bethany/Stilts for a moment. Aoife tried to use the seconds that he spent staring to lift the attaché case and make a getaway. She wasn't quick enough, though. Either that, or Stilts wasn't as transfixing as Aoife had imagined.

'Wait a minute.' The reedy voice had an English inflection to it. 'What's in the briefcase, Bethany?'

'What?'

'If these girls are your friends, then tell me what's in their briefcase.'

Stilts shrugged. She looked a bit less sure-footed now, as she tottered backwards into the semi-circle of pupils that had formed around Aoife, Becky and the teacher.

'You can tell me, then.' The teacher pointed to Becky. 'What's in that *man's* briefcase?'

Becky looked at Aoife. Aoife looked at the teacher, then at the semi-circle, trying to assess their options. They could make a run for it, but she doubted they'd get very far. Stilts seemed to have lost her influence, and the clutch of schoolkids who had found entertainment in hanging jewellery on one another might find it equally entertaining to chase the two Catholic schoolgirls off the premises and back to Lower Ormeau. With a shrug, more lopsided and awkward than the one Stilts had given a moment before, Aoife flicked open the case and held it out for inspection.

'It's jewellery,' she said softly. Then, with a flash of inspiration, she added, 'We're selling it for charity.'

'Is that right? Which charity?'

Aoife trawled through her memory.

'Amnesty International,' she replied, brightly. She had a vague recollection of them being mentioned on the telly from time to time when Civil Rights were brought up, or when they were on about allegations of torture up at Castlereagh Interrogation Centre.

'Well, if it's for a good cause.' The teacher smirked again, but there was no sarcasm to his voice this time. He reached out towards the few remaining items in the case, pointing to a necklace with a barbed wire and blue-stone pendant. 'I'll take this one for my wife, please.'

Aoife had to work hard to conceal her surprise, both at the fact that he had swallowed her story and at the notion that he had a wife. She lifted the necklace and trailed it into his hand. Tucking it into the pocket of his tweed jacket, the schoolmaster held out a crisp five-pound note. A Bank of England note.

'Keep the change,' he said. 'And tell them to keep up the good work.'

'I'll be sure to do that,' Aoife replied. She had nowhere to put the unexpected fiver, so she crumpled it into the palm of her hand. Then she clipped the case closed and, with a fixed smile on her face, turned to leave.

'Fancy an ice-cream, Becky?' she asked, as they walked back through the Botanic Gardens. 'My treat.'

Becky nodded eagerly.

'Hold this, then.'

Aoife handed her the attaché case and left her standing by the hot-house while she wandered over to the ice-cream van. As she queued, Aoife watched the students lounging about on the grass. They were older versions of Stilts and the rest of the Methody girls, and the boys, although that bit older than the Methody boys, were working just as hard to impress. They all had footballs or frisbees or books as props, but they seemed to spend half the time squinting over at the pretty girls to see if they were being watched. None of them looked over Aoife's way, though. Even the fair-haired boy serving the ice-cream barely looked at her as he handed her the two '99 cones.

Licking at the ice-creams as they walked, the two entrepreneurs made their way home. They took the short-cut through the Holylands, with Becky struggling to keep the jewellery case tucked in at her armpit whilst at the same time carefully using her tongue to gouge the ice-cream out from around the chocolate flake. She ended up with a moustache and beard of ice-cream, like those on babbies who couldn't feed themselves. Aoife stopped for a moment, as they walked down Lawrence Street, to wipe at Becky's face with the sleeve of her blazer. Becky didn't say a word at that, just stood and waited for Aoife to finish. She also didn't say a word when she lost the flake from her cone. It happened as they clambered through the hole in the fence and slipped and slid down the muddy slope onto McClure Street. Aoife didn't see it happen, but she noticed that, by the time they'd both skated to the bottom, Becky's chocolate had disappeared, leaving a deep crater in the remaining ice-cream. She expected to see Becky's face crumple at that, to see the waterworks starting. Becky just sniffed, and set to nibbling at the cone. Aoife was wile impressed, so she was, because it showed that Becky was growing up. A couple of months before, she would have started up rightly and there'd have been tears all the way up the street, but not now. Licking at her own sticky fingers, Aoife lifted her flake from the cone and handed it to the younger girl.

'Take mine,' she said. 'You deserve it, anyway, for your work back there.'

Becky smiled and took the flake. She stared at it, brown pools forming against her meltingly hot fingers, and then snapped the chocolate in two. She handed one half back to Aoife, and used the other to scoop the slushy ice-cream from the cone. They walked in silence until they parted ways by Becky's front gate.

With half a flake between her teeth, held there like a fat cigar, Aoife made her way up the path to her own house. She glanced in at the front window before reaching up to put her key into the lock. The flake fell from her lips, then, to break against the concrete of the doorstep. Seated side by side on the sofa, in the front room, were her daddy and Ciáran. They both had a can of beer clasped between their knees.

'You wee ratboy, you,' Aoife breathed, wrenching the door open and striding on into the front room. Ciáran and her daddy both looked up at her, smiling, as she came in. Ciáran didn't even have the good grace to look guilty. In fact, he had that much of a lack of grace that he slowly closed his right eye into a wink. Deliberate, it was, because he knew it would do her head in.

'Aoife, love,' her daddy said, 'get us another beer, will you?'

Aoife ignored the can that was waved in front of her, back and forth like a silent servant's bell, and spoke directly to Ciáran. 'What are you doing here?' she demanded.

'I'm visiting with your da, just,' Ciáran replied, placing his empty beer can down on the floor and setting the sole of his trainer on the top of it. He paused a second, for effect, before crumpling it down into the carpet. 'I'll have another one as well – cheers.'

It's the bomb at Canary Wharf that gets us going on the fourth. The end of the ceasefire. Baldy thought it best to lie low for a while after Whitey, to let the dust settle. Then there'd been all that false dawn of Clinton walking down the Falls Road and shaking hands with Gerry Adams, all the talks of meetings between the Shinners and the British. The British still fucking the Nationalist community, just lengthening their stroke. The war is not over.

It has to be carefully scouted, this fourth job. Baldy insists on it. So we take our time. We're selective. From a pool of candidates we choose Dave Gibson, a wee dumpling of a man with a receding hairline that he tries to cover with a wispy fringe. He's a British Army sapper from Cornwall who served two tours in the Province and then decided to retire to Bangor. Poor decision, that. He would've been better to have retired to Cornwall, or the South of France, anywhere but the North of Ireland. It's the first time I've operated outside of Belfast, but I'm willing to make an exception because Dwarf Dave was on duty at the Orange March in July 1990. He was one of the soldiers on the street that day.

The deed itself is uneventful enough. In and out in a couple of minutes. Convincing Dinky Dave to come back to the house Benny provided is as easy as selling religion to someone on their deathbed. I've to use a lemonade bottle because they don't have any tonic in the pub, but it does the same job. Then I'm out the door and into Baldy's taxi to get a lift to a wash house down near the Brunswick Road.

Two days later, the full story comes out in the papers. Dumpy Dave walked into the hospital cradling what was left of his bits in both hands. The nurse who treated him told reporters that it looked like a roll of uncooked bacon rashers. Good description, that, I thought. The stories run for a few days, making every man and boy across the whole of Ireland cross their legs and wince into their morning cornflakes.

The peelers begin searching the wider Bangor area for a girl named Cassie who has shoulder-length straight red hair and a taste for vodka-lemonade. Wrong city, wrong drink. Still, worth leaving my hair curly and drinking rosé for a while.

A week or so later, the Newsletter *runs with an article that states that this untraceable Cassie character whispered, 'Fuck you, wanker,' into her victim's ear in the moments after the damage had been done. Lies. I never said that. I said* tiocfaidh ár lá. *Our day will come.*

It was coming up to marching season. The Unionist streets were like a tired auld millie getting ready for a night on the lash: new nails, hair extensions and carefully chosen outfit. The kerbstones were painted red, white and blue, bunting was hung from lamppost to lamppost, and Union Jacks appeared outside near enough every house. The drab concrete housing estates were dressed to the nines, so they were, ready for that one big night of the year when everything was let loose. The Nationalist streets were getting ready as well, but there was no celebration to it. It was war-paint rather than make-up. The Tricolours came out, the murals of the Hunger Strikers were retouched, and bricks were split in half so as they were that wee bit easier to throw.

It was for the last of these community projects that Ciárán was useful. At all hours, he was to be found walking back and forth between the Short Strand and the Markets, catching the bus between Lower Ormeau and Andytown, or hitching a lift with one of the taxi-men out to Twinbrook or Poleglass. Not that he was in the INLA yet; not that he was running guns or scouting out operations. This Baldy one was just making use of him to fetch and carry between the different areas, maybe to take a gallon of petrol here or a length of fuse-wire there. After all, it was a busy time of year for those boys; they couldn't be expected to be running errands all day. The only difference, then, between what Ciárán was doing and what he had been doing down at the bar, day in, day out, was that it was over a greater distance and that, if he got lifted by the peelers or – worse – a Loyalist death squad, he'd be treated like a Republican paramilitary rather than a schoolboy.

It was those kinds of differences that set Aoife to worrying. The way she saw it, he was taking on all the risk of being one of the boys without actually getting the status of it.

To make matters worse, Damien took to keeping Ciárán company on these runner jobs. Like a faithful Robin to Ciárán's Batman. A good couple of feet shorter than Ciárán, and with a tangled mess of brown curls on his head rather than the shorn skullcap of the older boy, he skipped alongside to keep up and eagerly carried anything and everything that Ciárán handed off to him.

Aoife did whatever she could to stop him. She made sure that her brother went to school in the mornings – in fact, she marched him right up through the gates and into the classroom itself – but she couldn't keep him from seeking Ciárán out after school or at the weekends. And it would soon be the holidays. Two months of freedom, with the Twelfth of July week right at the start of them. Aoife was certain that the summer would wind up with either Ciárán or Damien – or both – up before the courts.

What Ciárán didn't seem to understand was that wee Damien was still a child. What it amounted to was a fifteen-year-old leading a ten-year-old into harm's way. Not that Ciárán was shooting at soldiers or trying to plant bombs on the undersides of cars, but he was still trying his level best to get himself involved in the riots that would, without question, take place when the Orangemen came and tried to march through the Catholic areas of Belfast. Aoife had seen the stand-offs that took place year on year. She'd seen the police in their head-to-foot riot gear, the Orangemen with their bowler hats, their suits, their sashes, and their snarls. She'd seen the teenagers from round her way with the scarves up over their faces and the petrol bombs being fed into their hands by the older men who stood in the shadows of the houses and watched approvingly. It was no place for a ten-year-old, that was for certain.

'Daddy?' Aoife said, sliding onto the arm of the sofa next to him. She had brought him a can of beer and a packet of crisps to soften the blow of pulling his attention away from the Liverpool match on the telly. It was only some end-of-season testimonial game, but, as he always said, a match was a match.

'What, love?' Shay replied, opening the can.

'I'm wile worried about Damien.'

'Is that right?' He opened the crisps and held them out to Aoife. 'Why's that?'

'You know that Ciáran's working for Baldy – '

'I work for Baldy Carroll too, love.'

'I know.' Aoife chewed thoughtfully on the crisps. 'It's different, but.'

'Listen, no harm will come to Ciáran.' He pulled Aoife down into a half-hug, half-headlock. 'Are you worried for your boyfriend, is that it?'

'That's not it at all.' Aoife wriggled herself free. She could feel her face reddening to the colour of the Liverpool jerseys. 'I'm worried about Damien, I said. He'd follow Ciáran into the Irish Sea if Ciáran took a notion to swim to Scotland.'

'Wise up, Aoife.' Her daddy leant forward in his seat as John Barnes set off on a mazy dribble towards the opposition box. 'Ciáran's got his head screwed on.'

'Maybe, but – '

'Listen, what are you wanting me to do, wee girl?' The question hung in the air. A chipped shot from Barnes looped up over the goalkeeper, clipped the post, and rolled wide. Shay turned to Aoife accusingly. 'Fuck sake,' he said. 'Are you wanting me to have a word with your man Ciáran, is that it? Or maybe a word with Baldy?'

'A wee word with Ciáran, maybe.'

'Will you give my head peace, if I do?' he muttered. 'Fuck sake. I'll mention it to him next time I see him, then, if that'll make you happy.'

As far as Aoife knew, though, words were never exchanged between the two of them. In fact, Damien began spending more and more time over at the Gildays' house. As the Twelfth week grew close, Ciáran and the other boys started wearing their GAA shirts and Celtic strips. Ciáran even gave Damien a Celtic away kit to wear, one from a couple of seasons back. It was like a dress on him, so it was. Someone had written 'McStay' on the back of it in permanent marker. Aoife wasn't best pleased about her brother wearing it, but there was little she could do about it, short of tearing it right off his body. Still, she let it be known – to both Damien and her daddy – that she didn't approve. After all, there was nothing as likely to get a boy a kicking from Loyalists as wearing a Celtic dress.

In light of her experiences with the two men of the household, Aoife wasn't keen on spending time over at the Gildays', but she was wanting to keep an eye on Damien, so she recruited Becky as a spy. It wasn't touting, she told the younger girl, because she was only looking out for her own brother. Besides, now that school was over, Aoife had no need for such a steady supply of jewellery, and if Becky wanted to keep picking up her share of the savings then she'd need to earn it in this way instead. So Becky began trailing around after Damien, who trailed around after Ciáran, who went wherever that Baldy one told him to go. Like a family of ducks, they were, getting progressively smaller towards the back of the group.

Aoife spent the first week of her holidays tidying, cleaning, seeing to dinner, and getting hourly reports from Becky. She was somewhere between an MI5 agent and a housewife. She couldn't really be annoyed doing all the housework, but it wasn't like anyone else was going to take it on. Her mammy still only moved whenever the dishwater got cold, and her daddy was out on taxi fares more often than he was at home.

Aoife followed her usual routine and straightened out one room at a time: first the front room, then the kitchen, then Damien's room, and then her own. She always left the bathroom for last – because it was always in the worst state, with a crust around the rim of the toilet bowl – and she never went near her parents' bedroom. It wouldn't have been right, she reckoned, to go rummaging through her mammy and daddy's things, even if she had the best of intentions. Better to just leave it be. So, she would run the vacuum cleaner right up to the door and then leave it standing there for her daddy. He could finish the job whenever he got the chance.

By the sixth day of the school holidays Aoife had managed to bring the whole house – except for her parents' bedroom – back up to scratch. It shamed her that she'd let it turn into such a hole, but, then again, she had been at school. It wasn't Aoife's fault if her mammy stood all day with her hands deep in warm, soapy water and didn't even take the trouble to lift a dish from the counter to give it a quick rinse. She couldn't be blamed for the fact that, even though they got through a squeezy bottle of washing-up liquid a week, the whole place was filthy from floor to ceiling.

Aoife found herself at a loose end on that sixth day. It was meant to be the seventh day that was for resting – according to the Bible – so she decided to fill the extra day by tidying up her mammy.

Working Saturdays at Cliona's salon had given Aoife a brave bit of experience at hairdressing. True, she never got to cut the hair, just wash it and sweep the curls of it up from the lino floor whenever Cliona was done, but she felt that she was bound to have picked some of it up – by osmosis, if nothing else. She could give her mammy's hair a quick trim. Besides, it wasn't like her mammy ever went outside, so if she ended up butchering it then so be it.

It all started off professionally enough. Her mammy was by the kitchen sink anyway, so Aoife didn't see the point in leading her off up the stairs to the bathroom. It was just a case of levering her round, by the waist, until her back was to the sink. Her hands dangled dripping in front of her, still in the position they had been a moment before, when they were plunged into the sink with the palm flat-down against the bottom of the basin. Gently, Aoife dried her hands off and then draped a towel over her shoulders, the way she had seen Cliona doing a hundred times down the road at the salon. Aoife reached behind her mammy, then, and drained the soapy water from the sink. She had to leave the tap running to get rid of the bubbles before she could fill the sink again. Inching her mammy back, until the ends of her near-waist-length red hair fell into the water, Aoife began smoothing shampoo up and through the wiry strands. It hadn't been washed for months. It felt like touching meat, so it did; knots of gristle beneath an oily sheen. As she poured glassfuls of water down through it, the clear water in the sink rapidly turned the familiar grey of dishwater.

'Now, Mrs Brennan,' she said, grandly. 'What'll it be today?'

There was no answer. Aoife had been hoping that the change in routine, the sensation of having newly washed hair, would waken her mammy. Cathy tended to come out of her daze when something out of the ordinary happened.

'The policy of this salon is to shave the head entirely unless we're told otherwise. Right down to the bone. Is that OK – does that suit you?'

No answer.

'Really, Mrs Brennan?' Aoife lifted the kitchen scissors from the counter. 'I can really do whatever I like, can I?'

Nothing.

'For fuck sake, Mammy.' Aoife lowered her voice for the swear-word, censoring herself. 'You'd think you'd care about having a shorn head. Honest to God, I sometimes wonder if there's any woman at all left in there.'

The scissors set to clacking. Wisps and licks of red hair, like embers from a bonfire, drifted slowly to the ground and settled there by Aoife's feet. A rug began to form across the lino. From somewhere, far off in the distance, came the steady beating of Lambeg drums. If Aoife had cared to open the window she might even have caught the faint whistling of the flutes and the rasp of the snares. At that time of the year the whole city had the Orange bands as background music, like the radio turned low. Once the marching season really began in earnest, the volume would be turned up.

It only took ten minutes for Aoife to finish. It normally took Cliona longer. That was because Cliona paused often to consider progress, to set her head on its side or to set the client's head on its side, and to see how she was getting on. Aoife didn't do any of that. She cut for ten solid minutes and then she stopped. There was silence. No scissors clacking, no flutes or drums. Her mammy's hair looked like one of the mullets on those footballers that her daddy watched on the telly. It was uneven and it was spiked on the top and there seemed to be a layer missing on the left-hand side. Still, it wasn't too bad for a first attempt. With a bit of a tidy-up, it'd be grand. Problem was, Aoife wasn't too sure how to do a salvage job on it. She could have asked Cliona to call round, or Becky's mammy, but she would have been too embarrassed to show them it as a work in progress. No, it was easier to just make the best of it there and then, over the kitchen sink.

Rat-a-tat-tat. The sudden sound nearly caused Aoife to take her mammy's ear off with the scissors. *Rat-a-tat-tat*. Like a snare drum, but close at hand. Aoife looked up to see Becky's face at the window, behind the smudged fingermarks she'd left on the glass. The wee girl looked odd, her face twisted somewhere between excitement and worry. She was dancing from foot to foot. Aoife motioned for her to come round to the front door.

'What're you at?' Aoife demanded. 'You scared me half to death.'

'Sor-sorry,' Becky gulped as she tried to catch her breath. 'You need to come quickly, but.'

'Why?'

Becky pulled at Aoife's sleeve. 'Ciáran and Damien are down under the Ormeau Bridge, down by the banks of the Lagan.' She gulped again. 'And they're filling milk bottles and then tearing strips from bedsheets and stuffing them in on top.'

Aoife frowned. 'Filling them with what?'

Becky opened her mouth to answer. Aoife didn't need her to, though. She'd caught on. Petrol. Without another word, Aoife was out of the door and off down the road at a half-sprint. It would have been a full sprint, but wee Becky kept her grip on Aoife's sleeve. They must have made for a strange sight as they hurried on past the shops on the Ormeau Road, with Aoife half dragging, half carrying the younger girl behind her.

'Are you wise, Ciáran Gilday?' Aoife slid down the muddy bank on her arse, leaving a long brown streak-mark down her jeans. She was past caring about that, though. Ciáran was holding a petrol can, tipping it towards a waiting milk bottle – still stained with a white swirl of cream – whilst Damien was crouched by his side, burying the finished petrol bombs – up to their neck – in the soft mud. They were both bogging. The chemical smell of the petrol stung at Aoife's nose and throat, but it didn't completely cover the smell of sewage that rose from the water.

'The wisest there is,' Ciáran replied, continuing with his work. 'Isn't that right?'

Damien looked up, tongue hanging out his mouth. 'Aye, right enough.'

'What if someone struck a match?' Aoife asked.

'Aye.' Ciáran wiped his hand on his jumper. 'Because people often jump over a fence, slither down a fucking deathtrap of a hill and hide themselves under a bridge just so as they can light a match, don't they?'

'What if the Army came past, then?'

'Then we'd be the ones lighting a match.'

'Bullshit, you'd shit your cacks – '

'You're all about the what-ifs, wee girl.' Ciáran put the petrol can down and tore a length from a dirt-streaked sheet. 'What if the Orangemen march right through Lower Ormeau, right up your path, into your house and take a piss up the curtains? What if they beat your daddy and rape your mammy? Those are the what-ifs I'm looking at.'

'You're not right in the head,' Aoife replied. She found herself chewing at the insides of her cheeks, tasting blood. 'And you've no right to be bringing my wee brother into it. He's only ten, after all.'

'No one forced him to come,' Ciáran replied, picking up an empty milk bottle.

'He's not old enough to know better. Neither are you, come to that.'

'We're both of us old enough to throw.'

Aoife was over to him in a single stride. Her arm drew back. She realised she was still holding the kitchen scissors in her hand. She let them drop down, to be swallowed by the riverbank, and hit Ciáran across the face with her open palm. He hadn't been expecting that. He drew away from her and the empty milk bottle fell to the mud and rolled on down to meet the dirty waters of the Lagan.

'You're just after hitting me,' he said. His hand went up to his lips and came away with a red spattering of blood.

'If you're old enough to throw, then you're old enough to be slapped,' Aoife replied. Her hand stung. She didn't know where to look. It might have just been the petrol fumes that were causing tears to pool in her ex-almost-boyfriend's eyes, but it didn't seem decent to examine too closely. 'Come on, Damien,' she said. 'You're to come home now.'

Becky was behind Aoife, looking unsure as to whether she should go over and see to her brother or stay where she was. Aoife made up her mind for her. Grasping hold of her arm with one hand, and Damien's with the other, Aoife led them out from under the bridge. She stood at the bottom of the bank and wondered how she was going to get back up to the road without having the use of either of her hands. It was going to be tricky to get the three of them up safely without at least one of them ending up skiting all the way back down and landing in the river. She didn't trust that either Becky or Damien would necessarily follow her if she was to let go of her hold on them. The split-second of indecision was all that Ciárán needed to catch up.

'You can't make him go,' Ciárán said. 'You're not his mammy. If Damien wants to stay, then he stays.'

'Catch yourself on,' Aoife replied. 'He's coming back with me.'

'I want to stay,' Damien said, softly.

'I'm taking him back and I'm watching him like – ' Aoife began.

'Did you not hear what he says, but?'

'I want to stay,' Damien repeated.

'Give me strength.' Aoife looked down at her brother. Mud clung in clumps to his curly hair and tears were beginning to make tracks down his dirt-stained face. He looked for all the world like any other young boy who'd been out to play and managed to get himself a second skin of dirt. The difference was the reek of petrol that rose off him.

'You can't stay, Damo,' she said. 'It's dangerous, so it is.'

'It's not,' he replied.

'It is.'

'It's not.'

'Fuck sake,' she breathed. Damien was pulling and straining at her arm now, trying to get away from her. She had a fistful of his Celtic shirt, but precious little hold of Damien himself. 'You know what your mammy would say, Damien Brennan, if she could see you?'

'She never says anything,' Damien replied.

It was hard to argue with that. 'Your daddy, then.'

Damien shrugged. Then, with a final wrench, he pulled away from his sister. With a hiss of ripping fabric, the sleeve of his shirt tore up to the armpit. The crying started properly then.

'You're coming with me,' Aoife said, 'and that's that.'

'You can't make me!' he howled at her.

'I can.' There was no conviction to Aoife's voice, though. She didn't doubt that she could get a hold of another fistful of Damien's shirt and she didn't doubt that, for all his acting the big man, Ciáran wouldn't physically stop her from taking her wee brother. It was the getting back up onto the Ormeau Road that would give her problems. It seemed likely that she could carry a screaming ten-year-old, and it seemed likely that she'd eventually be able to clamber back up the slip-slide of the riverbank, but she doubted that she'd be able to do both at the same time. Aoife knew when she was defeated.

'Wait here, then,' she said. 'I'll be back with your daddy, and then you'll be sorry.'

Any dignity she tried to give to this warning was removed by the graceless way she clawed her way, hand and foot, up the bank. She dug her fingernails into roots and weeds, using the toes of her trainers to chisel footholds into the smooth clay. Becky scampered up behind her. Then they were off again, back the way they came, both of them looking as though they hadn't had a wash since the day they were born.

'Jesus, Aoife,' her daddy said, as she strode into the front room, tracking dirt onto the carpet that she'd so carefully cleaned just days before. 'Did you just decide to bathe in shite, or what?'

Judging by the fact that there was only one empty beer can at his feet, he had only just finished his shift. He was still sober enough to drive, then, as long as he hadn't been in at the bar on his way home.

'You-need-to-come-and-get-Damien,' Aoife said, all-in-a-rush. She was as breathless as Becky had been earlier. 'He's down under the Ormeau Bridge.'

'Is he hurt?' Shay rose quickly from the sofa.

'No, he's not hurt.'

Shay collapsed back down onto the cushions. 'What's the matter, then?'

'He's making petrol bombs.'

'Petrol bombs?' Shay lifted another can of beer from the blue bag on the cushion next to him. 'Is Ciáran with him?'

'He is.'

'Jesus, love.' Her daddy sighed. 'I'm not wanting to go chasing your brother halfway round Belfast – can you not bring him back?'

'He'll not listen to sense.'

'Can you not just leave him be, then?'

'Daddy!' Aoife was genuinely shocked. It had been bad enough that her daddy had been willing to see Ciáran get involved with the paramilitaries, but she'd never have thought that he'd be willing to see his own son go the same way.

'It's not that I don't care, love.' Shay kicked at the empty beer can at his feet. It flipped over and a dribble spilt out onto the carpet.

'He's making petrol bombs, Daddy!'

'I know, love, I know.' He tapped at the top of his fresh can of beer with his fingernail. 'Where's Declan Gilday at? Can he not go and get the two of them?'

Aoife just shook her head. She could feel the tears squeezing themselves out of the corners of her eyes, seeming to bubble and boil out with the frustration of it all. She felt like leaning over and giving her daddy the same open-palmed slap she'd given to Ciáran under the bridge.

'Well…' Shay was obviously struggling with the decision. He remained slumped in his seat, but his eyes kept on flickering guiltily up to Aoife's face.

'What's going on through here?' The voice of Aoife's mammy came from the doorway. She stood there, using the towel draped over her shoulders to rub at the tufts and slicks that had once been her hair.

'What happened to you, Cathy?' Shay sat up again. 'Has everyone started living in a bog or what? You both look a right fucking state.'

'What's going on?' Cathy repeated.

'Since when were you back in the land of the living, anyway?'

'Mammy,' Aoife began, 'Daddy's not – '

'Fine.' Aoife's daddy stood. He'd been sitting with his feet half in, half out of his shoes while he decided on what to do. Now that his mind was made up, he hooked his heels into his trainers and picked up his car keys. 'I'll go and fetch him.'

'He's under the bridge,' Aoife said.

'I'll give that Ciárán one a bollocking, anyway,' Shay replied, as he made his way out. Aoife had to bite her tongue to keep from shouting after him that if he'd done that when she'd first asked then he'd still be sat on the sofa sipping on his second beer. It wasn't her place to be scolding her daddy, though, just as it wasn't her place to be cleaning his room.

'Hi, Mammy.' Aoife turned to Cathy and smiled. Strands of cut hair were patterned like wrinkles across her mammy's face and a rash had formed on the back of her neck. Still, her hands were dry and her eyes were clear. Maybe the fright of seeing her new haircut in the reflection from the kitchen window had been all she'd needed to waken her up.

'Come away into the kitchen, love,' her mammy said. 'You too, Becky. We'll get the both of you cleaned up at the kitchen sink.'

One of the Sunday papers flies a journalist over from London to interview Dave Gibson, a month or so after the event. There's interest in the wee sapper, so there is, because no one's too sure whether his story is a gruesome detail within the day-to-day brutality of Northern Ireland or whether he's just invented the whole thing for a bit of publicity. He's no proof for them save for the mangled mess in his trousers, but that's convincing enough for them to piece together one of those identikit photos of his attacker and print it beside the interview.

The photo looks nothing like me, but the stress dreams start the week after it runs in any case. I'm feared that Billy, my first, will come forward to show his war-wounds or that Whitey will step out of the shadows. Most of all though, I'm feared of Nigel, my second. He's enough of a sneer and a swagger to him that he'd lap up the attention, and there's no shame to his story either. He can tell it however he chooses. She targeted me, he can say, but I fought her off when I realised what she was at, and here I am today, dick intact, whilst that wee sap Dave dribbles a mix of piss and blood into his bandages.

It's Nigel who haunts my dreams. It's Nigel who comes up to me and taps me on the shoulder as I sip at my vodka-tonic, who says, 'I saw your picture in the paper, love,' in that same hoarse hiss of a voice that he used when he lamped me in the hallway at Damascus Street. Then there's a flashbulb goes off, like you'd get on an old-fashioned camera, and, as the searing red of it fades, I see the four of them lined up – Billy, Nigel, Whitey and Dave. And when I get up to run I find that the twisting vines of Nigel's shirt, in blue and white, have grown out onto the floor so as they trip at me as I stumble to the door.

Then I'm out into the back streets of Belfast, down beyond the Holylands and out onto the Lagan pathway, up towards Ormeau Road. And as I get closer to home I know that there should be someone I know, someone close at hand, someone with connections. There should be a taxi that can speed me away from the sound of steadily tramping feet behind, that can put distance between me and the footfalls that keep time to the marching beat of the Lambeg drum. But there is no one, no taxi, and the marchers behind have multiplied so as now they number in the hundreds or even the thousands, all in their suits and their sashes. And at the front of them, leading them, is Nigel – my second, the one that got away – who winks, and raises his hand as if to strike at me.

After her experiences that summer, Aoife swore off boys in general and Ciárán Gilday in particular. That wasn't to say she was for turning the school back into a full-fledged Convent, just that she turned her attention to men. Full-grown men with scruffy beards, ill-fitting blue shirts and a tendency to punctuate sentences with tuts and sighs, like Mr O'Toole, the newly qualified lay teacher who taught Aoife's class for GCSE history.

Around the middle of each and every period he took, Mr O'Toole would puff out his cheeks, let out all the air in his lungs and look at the back cover of the textbook they were working from as if expecting to find a disclaimer for the lies and half-truths he'd just been reading out. Then he'd set the book down on the desk, massage his beard with his hand and, with a 'Here's what you need to know', launch into an improvised lesson that had more detail than any of the exercises and essays in the textbook. About how the first planters to come from mainland Britain to Ulster were known as Undertakers – 'and didn't they live up to that name' – and how the Protestant King Billy had actually been supported before the Battle of the Boyne by the Pope of the time, Innocent XI. In talking of the Easter Rising in 1916, he told them about the so-called 'black diaries' of Sir Roger Casement who'd attempted to secure German support for the Irish rebellion and been hanged for treason. The diaries, Mr O'Toole told them, had been written by the British to support the rumour that Casement was a homosexual. It wasn't the first dirty trick the British had played in Ireland, he said, and it wouldn't be the last.

As he got closer to the present day, moving through the Civil Rights campaigns of the late Sixties and the subsequent outbreak of violence in the Province, as he spoke of the ambush of the People's Democracy march at Burntollet Bridge, the burning of Bombay Street by Loyalists and the Battle of the Bogside up in Derry, Mr O'Toole worked himself into such a passion that specks and sprays of spittle had the girls in the front rows holding their folders up in front of their faces as shields.

It was as he spoke about Bloody Sunday, and the whitewash of the Widgery Tribunal that had cleared British soldiers of blame in spite of the 'photographs, eye-witness accounts, newspaper reports and, most of all, bloodied corpses', as he banged the edge of the textbook on his table like a gavel, that Joanne leant across to Aoife.

'Have you ever seen sweat like it?' she whispered.

'What?'

'There's great patches of it, Aoife, and he reeks to high heaven.' Joanne frowned across at her. 'You must've noticed, surely?'

Aoife had been too engrossed by what Mr O'Toole was saying to pay attention to the steadily spreading stains which had formed small islands across his blue shirt and were now beginning to merge into continents.

'It'd not be so bad if he'd change his shirt more often,' Joanne continued.

'He's more important things on his mind.'

'You're not – ' She rocked back in her seat. 'You never – '

'Wheest, Joanne,' Aoife hissed, reddening.

'He must be nearly *thirty*,' Joanne replied.

Aoife held a finger to her lips and, later, tried to repair the damage by joining in the laughter as two of the girls up at the front exaggeratedly wiped at their faces with their handkerchiefs whilst Mr O'Toole's back was turned, but she continued to hold a flame for him. She'd a particular fondness for the odd occasion when he'd turn up with a copy of the *Irish News* instead of the textbook and read to them about the acquittal of the Guildford Four, who'd been wrongly convicted of terrorist offences over in England, or about the Stevens inquiry into collusion between the British security forces and Loyalist paramilitaries.

As they moved into 1990, Mr O'Toole dispensed with the textbook entirely and took to predicting the future rather than telling them the past. He'd a fair bit of excitement to him about the noises made by Peter Brooke, the British Secretary of State, towards having talks with Sinn Féin. But it was the upcoming release of Nelson Mandela that got him pacing from one side of the blackboard to the other with his hands making wee stabbing motions as if he was fighting it out with his shadow.

'The African National Congress is Sinn Féin,' he jabbed. 'And the Spear of the Nation is the Irish Republican Army. And Mandela is Gerry Adams, and President de Klerk is Margaret Thatcher. And the British...' he paused before swiping out '...are always the fucking British.'

There was a gasp. A collective intake of breath that had Mr O'Toole blinking for a moment, before he realised what he'd said.

'He can't say that,' Joanne hissed into the silence.

'Well.' Mr O'Toole cleared his throat. 'A momentous event, anyway, girls.'

Aoife hadn't known the first thing about Mandela or about South Africa, but she saw an opportunity to show Mr O'Toole what she'd learnt, to put into practice his mantra about history happening in the here and now, about the lessons he gave being history and politics – *agus polaitíocht*, with a stress on the Irish words. With some of the jewellery money, she set to organising a street party for that weekend to celebrate the release of Nelson Mandela, getting Becky to down tools for an evening so as she could help with the handwritten invitations instead.

A folded note went through every door on the estate and onto the desk of near enough every girl in Aoife's year, but she kept Mr O'Toole's invitation until last and delivered it in person at the end of the Friday classes. She'd decorated the corner of it with a wee silhouetted springbok, leaping up as if trying to escape the page.

'What's this in the corner?' Mr O'Toole asked, when she handed him the invitation.

'A springbok,' Aoife replied. 'I've a book out of the library that says it's a symbol of South Africa.'

'Of apartheid South Africa, yes.'

Aoife nodded down at the desk and watched as the invitation was set to the side. Mr O'Toole let out a breath and lifted his pen towards the pile of essays in front of him. Aoife's essay on the Irish Civil War was in there; she'd spent a fair bit of time on it, sourcing quotes from Sean O'Casey and W.B. Yeats to show that she'd understood the significance of it all.

'Would you be interested in coming at all?' she asked. 'It should be a good day.'

'I'll try to make it along, yes,' Mr O'Toole said, waving in the direction of the invitation.

'Excellent. It should be a good day, right enough.'

That Sunday, out along McClure Street, there was a barbecue with blackened sausages in buns, chicken drumsticks done in the oven and then seared on the heat and thin burgers that curled up at the edges but stayed pink in the middle. There were cans of beer for the men and lemonade for the youngsters. The rain kept off, but the breeze was still brisk enough that folk huddled in the doorway and around the barbecue rather than standing out on the grass at the front and chatting animatedly as Aoife had imagined them doing.

It was as she helped her mammy set out the marshmallows, on dampened wooden skewers ready for toasting, that Ciáran sauntered over. He had an opened can of beer in his hand and enough of a sway to his walk to let on that he was half-cut. Even with the Dutch courage of the alcohol, though, he couldn't meet her eye. His gaze slid off towards the men gathered around the barbecue.

'Alright, Aoife, what about you?' he began.

'You're looking wile suspicious.' Aoife squinted over at him.

'Is that right?' Ciáran attempted a laugh.

'What's the matter with you?'

There was a long pause then, a silence that was filled by the distant noise of the television from the living room. Aoife's mammy watched on, with a pink marshmallow held suspended above a skewer. She'd been much better in recent months, although Aoife was never certain how much she understood, how much she caught on to what was happening around her.

'Come away over here,' Aoife said, smiling reassuringly at her mammy and leading Ciáran over to the grass.

'I've some news,' he said. 'I've decided that I'm as well to leave school at the end of this term.'

Aoife stared at him. There was a cheer from the television, and laughter from those watching it. Cathy had gone back to threading the marshmallows, pausing only to pop the pink one she held into her mouth.

'After all,' Ciáran continued, quickly, 'it's only the rare occasion that I'm there in any case.'

'You've your GCSEs in the summer, though.'

'I've not much chance of doing well in those, though, and I've no hopes of going on to do my A-Levels, have I?'

'Why not? It's only February.' Aoife gripped at his arm. 'You can get a run at the books between now and the summer and get the results to stay on.'

'That was the plan originally...' He tailed off.

'Well?' Aoife demanded. 'What changed?'

He shrugged. His thumb was denting the side of the beer can, making a dull clicking sound. He pressed away at it as if trying to send an SOS.

'Are you going to be a full-time paramilitary, is that it?' Aoife hissed, her voice loaded with sarcasm. 'You going to be a professional terrorist?' she asked, her words getting louder now, getting towards a shout. 'A gunman has no need for an education, is that the thinking?'

The can-clicking stopped, as did the conversations going on at the doorway and around the barbecue. Aoife's mammy was staring across at them, chewing away at her marshmallow as she watched.

'Wise up, wee girl,' Ciáran snapped back.

'You've not a thought in your head, Ciáran Gilday, have you? Not a thought about what might happen – '

'There are better ways of – '

'Let me stop you there,' Aoife stepped in towards him. 'There's no call, no justification, for anyone who doesn't understand the history of it, who doesn't believe in a united Ireland, at the very least.'

'Is that right? Do I not believe in a united Ireland now?' Ciáran waved the crumpled beer can in her face, so close that she could hear the beer sloshing around inside. 'Because I've not got my exams, does that mean I'm not able to see the foreign soldiers on the streets? Does it blind me to the fact that there's a shoot-to-kill policy against my own people?'

Aoife chewed on her lip, but didn't answer right away.

'You could be an educated volunteer,' she said, after a moment. 'Able to argue the cause instead of just fight it.'

'Away on, it's the gun that does the talking.'

Aoife shook her head. 'You could be a true revolutionary, like…'

'Like who?'

She looked off down McClure Street, down towards Ormeau Road and then off towards Botanic. The night was beginning to draw in.

'No one,' she said, softly.

'Listen, I'm leaving school,' Ciáran said, in an undertone. 'And you've no claim on me and no right to think you can be scolding me about it.'

'I'll not scold you, then. From now on I couldn't care less. I'd not spit on you if you were on fire.'

He looked taken aback by that for a moment, but only for a moment, before he regained his smirk and his swagger. 'I've no interest in you anyway, Aoife Brennan, in spite of the high opinion you have of yourself.'

'Good,' Aoife replied, lifting the marshmallows and making her way across to the group by the barbecue. 'Away and get yourself shot, then.'

7

When she smelt the milk going sour Aoife caught on to what was happening out on the streets. She checked the fridge first, of course, hoping that it might be one bottle on the turn rather than the whole city. No such luck. The smell of it was coming in at the open window, in waves that were strong enough to cause even her mammy to wrinkle her nose and sniff questioningly at the air.

Tucking her hair in behind her ears and peeling off the yellow Marigold gloves that she had been wearing to clean the cooker – her head had been right in the oven like Big Gerry's sister Caoimhe – Aoife made her way out of the house. As soon as she was out of the gate, she knew for certain that something was happening. She could hear it drifting through the streets: that murmur of revving engines, slamming doors, sharp shouts, breaking glass, and far-off cheers. Then there was the drone of a helicopter, circling off in the west, providing a constant background hum. And in the lulls were the drums and flutes striking up the usual jaunty tunes that sent a shiver up her bare arms. The sounds of the Twelfth of July. It was all of these mingling with the faint aroma of spoiled milk that quickened her step. At that distance it was all just a simmering noise, but as she turned onto the Ormeau Road it got closer and closer to the boil.

The sun was high in the sky above Belfast, with only those wispy threads of clouds – like the wee swirl in the centre of a marble – twisting amongst the blue. Baking hot, it was, to the point that Aoife felt overdressed in the white T-shirt, knee-length shorts and sandals that she'd been wearing to clean the kitchen. She could feel the warmth of the sun sticking the fabric of her T-shirt to her, between her shoulderblades.

Already there was a roadblock forming at the junction with University Street. A car was driving up to it as Aoife passed, the tyres skidding and screeching to a halt. The doors flapped open, driver and passenger folded themselves out, and youths with scarves up over their faces ran forward to douse the seats in petrol and set them alight. Elderly residents had come out of the houses that lined University Street and were watching on, talking amongst themselves. They weren't going to raise any objections. They knew that the ones who were forming the barricade were wanting to stop the police or the army from entering the area, and they'd rather have a few young bucks hijacking cars and setting them ablaze than have soldiers shouldering in their doors or peelers smashing in their windows with the water-cannon. They knew which side their bread was buttered, so they did, and even if that butter was churned from the same sour-smelling milk as filled the air they were grateful for it.

So far the barricade consisted of a scorched white car with flattened tyres that had been toppled onto its side so as the pipes and mechanisms of its underside were on full show, an estate car with a roof that had been jumped on until it sagged down to near enough the head-rests, and a burning white van with the back doors open. The car that had just been driven up was added, at an angle, to the side nearest the doctor's surgery, so as near enough the whole road was blocked. As Aoife hurried on, she tried not to breathe too deeply at the acrid aroma of burning rubber and singed metal. The white van, though, was a butcher's van. The hanging carcass of a pig swung from a hook in the back. She paused as she passed, her mouth watering as – just for a second – the roasting pork overpowered the other smells that swirled about the street.

A clutch of young ones stood at the entrance to Hatfield Street, peeking out around the corner of the bookmaker's. They were looking down towards the bridge, to the RUC officers who stood, three-deep, across the mouth of the road. Lined up like Lego men, they were, none of them moving, all of them helmeted, bullet-proof-vested and plastic-shielded. Behind them was a row of armoured Land Rovers, parked nose to tail, so close together that only one Lego man could fit between. The sight of the sun reflecting off the black helmets reminded Aoife of burnt-out lightbulbs, black around the edges but with a glassy sheen on the top of them.

Behind the lines of policemen, a marching band was coming down the dip in the road by Ormeau Park, making its way along the contested route from Upper to Lower Ormeau, from Unionist-land to Nationalist, down towards the police blockade. Some of the ones walking alongside, in their Rangers or Northern Ireland shirts, had stopped paying attention to the tradition of filing along behind the suited men with the bright orange sashes and the bowler-hats, and had started running down towards the bridge. This hurry to get to the frontline seemed to work its way back to the drummers, who quickened their beat to a steady pulsing. Quickly, a brave crowd assembled on the Upper side of the wall of Lego men, a mirror-image of those gathering on the Lower side, except that one side was flecked with orange, white and blue and the other was assorted, but with a fair few green shirts and the odd white-collar-against-black of a priest.

Aoife was making for the clutch of young ones by the Hatfield Bar, because she'd spotted Becky in amongst them. She was wanting to ask where Damien could be found, although she did have a bad feeling that it wouldn't have taken her too many guesses before she lighted on the right answer in any case. She had a notion that the smell of turned milk and her unaccounted-for brother were linked because, in among the residents that had gathered, there were pockets of teenagers who were hurling milk bottles at the lines of Lego men. Not petrol bombs, just ordinary cow's milk. It was splashed like spilt whitewash across the five feet or so of no-man's-land that stretched between the natives and the security forces. The sun lifted a fearsome stench from it.

Soon enough the milk-filled bottles would be swapped for petrol-filled ones, and Aoife was anxious to get Damien out of there before that happened. Problem was, the crowd was ever-thickening. For the most part it was just men who had the slur of drink on them; student-types who were handing out leaflets; women who screeched insults and scratched at the sour-milk air; and scores and scores of teenagers with bottles or stones in their hands. The men – the boys with the connections – would still be in the pubs or off getting the roadblocks sorted. They knew that they had a bit of time before they were needed. It was only when the crowd of Loyalists on the other side swole up, when the army turned up to widen the buffer-zone, when the bile of it had risen to a certain pitch. Then, and only then, would they come forward and start feeding the petrol bombs into willing hands, organising and mobilising, getting the guns they could spare to those who knew how to use them. It was only when the protest became a riot that they were really needed, and they knew that rightly.

'Where's Damien?' Aoife went straight up to Becky.

Becky shrugged. 'How am I supposed to know?' she said.

'You're supposed to be keeping an eye out for him.'

'If you wanted it done, you should have done it yourself.'

'What did you say?' Aoife asked. She was genuinely taken aback by this reaction from the wee girl. True, she'd not seen much of Becky in recent weeks, but she'd taken her loyalty as a given.

'I'm sick of you bossing me around, so I am.' Becky started out on this sentence strongly, but trailed off towards the end.

'Is that right?'

Becky nodded.

'I've not got the time for this, Becky,' Aoife sighed. She knew rightly that she'd not treated the girl well, but she also wanted to find Damien quickly. 'Wise up and tell me where he is.'

Another shrug. Aoife reached forward and took hold of the younger girl's pigtail. She twisted it around her knuckles, so as Becky's head was pulled sharply to the side. There was a squeal and then a gasp from the audience. The wee ones were being treated to some show.

'Why didn't you come and tell me?' Aoife demanded.

'You never say anything whenever I do, anyway.' There were tears in Becky's eyes. 'I come and tell you and you just nod. There's no thanks or – '

Aoife twisted the pigtail again. 'I've no time for this,' she repeated. 'I need to find Damien, OK?'

'He'th in there.' A girl with a rash of freckles over her nose spoke up. She was sooking on a purple-coloured ice-pop. She pointed it into the crowd and spoke with a lisp. 'We theen him and Ciáran earlier, back when the polithe arrived.'

'You should have come and found me, Becky,' Aoife said, releasing the pigtail. Becky hung her head and whispered something that might have been an apology. Aoife decided that it was easier to just take it as one and get on with finding her brother. She turned and moved back into the slipstream.

She needed to use her elbows to make progress. Most of the folk were just standing still, and they weren't in the mood to be moved, so Aoife had to squeeze between, edge around, and push past. Sticks and stones went flying over her head as she shoved her way forward. They were no longer being thrown at the peelers so much as being lobbed over the shields and helmets towards the mass of Orangemen beyond. Retaliation came in the shape of half-full beer cans and clods of stone-filled earth from the riverbank. The back-and-forth missiles had the effect of thinning out the crowd, with those who had no taste for rioting stepping to the sides of the street or retreating to watch from the shadows of the shops along the Ormeau Road. The shutters of the newsagent and the side wall of the bookmakers were already scarred with the scorch marks from riots that had taken place the month before. Like birthmarks against the metal and red brick, so they were, birthmarks that faded every winter and then flared up again in the summer. Marching season wasn't a one-day event, a twenty-four-hour flashpoint. It wasn't only the bonfires on the Eleventh night and the stand-off on the day of the Twelfth. There was more of a build-up to it than that, more of a sense of momentum that started with skirmishes and protest marches and escalated as it got nearer to the day when the security services would try to force the Orange march down through the Nationalist Lower Ormeau. It always followed the same pattern, Aoife knew that as well as anyone, and it always ended like this. Always.

She'd tried her best to keep Damien in the house that day; she'd even worked out a plan to keep him distracted from the ructions that would be taking place out on the streets. There'd been a man out repainting the mural on the gable-end wall the day before, and Damien had stood watching him for hours. The mural itself had been simple enough, just 'Lower Ormeau Says No' written in black letters and a picture of a bowler-hatted Orangeman with a red circle around him and a red line through him, like you'd get on a 'No Smoking' sign. Still, Damien had watched every brushstroke. When the painter was finished, Aoife had gone up to him and bought the remainder of his red paint and an old paintbrush from him for a couple of pounds. She'd hidden the paint under her bed overnight. In the morning she'd given it to Damien and told him that he could paint whatever he liked onto the far wall of his bedroom, the wall behind his bed. They'd even pulled the furniture over to the window and spread newspaper out on the carpet underneath the skirting board. Damien was elated; a wide grin spread across his face as he dipped the brush into the paint and contemplated the massive empty space of the white wall.

Thinking that the project would keep him occupied for at least a couple of hours, Aoife had taken the opportunity to run a few messages – just getting dinner in for when her daddy got back from the pub and stocking up on washing-up liquid to get her mammy through the summer months. She'd been gone for no more than half an hour. When she got back, she went in to check on the progress of Damien's mural. He was nowhere to be seen. Ciáran and the other boys must have called for him while Aoife was out, and he'd just dropped everything and followed them out to make preparations for that afternoon. The only sign that he'd been there at all was to be seen in the three-foot-high letters on his bedroom wall that read 'Celtic FC'. The final C was more like an I, though, because he'd run out of space and had squashed it in before the wall reached the corner. Trails of red paint had dribbled down from each of the letters: globules of it were caught between the mouldings of the skirting board and pools had dried in patches on the newsprint.

As Aoife reached the front of the crowd, she felt something strike her on the shoulder. It could have been something thrown from the other side, but, if it was, then it had been trampled underfoot or quickly lifted to be chucked back across. There was no sign of a missile on the ground around her. Aoife looked up then, into the face of a policeman. He was no more than a couple of yards away. He stared over the top of her head. He had the white collar and cuffs of an office worker on underneath his riot gear. It could have been the baton swinging loosely at his side that she'd felt. Aoife reached up to unstick the material of her T-shirt from her shoulder. She couldn't tell if the dampness was blood or just sweat. She stopped worrying about it, though, when she saw what was happening to the left of her.

There was one man who was taller than the rest. He had brown hair, balding at the crown, and was dressed in a denim jacket and suit trousers. Stepping out from the rest of the protesters, he towered over a female officer who was standing facing them all. Not that he was jostling her, or even saying anything; he just loomed over her. It was as if he was trying to look down over the top of her plastic shield to steal a peek down her bullet-proof vest. She reacted as though that was exactly what he was doing, swinging her baton up to strike at his side. He stood firm against it, immovable. In fact he barely flinched as the baton sought out his kidneys. For several seconds he stayed upright, as calm as if he was standing waiting on a bus. Then another peeler took up the challenge, and then another, and then the one who had been standing in front of Aoife joined in. Close up, they didn't look so much like Lego men. Their movements weren't stiff and their faces weren't smiling. They breathed heavily and even let out a few grunts as they beat the tall man to the ground. Once he was down, they swarmed around him and batons rose and fell at a speed that would have wrenched a Lego man's arm from his socket. Aoife turned away.

There was a surge forward then. The noise that went along with it sounded like a collective growl, starting low and rising until it rang in Aoife's ears. The weight of bodies from behind lifted Aoife from her feet and carried her into a waiting plastic shield. It pushed back. The breath was forced out of her lungs in one wheezing cry for help. It was swallowed by the shouts from both sides, by the beating of the drums and the sound of breaking glass. Her arms flailed. Her legs kicked. One of her sandals slipped loose. She tried to fight her way free, tried to move either way – backwards or forwards – but she only thrashed against plastic on one side and the warm press of bodies on the other. She was part of the swell, caught on the undercurrent. Panic seized her. She swivelled her head, but the angle of her body meant that she could only see the searing sun. Red blotches smudged her vision, caused her to screw her eyes shut and scream out. It was then that she felt someone grasping at her hand. It spun her round, but she was still carried backwards into the riot shields, her spine slammed into the plastic. The grip stretched, but wasn't broken. As the crowd ebbed and flowed, she caught sight of Ciárán beside her. He was clinging grimly to her hand, his jaw clenched and his wiry frame set against the crushing crowd. As their eyes met, he winked at her, slowly.

'I didn't think you had it in you,' he said, after they'd worked their way free.

'What?'

'Attacking the peelers like that – I'm wile impressed.'

'Wise up,' Aoife replied, walking over and seating herself on the kerb. She had to clasp her hands between her knees to stop the shaking. 'I was looking for Damien.'

'Aye, well, it certainly didn't look – '

'Where is he?' Aoife interrupted.

'He's fine.'

'Where is he, but?'

People were moving both backwards and forwards among the knot of protesters, trying either to get towards the police or to get away from them.

Ciáran gestured vaguely at the scrum.

'He's around, so he is.'

'It's not safe for him,' Aoife said, trying to gulp enough breath into her lungs so as she could get back to her feet and get back to looking for wee Damien. 'He's too young.'

'It's only a bit of aggro,' Ciáran replied. 'We're only letting them know that those Orangies aren't to be marching through here.'

'He's too young,' Aoife repeated.

'There are stewards and all.' Ciáran placed a hand on her shoulder, which she promptly shook off. 'They'll see that no harm comes to him – '

'Here, lover boy!' The shout came from an open window above the shop behind them. A man with a cigarette dangling from beneath his thick moustache hung out and pointed down at Ciáran. 'Stop your courting and get back in there!'

'He one of your stewards, is he?' Aoife hissed.

'Away on,' Ciáran replied. He looked uncomfortable as he turned to shout back up at the window. 'Give me a minute,' he called. 'And tell Baldy that – '

Aoife never got to hear what Baldy was to be told, because the army arrived before Ciáran could finish his sentence. The window was slammed shut and Ciáran sprang to his feet, as though he was standing to attention so as he could salute the Saracens that were pulling up behind the lines of RUC officers.

No chance of that, though. Ciáran started shouting, 'Fuck off back to where you came from,' at the soldiers who came tumbling out of the backs of the Saracens. All dressed up in camouflage, they were. They certainly looked out of place on the streets of Belfast, dressed up in their green and brown flecked gear, among ordinary residents in baseball caps and tracksuit tops. A rack of men, including Ciáran, spat insults at them in an accent that they probably didn't understand, and a jeering started from the middle of the crowd. It spread in a rippling wave that ended with a chorus of 'The Fields of Athenry':

Low lie the fields of Athenry –

The song struggled to make itself heard over the noise of the army's arrival.

Where once we watched the small free birds fly –

The helicopter that had been over West Belfast circled around until it was directly overhead.

Up the 'RA – fuck the Queen –

The up-draught from the helicopter whipped Aoife's hair out from behind her ears.

Our love was on the wing, we had dreams and songs to sing –

Aoife stood up then and started to wade in, clawing and shoving with the best of them.

It's so lonely round the fields of Athenry –

She wasn't for caring whether Ciáran followed her or not, whether she was crushed or trampled, or whether she was hit by objects thrown from the other side. All she wanted was to find Damien. Get him away and to safety. Problem was, she had to fight for every inching step forward; she had to prise wedged shoulders apart, duck low to wriggle through a wee window of space, turn sideways and breathe in to wring her body through the mangle of people. As she got towards the centre, though, it suddenly started to get easier. The crowd began parting in front of her; people peeled off to the sides or sprinted back in the direction she'd just come from. She looked up and saw an elderly woman with deep worry-lines set among the shallow wrinkles of her face. The woman was bellowing out a series of Hail Marys as she hobbled past. Aoife stopped and listened. All around her was screaming and confusion. The singing had stopped, the chants had stopped, the drums had stopped, the flutes had stopped. Nothing but the banshee wails of the women hurrying off in the opposite direction. Many of them were stooped down low, their hands covering their heads.

'What's happening?' Aoife called. No one paid her a blind bit of notice. She saw for herself soon enough, though. A soaring milk bottle arced over her head and smashed against a Saracen. Flames licked at the armoured vehicle, the flickering heat-haze around it shimmering with out-of-focus soldiers running to and fro. Another petrol bomb followed, and then another. One grazed her shoulder. She leapt back from the explosion of it, her movements the mirror-image of a policeman who stood just in front of her. She was quicker than he was, though. Fire caught at his trouser cuff. He danced maniacally for a moment, whilst Aoife looked on open-mouthed, before he fell to the concrete and rolled frantically from side to side until the flames smouldered and died.

'They've the plastic bullets out, love.' A woman with her hair in curlers grabbed at Aoife's arm and tried to drag her away from the policeman, who was now trying to kick himself upright again.

'What?'

Aoife shook her head and tried to concentrate on what the woman was saying.

'They're using the plastic bullets,' she repeated, tugging on Aoife's elbow. Struggling against the unwelcome grip, Aoife tried to continue on into the chaotic crowd. As she was being pulled and pushed one way whilst desperately trying to move in the other direction, Aoife caught sight of Damien:

A policeman stands facing the crowd – one foot in front of
    the other – balanced
and ready. The barrel of his gun holds steady – shoulder
    height – level
with chests and torsos. It swings round – swivels and seeks
its target: a boy – one amongst many – ready to throw.

The boy has his mouth open, ready to shout as he turns
    – body twisted – ready
to run. The milk bottle in his hand arcs upwards –
    spilt milk curves
to form an empty speech bubble.

The shutter clicks to leave every detail exposed – and
    Aoife knows – knows
what will happen next.

I step into the multi-storey city centre restaurant and brush off the maître d' or whatever you call him. 'I know where I'm going,' I say. Then I make for the stairs, moving carefully so as my skirt doesn't hitch up too far. Level two I'm looking for, for the gathering of Loyalist politicians sitting down to their dinner after a day out at Senator Mitchell's peace talks.

  A good few months have passed since the fourth. No sight or sound of Cassie. Healing time. Time for the news stories to die down and for folk to start in with the gossip that maybe the wee

Cornish sapper has just made it all up for the publicity – just an urban legend.

Maybe that, or maybe he's an escaped mental patient from the Mater Hospital.

By the summer, when the peace talks begin, I've been forgotten rightly and it's then that I begin to scout for this UVF gunman-turned-politician, Willie Kitchener. Silvered hair, silvered tongue, but a brassy Prod killer beneath it all. A Prod known to have a wandering eye. A Prod politician who, by the end of the night, will have a choice between keeping a secret that means living the rest of his life with an open, pus-ridden wound instead of his manhood, or seeking medical help and having to admit he's cheated on his bottle-blonde wife. Give up either his cock or his political career. Win-win.

It doesn't take long before I catch sight of him, so I sit at the bar and order a vodka-tonic, and it isn't long before he catches sight of me. Looking over, time and again, obviously half-cut, browsing my legs and window-shopping at my low-cut neckline. I hold my breath in and meet his eye – one, two, three – imagining bringing the bottle down against the sink, then lifting the shards, one by one, from the floor. I imagine his screams. Closing my eyes, savouring it. I open them to find him stumbling across towards me. A wee flicker of excitement inside. Maybe tonight –

But the maître d' is looking over and he's in a whispered conversation with a brick shithouse in a suit – maybe a manager, maybe security detail, maybe a peeler – and then the shithouse starts towards me, the maître d' reaches for the phone and I reach for my jacket.

'Alright, love – ?' Kitchener begins.

'Not tonight,' I reply, shouldering past him towards the back stairs, picturing the map that Baldy drew, remembering the three flights of stairs, the swing doors to the basement kitchen, the turn right past the freezer and then the fire exit round by the bins. Remembering to turn left and then left again when I come out the back alley. My steps quicken, my teeth

136

*biting at my lower lip, until I catch sight of Baldy's taxi, engine
running, at the end of the street.*

Maybe I've not been forgotten, after all.

It took Aoife a few seconds to make her way across to where
Damien lay. Those few seconds were all it took, though, for
the Lego man to be swallowed back into the lines of Lego
men, and for a clutch of people to swarm around the slumped
figure of her brother, for a piercing scream to ring out from
where Damien lay, and for the blood to start flowing. Just a
few seconds.

Aoife stood, looking down. People stooped, knelt, stretched
out to lie beside wee Damien, to whisper softly in his ear
or smooth his brown curled hair away from the cascading
blood. People Aoife knew, and people she didn't. Some of
them remonstrating, shouting, or even weeping. All united in
anger and concern. Except for Aoife herself. She just stood,
motionless, and stared down at Damien's shoes, which were
bucking as he writhed in pain. She knew them well. Black
plimsolls, they were, with a sole that had flapped loose at the
toes of the right one and a worn slant to the fabric at the back
of the left one from Damien walking on his instep. They were
cheapies that Aoife had chosen for him, from Dunnes Stores.
She'd scraped fields' worth of mud from them, she'd held a
match to a hole in the sole to melt the plastic back together,
and she'd replaced the frayed black laces with the rounded
brown ones from her daddy's dress shoes. She was used to
seeing them, each and every day, beside the mat at the front
door. They were always askew, and Aoife would bend down to
straighten them. They were askew now, as they kicked at the
air. All Aoife could focus on, though, was the fringe of creamy
milk along the lip of the right one. She'd need to scrub away at
that until the fabric was worn to a single thread if she wasn't
wanting her wee brother to be reeking of sour milk the whole
year through.

'Give him some air,' someone called, and a hollow began to form around Damien. He looked tiny, so he did, curled into the vast folds of his torn Celtic strip as if the shirt had been a perfect fit a moment before but then he'd shrunk inside it as he lost blood out of the cut across his right eye. One side of his face was tears, the other blood. It was more blood than Aoife had ever seen before, folding down the ridge of his cheekbone, forming a sheen that looked like a garish Hallowe'en mask. Aoife couldn't see the wound itself, couldn't see his injured eye, or his cheek. Only blood. She could see his left eye, though. It was near rolling in its socket as it frantically searched the crowd, as it sought out something on which to rest. One eye, lined with the red raw shadow of pain and glittering with unshed tears. It fell on Aoife. On his big sister. And all Aoife could do was return the pleading gaze. She couldn't step forward, or back, couldn't smile encouragingly or even set to crying.

'Aoife,' a voice said. 'Come you forward and hold his hand.'

She looked up and saw Big Gerry. He had emerged from those gathered around, unbuttoning his shirt and advancing on Damien like Superman come to save the day. There was no brightly coloured costume on underneath the shirt, though, only a grey-looking vest. As he pulled his shirt off, Gerry seated himself on the road, right in the midst of the gutter-flow of mingled milk and blood, and lifted Damien's head up on his lap. With gentle fingers, he pulled Damien's clutching hands away from the wound and set the white of his shirt against the blood. Then his eyes came back up to look questioningly at Aoife. He was a thick-set man, Gerry, with a thin moustache that looked like an eyebrow and bristling eyebrows that looked like twin moustaches. Aoife moved forward and did as she was told.

'Now,' Gerry said, to everyone and no one, 'has anyone thought to look for an ambulanceman or a doctor? The wee lad's bleeding and we're all standing shouting about it or watching as if it's on the telly. Come on to fuck, someone make themselves useful and get an ambulanceman.'

Aoife didn't hold Damien's hand so much as caress it. His fingertips were a maze of shallow scratches and rough, uneven skin from where he'd bitten and bitten at his nails. The skin either side of the nails was torn and shredded, and the cuticles had been pushed back until they formed definite lumps, like second knuckles. At the base of his index finger was a scar from long ago, a curving half-moon he'd slitted into existence on a piece of broken glass down at the concrete playground. Aoife traced it, then followed the lines of his skin down into the moist palm, clearing the tackiness of the blood away from his curving lifeline. His fingers twitched to her touch, but he didn't grip and cling to her as she would have expected. She continued to sketch rough circles in the palm of his hand, thinking to herself that her wee brother's hand wasn't like her mammy's hand, wrinkled and coarse, nor like her daddy's, tobacco-stained and with the hard pads of calluses around the edges. Damien's hand was soft and smooth. And it was small. Aoife felt the tears welling, felt them rising from deep inside of her. She gulped and bit at her lip. His hands were so small that she could fold the fingers in on top of the palm and clench the whole thing in her own fist. She could hold his hand in that way she remembered from childhood, back when her daddy's hand enveloped her own. Back when she could feel his work-worn skin against her fingers, the thickness of his wedding band against her knuckles and the tips of his fingers against her wrist.

'Fucking useless, this is,' Big Gerry said, handing the bloodied shirt to Aoife and peeling off his vest instead. Bare-chested, he pressed the vest against the wound and looked about himself. 'Is there not an ambulance to be had?'

'There's a St John's ambulance,' someone replied. 'But it's parked at the end of Rugby Avenue and it can't get down here.'

Gerry took this in, nodding and looking down at the boy splayed across his lap. He scooped Damien up into his arms and started shouldering his way through the thickening crowd.

Aoife quickly rose and followed close behind, keeping her eyes fixed on the strands of hair that curled across Gerry's broad shoulders. She had to keep blinking the tears away so as she could focus. As she went, Aoife waved the once-white shirt in front of her. She had a vague notion that this was meant to be done when moving through with an injured person, so that no more shots would be fired and so as the people to either side cleared a path. She'd seen the black and white photos of Bloody Sunday, with the priests walking in front of the wounded waving bloodied handkerchiefs. This was different, though. Firstly, because she was behind Gerry and wee Damien, not in front, and secondly because Big Gerry had been right about the shirt being useless. It hadn't sooked up any of the blood, just gathered it in amongst the folds of fabric so that, as Aoife flapped it around in front of herself, it sent a splitter and spray of blood up onto those who had stepped aside to let the three of them through.

The St John's ambulance was manned by two volunteers in green and yellow jackets. As Aoife fought her way to the front, Gerry was lowering wee Damien down onto a waiting stretcher. One of the volunteers – a matronly woman with her hair up in a scarf that was knotted beneath her chin, as if she had a toothache – peeled away the ruined vest and replaced it with a fistful of cotton wool. Wisps of the dressing flew up, catching the breeze and drifting away like dandelion seeds. Back when she was young, Aoife's daddy had always reached up to catch the floating seeds for her, carefully transferring them into her cupped hands and telling her to make a wish as she released them. She had an urge to jump up and catch at the cotton wool wisps now, but they were too far above her.

'Who're you?' a quavering voice asked her. She looked up into the face of the second volunteer, a young boy who looked no older than Aoife. He was near see-through with whiteness, ready to retch as he looked across at the blood pouring from Damien's eye.

'I'm his sister,' Aoife replied, pointing to Damien.

'Right.' He waved her on, keeping his eyes fixed on her face.

Before Aoife could grasp at her wee brother's hand, though, the stretcher was lifted up into the back of the ambulance. The young gawky boy clambered in after it. He held his hand out for Aoife to follow him, but the matronly woman stepped across between them.

'Family only,' she said, sternly.

'I'm his sister.'

She looked Aoife up and down. 'You're too young to travel with him,' she said. 'Phone your parents and we'll meet you at the hospital.'

'But – ' Aoife began. She felt herself bristle with anger, her body near itching with rage. It couldn't be expected that wee Damien would go through the trip to the hospital alone, nor that Aoife would just stand back and watch her brother being packaged up and shipped off. The doors slammed and the engine started. Aoife reached up to pound her fists against the back of the ambulance, to bang on the metal until they opened up and let her in. The faint slapping noise of her hands against the door was lost beneath the screech of the siren.

Aoife looked around for Gerry. He could sort it, surely. In spite of his lack of Spandex or Lycra, or whatever it was that Superman's costume was made from, Gerry had certainly been a bit of a hero. Not that Aoife was expecting him to lift the ambulance clear off the road or fly her to the hospital or anything like that there; she was just hoping that he'd know what to do next. Gerry was gone as well, though.

'What the fuck am I meant to do?' Aoife asked the empty street.

She should run home and fetch her mammy and daddy. Although her daddy hadn't been in the house when she'd left and her mammy had only just refilled the sink. Aoife wasn't wanting to waste time trying to pull them away from the places she knew they'd be – from the kitchen and the pub. Aoife had been sitting one afternoon many years before, on her school holidays, watching an old Western film with her daddy, and had asked why they all kept talking about whiskey as 'firewater'. He'd chuckled a bit at that, and then replied that it was brewed from a mixture of fire and water and that you didn't want to go drinking too much of it or you'd end up bursting into flames right there on your bar stool. It could happen if you drank so much that there was more fire in your system than there was water. She'd only been eight or so when he told her that, but she knew now, at the age of fifteen, that if her daddy's story was true then he would have been burnt to ashes long ago. He was as fond of his firewater as her mammy was of her dishwater, and Aoife hadn't the time to go chasing around after him. No, she'd just ring the house like the toothache woman had suggested and then make her way to the hospital as quickly as she could.

The nearest public phone was on the other side of the Botanic Gardens, so Aoife had a fair distance to run before she reached it. A fearful smell of piss wafted out at her as she opened the graffitied plastic door. It looked as if someone had tried to wrench the phone itself from its setting, but there was still a dialling tone when she lifted the receiver. It had probably just been some hallion wanting to strip it for parts to fling at the peelers, and they'd given up when they realised there were all sorts of bolts and wires holding it to the back of the phone box. They'd have moved on and found something easier to throw. There wouldn't be any shortage. Everything in Belfast was a potential missile, especially around the Twelfth.

Fumbling a coin into the slot, Aoife dialled her home number. It rang. And rang. In the gaps between, Aoife could hear the drums starting up again down in the direction she'd just come from. There was no answer. Hanging up, she considered what to do next. She could still run back to the house and try to raise them that way, but that meant doubling back on herself and she wasn't wanting to leave Damien all on his own while she wove her way through the streets of Belfast. No, it was better to make her way to the hospital, make sure that Damien was being seen to, and then phone again from there. Better to take care of it herself. That way she'd know whether it was worth the trouble of raising her half-cut daddy and her mute mammy.

Decision made, Aoife was off again, setting off at a gowly half-run that skipped, tripped and stumbled her along that wee bit faster than just walking. Her tears had dried, but Aoife could still feel the puffiness up around her eyes. She wasn't wanting to focus on the questions that spun into her head – *what had been the last thing she'd said to Damien before he'd been loaded into the ambulance?* – instead just wanting to concentrate on setting one foot in front of the other – *what damage could a plastic bullet do to an eleven-year-old boy?* – trying to think of the quickest way through the mass of people that had come out to see the parades – *was it just a cut or would he be needing to have surgery?* – trying to edge past them with hurried shuffled steps – *did he at least know that she was coming, that she'd follow close behind?* – not looking up into their faces, not reading their banners or listening to their cheers – *which hospital was he being taken to?* – not caring that she was kicking the empty cans and bottles as she squeezed through – *which fucking hospital was it?* – not caring that a fluttering Union Jack trailed over her shoulder as she came up towards Shaftesbury Square – *which fucking hospital?*

She was aware, though, that one or two folk had been looking at her strangely as she pushed her way through. She'd thought nothing of it. Maybe they could just smell the Catholicism coming off her, a scent of incense and fish-on-a-Friday. It was only once she reached the pavement-lining of people waiting to watch the bands coming from up Donegall Pass that she realised she was still holding the bloodstained shirt in her hand. That was the reason people had been frowning at her and stepping out of her way. She'd not been waving it about in front of her or anything like that there, but it had still cleared a path. Aoife allowed herself a bittersweet smile as she let the shirt drop onto a pile of rubbish by the side

143

of the road. There were crushed cans, plastic bags, sandwich wrappers and burnt-out disposable barbecues lying there already, so she didn't see that a bloody shirt would make too much of a difference. Messy bastards, those Prods.

Having made her way to the front, Aoife was faced with a far bigger problem. She needed to get to the far side of the road so as she could make her way up to the Royal Victoria, but the parade itself was in her way. A steady succession of men in orange sashes with a blue trim walked past: some of them taking it deadly serious with their bowler hats set firmly on their heads and their eyes set firmly in front; some of them enjoying the moment, sauntering along like royalty and giving a wave one way and then the other.

Standing there, chewing at her lip, Aoife considered. She didn't have the time to go skirting around the outside of the marchers, seeking out the end of the line so as she could dart across the road. Besides, she was a teenage girl – surely no one would mind her quickly nipping across the street. There was no one would think that she was a threat, surely, especially now that she'd left the bloodied shirt behind. There was a gap coming up, between the ragged tail of one Lodge and the twirling baton of the next. Aoife decided to take her chances.

Breaking from the crowd, Aoife dashed out into the street. She swung her head to the left, to look at the oncoming marchers. At the front was a young lad with white gloves, twirling his baton and throwing it in the air to catch it again. His eyes met Aoife's and, in that moment, she could see the fright on his face. His hand missed the baton. There was a split-second of discord as the band behind missed a step and waited for him to pick his baton up off the ground. For a split-second, no more, Aoife stopped an Orange band in its tracks. She held her breath through it, hurrying on in a crouched run, expecting a shout from behind – 'Get your hands up, you bastard!' – waiting for the swivel of the gun, level with her torso, her chest – knowing what would happen next.

It didn't, though. One moment she was out in the midst of the parade, and the next she was on the other side, elbowing her way through the onlookers. She let out her breath. Shoulders jostled her and a set of grasping fingers clutched for her T-shirt. The material stretched, but didn't tear. Then, the fingers let her go and she was free. She was moving through the thinning crowd with enough adrenalin in her to carry her, at a sprint, all the way to the Royal Victoria up on the Falls Road. She just needed to pray that it was that hospital that they'd taken him to.

I wake to find a film of sweat between my body and the sheets, a dampness to the pillow and a hollow scream lodged halfway up my throat. I swallow it down and turn the pillow, so as it's cool to the touch of my cheek, then I settle back down and try to coax my mind towards dreamless sleep –

It's Nigel again, it's always Nigel, but now he's got Kitchener beside him, and the journalist who wrote about me, no more than a shadow, follows close behind. They lead an army of suited men; all of them wear orange sashes with blue and white trim and all of them have their faces hidden beneath the brim of their bowler hats. There is no steady marching to them now, no rhythm. They are sprinting, full-pelt, down an empty road to the accompaniment of the shrill shriek of flutes – tuneless and reaching a pitch that would set your ears to bleeding –

And there I am, at the front of them, never more than a stumbled step ahead, feeling their fingertips grasping for a handful of my clothing, waiting for the grip that will hold and slow me, dragging me down beneath the undercurrent of the oncoming tide –

Lying on my back, then, I feel the coarseness of gravel beneath me instead of the soft give of the mattress. Stones and shards of glass dig into my skin, graze the surface as I shift and stir. I lie still and wait, confused now as to whether I'm praying for death or waking. I can hear their whispers in the silence,

Nigel's the loudest and most insistent, as they decide what to do with me. And I know the options – I know that they've the razor blades to shear my head, the tar to coat my body, the rope to string me up from the nearest tree. I know that they've discussed the simple gunshot to the head, that they've dismissed the idea of choking me with their bare hands or slicing at my throat with a rusted knife. The longer they wait, the worse it will be. They'll get creative –

A man looms over me. He wears a surgical mask. There is a grin beneath, I know; there is Nigel's grin beneath. There will be drills and pliers used; he will set about me with tools of a trade that he doesn't know. He's wanting to leave me without even dental records – metal filling in lower back right molar, resin crown to upper left incisor, impacted lower wisdom tooth growing in at an angle – so as they won't be able to identify the corpse, so as there's nothing left of me –

I lurch awake. It takes a disorientating second for my mind to stretch itself towards wakefulness. A moment in which I'm still praying for a quick execution. Then I lie awake in the darkness of my bedroom, staring into the night and grinding my teeth through the silence.

Aoife didn't have time to rush up to the A&E receptionist to ask after her brother, or to run frantically from ward to ward searching for a wee boy with his face swathed in bandages. She wasn't wanting to tug at the sleeves of doctors who would dismiss her with a wave of the hand, or to press her face against the glass window of the operating room while they sliced into Damien's eye. She dreaded leaving the Royal Victoria, having found no trace of him, and having to decide whether to turn one way, to Belfast City Hospital, or the other, to the Mater.

As it turned out, though, she didn't need to do anything other than push at the door to Accident and Emergency. The first thing she saw, when she stepped into the waiting room, was her gathered family seated on a row of grey plastic seats. Her mammy, her daddy and wee Damien himself. Her mammy had her head in her hands, her shoulders shaking with sobs. Aoife looked at that with her jaw near hanging to the floor.

Shay Brennan, spotting his daughter at the doorway, levered himself up from his chair and held his arms out to her, the way he used to do when he returned home at the end of a working day. Running full-tilt across the waiting room, Aoife flung herself into his arms. He swayed slightly as he took the impact, either age or drink making him more unsteady than back in the day. When she was younger, the bear-hugs Aoife's daddy gave her used to leave her dangling toes stretching down towards the ground like those of a ballerina.

'Where have you been, love?' he asked, softly.

'What?'

'Where have you been? Big Gerry came to fetch us and said you were in the ambulance with Damien, and then we get here and he's sat all alone.'

Aoife pulled away from her daddy. She felt the tears burning at the corners of her eyes, frustration boiling up to spill them down over her cheeks. She looked beyond her daddy, at her brother. Damien was lying across two chairs, with his head propped up on pillows. The blood had been cleaned away and the wound dressed with clean white bandages that were beginning to turn pink with seeping blood. The bandage covered the eye itself, but beneath that was deep purple bruising that had swollen up to the size of a golf ball. The hot tears sliding down Aoife's cheeks reached her chin and began to drip down to her T-shirt.

'I tried to, Daddy,' Aoife whispered. 'But they wouldn't let me.'

Her daddy folded her back into a hug and stroked at her hair. There was a trace of whiskey-breath about him. The peaty smell of it was comforting and familiar.

'Is he going to be OK?' Aoife asked, in a small voice.

'They've made him comfortable, so they have,' her daddy replied. 'There's a fair bit of damage, so they're waiting for a

147

surgical consult. But he's been given something for the pain and they'll try to get the swelling down so as they can have a proper look at the eye itself.'

Aoife nodded, taking in these ready-made phrases that had obviously been given to her daddy by a doctor and then repeated word for word.

'Gerry's gone to get your Auntie Eileen,' Shay continued. 'And your mammy's pills.'

'Is Damien going to be OK, but?'

She wasn't wanting a medical opinion or anything like that there; she was just wanting her daddy to tell her that everything would work itself out. She waited, and then felt her daddy's nod bringing the tip of his chin down onto the top of her head. Squirming away from his grasp, she looked up at him. A nod wasn't enough; she wanted to hear it said.

'Is he?' she demanded.

'They think he might lose his eye, love.'

The sharp scream that Aoife let out caused Cathy to lift her head from her hands. She rose from her seat and came marching across to them. Shay caught at his wife's arm, but it didn't stop a finger being waved in Aoife's face. There was no sightless staring or sink-standing to Cathy now; she was fully awake.

'You stupid girl,' she spat. 'Why weren't you looking after your wee brother?'

'Come on now, Cathy.' Shay tried to keep the peace.

'It's a simple enough question. Why wasn't she looking out for Damien?' She stared at Aoife, hard, as she repeated the question.

Aoife stared back. She opened her mouth, but no words would come. The hypocrisy of it left her dumbstruck. She looked down at the bunched-up handkerchief in her mammy's hand and then back up to the tear-streaked face. With her reddened face and the manic gawk to her eyes, Cathy Brennan looked like an escapee from the hospital's psychiatric wards.

'Well?' she asked, jabbing her finger towards her daughter. 'I'm waiting for an answer.'

Aoife wanted to tell her mammy to wind her neck in. She wanted to ask if she even knew what age her son was, or what day of the week it was. Never mind whether or not she knew where Damien had been. Aoife wanted to scream that she shouldn't be the one looking out for Damien, that she shouldn't be needing to make him his dinner, that she shouldn't have to turn his socks inside out so as he could wear them for a second day. It wasn't Aoife that needed telling, it was her mammy.

But the words wouldn't come.

'Well?' her mammy asked again.

Instead of answering, Aoife crumpled. Her legs just gave way and she collapsed down towards the tiled floor. No warning, no reply to her mammy, just a slumping fall. Her daddy caught her underneath the armpits before she reached the ground and walked her over to the plastic seats.

'Go easy on her, Cathy,' she heard him whisper. 'She's been through a brave bit today.'

Aoife cradled her head in her hands and smeared away the tears that continued to well in her eyes. She waited, every nerve set on edge, for her mammy's reply. Concentrating on waiting for it, not taking any notice of the calming hand her daddy placed on her shoulder, not wanting to look over at Damien, who let out a moan through the breathless silence.

'Damien's only eleven, though,' Cathy hissed. 'She should be looking out for him.'

'So you know what age he is, then?' Aoife's head snapped up. She glared at her mammy, her irritation only growing when she noticed the shock etched across her mammy's face.

'Of course I do.' Cathy frowned. 'I'm his mammy.'

'Is that right?' Aoife let out a short, sarcastic laugh. 'When was the last time you made his dinner, *Mammy*? Or the last time you washed his clothes, *Mammy*? Or tucked him in, *Mammy*? Or even bloody spoke to him?'

'I have my bad days,' her mammy replied, softly.

'Every fucking day – '

Aoife had risen now. It was her turn to point a finger in her mammy's face, her turn to feel her daddy's staying hand on her arm.

'Come on, now,' he said. 'Don't be saying things you'll regret.'

'I'll not regret them,' Aoife replied, quickly, looking her mammy square in the face. 'Mammy,' she said, 'it's your fault that wee Damien's in here. Not mine. Yours.'

With that, she was off. Swiping out at her daddy to get free of his grip, she made contact with him up around his mouth. She felt him recoil, heard the pain and surprise in his voice as he called after her. She wasn't for stopping, though. Blindly, she strode off down corridors. She wasn't for caring that orderlies had to wheel beds to one side to make way for her, that patients on crutches were hobbling quickly out of her path, or that nurses were having to flatten themselves to the walls so as she didn't clatter into them. She barely noticed that the sterile white walls with brown tiles changed to light blue walls with carefully painted pictures of cartoon characters and then changed back again. She didn't read the signs as they flashed past.

When she finally came to a stop, she looked up to find a sign that read 'General Surgery'. There were two blue-cushioned seats there in the corridor. Aoife sat herself down on one of them and set to scratching at her forearms. When she looked up again, she found a man in a white coat sitting in the seat next to her. He was watching her intently.

'You having a tough day?' he said, with a smile. He had an English accent, the kind where every word was perfectly clipped into shape before moving onto the next. Proper Queen's English.

Aoife nodded and looked him over. He was young, but with a shadow of stubble across his chin that stopped him from looking boyish. Gaunt in the face, with lank black hair that hung down over his ears. Handsome enough, but in need of a good feeding.

'What's the matter, then?' he asked, again with a smile. Aoife found herself smiling back, in spite of herself. A flush and flutter came over her, reddening her face.

'My wee brother, just,' she replied. 'He was hurt out on the street.'

'Bloody marching season.' He put his head on its side and peered keenly at her, his eyes still holding the warmth of the smile. 'Is he badly hurt?'

Aoife sniffed. Looking down at her hands, she twisted her fingers around and through one another. The silence between them was filled with clanks and beeps and distant voices. It wasn't the whirr of machines that Aoife hated about the hospital, or even the faint sourness of disinfectant. It was the constant thrum-hum of the strip-lighting from the ceiling – a noise that followed you right through the corridors, a noise you couldn't get away from.

'I'm Tom, by the way,' the man in the white coat said, holding out his hand. There was a tremble to his fingers, just a wee shiver of nerves.

'Aoife.' She took his hand. 'Pleased to meet you.'

'So, is your brother in surgery, then?' Tom asked, shifting his weight so as he could sit on his shaking hands.

Aoife shook her head. 'Accident and Emergency,' she replied. 'He was hit in the eye, or just above the eye, with a plastic bullet. We're waiting on them seeing to him. They say he could lose the eye, though.'

'What's his name?'

'Damien. Damien Brennan.'

Tom nodded thoughtfully. 'I think they've requested a surgical consult. I'll ring down when I go back in and see if I can speed it up a bit for you.'

Aoife looked up, into his eyes. 'Thank you,' she said.

She thought that he coloured a bit at that. Aoife wanted to reach out then, to grasp at his hand or trace the lines of his smile with her fingertip. Inappropriate, guilty desire stirred through her. He could only be mid-twenties, could be no more than ten years older than her. Besides, out of school uniform, Aoife could – at a stretch – pass for eightteen. She shifted in her seat, tucked her hair in behind her ears, and searched for a question that she could ask without her voice catching or her face turning beetroot-red.

'Are you a surgeon, then?' she said, finally.

'I am,' he replied. His hands came out from under him then and he held them out, palms towards the ground the way Aoife and Damien used to do whenever their mammy wanted to check their nails. It had only ever been Damien's nails that were marbled with dirt, never Aoife's. Tom's nails were clean and well trimmed, but his hands still had the flicker of nerves to them. 'I'm a surgeon with the shakes,' he said.

Aoife drew in a breath. 'Are you nervous, is that it?' she asked, trying to make her voice coy but succeeding only in making it high-pitched.

He wrinkled his nose and nodded.

'Aw, bless.' Aoife reached across and set her hand on his. She moved her index finger back and forth across his knuckles, the way she'd seen some of the girls doing at the Convent whenever they wanted something from Extra Anchovies. If they wanted a bottle of cider or tonic wine bought for them, they'd send the prettiest girl off to ask the laboratory assistant, in her most tactful and tactile way. Not that Aoife was wanting anything like that there from Tom. She was wanting nothing other than to see him smile again.

'Thanks.' His other hand came up and patted at hers.

A small tremble transferred itself to Aoife's fingers and travelled up her arm.

'It's a problem I had all through medical school,' he said. 'I can control it reasonably well, but it's a nuisance. It happens when I get overwhelmed by the precision and concentration of it all.'

'So, it's caused by the pressure of your job, then?' Aoife asked, pulling her hand away and trying to keep the disappointment from her voice.

He smiled ruefully. At least she'd succeeded in making him smile again. 'Have you ever heard of a surgeon with the shakes?' he said. 'It's ridiculous, I know, but I've never had it in the operating room. As soon as I get in there I'm fine. Touch wood.'

They both looked about themselves for a wooden surface to touch for luck. There was none to be found though. It was all tile, plastic and painted plaster. Tom settled for tapping at his head. Aoife smiled, uncertainly now.

Tom spoke first. 'The sooner your brother gets his injury seen to, the more chance we have of making sure he doesn't lose the eye itself.'

'Is it likely that he will lose it?' Aoife asked, quickly. The sharp guilt of having forgotten – even just for a second – about her brother and his injured eye added a note of urgency to her voice.

'It depends on where the thing hit him.' Tom spoke softly, calmingly. 'Those plastic bullets are vicious things. What I was going to say, though, is that I'll come back along with you now and do the consult myself. We'll get things moving that way, OK?'

Aoife tried to keep the doubt from her face. She wasn't wanting to offend, but she also wasn't sold on the idea of a nervous surgeon, who looked as if he wouldn't be able to hold a knife and fork without them rattling against his plate, prodding around her brother's damaged eye.

'Ee-fah,' Tom leant in towards her, pronouncing her name carefully and uncertainly, 'I'm one of the best reconstructive surgeons there is. That's why I'm over here. They hired me because I can piece together a kneecap better than anyone else in the world. It's a rare skill, that. Almost useless outside of Northern Ireland, fair enough, but a skill nonetheless.'

'Why *did* you come across here, though?' Aoife asked.

He looked taken aback by that, by the force of the question and by the bile that was behind it. Blinking, he slowly rocked back in his seat.

'I don't mean it like that,' Aoife said, quickly. 'All I was meaning was, why come over here when half the knees you're putting back together are the knees of people who hate you?'

'For being English, you mean?'

Aoife nodded.

'I think the majority of people have more of an understanding of the situation than that. I'm not the enemy just because I'm English, surely?'

He left the question hanging there. Aoife didn't answer and Tom seemed to take that as a sign that the last word had been said on the subject. He stood and made a crook of his arm for Aoife.

'Shall we?' he asked.

8

The doctors called it a blow-out fracture. As if the eyeball and all that there had exploded outwards, like a planted bomb, leaving a deep crevice in the right-hand side of his face. Aoife could have understood that, if there'd been a scorched hollow between his cheekbone and his forehead, a crater like the one she'd seen whenever she'd walked, looking-and-not-looking, past the bombed building up on the Donegall Road.

They'd followed the smoke that day, her and Joanne. It was a weekend, so they weren't needing to worry about their school uniform giving away their Catholicism. It had been earlier that same year, back when they were selling enough jewellery during the week that they could indulge in wee trips into town to flick through the sales racks on the Saturday. They'd been holding dresses up against one another – paying a compliment and then waiting for one in return – when they felt the shake and heard the rumble. Thunder in the spring. They'd made their way outside and followed the billowing, dirty smoke to a builder's merchant's just off the Donegall Road. A deep and sunken scoop had been taken from the side of the building, shards of brick and glass were strewn out and across the road and the timber piled in the yard beside had been scorched by the blast. Flames licked at the roughly hewn edges of a wall that had been torn away to leave a ground floor bathroom open to the street. The toilet now looked straight out onto the mangled metal of the car that had been used to plant the bomb. Toilet tissue flapped and uncurled in the wind.

Aoife had watched the local news later that night and been told that the IRA had claimed responsibility for the bombing. The builder's yard had been identified as a target, they'd said, because the Nationalist owner was tendering for work from the security services.

Damien's face wasn't like that, though. It wasn't like a blow-out, like an explosion. The surface hadn't been stripped away to show the details of the inside, to show those bits that you were never meant to see. The bricks and mortar of his face weren't missing, hadn't been scattered out and over the pavement. Falsely named, so it was. Not an explosion so much as an implosion. The bullet had laid waste to the arching bone above the eye and the whole thing had shifted downwards. It had 'compressed', the doctors said, causing an 'orbital fracture'. His cheek, beneath the eye, had collapsed as well so that the whole right side of his face seemed to be slipping. It wasn't like a bombed building at all; it was more like one of those ones further down the street that had been shaken to its foundations by the blast, one of those ones where the walls began slowly leaning inwards, where the plaster started to crumble and the tiles slid down from the roof to shatter against the pavement below. Structurally unsound, he was. The bullet had struck and everything had been crushed and squeezed backwards into his beautiful face. Beneath the skin everything was crumpled and disfigured, whilst on the outside it only showed whenever he tried to smile, or laugh, or frown, or sleep, or cry. Or look up.

It probably wouldn't really be noticed, or at least not too badly, if he'd just sat there expressionless, day in, day out. It was when he glanced up at whoever was talking to him, though, or if he tried to let his eyes drift off in the thinking of something. Then it became wile obvious. His left eye would go dandering off, happy enough, but his right eye stayed where it was and the pain of its not moving caused him to flinch his face around it as though he'd an odd wink on him. The bullet had also left him blind in that eye. It was as useless to him as a conker or a marble would have been in its place, but they weren't wanting to remove it from him because they were feared that the socket would collapse and close over. So the eyeball remained there, sightless and swollen. As the bruising went down, it showed itself – the iris no longer coloured the blue of the sky but clouding over with a milky white.

They kept him in the hospital for a couple of weeks, trying to put pins in around the eye to stop it slipping further. Best reconstructive surgeons in the world in the North of Ireland, could piece together a shattered elbow joint or straighten a battered leg. They'd had plenty of practice, after all. An injury to an eye was different, though. With an elbow it didn't matter if you could see the joins or if the scars were visible, and with a leg it didn't matter if it was lumpen or if the patient had to spend months on crutches, so long as the muscles became strong enough to support the weight. A face was altogether different. It was always going to be seen by the world. And Aoife wasn't wanting a wee brother who looked like a melting waxwork.

He was sent home towards the end of July 1990, just as the simmering tension around the Orange marchers being forced through the Lower Ormeau on the Twelfth was beginning to fade. The homecoming was perfect for those who wanted to rake over the coals. There were plenty of visitors to the house in those first few days – journalists wanting copy, community activists wanting a cause, paramilitaries wanting an excuse. Not many of them wanted to help. At least, not in a way that Aoife would have seen as helpful. There were no hand-outs or offers to fly the family off on an all-expenses-paid holiday. None of that there. Precious few of them even stayed for the time it took to drink a cup of tea with Aoife and her mammy, and none of them ventured upstairs to the room, with the curtains drawn where Damien lay and stared, through his one good eye, at the far wall: 'CELTIC FI'.

All the attention stirred a change in Cathy, though. Having an invalid for a son seemed to suit her. She'd not taken a single pill since Damien got injured. Whether she'd been stung into going cold turkey by the sight of her youngest child in a hospital bed or by her eldest child's outburst in the waiting room was open to debate but, either way, she'd not filled the kitchen sink since that day. Instead, she took the time to go to Cliona's salon to sort herself out with a new haircut and then took a bus into town with Eileen to get her first set of new clothes in many a year. Certainly she needed to take out a small loan from the Credit Union to fund the shopping trip but, as she said, you need to make an effort if you're expecting visitors.

To be fair to her, Aoife noticed that she was also working hard on being a mammy to Damien. She bathed his face with a cold flannel whenever he woke up screaming, and mopped up after him whenever he left a dribbled trail of urine over the toilet seat. The doctors had said that might be a problem – depth perception. She went up and read to him before tucking him in for the night and carried the telly up for him to watch whenever his daddy was out on a taxi run. There was one aspect of this nursing routine, though, that took precedence over all the others, one thing that Cathy spent the majority of her time on. Because Damien couldn't chew and because even swallowing caused him a fair amount of pain, the doctors had recommended that he be kept off solid foods for the time being. If it had been up to Aoife, that would have meant going to the shops and finding the dented, discounted tins of soup and then heating them on the stove. Not for her mammy, though. Cathy was determined that her brave wee boy should have nothing but the best. So she took to making him home-made soup. All types and flavours: potato and leek, tomato, fish broth, winter vegetable, carrot and coriander. With a kind of manic energy that Aoife had never seen in her mammy before, Cathy threw herself into cooking up vast batches of the stuff. Whereas before she'd stood motionless at the sink, she now bustled from sink to worktop, to cupboard, to fridge, back to worktop, to stove, to sink, to stove. A flurry of movement she was. All action. Except for when it came to the washing-up. That was left for Aoife. Not that Aoife minded: she was relieved that her mammy had given up the soap for soup and she wasn't wanting anything to remind her of her former passion, even if it was only for the minute or so it took to scrub at a pan.

The Brennans began having soup for almost every meal. It wasn't only Damien who was expected to slurp away at it. They'd have pea and ham for lunch and cream of chicken for dinner. Pots of it bubbled on the stove at all hours of the day and night, casserole dishes of it sat keeping warm in the oven, and Tupperware bowls of it were tucked away into every available space in the fridge and freezer. Every penny that Aoife's daddy brought home was spent on ingredients. Shay began working extra shifts just so as they had enough for another pound of tomatoes or for the shoulderbone of a lamb from the butcher or for a quart-jug of cream. He wasn't for complaining, though; he just seemed pleased that he finally had his wife back.

Those who visited within the first few days of Damien's being allowed home had been given only a cup of tea, but those who kept coming back, in the days and weeks that followed, were handed a steaming bowl of soup. Aoife started near dragging well-wishers in from the doorstep so as she could get rid of the three-day-old Cullen Skink or the cream of spinach that had developed a skin on the top.

It was Father O'Neill who came up with a practical solution for what to do with the leftovers. The visitors had by that time thinned to a trickle, but Father O'Neill was still getting through at least four bowls of sweetcorn chowder, or minestrone, or cream of celery in a week. He was the priest who gave Mass at Damien's school, so he'd taken it upon himself to visit regularly. At first he'd only murmured platitudes or whispered prayers at the bedside, but, as the weeks had gone on, he'd taken to sitting for a bit longer over his lunch and talking things over with Aoife and her mammy.

'Very tasty,' Father O'Neill would always say, after the first spoonful. 'Very tasty indeed.'

Aoife's mammy would nod and smile, while Aoife sat silently and tried to ignore the groaning of her bloated stomach. It had got to the stage where she was near certain that, if she were to run down the street, she would hear the ebb and flow of her liquid diet sloshing around in her belly like the waves out at sea. She had even taken to eating slice after slice of dry bread between meals to try to sook some of it up.

'Very tasty,' Father O'Neill said, as usual, one day about three weeks into his soup vigil. He paused for a moment, then changed tack. 'I don't know where you get your ideas, Mrs Brennan,' he said. 'But I don't think I've ever had the same flavour twice.'

Aoife swallowed. 'We've enough of it frozen to see us through the next four or five winters, Father,' she replied, with a tight smile.

Cathy frowned across at her daughter. 'I enjoy making it, Father,' she said. 'It keeps me busy.'

'I see.' He smiled, softly. 'Can I ask a delicate question, then?'

Cathy nodded.

'Do you have any use for the excess?' He hesitated. 'That is, is there any going spare?'

Aoife looked up at him over the rim of her bowl, at his earnest brown eyes beneath the thinning hairline. She'd never thought of priests as going hungry before; she'd always assumed that they were near enough the only people in any parish assured of a hot meal at night. Sure, she even had a vague memory of Mr O'Toole, in a lesson about the potato famine, saying that the poor often went to the parochial house in search of a decent feed. Aoife knew that the nuns at the Convent were always complaining that Ireland was fast becoming a Godless country, but it seemed unlikely that things had become so bad that Father O'Neill would need to rely on charity so as he didn't starve.

'It's not for me,' Father O'Neill said, quickly, as if he'd read Aoife's thoughts. 'It's not for me, Mrs Brennan. Although it is very tasty indeed. No, it's for the poor and homeless in my parish up at Clonard.'

Aoife let a smile seep out at the corners of her mouth, some deeply ingrained Catholic guilt assuaged by the fact that the priest wasn't living in abject poverty.

Cathy considered for a moment. 'Why not?' she said. 'It may as well go into hungry mouths rather than down the drain.'

'Excellent.' Father O'Neill smiled brightly. 'We'll pay for the ingredients, of course. As it is, we hand out tinned soup every Wednesday and Friday, so it'll be nice to give people proper home-cooked food.'

'Shay could run it up to you in his taxi, I'm sure,' Cathy said.

'When did you want to start?' Aoife cut in.

'Tomorrow, if possible.'

'I think we can manage that,' Cathy replied, ignoring the squeak of protest that came from Aoife. She collected the empty bowls and rose from the table. 'I'm certain we can.'

The next day, the troops assembled: the Brennan family and two recruits from the Gilday household. Becky was feeling sheepish about not reporting back to Aoife on the day Damien got injured, so she'd have carried the soup across Belfast on her back if she'd been asked. For his part, Ciáran was the quietest that Aoife had ever known him to be. He'd been all repeated phrases and stuttering excuses when he came over to apologise to Damien in person. In spite of his suffering, though, Aoife thought that he was getting off lightly enough if his only punishment for getting Damien involved in the rioting was to be helping with the soup run. He could count himself lucky, because it was rumoured that Big Gerry had wanted him to be trailing a broken leg behind him rather than a soup tureen.

The soup they had frozen was all different flavours, so they decided to cook up some batches of the same type so that the volunteers who doled it out weren't needing to remember the names of more varieties than Heinz. Cathy was in charge of the kitchen; Becky and Aoife would help with the cooking and then ladle the soup into the two enormous metal tureens that Father O'Neill had sent round that morning; and Aoife's daddy, Damien and Ciárán would lift the tureens into the taxi and drive them on up to Clonard.

For Shay, the day of ferrying soup was the closest thing he'd had to a holiday in months, so he eagerly fetched and carried and followed his wife's instructions. Aoife had a feeling, though, that all the while he was thinking about the money for ingredients that would be coming his way at the end of the half-day. She knew rightly that a fair portion of that money would go behind the bar of some wee Fenian pub up the Falls Road. Still, she couldn't blame her daddy for wanting to get half-cut – he must have been beat to the ropes with all the hours he'd been working.

As for Damien himself, Aoife wasn't too sure how willing to help he was, but it was good to see him distracted. As he lifted the punnets of mushrooms into the kitchen, for Becky to clean and slice, there was a set concentration to his face. There was less of the crumple of pain whenever he was focused on what he was doing – only the odd twitch, like a reflex, as he blinked.

Lamb broth and cream of mushroom, they were making. Litres of the stuff. Enough to fill the big stainless steel tureens, that looked more suited to holding milk at a dairy than taking soup to the poor; enough that they had to get Becky's mammy to lend them flower vases, punchbowls and Thermos flasks so as they could store it while they waited for the boys to get back with the tureens.

They had to make three round trips before the last drop of soup had been drained from the measuring jugs and old fizzy drink bottles that littered the kitchen. They all worked hard at it for two hours and then, suddenly, it was done. The two tureens were loaded for the final run and Becky was filling the sink to get started on the dishes.

Aoife decided that Ciárán should stay behind and help his wee sister. He didn't give a word of protest. Aoife took his place in the taxi for that last run. It wasn't that she didn't trust her daddy to bring home some of the pay cheque, more that she didn't trust him to budget well. It was safer to give him pocket-money rather than expect him to portion it out himself.

'It's a grand job, Aoife, very tasty,' Father O'Neill said, as he counted out the notes. A cash-in-hand job, it was – even the Church did its level best to avoid tax and paperwork. 'Very tasty indeed.' He paused a moment. 'If you're able, I know that Fisherwick up on Malone would be keen on a similar arrangement. They would pay better than we could as well, I'd say.'

'Is it not a Protestant Church, though?'

'Presbyterian, yes.' Father O'Neill looked at her sternly.

'Not that it matters,' she mumbled, looking down to the floor. 'I'll need to ask my mammy,' she continued. 'But I don't see why not.'

'Feel free to say no, now. It's a time of great strain for your family, after all, and I'm not trying to – '

'No,' Aoife interrupted. 'The money will come in handy. Besides, the work seems to be doing my mammy some good.'

'Like I say, they'll be able to pay a bit more.' Father O'Neill's eyes met her own and a covert smile passed between them. An unspoken thought went along with it: it's best not to take a profit from your own, but if you can squeeze a penny or two from the other side, then where's the harm?

'It's best to keep busy,' Aoife said.

Baldy drives quickly, his eyes fixed on the road. When we reach my house, he turns to me. He isn't smiling; his face is dusted with tiredness and creased with lines of age.

'You can leave for a few weeks without anyone noticing?'
I nod.

'Pack a bag, then,' he says. 'A light one. You've a passport?'
I shake my head.

'Find some ID. Birth certificate, bank book, anything that says you're not Cassie. Go.'

I do as I'm told. Out of the car and into the house. It's empty. There's only my daddy to realise I'm gone, and he'll either not notice or not say. I move from room to room. Bathroom, make-up off. Bedroom, clothes in a bag. Bathroom, gather my toiletries. Bedroom, get my savings book out of the drawer. Hallway, slip runners on instead of my high heels. Living room, stand in front of the mirror to tie a scarf under my chin so as it covers all but the stray strands of my straightened hair. I'm stripping Cassie down as much as is possible, leaving her behind for a few weeks. On the run from her as much as from the peelers.

Back in the car, Baldy nods once. I'm wanting to ask if my scarf makes me look more like a film star or a housewife, but I know I'd get no answer. There is a fair amount of tension to him as he steers the car onto the main artery road out of Belfast. My mouth is dry, tacky with fear and unanswered questions.

'You've done this before?' I ask, finally. 'Gone on the run, I mean.'

He sniffs, keeps his eyes dead ahead.

I try another line of questioning. 'Where are we going?'

'You'll see shortly,' he replies.

We drive up through the narrow country roads of County Tyrone, through backwater towns, making for the weaving border-line of the River Lifford. The road signs change from miles to kilometres, then back again. It's not until they've all changed again, though, not until they're all in kilometres, that Baldy relaxes. Into the Free State.

'In my day you'd be lucky to get a draughty barn to sleep in, of a night,' he says. 'But you're in the lap of luxury, so you are.'

'Is that right?'

'Just you wait and see.'

It might have been more luxurious than a barn, but not by much. A caravan down at the bottom of a field near Ballybofey, rust scarring the underside of it. Nothing for miles but sheep, sagging telephone wires and a solitary farmhouse. Not what I'd been hoping for – not the rolling hills or the sprawling beaches of Donegal. Then again, it isn't like I'm off on my holidays.

'We can lie low for a good while here,' Baldy says. 'I know the farmer well.'

'What do we do, though?' I ask.

'We make use of the time as best we can.'

The social worker recommended that Damien take up a hobby to help with his recovery. Writing or painting or stamp-collecting – the kinds of activities that Aoife could imagine English children in bow-ties doing in the grounds of their parents' country mansion. Not things that she could imagine her odd-sock-wearing, jam-in-the-corner-of-the-mouth, twigs-tangled-in-his-hair brother doing. Not hurling or football or anything that he'd enjoyed before the injury – nothing that might send him flying or earn him an accidental elbow to the side of the head. Quiet pursuits, was how the social worker put it – nice quiet pursuits.

Lorcan, you called the social worker – Lorcan Mannus. He was a large man, not older than thirty but with enough pits and sunken shadows to his face for someone twice his age. All mottled skin and anxious frown, although Aoife found it difficult to tell whether the tremble to his hand was from nerves, like Tom, or from drink, like her daddy. She had her answer soon enough, though. When he slurred the word 'catharsis', slurred it so as Aoife – who hadn't a notion what the word meant – had to go flicking through the c-words in the dictionary until she found it, then she knew it was the drink.

She was fair worried, on that first visit, that he might want to investigate the steamed-up kitchen window or the smell of frying onions that drifted out from the edges of the tightly closed door through to the kitchen. She dreaded him turning round and saying that the neighbours had passed comment on the window, near white with steam, and the smells that came out of the house at all hours of the day and night. After all, the social worker wasn't to know that it was only a soup kitchen. He might already have called it in and just be talking to Aoife about getting Damien a hobby so as the peelers had time to surround the house and organise themselves for the raid. The way they had back on the day when Eamonn Kelly was shot.

Lorcan seemed to have no desire to see the kitchen, though. In fact, he even seemed reluctant to make his way upstairs to visit with Damien. He spent most of his time talking to Aoife and her mammy about the benefits of building model cars, or of collecting wild flowers from the side of the Lagan, or even of crafting fishing lures from wire and painted glass. He eventually trudged up the stairs to talk with Damien face to face, but he didn't stay long enough to work through even half of the activities on the list of hobbies he'd given Aoife and her mammy.

After Lorcan had stumbled on to his next visit, Aoife went up the stairs to ask Damien which hobby he fancied taking up. She was insistent about pressing him for an answer, because she desperately wanted to see him talking again, to see him laughing. She knew that it hurt him to talk, that it hurt him to laugh, but there seemed something unnatural about a young boy lying in a darkened room. Problem was, no matter how many times she asked, all he did was shrug. It didn't hurt him to shrug.

For a few days, Aoife set him up with one thing or another in the mornings, before she went off to school. He was to be off sick for the term, which would have been his first at St Joe's, and she wasn't wanting him to brood on it.

On the first day, she laid down a blank sheet of A4 paper and a clutch of colouring pencils and asked him to draw a picture. She'd been on the cusp of giving him the wee pots of paints that she used to use with her mammy, but she was still mindful of what Damien had done with the tin of red paint she'd given him during the marching season. Once her daddy finally got round to it, it had taken two coats of emulsion to cover over the spidery letters that Damien had left on his bedroom wall. Colouring pencils were a good deal safer.

When she came back up to check on him in her lunch hour, he'd only managed to leave a mangled mess of swirling colours on the page and a small pile of broken pencil tips beside. He was sitting staring blankly at the black hole he'd created. With a sigh, Aoife took his hand and led him down to the kitchen, where he spent the rest of the afternoon peeling the skins from piles of roasted tomatoes.

The next day, Aoife again sat Damien down with a blank sheet of paper, but this time she asked him to write a story. She had even less luck with that idea. Within ten minutes he was down in the kitchen, lifting handfuls of chopped carrots and holding them out so that his mammy could take them and drop them into the simmering pot.

After school on the third day, Aoife got her daddy to drive her down into town and she picked up four plant pots, some bags of seeds and the smallest bag of soil they had. She had to dip into the attaché case of jewellery money to fund it all, but she was fairly confident that it would be worth it in the long run.

'What's all this?' Damien asked, when he saw it lined up the next morning.

'I thought you could plant your own herbs.' Aoife smiled down at him. 'You've got rosemary, parsley, basil and mint there.'

Damien looked up at her, but didn't say a word.

'That way you can help with the soup-making.'

He nodded.

'It'll be that bit more special for mammy,' Aoife continued, 'if you've grown the herbs that she uses, won't it?'

Still nothing.

'Well?' Aoife asked, irritation rising in her. After all, she'd put a brave bit of thought into the idea. 'Isn't that something you'd like to do?'

Damien didn't reply, but he did crouch to his knees and begin examining the packets of seeds. The anger leaked out of Aoife at that, because he was holding the packets, one by one, up to his good eye and squinting at the instructions so as he could read them. Aoife pulled the bedroom door gently closed and went downstairs to get herself ready for school.

She'd not even finished her breakfast when, twenty minutes later, Damien came wandering into the kitchen, with a wee curling smile to his lips and a smudge of soil across his cheek. He didn't speak a word, but there was dirt clumped in underneath his fingernails.

'Well?' Aoife asked. 'Are they all planted?'

He nodded.

'That didn't take you long.'

He shrugged.

'Wash your hands, then, and you can help Mammy.' Aoife waved over in the direction of the sink. 'You'll need to remember to water them every day, now,' she added, as an afterthought, 'if you're wanting them to grow.'

He nodded again and dragged his feet over to the sink.

Aoife turned back to her breakfast. She hadn't really thought the herb-growing hobby through, she realised. It had kept him occupied for a spell, certainly, but it would take him no longer than a couple of minutes to water them every day. It was likely that with only four wee pots he'd lose interest before the seeds even started sprouting. So, unless she wanted a fragrant jungle up there in his room, she'd need to find him some other project to keep him busy.

For her part, Aoife was near rushed off her feet with soup runs up to Fisherwick on a Monday and a Wednesday night and runs to Father O'Neill on a Tuesday and a Thursday. Every evening after school was spent chopping, dicing, slicing, braising, boiling and ladling. At the weekend, when her classmates were taking time off, Aoife and her daddy would take the taxi down to St George's Market and buy a carful of vegetables, herbs, meat, fish and other ingredients.

In spite of spending each and every moment of the school day fretting about it, scribbling down ideas in the margin of her maths jotter and answering the teacher with 'Maybe scrapbooking, sir,' when he asked her for the difference between a presidential and a parliamentary system of government, it was four weeks into the new school term before Aoife landed on a hobby that might actually keep her brother occupied. By that time, with the soup-making to distract her as well, she'd fallen behind the rest of the class and been handed back several homework assignments that were more red pen than white page.

'Is that batch ready?' Aoife's daddy asked, as he came in that evening.

'Not yet.' Aoife looked up at the clock. 'We've still got a bit of time.'

'Right.' Shay sighed. 'Can we hurry it along? Mrs McGrath is out there looking for a taxi ride up to her sister's house and I'm not wanting to take her. It's nicer having the smell of soup in the car than the smell of piss.'

'Don't go taking her or the soup itself might smell,' Cathy said, from over by the stove.

'There's plastic sheeting down for the soup, though, so maybe – '

'No,' Cathy insisted.

'Alright, love.' Shay gave her a quizzical look.

'I'm not wanting the Prods thinking that we've pissed in their soup, is all,' Cathy explained. 'So sit you down and Aoife can wet the tea-leaves. Mrs McGrath can find some other taxi-man to take her.'

'I've no arguments with that,' Shay replied, reaching down to ruffle Damien's hair. As he squirmed away, Damien's damaged eye twitched and, as he tried to smile up at his daddy, that whole side of his face flinched with pain.

'Have you found something for the wee lad to do?' Shay asked, sitting and turning the volume up on the radio. Aoife kept it on low all through the evening, tuned to a local station. She'd taken to having it on to fill the silence.

Aoife looked sidelong at her brother, waiting for him to answer for himself, not wanting to talk about him as if he wasn't there. He might as well not have been there, though, for all the attention he was paying them. Instead of listening to the conversation, he was standing next to the radio listening intently. Nodding her head towards him, Aoife shared a smile with her daddy. They both watched as Damien leant further in to the speaker so that he could hear the music beneath the hiss of the kettle and the bubbling of the saucepans. It took Aoife a moment to place the song, although the tune was familiar. Bob Dylan it was, singing with Johnny Cash, on 'Girl from the North Country'.

'Maybe that's the answer,' Aoife's daddy said. 'We could get him a guitar.'

Aoife nodded. 'Are they expensive?' she asked, pouring water in on top of a teabag.

'I'd say they are. And we'd need to get him lessons on top of that.'

'It's a nice idea, though.'

'I'll keep an eye out,' Shay said, winking as he took the cup of tea from her. 'Thanks, love.'

The sex is a release. Of tension, of frustration, of boredom. It is urgent and unpunctuated by caressing or whispering. He keeps his socks on and I keep my bra on. No need to be fully naked. It is quickly over.

It's only afterwards that I trace the scar up near his collarbone with the tip of my finger, that I hear the rainwater drip-dripping into the saucepan we laid out to catch the leak and the wheeze of the wind through the vent above the chemical toilet.

'When did you get this?' I ask, meaning the scar.

'Probably before you were born,' he says, then clears his throat, thinking perhaps of the implications of that. '1976.'

I nod. 'How did it happen?'

'Interrogation,' he says. No more than that.

The very next afternoon, just minutes after she arrived home from school, the doorbell rang and Aoife opened the door to Ciáran, who stood there awkwardly holding an oddly shaped parcel wrapped in black bin-bags. He didn't meet her eye, but spoke to the fringe of weeds that lined the path.

'I heard you were wanting a guitar,' he murmured.

'Aye, we're on the lookout for one. How did you know – ?' Aoife stopped short of asking the question. It must have been Becky that had told him, good old dependable Becky. 'You've not stolen it, have you, Ciáran Gilday?' Aoife asked instead.

'No.' His eyes darted up to meet hers, then slid away. 'It's Declan's, so it is. That is, it belongs to my daddy.'

'And will he not miss it?'

'He's never used it, so far as I know. It's been up in the attic for the past four or five years gathering dust. I had to replace two of the strings.' There was a note of pride to Ciáran's voice. He quickly swallowed it. 'But it probably still needs a good tuning.'

'Thanks, Ciáran,' Aoife said, stepping to one side to let him in at the doorway. 'Why don't you come in and give it to Damien yourself?'

Ciáran smiled, nodded and wiped his feet on the mat before stepping inside. Aoife had to bite her lip, to stop herself from snapping at him to hurry on, as he carefully scraped his toes and then his heels on the doormat. He obviously wasn't wanting to give her any excuse to throw him out. There was an awkward moment, then, as he edged past Aoife and on into the living room. Aoife broke the silence by calling up the stairs for Damien.

'Damien!' she called. 'Come down here a minute.'

It was a blessing for Aoife to watch Damien as he opened his present. To see him frowning and flinching as he tiptoed warily up to it, to see him start to rip at the plastic like a fox at the bins. Then, as the fret-board showed itself, to see the smile on his face creasing at his bad eye but him carrying on regardless, the smile only getting bigger as he pulled the guitar clear of its wrapping and stroked at the gleaming, red-hued wood of it.

Aoife made her way over to him and positioned his right hand over the strings, bringing it down so that it struck a tuneless open-chord. She knew then that they'd found a hobby that would occupy him rightly. He sat there, with the fingers of his left hand pressing here and there on the fret-board and the thumb of his right hand strumming non-stop at the strings. As he thrashed away, his good eye focused on her with a gratitude that didn't need any contorting of the face.

'Are you not going to thank Ciáran?' Aoife prompted him.

'Thank you,' Damien whispered, his words lost beneath the noise of the guitar.

'Like I say,' Ciáran tried to shrug it off, 'Becky says you might have a use for it, and it was only collecting dust over at our place.'

'Still, it was kind of you.' Aoife laid a hand, briefly, on his arm. 'I'll need to remember to thank Becky when she arrives as well,' she continued, briskly. 'She's a thoughtful wee girl, that one.'

Damien took his guitar up to his room and spent the rest of the afternoon raising sounds that were fit to set a banshee running for cover. Down in the kitchen, they had to turn the volume on the radio to full blast just to drown out the worst of it. Even then, they could hear the faint clattering and clanging of notes beneath the radio music.

Aoife's daddy was right about them not having the money for lessons. After the tureens of soup had been piled into the taxi – and after Damien had been persuaded to lay down his guitar and help his daddy with the delivery – Aoife made use of the peace and quiet to make some calls. She sat herself down with the *Yellow Pages* and rang every listing they had. There were community centres where he could learn it as part of the activities they provided, evening classes he could pay for on the door, individual tutors that charged by the hour, and one or two intensive residential courses he could have gone to down in Meath or Wexford. Each option, though, was more expensive than the last. Things were tight enough as it was – even with the money from the soup runs – and if they forked out for the guitar lessons then Aoife reckoned that they'd need to cook soup morning, noon and night just to cover the cost. She didn't doubt that her mammy would happily spend every waking minute at the stove, but Aoife herself was fast growing scunnered of the whole business. Besides, they were well into the new term at school and there was a queue of girls wanting bracelets, bangles and necklaces. Aoife had kept Becky off the jewellery-making this long, but she wasn't wanting to make the switch permanent.

Rather than paying for lessons, then, Aoife asked her daddy to drive her round the charity shops that weekend. She was looking for a book or a tape or something like that there, to teach Damien the basics. There was bound to be a Johnny Cash or Bob Dylan songbook going begging, surely? The best she could find, though, was a paperback in a St Vincent de Paul shop out in the farthest reaches of the Wild West of Belfast. *Fingerings*, the book was called. Aoife had giggled a fair bit at that, but she wasn't wanting to share the joke with her daddy, so she carefully covered the title over with her thumb and paid the fifty-pence asking price. She would give Joanne a call later that night, she decided, so as they could work out who in their right mind would give a guitar book that title.

Damien took the book gratefully, and began studying it at all hours of the day and night. Aoife would walk past his room on the way to the toilet, in the small hours of the morning, and see his door outlined by the light coming from inside. She'd clamber out of bed the next day, bleary-eyed, and hear the rustle of the pages being turned. Then she'd take soup and a sandwich up to him when she got home from school, thinking he should eat something, and find him asleep, with his nose still in the book. The strange thing was, though, that he didn't pick his guitar up once. For over a week he did that, looking through the diagrams and making the shapes with his hand but leaving the guitar lying on the mattress beside him all the while. As the days slid past, Aoife began to worry that he'd taken up air-guitar instead of the real thing.

It had just been his way, though. Soon enough, he set the guitar on his lap and began to put his learning into action. With his tongue sticking out from the corner of his mouth, he moved through the notes: from C to D to Em to G to G7 to Am. There'd always be a long pause, while he twisted and wrestled the F from the guitar, before he could move his wee finger back and play an Am or a G or a C again. The chords rang through the house, over and over again, from when he got up in the morning through until the time when Aoife edged into his room and, reluctantly, tucked the guitar into its case and slipped Damien in underneath the covers.

As the weeks passed, the lulls between the strumming of the chords got shorter. Even the F began to seamlessly merge with the Am on the one side of it and the Em on the other. Wee tunes formed, sequences of notes that Aoife found herself listening out for as she chopped at an onion or plucked chicken from a boiled carcass.

Soon Damien started writing. Scrawled lyrics, normally only two or three lines at a time, would be noted down on the edges of newspaper columns, the fly-leaves of school books, the block-borders of posters, wherever there was blank white space. Damien would write them all down, the procedure requiring not only his tongue to be hanging out of his mouth, but his teeth to clamp it in place as well. Once he'd got his thought down, however short it was, he'd tear the corner of paper – from the newspaper, from the school book, once even from the bog-roll – and add it to the rest of the pile. A tiny mound of oversized confetti became a hillock, became a hill, became a mountain, became a mountain range. The paper would drift and then settle in the draught from the door opening and closing, so that the peaks of it were always changing and ever-spreading across the bedroom. Above each word or each lyric would be a chord – a D or an Em or a G7 – that was to be played as the words were soundlessly mouthed, but it would have been near enough impossible to have scooped up a handful of scraps and come up with anything even close to a song. It would have been like flicking the dial constantly through the radio stations and catching only snippet after unrelated snippet.

There was a problem with the chasing of the Johnny Cash dream, and it was a fairly fundamental one: he hadn't a note. From his soundless mouthing, Damien moved on to whispering the lyrics with these wisp-wheezes of breath that were like the noises Aoife's daddy made whenever he fell into a whiskey-soaked sleep in front of the telly. That hadn't been too bad, though. Aoife had at least been able to tune it out. It had even been passable enough as it worked its way up to a kind of stutter-mutter. But when Damien took a sudden notion to belt his words out with all the breath in him – like an opera singer trying to pop a lung – then it was murder.

The writing on the wall started by accident. Aoife had been down in the kitchen, stirring the cream of parsnip for that evening's soup run, when Damien came running in and tugged at her sleeve.

'What's the matter with you?' Aoife asked.

Damien didn't answer, except with another tug.

'What's that, boy – someone's fallen down the old well?' She accompanied her sarcastic words with a hand-on-each-knee crouch. She immediately regretted it, though, when Damien let out a pitiful wee whine that Lassie herself would have been proud of. She hadn't meant to hurt him, it was just that she wasn't wanting him to revert back to dumb shows.

'Just come,' he whispered.

Aoife followed Damien up the stairs. He went quickly and kept swivelling round to check that she hadn't fallen behind. When they reached his room, he pointed a trembling finger over towards a patch on his recently emulsioned white wall. It was like a graze against the white, a faint black mark. Aoife had to move in close, kneeling down on the carpet, before she could make it out.

'What is it?' she asked.

'Pen,' Damien answered, in a small voice.

'How did it happen?'

'I was jotting something down and I leant on the wall.' He held up a marker pen. The black of it was stained across his fingertips. 'It's wile inky. I didn't realise, Aoife, honest.'

'So it soaked through the paper and onto the wall, then?'

He nodded.

'Right.' She smiled up at him. 'And?'

'And now it's all over the wall there.'

'Who cares? Work away.'

'Really?'

'Absolutely.' Aoife rose to her feet. 'Is that why you didn't tell me down the stairs? Because you thought Mammy would hear you?'

He nodded again.

'Don't be worrying about that, Damien. Mammy's not going to notice. Half the time I'm the one who cleans your room anyway, and I'm not going to give you any grief about a bit of ink on the wall.'

'Serious?'

'Deadly.'

Damien was still more than a year off becoming a teenager, but he'd learnt rightly that if you're given an inch then you take a mile. Far from just leaving the faint tracings of one lyric, he began copying the words from each and every scrap of paper onto that white wall. He started forming a mural with the lyrics. As he went, Damien scrunched his pieces of paper into tight wee balls and dropped them out of the opened window. The mountain-range became a mountain, became a hill, became a hillock. Then even the hillock disappeared, to be scattered like hailstones across the soil of the barren flowerbed beneath his window.

To Aoife's eyes, the assortment of collected words looked beautiful. After the black marker had run to grey, Damien picked up the next pen that came to hand. It was red. Then he began using the colouring pencils – those with unbroken tips – that Aoife had given him: first green, then brown, then yellow, then back to black. The different colours formed a patchwork that reminded Aoife of all the leaves that used to gather along the pavements up the Malone Road, the piles of leaves she'd cycled through two years before when Ciárán had been training. She'd told Joanne about the writing on Damien's wall at school one day, and Joanne had grandly announced that it was called a mosaic or a montage, depending on whether it was about the different colours that had been used or the various clutches of words. She had a cousin who was an artist, did Joanne. She seemed to have one relation or another who did near enough everything. All Aoife knew about the writing on Damien's wall was that it filled her with the same joy she used to feel whenever she looked out of the window to see the first falling leaf of autumn spiralling down towards the ground.

Baldy seats himself on the thin fold-down mattress, with his back to the curved metallic wall of the caravan. A sheet is draped across his naked shoulders. His hair, slicked back, shows his receding widow's peak. Maybe there is more to his nickname than simple irony, after all. Reaching down to lift his shirt from the floor, he takes out a cigarette and lights it. Without his glasses, he has to squint and peer. He begins to talk.

Sean McGinn was ten years old in 1969. Not Baldy, at that stage, but Sean. From the streets around Clonard, off the Falls Road, the area that saw the worst of it that summer, on those first nights when the Loyalists gathered. Like a chip-pan fire: one moment the hissing, then a spark that catches and the whole area is up in flames.

Sean fled with his mammy and three sisters. They left their daddy behind and hitched to the camp at Gormanstown, County Meath, along with five thousand or so others. I Ran Away: IRA. Even if he had been old enough to fire a gun, there was none to be had. His daddy fought bare-knuckle alongside his cousin Kevin. Hand-to-cudgel, as the circles of Hell burnt behind.

The McGinn family were reunited once the Army got control of the streets. Sean came back to Belfast to see his daddy lifted in the first wave of Internment in '71. He was old enough to throw stones. He heard his cousin Kevin develop a stammer from the CS gas the Brits used. Old enough for petrol bombs. He smelt the urine as their home, with scorch marks still on the walls, was torn apart in '75. Old enough for the gun. Lifted by the RUC in '76 and sent to Long Kesh. Not Sean now, but Baldy.

He tells it all flatly, without emotion. Not a litany, but a rationale. He tells it, then snuffs out the half-smoked cigarette between finger and thumb. Normally it goes in his shirt pocket, but he tucks it in behind his ear instead. He'd have done that in prison. He'd have sat in a chill room smaller than this, with only a blanket rougher than the sheet.

If he chose to, he could list more grievances, more scar tissue. He's calm, though, is Baldy. Considered. Everyone has their reasons, Republican and Loyalist alike. Everyone has a stammering cousin Kevin, a gutted childhood home, a martyred friend or family member. This is the oil that gets poured on the chip-pan, and the flames keep spreading, and it's all sides that are pouring. But we all know who set off that first spark. We all know rightly.

9

In what, to Aoife, seemed like an equal but opposite reaction to Damien's discovering the links and movements between his guitar notes, Cathy started forgetting certain ingredients in her soups or failing to make the connection between the chopped carrots bubbling away in the boiling water in front of her and the handful of coriander on the worktop to the side. As the sounds from upstairs began to develop a rhythm and confidence, Cathy began substituting muesli for mint or introducing a handful of raisins into her lamb broth. There were coffee granules in her cream of spinach and clingfilm floating, like a skin, on top of her minestrone. During the Christmas holidays, Aoife was close to hand and was able to rescue the situation by fishing the extra ingredients out with a spoon. There was one tureen of potato and leek, though, that went out sweetened with caster sugar, and a compliment came back to them about the 'spicy taste' of the cream of sweetcorn soup. Aoife knew for a fact that there wasn't supposed to be anything in the least bit spicy in that soup but, since it had already gone out, she could only send back a word of thanks and silently pray that it hadn't been anything more poisonous than chilli powder that her mammy had added.

Making soup with her mammy became a case of running interference while Becky got on with mixing the correct ingredients and filling the tureens. Aoife would follow her mammy to the cupboard and take the can of golden syrup from her before it could be added to the oxtail, or she would catch at her mammy's wrist just as she began tipping the box of washing powder down towards a simmering pan of mushroom soup. Once Aoife even had to pull the scissors from Cathy's hand to stop her from adding a lock of her own hair to the fish broth that was sitting on the table waiting for its taxi ride up to Father O'Neill. All the while, as Aoife chased her mammy here and there across the kitchen, the strumming of chords from upstairs got faster and faster, as if Damien sensed the need to provide a fitting soundtrack to the slapstick going on downstairs.

It quickly became too much of a head-melt for Aoife, and she sent a note up to Father O'Neill to tell him of the change in her mammy. As the Christmas holidays drew to a close, the soup kitchen ceased full-scale operations. The stove was partly decommissioned so that it was once again used only for small batches of Cathy's concoctions. As the spring term started, Aoife went back to selling jewellery to her classmates and her daddy went back to ferrying paying customers to and fro. They'd to give the soup tureens back to Father O'Neill, but Aoife's mammy still did her best – on her own – to fill pots, pans, jugs, casserole dishes and the like. Aoife, whenever she got back from school of an evening, had to set up a checkpoint like the one the Army often set up on the road further up beyond the gasworks. She wasn't looking for armalites in beneath the floors of the cars, though, but hairpins in the cream of tomato; not for a mortar in behind the false back of an articulated truck, but for a cutlery set in amongst the potato and leek. The Brennan family would eat the small amounts of soup that Aoife waved through as posing no risk, and the rest of it was poured down the drain.

Truth be told, Aoife was pleased to be shot of the soup-making. It had been a tidy enough income, but she preferred skipping the last two classes of the day to sell bracelets and bangles up at Methody or missing the morning lessons so as she could sell a necklace or a pair of earrings to the students milling around outside the Whitla Hall up at the university.

Besides, Aoife always knew where she was with Becky – you could ask her for twenty new bracelets and fifteen new necklaces and she'd spend the evenings after school twisting wire and threading beads, and the weekends plaiting threads and setting stones, until she had them finished. There was no need for a checkpoint with her, either: the final pieces were always near enough perfect.

Aoife was also relieved to be back focusing on her studies – despite her late arrivals and early departures – because it distracted her from worrying about Damien, who had finally gone back to school after missing all of the first term. While she was trying to learn about trigonometry, she wasn't imagining Damien's teacher calling him to the front of the class and asking him to explain why he kept winking when she asked him what the capital of Peru was, or fretting about the teasing that Damien might get out in the playground, with the older boys all standing around him and pulling faces to mock his involuntary twitches. Concentrating on her lessons was also a good way of keeping from thinking about whether her daddy was spending the day making money behind the wheel of his taxi or spending it in beside the stout tap in the bar.

For six months or more after Damien's accident, Shay Brennan had played the part of loving husband and father, working away at his taxi-driving and then helping with the upkeep of the house in the evening. As the months had passed, though, he'd started getting home later and later into the night. With the extended shifts over the Christmas period he had taken to driving a double shift and sleeping on the wooden bench in the depot between jobs, and that became a pattern that continued after New Year. At least, that was what he told his daughter whenever she asked. Aoife thought it more likely that he was doing an early shift in the taxi and then a late shift in the bar, although she didn't doubt that he often found himself sleeping on a wooden bench in one place or another.

It was around the time of the Provos' mortar-bomb attack on Downing Street, at the beginning of February 1991, that

Aoife's mammy took a turn for the worse that stopped the soup-making altogether.

Aoife came down to the kitchen one morning and found her mammy moving between the sink, where she was blending sliced mushrooms with cream, and the stove, where she was stirring two massive pots of boiling, soapy water. The bubbles were overflowing, hissing and evaporating on the red-hot hob, but she still kept right on with adding liberal squirts of washing-up liquid from the squeezy bottle in her hand. Something had clicked in her mind, some wee switch that couldn't be reset, and washing-up and cooking seemed to have permanently changed places for her.

There was nothing for it but to lead Cathy firmly from the kitchen, lock the door behind her, and call the doctor out. Truth be told, Aoife had been half waiting for an excuse because she was getting tired, by that stage, of fishing Damien's old Matchbox cars out of French onion soup or finding a stringy shoelace in the fish broth. At first the manic cooking had been better than the standing at the sink with her hands plunged in warm water, but Aoife was beginning to re-think and pine for the days when she'd known, from one hour to the next, from one day to the next, from one week to the next, that her mammy would be standing still, staring out of the kitchen window.

The doctor listened impatiently to the symptoms Aoife described, nodding as though it was the most common illness on the planet – no more serious than a head cold – and he was therefore only wasting his time making a house-call about it. Then he set to examining Cathy, and it was Aoife's turn to stand impatiently waiting. She didn't see why, given her mammy's medical history, he couldn't just give her the exact same pills – the ones that left her chained to the sink – and be done with it.

After the examination, though, the doctor prescribed new pills that came in massive purple capsules. They were just the thing, he said. There was a drawback to the new medication. Cathy wouldn't take it and, whereas the last pills had been easily slipped under her tongue or tucked in with a mouthful of food, the purple pills were too large and unwieldy to be given without her noticing. The only method that seemed to work for Aoife was adding the powder from the insides of the capsules to a lukewarm mug of tea and then putting the tea into her mammy's hand. Once she'd done this, Aoife didn't even have to force the issue. Her mammy happily sipped away at the tea and swallowed even the dregs of the medicine, as though something deep within her – something ingrained in the genetic code of a Belfast woman – saw to it that she took the mug that was offered to her, and that she drank every last drop, right down to the purplish sediment at the bottom.

The new pills didn't take Cathy Brennan back to her sink-standing days, though. On day one, Aoife thought that her mammy followed her from room to room as she did her weekly cleaning because Cathy had taken it into her head to help her daughter. Even when she followed her husband out of the house on the morning of day two, and right down the path to the door of his taxi, they thought that it was because she was wanting to see him on his way. When she sat and listened to Damien playing his guitar for four hours straight on the afternoon of day three they assumed that she was just taking an interest. It was only when she decided, halfway through following Aoife around the supermarket on day four, to turn her stalking to a wee girl who was seated on a trolley pushed by her mammy, only when she took a notion to follow the fearful smell that auld Mrs McGrath carried to Cliona's salon on day five and when Father O'Neill came to call on them during day six and found that, on his way back to Clonard, Cathy was a step behind him the whole way... it was only then that they realised that the new medication was causing her to fixate on people and follow them from place to place.

Aoife looked at the small print on the bottle, spoke to the woman in the chemist and even phoned the helpline for the pharmaceutical company. There was no mention made of this side-effect, though. It seemed to be specific to her mammy and to her mammy only. At least when Cathy had had her fascination with the sink Aoife had always known where she would be, and there had always been the prospect of her wakening up for a spell and participating in the life of the household. Now, though, she showed no awareness of anything other than the person she'd chosen to follow, as if she had the blinkers on from the moment she spotted someone of interest. Aoife had to keep an eagle-eye on her or they'd end up hearing on the evening news about the middle-aged woman who'd followed an office worker onto the train back to Lurgan, or an electricity linesman up a pole to fix the line, or Peter Brooke, the Secretary of State, onto his plane back to London.

'Does she show any sign of being a danger to herself or others?' the doctor asked, once Aoife had finally got him on the phone.

'I wouldn't say so, no.' Aoife paused. 'But we don't know where she'll go from one minute to the next and she shows no sign of being aware of her surroundings.'

The line was quiet, although Aoife could hear a whispered conversation at the other end that didn't seem to be about her mammy. She could have sworn, in fact, that it was the doctor giving his lunch order to his secretary.

'It's much worse than it was before, with the other pills.' Aoife paused. 'Is this meant to happen? That is, have you ever known it to happen?'

'No,' the doctor replied. 'But your mother's been off her medication for a long while, and it takes time for a new prescription to take effect. You just have to persevere, keep a close eye on her and she'll soon adjust.'

One way and another, they managed to keep her indoors. Damien was a great help with looking after her, because he had a brave bit more patience than Aoife. He would calmly turn around, if he saw her following him out of the house, and lead her back in, whereas Aoife was more likely to just walk on and leave her mammy to her own devices, knowing that sooner or later the two of them would come full circle and arrive back at the house.

They took to locking her in during the daytime and then taking her out for a walk, as you would with a dog, in the evenings. There was no harm in leaving her on her own during the day, Aoife reckoned, although she had a feeling that her mammy spent the time walking from one side of the living room window to the other, to follow the passers-by on the street outside, or taking dashes at the telly to try and follow the daytime soap characters as they strode away from the camera. So long as the front door was locked, though, then Cathy couldn't do any more than that.

Through the run-up to her GCSE exams, Aoife needed to sell jewellery to supplement her daddy's meagre contribution and scrape together enough money for housekeeping. The difference was that she couldn't cut lessons any more or she'd risk finding herself far behind the rest of the class. So she took to going round the houses of the girls in the evenings, after the school day was over. She only went to the houses of those she knew at first, the homes of the girls from school. Soon, though, she realised that while she was calling on Paula at number thirty and Mary-Thérèse at number thirty-eight she might as well call in at numbers thirty-two, thirty-four and thirty-six as well. She didn't know the folk she was calling on, but she was going to the doors around the Falls Road, so she knew that those inside were safe enough – there weren't going to be any Prods lurking behind the door, waiting to jump out at her.

Within a few weeks, during which her exams came and went, she was knocking at each and every door that she came to, no longer bothered about whether the women inside welcomed her or chased her off, providing they had necks that needed necklaces, wrists that needed bracelets and ears that needed earrings.

There was the odd housewife who refused to answer their doorbell once it got dark outside, thinking it was more likely to be boys in balaclavas than a young girl with crinkled red hair selling jewellery. Those jumpy ones were few and far between, though, because things seemed to have settled a little in Belfast. All the major political parties – with the exception of Sinn Féin – were seated at the table with one another and the talk, after a fashion, was all about ceasefires and settlements. Aoife only picked up on the news in the snatches and snippets that she gleaned from the conversation of those she called on, or from the low mumble of the telly that was on in the background, but she knew enough to know that it was over in mainland Britain, with the stepping up of the Provos' bombing campaign, that the real trouble was stirring.

John Major had been in office for less than a year, but he'd already had to deal with the close call of that mortar-bomb attack and, as the year came to a close, with a spate of bombings in central London. Maybe he was a soft touch after the Iron Lady, maybe he didn't have the ruthless streak that Maggie Thatcher had... maybe that was why the violence had moved to the streets of the capital.

Aoife remembered her daddy sitting watching the news back in '81, back when Bobby Sands passed away. She was only a wee girl of six at the time, curled up against her daddy's chest on the sofa.

'Why did he die, Daddy?' she'd asked, looking up at him.

Her daddy had thought for a minute. 'Well, love, see that lady there with the starched hair?' He pointed at the telly, where Maggie Thatcher had just come on screen. 'She's a greedy monster, so she is, and she ate all of our Bobby's meals.'

'Really?'

'Every last one of them. Breakfast, lunch and dinner. Double servings for her and none for him.'

'That's not fair.'

'It's not, love.' He smiled softly at that. 'He could have got scraps, but. If he'd only begged for them.'

Aoife hadn't fully understood what was happening, but she thought she had a fair idea now that she was a bit older, sixteen and with a GCSE in history to her name. The reality of the hunger strikes, she now knew, was a good deal more intricate than her daddy had made out. She'd learnt, over the years, that the political situation was always more complicated than her daddy let on.

'Things have changed,' Baldy says.

Twelve weeks pass.

'Things have changed,' he says, again.

The Good Friday Agreement goes to a referendum, so as the whole of our wee Province can agree to disagree. Sixty-five pages of it come through the door, but I don't read it. I just judge whether or not to vote 'yes' by the reaction of Ian Paisley. Trembling with anger at it all, so he is. Trimbling maybe. So I vote 'yes' on the twenty-second of May on the basis of that. It isn't going to change what I'm doing in any case, in spite of what Baldy might say. I'm not for stopping. There's no reason for me to. After all, each one of the targets we select is carefully chosen. They've all done something to deserve the thing inside me – they're all worthy of it. Nothing in the sixty-five pages can change that, it can't rewrite the past, can't alter what's already been done –

The fifteenth of August 1998. Omagh. It is a Saturday afternoon, two weeks before school term begins. The streets are filled with shoppers. There is a busload of exchange students from Spain. Mothers have their children with them so as they can buy them their school uniforms. Later that day a carnival is due to arrive in town. At two-thirty pm the first of the warnings is phoned in to Ulster Television. Two minutes later another warning is called in to the Samaritans. Then Ulster Television is phoned again. All calls use the Real IRA codeword: 'Martha Pope'. Main Street, the first warning says, but there is no Main Street. Near the Courthouse. The peelers begin moving people away from the area around the Courthouse. But the car bomb isn't at the Courthouse, it's a red Vauxhall Cavalier parked on Market Street, the main shopping street. Fertiliser-based explosive with a trigger of Semtex. It detonates at three-ten pm. And –

And Baldy is right, it changes things.

Twelve weeks and twenty-eight men, women and children slaughtered.

'Things have changed,' Baldy says, again.

When Aoife went out on her nightly sales run, it was Damien who was left in charge. Aoife intended that he should watch his mammy, but he'd been so distracted since the end of the winter term that she wasn't too confident whether he'd have noticed if his mammy did wander off. He'd probably just stay seated in at the wide windowsill where he always sat, curled up with a book, and only realise she was missing when the news came on the telly and the presenter announced that a Belfast woman had followed a scuba-diver into Lough Neagh and drowned, or that a housewife had fallen to her death after sharing a lift to the top floor of the Europa Hotel with an abseiler. With that in mind, Aoife took to slipping the key into the lock whenever she left the house and smoothly turning it to leave both Damien and her mammy locked inside.

It was fair enough that Damien was distracted. As Aoife had feared, he was getting a rough time of it at school. Not that he talked about it to his older sister, but he told Ciáran about it and Ciáran told Becky who, in turn, told Aoife. There might have been an element of Chinese whispers about it, but by the time it reached Aoife's ears the bullying sounded vicious. Becky stood up for her big brother, saying that Ciáran had spoken to some of the boys who were still at school and told them to look out for Damien but that, without actually being there, there was precious little he could do when the name-calling began.

According to Becky, the thing that caused Damien the most grief was the presence of the Convent girls at the gates of St Joe's at the end of the school day. He was at an age where he was starting to show an interest in the girls, their necks festooned with Becky's necklaces and their ears hung with the earrings Aoife sold them, and it was their reaction to his injuries that sapped the last of his confidence. It wasn't that they ridiculed him, or pulled faces or any of that there. It was that they reached out to touch him gently on the arm, made wee clucking noises with their tongues, and whispered one to the other, 'Aw, bless.'

It broke Aoife's heart to see the effect it all had on her brother. He stopped playing his guitar almost entirely and lapsed into a silence that was only broken by a 'yes' or 'no' whenever Aoife asked him a direct question. Every hour that he wasn't in school he spent curled in at the windowsill sullenly reading from the histories and biographies – about Elvis Presley, John Lennon and the like – that he checked out from the library and, later in the year, scanning the obituaries of Freddie Mercury, as though he'd decided to absorb the talent of musicians from the pages of books and newspapers rather than taking the trouble to actually learn the instrument.

Once school started up again in the new year, Aoife tried her best to get wee Damien up and out of the house in the mornings. He wouldn't respond, but just lay there with the covers up to his chin and with his damaged face buried deep into his pillow. Even if she whipped the covers off, leaving his pyjama-clad body shivering against the bare mattress, he still dug his toes into the springs and clung onto either side of the bedframe with curled fingers. He wasn't for moving, wasn't for getting up to have a wash so as he could join his daddy and Aoife for breakfast.

Joanne likened it all to the Blanket Protest. They were doing their A-Levels by that time, and Joanne was hoping to go on and study history and political science down at Trinity College afterwards. Aoife hadn't decided what she'd be studying yet, but she was near certain that she'd be applying to Queen's University so as she could stay close at hand for her brother's sake.

'Maybe he wants something,' Joanne said, one lunchtime. 'Like the Republican prisoners back in the late Seventies and early Eighties who went on Blanket Protest. They wanted to be political prisoners, so they did, so as they had the right to wear their own clothes and the right to free assembly – '

'Jesus, wee girl,' Aoife cut in. 'Have you swallowed a textbook?'

'What?' Joanne looked hurt.

'Listen, Damien is in his own home, not some prison block.'

Joanne sniffed. 'I'm only saying. Maybe he wants something. And it'd be as well to find out now, because the Blanket Protest in the Maze soon escalated to a Dirty Protest, and if that happens then you'll have a job on your hands when it comes to cleaning his room, I'll tell you that.'

'Wise up – my wee brother's not going to smear shit on his own walls, is he?'

They both laughed at that, but, over the weekend, Aoife thought about what Joanne had said. The next week, when Damien refused to change out of his pyjamas, Aoife sat herself down on his bed and calmly asked him why he didn't want to go to school.

He shrugged and flinched. Then he pulled the covers up and over his face.

'Are you worried about them teasing you, is that it?' Aoife asked.

The covers creased up and down as he nodded.

'What do they know, Damien?' Aoife paused and chewed on her lip. 'The half of them probably don't even know how it happened, do they?' She paused. 'In fact, there's nothing to stop you telling your version of the story, sure there's not.'

A corner of the sheets lifted and his eye winked as he peered out at her.

'Tell them the truth,' Aoife said, laying her hand on the covers where she thought his shoulder might be. 'That you were there trying to stop an Orange March coming through the Lower Ormeau, that you were the last line of defence, with a bottle in your hand. Tell them that you hit a policeman with the bottle, maybe, and that you'd already taken two or three of them down and that they had to shoot you because you were picking them off one by one.'

'Is that not a lie, but?'

'No one tells the full truth in Belfast; it's all just half-truths and different versions of the same story.'

'But – '

'You were there, weren't you? You were throwing things.' Aoife smiled down at him. 'It's an exaggeration, not a lie.'

Sure enough, this pep-talk got him up and out of the house. Aoife wasn't proud of telling her brother to make a Republican martyr of himself, but it got the job done. Besides, it was surely no worse than the countless men who sat on bar stools throughout Belfast and told anyone who'd listen how they were on the run for this or that, or how they'd carried out a job the night before, when everyone knew well and good that they'd not left the bar stool in many a long month other than to fall into bed – or the nearest gutter – at the end of the night.

An uneasy peace held in the Brennan household. Aoife's daddy spent the majority of his time away from the house, telling his children that he was working shifts down at the taxi depot, although the rumour was that the few times he took a notion to get behind the wheel of his taxi he had to be pulled away from it because he was too hammered to get a grip on the wheel never mind steer it the right way. Damien said no more about mitching off school and no more about the teasing, but, if truth be told, Aoife had precious little time to ask him about it because trying to get any information out of him was like conducting a Castlereagh interrogation – she'd have needed changing shifts of peelers, sleep deprivation, threats of violence and maybe violence itself to get more than a whispered word. He spent his evenings tucked away in the window seat, reading his biographies of Jimi Hendrix and Buddy Holly, while his mammy sat herself on a chair at his feet and waited patiently for his next move. She seemed wile fond of her youngest. If he rose from his perch to go into the kitchen and get a drink of water she'd follow close behind, and if he went up the stairs to the bathroom she'd trail after him and stare at the grain of the wood on the closed door until he came out.

It was this that would eat away at Aoife later when she thought about what happened on that Thursday evening in late April '92 – the idea that nothing that Damien did that night pierced through his mammy's medicated haze and wakened her into action; nothing she saw caused her to cry out until after it was all over. She had carried on as normal, moving with Damien from room to room, not speaking a word.

Aoife didn't go home after school that day, but instead took a few pieces of jewellery with her and called on some regular buyers on her way up to Joanne's house. Since February of that year, since the UFF had walked into the bookmaker's at the top of her road and killed five at random, she'd been more careful about the hours that she kept and the people that she called on of an evening. As Damien arrived home, she was probably with Mrs Lamont, waiting impatiently while the Frenchwoman decided between twisted wire earrings with fake diamond insert or dangling peacock-feather earrings with a blue-hued stud at the join.

Cathy would have been standing by the door waiting, when Damien wandered in from school and set his bag down beside his neatly arranged shoes. No words would have passed between them, but maybe a gentle smile from Damien, interrupted by a flinch contorting his face. Into the kitchen, Damien's mammy watching as he poured himself a glass of milk, maybe shaking her head when he offered her a gulp. After swallowing his own pain pills, and chasing them down with milk, Damien would have broken open two purple capsules and mixed the powder into his mammy's tea, making himself a ham and cheese sandwich as he watched his mammy slurping away at her medicine, and leaning across to feed strips of bread into her tea-moistened mouth.

Aoife stayed at Joanne's house for her dinner, unable to resist the offer of a fry cooked by Joanne's mammy, and then stayed for a spell afterwards to make a start on the politics project they'd been assigned on the general election. The election had been only a couple of weeks earlier and there was plenty to interest them, what with Gerry Adams losing his West Belfast seat and John Major staying on as prime minister, but Aoife and Joanne had been sluggish after the fry and had wound up talking about Mrs Lamont instead, speculating about what would convince a nice young Parisian lady to come across and marry a Belfast man.

At some stage, Damien decided to lay his book down on the arm of the sofa and make his way back through to the kitchen. Mother followed close behind son, watching as he rifled through the cupboards, knocking a tin of baking soda to the floor and collapsing a paper packet of flour onto the counter so that it spilt out over the dirty dishes. He found what he was looking for under the sink, where it had always been kept. If Cathy recognised the blue plastic bottle, then she never said.

Using the same milk-clouded glass as before, Damien poured himself a measure of thick, syrupy bleach. It was yellow in colour, and that, as well as the smell of it, should have stirred a memory in Cathy, should have triggered a reaction.

He would have tipped it, watching as the slow-moving liquid trickled down towards his mouth, taking a gulp and raising a hand to his throat as he swallowed and then fell to the floor.

If Cathy understood, then she never let on. She didn't dash out to the phone to call for an ambulance, or run out to the street to scream for help, or even try to get Damien to vomit the bleach back up. None of that. None of it penetrated through the purple-capsuled drugs; none of it caused her to catch on. Maybe in the past, with the previous pills, she would have realised what was happening and taken some action. Instead, as his hands clutched at his stomach, as his fingers tore at his windpipe, as he tried to wrench his seared flesh free from his body, she stood silently watching. As his groans became whimpers, his writhing curled him into the foetal position and his eyelids fluttered shut, Cathy followed suit and calmly lowered herself to the ground to lie directly behind him.

As they lay there, mother and son, some faint instinct caused Cathy to reach out an arm to cradle her dying son.

It was this scene that Aoife came back to. There was still bleach in the glass, which lay toppled in the centre of the tiled floor, and the whole room reeked of the stuff. Damien and his mammy lay spooned to one side, stretched out as though in sleep. It didn't take Aoife long to piece together what had happened – only a lurching split-second.

At first, though, she thought that her mammy had taken a drink of the bleach as well, that the two of them had both lifted a glass of the stuff and swallowed it down. She ran out to the hallway and lifted the phone – her hands trembling so as she could barely push at the buttons – asking for an ambulance and giving her address to the operator – the tears wrenching the words from her in gulps. It was only as she looked frantically about herself – her chest gripped by panic – that she realised that her mammy had risen from the kitchen floor and calmly followed her daughter out into the hallway. Aoife turned fully then – the phone cord flexing behind her – and slapped her mammy across the face.

'You stupid woman!' she screamed. 'Why were you not looking out for him?'

'Love, I know you're upset – ' the voice of the operator intoned down the line.

'Not you,' Aoife said, hurriedly, and covered the mouthpiece with her hand. 'Mammy, why were you not watching him? Eh? Did you not see him drinking the fucking bleach?'

Cathy didn't respond. The palm-print Aoife had left across her cheek was beginning to flare red. She stood in silence for a moment, then her hands went up and she began clutching and clawing at her hair, lifting fistfuls of it out by the roots. She moaned softly as clumps of it came free. 'You're not human,' Aoife hissed, and then lifted her hand so as she could speak to the operator again.

In the ten minutes or so that it took for the ambulance to arrive, Aoife fed her wee brother nearly a full pint of milk. It was the only thing the operator had been able to suggest – to dilute the bleach and protect the stomach lining. As soon as she hung up, Aoife left the front door open for the paramedics – little caring whether her mammy took the opportunity to wander off – and went through to the kitchen to seat herself on the floor, prop Damien's head up on her knee, and pour the milk directly from the bottle into his mouth.

He was conscious, but his eyes kept rolling up into his sockets and he let out a continuous moaning keen that would have grown into a scream if not for his facial injuries, which hurt him mercilessly whenever he opened his mouth more than a quarter-inch. The milk bubbled up and out with every cry, spilling over his lips and out onto the floor.

Aoife smoothed back his hair, dabbed at the spilt milk with her sleeve and recited the rosary from start to finish. Or, at least, what she could remember of it.

Three weeks after Omagh, the day after the twenty-ninth victim dies of his injuries, Baldy asks me to move in with him. There's no romance to the question; it's blunt and straightforward. He just comes right out with it and, as I'm spluttering an answer, he starts in about how everything's changed now and how the two of us have to be changing too.

I'll not lie, I'm nervous about it. I've never lived with a man other than those in my family. But there's excitement mixed in with the fear as well. I'll live with Sean and he'll look out for me and we'll live a normal life in a two-up, two-down in the leafy parts of South Belfast. I'll recycle empty tonic bottles and Sean will taxi businessmen between jobs.

The house that Benny finds us is down in Stranmillis, south of the city centre. I go for a walk to find it and sure enough it is a two-up, two-down. I'm all for planning what bedsheets I should bring and whether we should get a new cutlery set from Dunnes Stores, for looking at colour charts so as I can repaint the hallway. All for playing house, so I am, like when I was young and I used to pull all the cushions from the sofa so as I could build a house for me and my brother to move into.

It's not like that, though. It's white-painted walls and two single mattresses with grey-looking sheets set up in the back room beside a three-bar electric fire and a camping stove. If I want hot water then I need to heat it in a saucepan. 'It'll be safer living like this,' Baldy says. 'They'll be on the lookout, so they will, after Omagh. We're best to take no chances.'

Whenever I made the house out of sofa cushions it would always end up that my brother would set to hollering and firing an imaginary gun out of the gaps between the cushions. I would be left in the imaginary kitchen, right enough, but he would be out scalping people rather than being hard at work in the office, and, whenever he came back, all his talk would be of killing and looting rather than marriage and babies.

'The peace process makes it harder to go unseen,' Baldy says. 'They'll take more notice of what we're doing, maybe. Especially if they think it's sectarian.'

We move into the one room, to keep warm, but we use the front room during the day as well, to begin planning for number five, Kitchener's replacement. There's manila folders spread out over the floorboards and a colour-coded map tacked to the bare plaster wall. Baldy's gun sits beneath the windowsill, out of sight.

We're not setting up house and home; we're setting up a fort.

Damien survived the suicide attempt, but he was in the hospital for weeks. The bleach had eaten at his trachea and so he had to have tubing and bandaging across his throat that took away his ability to speak. Until it healed he could communicate with Aoife by writing on a pad that was left beside his bed. Not that he had much to say – the pad was always left blank and they could have managed just as well with only slight nods and shakes of the head, the way they'd been doing for months before.

They had to be careful about the foods that they gave him in those days after the – well, what could Aoife call it? – not accident; incident maybe, or attempt – because they weren't wanting to agitate the stomach lining and cause an ulcer.

Her daddy showed up at the hospital that first night, and stayed by Damien's bedside for hours at a time in that first week or so. He looked a broken man, sitting there with a hunch forming in his back from where he'd slumped over and fallen asleep in the upright plastic chair. When Aoife spoke to him he replied in a voice that was slurred, although she couldn't tell whether it was slurred from lack of sleep, from drink, or from lack of drink.

'Aoife, love,' he said, thickly, on that first night. 'I'm sorry that you've had to go through this. A parent – a father – shouldn't be leaving his kids to this.'

Aoife hadn't said a word to that, because she couldn't disagree with him, but because she also felt that it would be cruel to agree.

'And your mammy…' he said, although he left the sentence unfinished.

'We need to do something about her, Daddy,' Aoife replied.

He nodded. 'We'll see about getting her in somewhere where they can take care of her…'

Again, Aoife was silent.

'I'll look after it,' he continued. 'I'll pull my weight, love.'

'We need you to bring in your wages, Daddy.' Aoife's stern tone faltered a little; there was a tremble to her voice. 'I can look after Damien, I'm happy to, but I need money for messages.'

'I'll work double shifts,' he said, passing a hand through his hair. 'I'll get it sorted, don't you worry. There'll be enough money to keep us going.'

Sure enough, as soon as Damien was out of the hospital, the bundle of folded notes that their daddy left on the kitchen counter for Aoife started to grow thicker. He left it once a week, on a Thursday, and supplemented it with the illegally claimed dole money every fortnight, leaving Aoife to sort out both the bills and the housekeeping with what he provided. All the same, Aoife couldn't shake the feeling that the bundle of notes – however much it had thickened – was still not enough for the amount of time that he spent out of the house. He always left before Aoife woke in the mornings, and he was often back after she'd gone to her bed for the night, yet the folded notes were only ever enough to scrape by. Her daddy would come in dishevelled and yawning fit to dislocate his jaw, but would only have half a day's wages to show for it, leading Aoife to the conclusion that there were as many folded notes being placed on the counter of the bar down the street as there were being left on her kitchen counter. It wasn't a surprise to Aoife, right enough, just another of those things that wet the creases of her pillow at night, before she fell asleep.

Aoife never did get the chance to sit her school exams that summer, at the end of the lower sixth. Rather than spending her time in an overheated gym hall scribbling away alongside all the other girls, she spent days on end on a suicide watch for her wee brother. What made it worse was that she didn't want to let on that she was keeping a close eye on Damien, so the babysitting involved a great deal of ducking and diving into rooms, putting her ear up to the door to listen in, and trying to engage Damien in a kind of continuous idle chatter. Holding a two-sided conversation with her brother, even before the accident – incident – attempt – had been difficult enough, but now it had the added strain of Aoife standing in the kitchen, talking away about how it was no surprise to her that the stop-start peace talks had moved onto strands two and three without reaching any sort of agreement on strand one while she occupied herself with peeling the carrots for dinner, and suddenly realising that she hadn't heard even a word from Damien in at least twenty minutes – sitting there in the living room, with the iron in the cupboard that he could burn himself with, or the sockets in the wall that could electrocute. So she'd rush in to check on him, panic fluttering inside her, and he'd be sat there nodding along to every word she said, his nose in a book. She'd have to lift a cushion from the sofa then or a cup from the coffee table – 'Ah, there it is!' – as though that was the reason she'd dashed into the room in the first place.

Aoife tried not to resent Damien for keeping her away from school because, when it came to it, she'd rather have a brother than a qualification. Family was important. All the same, when Joanne came round to see her after the end-of-year English exam – all flushed with excitement and talking away nineteen to the dozen about how tired she was and how Aoife was lucky for not having to go through the sitting of exams and the pressures of it all – Aoife near bit the head clean off her best friend. *Snap*, it had been, words that Aoife couldn't even remember, about how Joanne didn't know she was born and how Aoife had worked harder than her through the year and how it was Joanne that was lucky because she'd eventually get the results to apply to university – maybe – while Aoife had all this useless knowledge and none of it was going to be of any use to her whatsoever – it was all just wasted effort.

Joanne left fairly quickly after that, her long plait swinging behind her as she angrily strode away up the street. Aoife, who watched from the living room window, knew that it was the last she'd see of Joanne unless she took a notion to apologise. Joanne was proud, and she held a grudge, although she'd not hold her tongue in telling everyone at the Convent about the change in Aoife Brennan, and she'd not darken Aoife's doorstep again without receiving an apology. Not that Aoife really minded – after all, she had more than enough to be getting on with, plenty to concern herself with, and no time to be worrying about silly wee schoolgirls and their tantrums.

In spite of the money that her daddy left for her, Aoife still found herself struggling for cash to buy everyday messages. She had three – sometimes four – mouths to feed, and her savings from the jewellery had all but disappeared. She didn't want to leave Damien alone, even for the time it took to sell a few bracelets, so she took to calling her regular customers – pulling the phone cord as far as it would go so as she could casually lean against the frame of the living room door and watch-without-watching as Damien read away in his window seat. If the women she called wanted anything, Aoife sent it round with Becky. She was a blessing in those weeks, taking on the responsibility of making the jewellery, delivering it, collecting the cash and using the money to buy food on the way back. Aoife felt a brave bit of guilt, because she knew that she was taking advantage of Becky's kindness and that she was taking a cut of the profits without putting in more work than a quick phone call, but she didn't know what else to do.

She spoke to her daddy about working out a rota, so that they could make sure that they took it in turns looking after Cathy and Damien, but he was quick to reply that if she wanted the housekeeping money then she'd need to accept him working each and every shift going. He didn't seem to realise the strain that she was under, caring for both her mammy and her brother. Aoife told him often enough, chided him to chase up the doctor about getting Cathy a treatment order, or the social services about getting her a nurse. No matter how many times she mentioned it, though, no matter how often she was in tears as she explained that she just couldn't cope, it always fell to her to see that her mammy was fed in the evenings and given a sponge-bath before she went to bed at night. The pills had Cathy so spaced, so meek and mild, that she'd happily feed and wash herself so long as Aoife mimed the actions for her. But the sheer tedium of it, the dumbshow she had to go through night after night, left

Aoife near climbing the walls. And all the while she needed to keep an eye on Damien.

It was Ciáran who came through with the solution. One night Aoife was seated up in Damien's favourite spot at the windowsill, keeping half her attention on her brother as he sat beside his mammy on the sofa watching telly and the other half on trying to identify anything up by the window that might be a hazard: the sash to the blind could choke him, she'd need to snip it short with scissors; there was a light switch to one side, but she didn't think it could harm him; a picture hook in the wall, but it wouldn't be strong enough to hold his weight. As her eyes scanned the room, the doorbell rang. Aoife went quickly through to answer it, thinking that it was her daddy having forgotten his key – although he was a good few hours earlier than usual – or Becky calling to see if she had any deliveries to be made. Truth be told, Aoife was pleased at the thought that it might be her daddy, because then he could watch Damien – without watching – and she could make a start on the dinner. They were only having mince and spuds for a feed, but Aoife knew rightly that the cooking of it took well over an hour with the constant dashing back and forth to the living room, so if her daddy was there then she could make it that wee bit quicker – unless her daddy fell into a doze on the sofa and Damien used his belt to –

Ciáran was at the door. He looked her in the eye and handed her a plastic shopping bag, sagged down with the weight of whatever was inside.

'What's this?' Aoife asked.

'Think of it as compensation. From the peelers, from the bleach company, from the Brits even – '

Aoife lifted a corner of the bag and saw a thick roll of notes – far thicker than any her daddy had ever left on the counter – tied with a rubber band. There was hundreds of pounds there, maybe even thousands. 'Where did you get this?' she asked.

'Ask no questions, wee girl,' he replied. 'You've a need for the money and I had some I could afford to give away.

Don't think beyond that. Take it and use it; don't let anything else concern you. And if you've a need for more then let me know.'

Aoife chewed on her bottom lip, considering. On the one hand, the money would let her get someone in to mind Damien and her mammy of an evening, so that Aoife could go out and sell jewellery. On the other hand –

It didn't bear thinking about. Ciáran was right – she needed the money and there had been plenty of talk on the news of folk who'd got compensation from this organisation or that government department over the past few years. Damien was due it, surely, only it took lawyers and time. It might take years to get what Ciáran had brought to her door in a plastic carrier bag that night.

'Thank you,' Aoife said, reaching out to clasp Ciáran's hand. He was wearing gloves, thick and woollen, even though it was mild enough outside.

'You're welcome,' Ciáran murmured, avoiding her eye.

Aoife counted the notes out into sets of £30 and put one set into every container she could lay her hands on. By the time she had finished, there were over fifty of the sets, spread out through the whole of the kitchen – hidden in the backs of cupboards, up on the counter by the sugar, tucked in where the bleach used to be beneath the kitchen sink. Aoife thought it was the perfect hiding place because she couldn't for a moment imagine a burglar – especially a male one – rifling through a cluttered kitchen in search of a small fortune. If anyone did break in then the likelihood was that they'd search until they found the first stash, think they'd found the housekeeping money, and go off to search the rest of the house.

The only downside Aoife could see to squirrelling the money away was that, if she forgot to lock the kitchen door behind her and her mammy took a notion to begin cooking again, then they'd all be having money soup for years to come.

Aoife put the word out that there was cash to be had for minding the youngest Brennan and his medicated mammy for an evening. There was no shortage of offers from schoolgirls who wanted a bit of pocket-money. The job itself was easy enough, after all: sit yourself down in front of the telly and make sure that the two of them never left your sight. Wee buns, really – couldn't be easier. All the same, Aoife had a couple of criteria that she expected the babysitters to meet. First, they had to be at least a year older than her brother. Second, they had to be pretty girls. Not knockouts, but nice girls to look at. Her thinking for this was simple enough – if the girl was good-looking then Damien would be trying to get closer to her rather than squirming away, so it would be easier for her to keep an eye on him without it being wile obvious. Boys of that age could be controlled by a pretty face better than by an iron fist – boys of any age, really.

In the end, Aoife took on two local girls from the dozen or so that came around to see her about it. Nadine, who covered Monday and Wednesday evenings, was a wee slip of a girl with the palest skin you ever saw and dark curly hair that tumbled down over her shoulders. Aoife decided on her because the first thing she did, when she turned up to ask about the job, was smile sweetly over at Damien. And the first thing Damien did was smile back. The creases of it would have hurt him, but he continued on with it in any case, right up until she left. She was what Declan Gilday would call a wholesome Irish girl, was Nadine, with a wrinkle to her nose whenever she smiled.

Caroline on the other hand – the second girl, covering Tuesdays and Thursdays – was a different matter altogether. She was taken on because Damien's eyes lit up the moment she wandered into the house. Near panting, he was – couldn't keep his eyes from her. She was a good-looking girl right enough, with blonde hair down to her shoulders and wide hazel eyes that widened still further when she saw the flinching that gripped Damien's face as he stared across the room at her. She was tactile too, placing her hand on Damien's arm as she spoke to him, or tousling his curly hair as she handed him a cup of tea. Cathy seemed to take to her as well, because she always brought a make-up bag filled with all variety of nail polishes and eyeshadows and spent her evenings giving Aoife's mammy makeovers that would never see the light of day.

The two babysitters distracted Damien rightly from his twitching and his brooding and left Aoife free to go out around the houses selling jewellery, filling still more kitchen containers with cash. It was only on a Friday and over the weekend that Damien seemed to get back into his dark moods, because then he had his sister watching over him instead of the two Catholic schoolgirls.

As the summer went on, he even brought his guitar down the stairs, pressed his fingertips against the dust of the fret and took to serenading the two girls, turn and turn about, with a succession of softly strummed chords. There were still no words, no lyrics, to it, but, with his gaze focused on Nadine and Caroline, he'd at least started playing again.

He stumbles along, clattering into litter bins and elbowing lampposts before turning to fix them with snarling sidelong glances, demanding an apology. He's drunk as a lord; he's been on the rip ever since he was released early under the terms of the Good Friday Agreement.

'We may as well just lift him here,' Baldy says.

'It's dangerous,' I say, frowning.

'More dangerous than you going into some Hun bar on your own?'

We're crawling along, down some side-street off the Cregagh Road. As we pull up alongside, he quickens his pace, tripping and swaying across the deserted pavement. He keeps his head bowed and his fists clenched.

'You going anywhere special?' I ask, leaning out of the window.

He shakes his head, stops, looks across. He needs to squint to get a good look at me. I flick my hair over my shoulder and smile.

'Fancy coming to a party with me and my friend?' I ask.

Within seconds he's into the back seat, peering forward at me, then at Baldy, then back to me. It makes you wonder why we've never done it this way before. I'd been dreading going into another bar, having dozens of sets of gleaming Orange eyes on me and not knowing whether they recognise me as a bit of skirt or as the one called Cassie that was spoken about on the news a year or so ago. I'm delighted not to have to go through with that part.

'Wait,' I hiss to Baldy. 'I've not got a tonic bottle.'

Baldy nods, calls into the back seat, 'You fancy a carryout, mate?'

As soon as we're alone, he's straining himself to pluck and poke at me around the bulk of the front seat. He's not gentle. It's as if he's tenderising meat. I let him get a good feel, though, gritting my teeth through the worst of it, knowing that I'll not be gentle with him either.

'Here.' Baldy slings a blue plastic bag into the back seat, towards the lap of our passenger. The hands jerk away from me as the heavy cans find their target and fold him in two. He lets out a growl of protest at that, but he doesn't take it to heart. The first spluttering can is opened.

I take the miniature tonic bottle from Baldy and lift it to my teeth to snag the cap of it free. Then I begin emptying it out the window.

'Now, let's get you two somewhere private,' Baldy says.

'Cheers, mate,' he toasts us from the back of the car, his grin spreading to fill the rear-view mirror as he settles back in his seat.

'You're welcome,' Baldy replies.

10

In spite of her daddy's continual assurances, it was Aoife who did most of the organising towards getting her mammy sectioned, just as it was Aoife who'd shouldered most of the burden of washing, feeding and caring for her mammy those past months. True, her daddy was involved at certain key stages, whenever they took Cathy to the appointments with the psychiatrist up at the Mater Hospital and with the second doctor out Dundonald way. As the 'nearest relative', Shay was required to sign off on each stage of the process, working towards getting his wife a treatment order, but it was Aoife who did the running, who made the phone calls, filled in the forms and arranged the final meeting with both of the doctors and the psychiatrist up at the Mater to finally get it sorted.

On the morning of the meeting, though, she had a hard time moving her daddy. He had just finished a night shift, or so he said, and was seated deep in the sofa watching a boxing match from the Olympics out in Barcelona. He had a can of ginger beer open rather than anything stronger, which was a small mercy, but he turned a deaf ear when Aoife tried to get him up and out of the house.

'I'm just wanting to watch this fight, love,' he said. 'It's a young lad from the Shankill fighting. Wayne McCullough, you call him.'

'We'll be late, but,' Aoife replied. She already had her mammy buttoned up in a cardigan for the taxi ride up to the

Mater. It was August, but there was still enough of a bite to the air for Aoife to fret about her mammy catching a chill.

'They can wait for the time it takes to watch this, surely. It's history in the making here. He's in with a shout of gold. Wee lad from the Shankill winning gold for Ireland would make a hell of a story, so it would.'

'If we miss the appointment, though…' Aoife didn't want to finish the sentence, because she knew missing the appointment would mean going through the whole head-melting process again, and keeping her mammy around the house for another rack of weeks. She was beat to the ropes with looking after both Cathy and Damien and she was sick to the back teeth of doctors cancelling appointments, referring her on and forgetting to mail off paperwork.

'You'll have left too much time anyway; we'll be early and waiting around.' Shay took a sup from his can. 'So I'd as soon stop here and watch the fight, go to the hospital in the gap between the fights and be back in time for the Michael Carruth fight after.'

Aoife stared at him. The frustration of it burned at her, the disappointment of seeing her daddy, who'd carried the world on his shoulders when she was a wee girl, for what he really was.

'She's not just a taxi fare, Daddy.' Aoife had to swallow to get the rest of it out. 'She's your wife.'

He looked up at that. With a guilty glance back at the television, he set his can down on the floor and stood. 'They'll maybe show a replay of the final rounds later, in the round-up programme,' he said.

By the time Michael Carruth won the welterweight gold medal for Ireland, Cathy Brennan had been committed to the Mater Hospital under a Section 3 treatment order. The whole process took only an hour or so, and then she was led away by a nurse whilst her husband signed the forms and chatted away to the doctor about the Olympics.

Getting her mammy off to the psych ward for a spell was a relief to Aoife because she could finally focus all her attention on looking after Damien and trying to get him on the mend before the start of the new school year. She had a hard time understanding her daddy's outlook, right enough, what with him being more interested in going from house to house, around the estate, asking if anyone had taped the McCullough fight instead of sitting down with his children and explaining how they were to cope without their mammy. It wasn't even as if McCullough had won gold like Carruth; he'd only managed a silver medal in the end.

In any case, Aoife made the most of her new-found freedom. During the day she saw to it that the house was kept tidy and that she took the time to play board games with Damien and talk to him about whichever book he'd his nose in that week. She even found the odd moment to listen to the news on the radio, or call round to McGrath's on the corner to pick up a newspaper. Then, in the evenings, she left Damien in the care of either Nadine or Caroline and went out around the houses with her jewellery case.

Shay Brennan also settled back into a schedule, of sorts, in those last few weeks of summer. He'd rise in the morning with his children, eat his breakfast with Aoife and Damien, and then go off to start the early shift at the depot. He'd not be seen then until after his late shift, which finished at ten at night. How he passed the time in between was anybody's guess, although anyone with half a brain would guess that he spent his time in the bar. Still, Aoife was past caring, providing he left his few folded notes on the kitchen counter.

With one thing and another, Aoife found it hard to make the time to go up to the Mater to visit her mammy. There had been one or two times – when the guilt ate away at her – that she'd wanted to ask her daddy if he'd come home earlier and give her a lift, but Shay always came in the door just too late – ten minutes after visiting hours had ended or just as dinner was being served.

So one evening at the end of August, with Damien safely engrossed by Caroline, Aoife took the opportunity to get the bus up to the hospital so as she could visit her mammy for the first time. Aoife wasn't too keen on hospitals, but the psychiatric ward at the Mater at least didn't have that smell of sickness and bleach about it. There were still strip-lights, squeaky floors and eerie silences to contend with, right enough, but less of the frantic action and bloody gauze than she had seen on her visits to Accident and Emergency.

'Excuse me,' Aoife asked a nurse with ringlets of brown hair hanging loose from her ponytail. 'Could you tell me where Catherine Brennan is?'

'Are you her daughter, then?'

'I am, yes – Aoife.'

'You're often spoken of.'

'Really?' Aoife tried to keep the surprise from her face, but it was a struggle. The hospital treatments must be fairly effective if Aoife's mammy – who hadn't seemed to realise who Aoife was for many a year – was sitting chatting away about her daughter.

'Follow me, then.' The nurse smiled. 'I'll take you to her.'

They walked in silence, with Aoife listening out for the wailing and keening that she had always presumed would fill psychiatric wards. The fear of encountering masses of gibbering, slavering mental patients had caused her, on the journey over, to grip the metal bar on the bus seat until her knuckles whitened. But everything was quiet and still.

'Here we are,' the nurse said, stopping beside a red-painted door. 'Your father's in with her now, but I'm sure he'll be glad of the company.'

'My father?' Aoife frowned. She stepped forward and peered in through the glass inset of the door. Sure enough, there he was – her own daddy – seated on a plastic chair to the side of the bed. Her mammy was sitting up on the bed and waiting patiently, with her lips parted and her tongue poking out, for her husband to feed her something from the bowl in his hands. As he lifted the spoon and blew gently at it, Aoife turned back to the nurse.

'She always has soup for her meals,' the nurse said.

'And is he always here to feed it to her?' Aoife asked.

'Yes.' The nurse nodded and let out a wee giggle. 'Lunch and dinner. Every day he's in here as soon as visiting hours start, seeing to her and going around the beds to have a chat with the other patients. Me and the rest of the girls often say that we'd be happy so long as we had a husband like that, who waits at the door for the ward to open and stays until the last second of visiting hours.'

'Is he here all day, then?'

'No, only for visiting hours. Truth be told, there are a few of us that would let him stay beyond, but he always says he has a shift to do.'

'Is that right?' Aoife said.

'Are you not going in, then?'

Aoife looked in again, at Shay lifting spoonfuls of soup to her mammy's mouth and then leaning across with the napkin to dab at the dribbles on her chin. He was talking away to her all the while, too softly for Aoife to hear from outside the door. His lips were moving, though, and his wife's lips were curling into a smile in response.

'No,' Aoife said, shaking her head. 'I think I'll leave them to it. He seems to have it under control.'

The runback is more complex than it's ever been before – out the back lane, doubling back on myself through a patch of wasteland and then cutting through the hedges at the back of a cul-de-sac to land at the entrance to a city council scrapyard.

I think there must be something wrong, because the headlights aren't on and the engine isn't running. I've a wee jolt of nerves in my chest at that, and a stumble to my walk. But there's a red pinprick of light from Baldy's cigarette, hanging there in the darkness, and as I draw close he unfolds himself from the driver's seat and starts towards me. He nips the cigarette at the end closest to his lips between index finger and thumb and flicks it down at the grating by his feet. Then he goes to move past me.

'Wait in the car,' he says.

He has the gun in his hand, swinging loosely by his side.

'Wait in the car,' he repeats, following the direction of my gaze.

'What are you doing, Sean?' I ask.

'We can't be leaving any loose ends,' he says.

'But – ' I begin.

'Wait in the car.'

Seated in the car, I bring my knees up to my chest and grip at them until my knuckles turn white. The angle's sore, though, it causes the thing inside to stab and tear at my insides, so I lean forward instead, with my forehead resting against the dashboard.

No loose ends. I retch. A dry heave that leaves a puddle of bile on the worn carpet at my feet, attached to my bottom lip by a beaded trail of saliva. Gulping in shallow breaths, I wait.

I'm hoping that the sound of the shot won't travel along the back lane, across the wasteland and through the hedges at the back of the cul-de-sac. I'm hoping that he'll not make it as far as the house, that he'll stop on the wasteland and turn back. I'm hoping that he'll trip and fall and lose his gun among the hedges at the back of the cul-de-sac.

In the breathless darkness, I wait for the next retch.

Aoife tiptoed around the subject of Damien going back to school, preferring to drop hints and ask him if he was missing his schoolmates rather than directly challenging him about it. She knew that it was a delicate subject and she was feared of pushing him back into the classroom before he was ready.

She even let him away with mitching off school for the first few days of term. She was wanting everything to sort itself out naturally, hoping that he'd find his strength of his own accord and that she'd not need to interfere beyond getting his uniform washed and dried for him and maybe packing him a lunch so as he didn't have to suffer the cafeteria food.

It was the visit from the truancy officer that changed things. That was fair embarrassing, so it was, having the red-faced woman with the clipboard knocking on the door and asking why Damien Brennan hadn't yet started his third year at St Joe's. It was even worse when the woman narrowed her eyes and asked why a bright girl like Aoife wasn't at school herself on a Thursday morning, and Aoife had to explain frostily that she was seventeen and she'd left school so as she could keep house for the family. It was the expression that flashed across the truancy officer's face at that – half scorn, half pity – that saw Aoife climbing the stairs the next morning and trying once again to convince Damien to go back to school.

'Would you not like a qualification or two to your name, Damo?' she'd asked.

She got no more than a shrug in response.

'Then you could maybe go on to college or even university and study music. You'd like that, would you not – being able to talk to other folk about all those guitarists you're always reading about?' She reached out a hand and caressed his damaged cheek. 'It'll not always be like this, you know; it's not always cruelty that shows through – '

For a couple of hours, Aoife rode a wave of joy at having convinced her brother to take up his schooling again. She fixed him a proper breakfast of buttered toast and orange juice and sent him off with clingfilm-wrapped sandwiches. Then she sat herself at the kitchen table and planned her next step. Now that Damien was out at school, she saw no reason why she couldn't sit down with her books from the year before and study to take her A-Level exams the next summer. Maybe she could even register to sit the exams through the mail, or get the examiners to come over to the house and give them a cup of tea while they waited for her to write her English and history essays.

That was the plan, anyway. For two hours, at least, maybe three at a stretch. Right up until Aoife set to cleaning up the living room – picking up stray sweet wrappers from the floor, and lifting stained mugs from the coffee table – up until she moved over to straighten the curtains, glanced out of the window and caught sight of Damien sitting on the grass verge outside, gazing over at the Protestant estate on the other side of the train-tracks. She didn't know if he'd been in to school and then left again, or whether he'd been sitting there for the duration, but it hardly mattered. Either way, Aoife knew that she still had a battle on her hands in getting her brother to go off to school in the mornings, never mind finding a moment's peace so as she could get a run at her own school books.

The social worker, Lorcan, was the next one to try to scold Damien into going to school. If Aoife's approach had been the carrot, then Lorcan's was most definitely the stick. He sat on the sofa beside Damien and told him that he'd grow up and find that he hadn't two brain cells to rub together, that he'd never get a job or a girlfriend, that he'd never have a family, or be able to hold a decent conversation with anyone other than the stray three-legged dog that hobbled around the estate begging for scraps of food. He'd be worse than useless, Lorcan told him, if he didn't go to his classes.

Damien sat silent-still whilst the social worker painted him this bleak picture of adult life, his face flickering with – emotionless – involuntary convulsions. Lorcan, for his part, got fair frustrated when his stories provoked no reaction. He might have been gratified to see the tears that slid down Aoife's cheeks as she stood in the shadow of the kitchen doorway and listened in. His words had an effect on one of the Brennan children – just not the one he was intending.

Aoife stood eavesdropping, letting the social worker start in about how Catholics never used to have access to education back in the day, how Stormont rigged the entire system to maintain the Protestant status quo, how Damien didn't know he was born. Back in the day, Lorcan said, Damien would have been out in the fields lifting spuds or down in the yards working on the ships – if he was lucky – and he would never have had the opportunity to go to school, never mind the possibility of carrying on to university.

Aoife silenced Lorcan the only way she knew how – by pouring him a large whiskey with the smallest drop of water glazing the surface of it. Then, seating herself between the social worker and Damien, she nattered away about how she'd personally sit him down with his textbooks and make a start on teaching him what he'd missed out on. Soon enough, she smiled, he'd be good and ready to return to school and, when he did, he'd come back at the top of his class. Although she knew fine well that there was precious little she could do if he refused to go to school in the weeks that followed. All the truancy officers and half-cut social workers in the world could come knocking on the door, but if wee Damien didn't want to go in, then Aoife wasn't going to force him to.

Months passed, then, in a steady enough pattern. Aoife sat down with Damien during the day and taught him what she could remember from her old jotters and folded-corner textbooks. Curling her hand over the page – to hide the scrawled, faded '*Ciáran + Aoife*' from her wee brother – she tried to decipher her own handwriting into something that was halfway teachable. The syllabus was formed from the pages where she'd been given a neat line of ticks along the sides and the tests that had a gold star tacked to the top of them. Anything with a cross or a looping question mark beside it, though, had to be discounted. And, often enough, Aoife found herself unable to answer even the most basic question. Whenever that happened, Aoife always suggested that they take a quick tea break, in the hope that either inspiration would come to her as she sipped away or that Damien would have forgotten the question by the time they went back to the books. It didn't take more than a week, though, for Damien to catch on to this ploy and he soon took to asking difficult questions every ten minutes or so, until the kettle was being put on to boil more often than a textbook page was being turned.

The teaching of Irish history, from the notes she'd taken in Mr O'Toole's class, was the worst of it. There was that much confusion to her scribbled paragraphs that Aoife wound up telling Damien that Eamon de Valera led the Siege of Derry, even though she knew that wasn't quite right, and that it was Oliver Cromwell who sent James Connolly to the firing squad after the Easter Rising, even though the dates didn't seem to match up. Without a textbook to turn to, Aoife followed the example of Mr O'Toole and began teaching her brother from the pages of the *Irish News*.

As they moved into 1993 there was plenty of material for her improvised lesson plans, with massive IRA bombs in Warrington and the UFF claiming responsibility for a clutch of shootings up in Castlerock. It was the revelation of secret talks between John Hume, the leader of the SDLP, and Gerry Adams that filled the pages of the *Irish News*, though. The idea that there might be a Nationalist consensus emerging led to a fair amount of excitement across the island of Ireland and Aoife and Damien, with the newsprint smudging the handles of their mugs of tea, joined in the speculation about the future of the North.

Damien took to snipping the articles that interested him from the newspapers and carrying a wee bundle of them up the stairs so as he could tack them to his wall. Over the weeks and months that followed, the lyrics gradually disappeared, to be replaced by a patchwork of headlines and press photographs. After the Bishopsgate bomb, over in London, he put up an entire row of photos of grey-looking buildings with their windows blown out, streets littered with rubble, and twisted carcasses of cars caught in the blast, so as it formed a kind of post-apocalyptic cityscape across the length of his bedroom wall. At eye level, it was, if he was sat on his bed.

It gave Aoife the shivers, when she walked past his bedroom, to see him sitting there staring morosely at the pictures up on his wall. She tried as best she could to distract him with schoolwork, but there wasn't much of a wide-ranging curriculum to Damien's home schooling. Instead, she took to getting him to thread beads for necklaces, tie leather straps for bracelets and attach hooks for earrings. True, they still sat down and read the paper together in the mornings, but the afternoons began to be taken up with doing the unskilled jobs in the jewellery-making process.

The routine changed so little from day to day that Aoife could have marked a calendar from one week to the next, from one month to the next, with exactly the same schedule – could have passed the spring and summer of 1993 crossing out identical plans with identical red crosses. That was, if she had troubled herself to buy a calendar to note down the monotony of it. There seemed to be no point to a succession of white boxes that contained little of note except endless tea breaks followed by countless bathroom breaks.

The only thing that interrupted this routine – or threatened to – was the violence out on the streets of Belfast which, on occasion, ground the clockwork of the Brennan household to a temporary stop. There was always the possibility of bomb alerts whenever Aoife was out on her sales calls, which meant she had to skirt around an area or wait for the peelers to wave her through, and there were those nights when she sat breathlessly waiting on her daddy coming home, even though she knew full well that he would have just been delayed at a checkpoint at one end of the town or the other.

For the most part, though, Aoife knew the whereabouts of each of her family members, knew what was happening from one day to the next, and that was a comfort to her as she crossed the days off – no calendar, no red pen – in her head.

Number six is a nihilist. He's been expecting this day to come. Maybe he didn't know how it would happen, maybe he didn't expect the intricacies, but he's resigned to his fate, so he is, before I even lower myself down onto him. There's despair behind the eyes before I grind down; there's a silent scream to him before he cries out; there's death shadowing him before Baldy pulls the trigger.

I'm never given his surname, just Phil. A man in his sixties now, who's served in the Ulster Defence Regiment and in the B-Specials before that. A state-sponsored Loyalist thug. He drinks alone, in the corner of the bar, because all of his friends have either been killed, jailed or driven from the 'No Surrender!' of it all by the peace process. The last man standing, is Phil, but he's waiting to fall.

He takes my hand as I lead him to the grim bathroom in the disused house, and he seems almost grateful as I mutilate what's left of his manhood. He stares at the tiled wall behind me, his jaw set. He's making his own peace, so he is, with the past and the present. There's no future, though, and he knows that. He looks up into the muzzle of Baldy's gun and mutters an Ulsterman's curse – 'For God and Ulster' – to all those who've betrayed him, who've sold him out and left him defenceless and broken.

I ask Baldy, afterwards, whether there's a need to continue with the shards of glass. Is there a need for the thing inside, I'm wondering, if I'm only a honeytrap? Is there a need for the slit and wrench when I'm only acting as bait? When a bullet follows soon after?

He answers it, though, before I've even finished asking. His eyes hidden behind the sepia tint of his glasses, he says that we've a signature now, that we've a way of cutting through all the pride and positivity so as to remind folk that the job isn't done, the war isn't over. We're sending a message that we'll not compromise. We're not for negotiation, not for decommissioning, not until the last occupying footprint has faded from Irish soil. We've no affiliation, no army behind us, no organisation beyond the two of us, but we'll strike out – again and again – until we're heard. He says all that, and more, in a short sentence that I can barely hear over the noise of the taxi's engine.

'Yes,' he says, softly. 'There's a need.'

When the Shankill Road bomb went off in October '93, Aoife narrowed her sales area back down to only local streets. It wasn't that the explosion was closer to home – although it was – or that the bomb had gone off prematurely in the bomber's hands – although it had. It wasn't that it killed ten people – although it did – or that one of the victims was a wee girl – although she was. It wasn't any of that. It was that the bombed building was a fish and chip shop, chosen because the UDA leaders were due to be meeting in the room above. It was that Aoife often got the dinner from their own local chippy, and now she couldn't walk into the shop, with its smell of melting fat and its curling shards of fish in underneath the heat lamp, without thinking of the bombing and getting this rushing panic in her throat that the UFF might target the Lower Ormeau chippy as they had targeted the bar up in Greysteel, County Derry, in retaliation for the Shankill Road bombing. And with thoughts of the Greysteel carnage on the evening before Hallowe'en, with seven civilians killed to the chilling sound of the phrase 'trick or treat', came a real desire to never stray far from her house – never more than fifteen or twenty minutes' walk – especially now that the nights were drawing in.

In any case, as Christmas approached she found that she could easily sell even her sub-standard stock locally, if only because housewives were desperate for stocking-fillers and for trinkets that they could give to those who were known well but not well enough to lavish any real amount of money on. Aoife had little doubt that there were many neighbours who might each give, one to the other, a pair of cheap earrings or a chain-link necklace bought from Aoife, and that they'd both know well and good that the neighbour had spent only the price of a loaf of bread on picking out their present but, because they were each as guilty as the other, they'd smile and coo and wear them for the whole of Christmas Day before tucking them to the back of their bedside drawer.

The day of the Downing Street Declaration started off normally enough, with Damien's tea-soaked lessons from the newspaper soon giving way to working on the pile of raw materials that Becky had dropped off as the makings of a batch of earrings. Becky had told them that all they would need was glue, but she probably hadn't reckoned on Damien gluing his fingertips to the wood of the table or Aoife having to chip the excess away from the ear hooks with a kitchen knife. It was meant to be simple, unskilled work but, even at that, the two of them – brother and sister – made the earrings look like something that might be found in the plughole of the sink or growing down the back of a sofa cushion.

By the time Caroline arrived, at five o'clock, Aoife was starting to get a fair bit of cabin-fever. She always seemed to get more and more restless as the afternoon passed, as the time of her escape out to the streets approached. She knew rightly that her sighing and her pacing to and fro unsettled Damien – she could see it in his twitches and flinches getting worse and worse – but she was always bored to tears by sitting in silence fiddling with wee bits of wire (or string, or fabric). By the end of those afternoon craft sessions she'd have gladly knocked on Ian Paisley's door, even, just for an excuse to get out of the house. Although the Reverend Paisley didn't live locally and she had a feeling that if she were to call on him he might denounce the tangled twists of jewellery, in that gravelly voice of his, as the work of the devil.

Aoife decided to call at the houses up around Sunnyside Street, just off the Ormeau Embankment. It wasn't Paisleyite territory, but some of it wasn't far off it. The Annadale Flats – a staunchly Loyalist estate – was just a bit further down towards the River Lagan and the spread of Unionism from it infected every fourth or fifth house along Sunnyside Street. The infection showed as a Union Jack flying from a pole above the door, a 'For God and Ulster' sticker in the front window, or an IFA pendant hanging from the rear-view mirror of the car parked in the driveway. In the normal course of things Aoife would have moved quickly past these houses – just walked past the gate to the next unadorned house – but the night was so bitterly cold that she decided that she was as well stopping at each and every house, crunching up each and every frost-glittered path, in the hopes of getting invited into the warmth.

Sure enough, it was at a neat wee house with a Northern Irish flag hanging limply from a flagpole to the side of the door that she was first invited inside. A middle-aged woman answered the door, her feet in slippers and her hair up in a net.

'God save us,' she said. 'You must be freezing, love, frozen to the bone. You'll catch your death, so you will.'

'I'm selling jewellery – ' Aoife began.

'Yes, yes.' The woman waved her inside. 'You're letting all the cold air in, love – come away inside, quickly now.'

So Aoife stepped into the house and followed the woman into the heat of the living room, seating herself on the sofa as she was told to and nodding gratefully when the woman offered her a cup of tea. She sat there massaging her numb fingers, taking in her surroundings, whilst the woman bustled around in the connecting kitchen. There was a stone fireplace with an electric heater in the centre of it, two bars on; a small television set in the corner showing the six o'clock news; a flowery three-piece suite – that Aoife was perched on – and there, above the mantelpiece, the sign of Protestantism that Aoife had been looking for – a portrait of the Queen. Aoife sniffed and silently wondered if that was the only difference between the wee terraced houses here and the wee terraced houses fifteen minutes' walk away in Lower Ormeau – one set had portraits of the Queen and the other set had portraits of the Pope, but the layout and furnishings were near enough identical other than that.

'What's your name, love?' the woman called from the kitchen.

'My name?'

Aoife couldn't give her real name or she'd find herself back out on the cold streets without having made a sale and without having had a cup of tea. Or, worse, she might find herself in some back alley with her frost-brittle hands broken by breeze-blocks, or her hair shorn by an open razor.

She tried to think of a Protestant name. That drew a blank, though. So, instead, she just tried to remember a name – any name – that wasn't obviously Irish Catholic. Anything other than Aoife. Her thoughts spun through her childhood surrounded by Catholics – and her schooling – in the Convent – and finally settled on some of the Greek mythology she'd read in her first year at the school.

'Cassandra,' she called, cringing as she said it in case that was a Catholic name as well and she just hadn't realised.

'That's a lovely name,' the woman replied, as she carried in two steaming mugs of tea. 'I'm Margaret, but call me Maggie.'

Aoife smiled tightly and took one of the mugs from her. She silently scolded herself for not having come up with a better Prod name. Margaret would have been perfect – much simpler and more obviously Protestant. Or – her gaze wandered up to the portrait of the Queen – Elizabeth.

'Have you seen this here, Cassandra?' Maggie asked.

Aoife looked across at the older woman, who nodded towards the television. There were pictures of John Major and Albert Reynolds on the screen – both suited and sombre – standing outside a black door.

'The Downing Street Declaration, you call it,' Maggie said.

Aoife shook her head. 'What's it all about?' she asked.

'As far as I can tell, they're saying that the lot of us can be handed over to Rome for all the English care.' She let out a wee chuckle and a slop of tea spilt from her mug and fell to the carpet. 'You're not a Papist, are you, love?'

'Me? No,' Aoife replied. She found it easier to lie to that question than she would have if Maggie had asked if she were a Catholic. To say you were a Catholic in Belfast meant that you were a Nationalist – that you were Irish and proud – whereas to say you were a Papist meant that you believed that some wee old Polish man was God's representative on earth. It was easier to deny allegiance to the Vatican than it was to deny association with Bobby Sands.

Maggie nodded, satisfied. 'All they're saying, really, is that if the majority of the people can agree one way or another then that's the way it'll go. Those are only words, though, so they are. They may as well ask a turkey and a goose to decide among themselves which of them should be had for Christmas dinner.'

Aoife smiled and sipped at her tea. This was dangerous ground and she wanted to lift the attaché case and start showing the older woman her jewellery instead, but Maggie was in full flow now. She obviously didn't get many visitors of an evening, and she was determined to take advantage.

'I'll tell you this, love,' Maggie continued. 'There'll need to be a lot of people cold and dead in the ground before Ulster is anything other than British, especially since any right-minded person can see that Gerry Adams is trying to bully his way to the negotiating table. If there are to be talks with those people – with those murderers – then they'll have a fair bit of outcry about that, I tell you.'

The tea was warming Aoife, but she still had a chill to her. Though she didn't see how she could possibly be exposed – unless Maggie were to ask her to recite the monarchs of Britain since the turn of the century, or start up the first verse of 'God Save the Queen' and expect Aoife to join in.

'Those men…' Maggie shook her head sorrowfully. 'And such a shame because I've lived all my life beside Catholics, good honest hardworking people for the most part, and then there are just those few who take up guns – just the worst of the community arming themselves – and then the worst in our community do the same and suddenly there's a war on. It seems like it all happened overnight, but we've been waiting for daybreak for a long while now.' Maggie stared through and beyond the telly, then let out a shallow sigh. 'Sorry, Cassandra, listen to me harping on. What is it you've got to sell, then?'

Aoife sold Maggie friendship bracelets for her grand-daughters and a pendant necklace for her sister, but she got more than the price of the three items in return. While Aoife sat over a second cup of tea, Maggie insisted on noting down the names and addresses of all her friends that lived up and down the street. There were thirteen names on the list, each one nudging the bottom of the one above.

For the next three hours or so, Aoife went from one name on the list to the next, doing a roaring trade with a series of housewives who all seemed the spit for Maggie – slippers, hair up in nets or curlers. She had never before seen the inside of so many Protestant homes – all neatly turned out, although only a couple of them with any sign of the Royal Family, in pictures on the sideboard or portraits on the walls. She'd also never before had so many cups of tea in such a short space of time – although her morning lessons with Damien had given her a fair amount of practice – or called upon women who were so immediately welcoming and so willing to put their hands into their purses for her jewellery. Her attaché case, on the way home, was noticeably lighter and her jacket pockets rustled with notes and clinked with coins.

It was with the satisfaction of a job well done that Aoife walked through the front door of the house just as the ten o'clock news came on the telly. There was no sign of her daddy, but Caroline, with her usual smell of freshly applied nail polish, was curled up on the sofa flicking through a magazine. Damien was up on the window seat behind her. He was asleep, with his book folded open across his chest and his head lolling back against the window-pane. Aoife put down her case and stepped out of her shoes, then moved across to stand behind the sofa and watch the headlines over Caroline's shoulder. It was the same pictures as earlier, and an English newsreader going on about 'mutual consent', 'self-determination' and the like. It all seemed like a carefully designed way of saying nothing, committing to nothing.

'How's he been?' she asked Caroline, in a whisper.

'He's been quiet.' Caroline twisted her head round to look up at Aoife and then across to Damien. 'He's been asleep for the most part.'

Aoife nodded, then frowned. There was something wet soaking into her socks. She lifted her foot and it peeled away from the sticky carpet. Leaning against the sofa, she took her white sock in her hand and examined the sole, her frown deepening as she watched the spreading stain –

'Has something been spilt back here?' she asked. Then she looked down, and began following the trail:

Taking a single stride across to the windowsill, to where
   Damien lay sleeping –
lifting the opened book from his covered arms, then
   letting it fall –
to the soaked carpet, staring eyes following the flow –
   from the inch-wide gashes on his wrists –
down the seam of his jeans.

Reaching out to touch his cold skin.

The nightmares are back. In the weeks after the sixth, the nightmares are back. Only they're different now. Now the marching men aren't chasing after me; instead I'm breathlessly stumbling after them, down that same empty road, my legs heavy and my lungs empty as I try to shout out a warning –

They find the body three days after the deed, in the upstairs bathroom of the wee terraced house where I left him. Only he's not as I left him at all. He's a single gunshot to the head as well as the shard of glass that's embedded itself deep, that's stretched the foreskin away from the wound as the blood swells up and over. And it's only the gunshot that the newspapers mention; it's only the possibility of a revenge killing that they're for speculating about. There's no talk of a link back to that Cassie one, no call to see if wee sapper Dave can shed some light on this latest killing. It's all about the gunshot – that's the wound that killed him, that's the one that saw him splayed out on the tiled floor, slumped against the outside of the bathtub, with his bound hands dipped in his own blood. They're not for complicating things by raking over the coals of a story that set them to shivering and flinching, that saw them crossing their legs tightly and promising never to dirty their dicks again with the loose millies and vacant-eyed hoors that they pick up whenever they're out on the rip. Keep it clean, keep it simple. A single gunshot wound to the head, nothing more.

It's the shot that sets me to shuddering, though, and it's the sound of it that jolts me awake and sees me lying in the dark in the wee hours of the morning with the lids scratching at my unblinking eyes. The dream itself stays flickeringly on the reel, replaying again and again. As I try to shout out a warning, with only the whisper of breath left in me, I hear the gunshot up ahead and I feel my legs buckle beneath me. In that moment, I know there's no need to be chasing the ones in front, that they are beyond helping now, and that the ones behind will catch up with me soon enough.

11

In Damien's room, Aoife had hung a framed photograph of her wee brother in the centre of the far wall. It was a school photograph from the year before the shooting – back when he could smile without his face creasing with pain. Around the photograph, the ink fading from the sun, were Damien's lyrics. The newspaper cuttings had long since been removed, although the tack from them continued to scar the words they had covered. Often, in the evenings after she got back from selling her jewellery, Aoife would spend an hour or two in the bedroom, sitting cross-legged in front of the photograph, quietly reading the words of the lyrics to herself. It reminded her of what she had lost, of the debt that still had to be settled, the injustice that had to be called to account. She would do it herself, if need be.

Aoife went into the bathroom and set the hot tap to running. The rubber plug had a slow leak to it, so the bath always took an age to fill, and even then she'd need to leave the water on while she lay there. Just a trickle, no more, sliding down against the brown-stained markings of previous baths, keeping the water level up so that it lapped against her chin.

While she waited, Aoife sauntered through to her bedroom and switched on the old black and white telly in the corner. As it flickered into life, she had no problem in catching on to what the young male presenter was talking about – the IRA ceasefire. They talked about little else these days. On the thirty-first of August of that year, 1994, the Provos had called a 'complete cessation of military operations' and all the news programmes had near enough wet themselves with speculating about a lasting peace. A new dawn and a new day, they said, for Northern Ireland.

There were two guests in the grainy studio, one of them sharing the presenter's excitement and the other staring at the camera with a dour frown – one Nationalist and one Unionist. It was a shame it wasn't Ian Paisley that they had on, because he was wile entertaining to watch, as he seethed and bridled and near spat at the suggestion that the Unionists and the British government should sit down with the Republicans and work out their differences. He would probably have cursed at the presenter on hearing the latest news that the Brits had lifted the ban on broadcasting members of Sinn Féin or the IRA. He would have knocked the young lad out for suggesting that it showed that John Major took the ceasefire seriously and that the government were expecting the peace to hold. As it was, the Unionist in the studio just sat there with his face tripping him and muttered about giving a voice to murderers and a platform for terrorists to spread their lies.

Aoife didn't see that the lifting of the broadcasting ban made much of a difference. She'd spent her teenage years listening to the paramilitaries' parts being read out by actors, with the voiceover coming a second too early or a second too late to catch the mouthings. Or the gunman would be seated in shadow, obscured from view, with an impassive Belfast accent speaking his words over the top of it. Or the newsreader would quickly and efficiently read a statement, attempting to let it be known – through the sternness of her lowered eyebrows or the disapproving tone of his voice – that he or she wasn't agreeing with what was being said, merely reading it out of a sense of professionalism. It made no difference who spoke, though. Aoife had always known rightly what the words meant. They meant no end to the violence until the twenty-six counties were thirty-two, until the Brits paid for the young Catholic men killed by

227

their soldiers, limped back across the Irish Sea, and left Ireland as a united island again. That was what had been said, and that was what had been meant – at least up until the ceasefire.

Folk like Gerry Adams and Martin McGuinness must have been on the news shows when she was a wee girl – if only on one of them there 'Wanted' posters like they used to have out in the Wild West – but Aoife couldn't remember seeing either one of them on the telly without their voices dubbed over.

She did have a vague memory of her daddy telling her that the word 'dubbed' came about because all those who spoke in the place of the Shinners were Dubs – or at least actors with a Dublin accent – and they'd told them to put on a Belfast accent to mock the Irish both north and south of the border. The story was like a long-ago rumour, though, that had never had the ring of truth to it. When she actually stopped to think about it, Aoife realised that it made no logical sense.

It wasn't Shay Brennan's only lie on the subject, anyway, and it certainly wasn't his most far-fetched. She remembered well the day, back when she was thirteen or so, that her daddy had come in late with breath that was thick enough to be used as lighting fluid. He'd collapsed himself down, head-first, onto the sofa behind Aoife, who was sitting quietly watching the telly. The reporter was up in the hardline-Republican Bogside in Derry and was having a fair bit of bother finding anyone who he could talk to without an actor's voice being needed. As a so-called community leader came on the screen and an actor started to speak on his behalf, Shay twisted his neck on the sofa cushions to peer out at the screen.

'Let the man speak,' he grumbled. Aoife didn't recognise the man being interviewed and she was near certain that her daddy didn't either, but he seemed to have taken up the cause as a point of principle. 'Let the man,' he repeated, with a slur, 'bloody speak.'

'Daddy,' Aoife said, softly. 'I'm trying to watch.'

'Aye, love, you're watching.' He attempted to tap his nose knowingly, but misjudged and ended up poking at his cheek.

'You're watching but you're only getting to listen – to listen – to what they want you to listen to.'

Aoife pursed her lips and kept her eyes on the telly.

'You hearing me, Aoife? It's censorship, is what it is. Chensore-ship. It's a violation of their human rights. Their rights as humans. Sure, didn't half the city vote for them?'

'In Belfast? Half of the West, maybe.'

'Still, we've members of Parliament – in Westminster, no less – who're near enough gagged, so they are.'

'They do voiceovers for the Loyalist paramilitaries as well, though.'

'They do, aye.' Her daddy's head lolled forward in a movement that might have been an attempt at a nod. 'But it's worse for our boys, so it is. They pick actors with wile whiney voices, simple folk with lisps and that.'

'They do not, Daddy.' Aoife couldn't help smiling.

'It's always been the way, I tell you.'

'Away on, you're half-cut.'

'I've a drink or two in me, no more than that.' He cleared his throat and levered himself up with his elbows until he sat as close to upright as he could manage. 'It's always been the way,' he repeated, waving a hand vaguely in the direction of the telly, ignoring the fact that the programme had finished and they had moved on to the weather forecast. 'All of that there has always been biased against our lot – against us.'

Aoife turned and gave him a look. She was wanting him to know from her eyes that she wasn't for having some bullshit story about how he'd run guns for the Stickies as a teenager, wanting to let him know that if he started in about how the weather was against them as well – that the Brits were controlling the rainfall over Belfast so as it fell mainly in the West – that she'd not believe even a word of it.

'It has,' he continued. 'You know back when you were wee they didn't even bother using actors' voices for the IRA men, they'd just use them squeaks, squawks and whistles like they used on that there kid's show about the wee moon-rat things.'

229

'They didn't, Daddy.' Aoife sighed.

'They did too.' He frowned. 'What is it you call that show?'

'*The Clangers*.'

'That's the very one.'

'You're not expecting me to take this seriously, are you?'

'I'm deadly serious. I wouldn't be shocked if they went back to doing it now.'

'They'd not do that, as well you know.'

'They would and they did. They're the ones with all the fucking power – mind the language, love – they're the ones with all the power, so they are. If they want to put whistles over the top then they can; if they want to change the words of the statements before the actor reads them then they can; if they want to put the voice of Hitler over the top then there's bugger-all we can do to stop them – '

'They'd not do that, either,' Aoife replied.

'No, they'd not do that,' her daddy conceded, sagging his head as a mark of respect. 'If only because there were that many Irish who fought with them in that war of theirs and they'd not piss on their graves like that. Fine Catholic men, like your grandfather, fought in that war. They'd not want to say anything against them, even if they have no problem with making out that the whole lot of us are all wee fucking moon-rats.' He paused, belched. 'Excuse me, love,' he concluded.

'You want a cup of tea?' Aoife had asked, rising. 'To quieten you down.'

'That'd be nice, now, a wee cup of tea would be lovely,' her daddy replied. 'Is your mammy still at the sink, I take it?'

Aoife nodded, but her daddy didn't notice. They played the national anthem at the close of programming on the BBC and her daddy had turned his attention to the turning globe that had appeared on the screen. He let out a screeching, tuneless whistle to fill the couple of seconds of silence before the national anthem began. Aoife reached across and flicked the telly off and, as if controlled by the same switch, the whistling stopped.

Aoife allowed herself a bittersweet smile now, as she rose to go through to check on her bath, at the memory of her thirteen-year-old self who'd wet the tea that night while grappling with the notion that her daddy might be right after all, that there might be a grain of truth to the idea that the British Broadcasting Corporation had played the soundtrack of *The Clangers* over the words of Republicans back in the day.

At the age of nineteen, though, she'd more sense in her head than to go believing all that she was told – by anyone. It was the ceasefire she fretted about: the idea that the Shinners were ready to let the Brits off the hook, ready to put down their weapons and start letting the whisperings of peace take hold. As likely as not it was all a ploy – on one side or another – and the Active Service Units were working away in the shadows, identifying legitimate targets, while MI5 still kept on their paid informers and worked out ways to assassinate members of the IRA Army Council.

Aoife had decided to take precautions though. Just in case the Provos were looking for an escape route, in case the talks between John Hume and Gerry Adams had all been in good faith and the entire military command was on the point of laying down the armalite and continuing with only the ballot box in hand. It was as well to be prepared: for the Republicans to abandon the cause, for the Brits to offer a settlement and for the leadership to betray the dead martyrs that stared down at them from the gable-end murals – hundreds of volunteers and civilians, old and young.

After all, she had the advantage of not needing to pay any heed to the politicians, to the community leaders, to the newsreaders, to her half-cut daddy. That was the beauty of her idea, so it was – there was no Army Council, no OC, no Active Service Unit. It was her and her alone. Or a version of herself, at least.

The water wasn't yet deep enough. Turning the cold tap on so that it thundered down against the steaming surface, Aoife perched herself on the edge of the bath and closed her eyes. She had some thinking to do, no doubt about that – but the outline of a plan was beginning to take shape in her mind. She would need to wait and see if the ceasefire would fracture, but if it didn't she'd be ready and waiting to seek her own revenge. An eye for an eye, a tooth for a tooth – wasn't that the saying? Biblical, taught to her from infancy, shown to her by the boys out on the streets who answered a vandal with a beating, a drug dealer with a kneecapping, an informer with a bullet in the head, a politician with a car bomb, an occupying force with a bombing campaign on the British mainland. An eye for an eye. That was all Aoife wanted; that was all she intended.

She opened her eyes, turned off the cold tap.

Two things that had seemed constant were now gone: her brother and the violence. Two events separated by only eight months, neither of which seemed real or permanent, neither of which she'd wanted or had a say in. Neither of which she'd accept. Not without a fight.

Turning the hot tap until it slowed to only a trickle, Aoife began to undress. She pulled her hooded jumper and T-shirt over her head in one movement and then reached around to unclasp her bra. Stepping out of her slippers, she quickly lowered her jogging trousers and pants. The clothing lay in a bundle on the lino floor. Standing there, naked, Aoife was aware that the cold was raising goose-pimples across her flesh. She didn't shiver, though. Staring down at the water, she knew that she was prepared – come what may, ceasefire or not – to search out those responsible for Damien's death and call them to account. She was an avenging angel. Prepared for peace, ready for war.

It always takes a while for the swelling to go down. That's normal. It's not normal, though, for the redness to harden and spread; it's not normal that the slashes and cuts glaze over but do not heal, or that I've to sit on the toilet for half an hour, a steady stream of tears streaking my face, trying to squeeze even a stinging drop of piss out of me.

I keep an eye on it. What more can I do? Morning and night I carefully, tenderly spread anti-bacterial cream, anti-fungal cream, anti-inflammatory cream. And after a few weeks the scratching worry of it becomes a tingle, and then the itching stops and the red-raw rash fades.

Breathing easily again. No more tumbling images of operating theatres, foreign hands holding cold retributive steel, blinding pain as they slice and dissect, as they carve into me. No more flashing nightmares of a mutant foetus, not so much growing in my womb as consuming it, his clenched fists tugging at the umbilical cord, his toenails growing into talons that scratch and claw their way downwards and out into the world.

I tell Baldy about it, once the worst has passed. It's the reason for my silence, I say, for the distance between us and the shiver-flinch I get whenever he tries to touch me. Although it's not the only reason. We both know that rightly.

It never gets easier to piss, in spite of the swelling going down. It still burns and throbs and brings tears to my eyes. And one morning I wake with a dampness, with a leakage. The pus is white and thin, like milk. Over the next few days, it begins to curdle. It begins to turn, thickening and separating into lump-chunks of solid along with watery liquid. Milk to yoghurt, to cream, to clotted cream, to cottage cheese. I've to scrape it off with the blunt edge of my index finger.

'Sean,' I say, after about a week of this. 'I need a doctor.'

He nods, but doesn't ask why. He's seen the emptied tubes of cream, the pans of clear water I've boiled on the camping stove turning cloudy as I rinse out stained flannels. In silence, he just nods.

The water was deep enough to cover the tips of her toes, deep enough for the overflow drain to begin gurgling, deep enough for her to immerse herself. Closing her eyes, holding her breath,

Aoife slipped down underneath the water. The silence groaned as the water plugged her ears, as the running tap burbled somewhere near-distant and the disturbed surface settled.

She held her breath until her chest began to tighten, until her thoughts began to turn to the idea of staying beneath and seeing what it would be like to flicker into unconsciousness as her lungs filled with water. Seeing what it would be like to drown – lying there in the warmth of the bath – all the while knowing that her next breath was only inches away, above the surface. All she would have to do was sit up, raise herself on her elbows, even just pull the plug free with her feet and she could breathe again.

Opening her eyes, then, she let out her breath in one stretched, distorted, bubbling scream. Water caught at the back of her throat like bile, was inhaled up her nose, shimmered and then reddened in front of her staring eyes. The clear, clean bathwater turned the consistency of something thicker, something that cloyed and coagulated, that settled in slicks and pooled in pavement-cracks. In her eyes, in her ears, up her nose, down her throat, forming like a second skin across her whole body.

Spluttering to the surface, Aoife drew her knees to her chest and took in a gulping breath, and then another and another. As the water rippled back to calm, Aoife closed her eyes and wept, softly and quietly, with the tears dripping from her chin to dimple the bathwater.

Damien's wake had been held in the living room. The table was carried in from the kitchen and placed by the window, on top of the bloodstained carpet. Aoife had not had the time or the heart to clean or replace the carpet, only time to take a pastel-blue sheet from the airing cupboard and spread it over the dried blood as a makeshift rug. The shadow showed through. It was better than nothing, though. The table went on top of it and the coffin went on top of that.

Only two days after Aoife had arrived home to find him, lifeless, sitting in the windowsill, she came down the stairs to find him lying in his casket. Dressed up in a suit, as neatly turned out as he'd been for his first Holy Communion. The undertaker had slicked his hair into a side-parting and tucked the curls of it in behind his ears. Aoife didn't like it like that. She wanted to reach into the coffin and unsettle his hair, ruffle it through her fingers until it was once again pulled into the tangles and angles that she was used to. The thought of the oily gel against her fingers, though, caused her to hold back. She wasn't wanting the feel of it and the smell of it on her for days, wasn't wanting her last memory of her brother to be the cheap hair-product that the undertaker had used. Instead, she kept her hands clasped in front of herself and looked down at her wee brother's hands, which were also resting, one on top of the other, across his front. She knew that if she were to turn them over she'd see the slashes to his wrists, now carefully stitched together no doubt, but just as long and ragged and final as they'd been two days before.

Aoife didn't stay beside the coffin for long. She didn't keen or wail or stand sobbing into a handkerchief like the other women who had gathered in the cramped living room. There was no need to shake her head or tut softly or murmur 'whatawaste… cryingshamesoitis… thepoorlad… hispoorfamily… neverbeenthesamesince… soyoungwhen… weknowwhotoblame… weknowrightlywhotoblame', the way the men did. Others stood for the required few seconds and then made their way over to the clutch of people standing close – but not indecently close – to the bottles of drink on the collapsible card table in the far corner, or wandered across to the plates and plates of sandwiches that Aoife and Becky had carefully buttered, filled and trimmed the crusts from the previous night. But Aoife just stood for a moment and then moved to the windowsill behind the coffin.

There were no bloodstains on the white paint; the surface shone. Becky had cleaned it, had straightened out the room and then come through to the kitchen to salt the ham sandwiches with her silent tears. Easing her body up into the window seat, Aoife sat where Damien would have sat, and watched the comings and goings of his wake.

Ciárán arrived on his own and immediately made his way over to the men by the card table. Aoife followed his every step with her eyes and she knew rightly that Becky, in turn, was watching her. There was an attempt made, by Becky, to lead her older brother over to where Aoife sat, but he shrugged off her guiding arm. When she persisted, he had only to show her his raised hand and she quickly retreated.

Cliona and another woman Aoife didn't know stood to the side and Aoife could tell, by their whispering and their sidelong glances, that they were talking about the state that Ciárán was in. They had reason to. He'd a stubble on him that would file your nails and a glassy pallor to his skin that seemed to reflect the whiskey in his tumbler.

'Can I get you anything, love?'

It was Father O'Neill who spoke. He would be the one laying Damien to rest the next day; he would be speaking by the graveside and answering to the Church if they questioned why a suicide was being given a Catholic burial. Not that they would.

Aoife shook her head.

'Come on, now.' The priest held up his own glass, which had a generous measure of something amber in it. 'It might do you good, Aoife.'

She nodded quickly. She'd caught sight of her daddy's return. He had left a half-hour before, taking the car keys from the kitchen counter on his way out. Aoife had known right away where he was going.

'Good girl,' Father O'Neill said, smiling and heading off to the far corner.

Aoife didn't reply. She kept her eyes on the door.

Following a few seconds and a step or two behind her husband, Cathy Brennan shuffled into the room. She looked bewildered, with her eyes flitting about the room as if she was seeing it for the first time. She'd shrunk and shrivelled since

Aoife had last seen her, and her hair seemed to be thinning along her neatly combed parting. A smiling nurse, sympathetic and apologetic, walked alongside to support her.

'Here you are.' Father O'Neill came back with a half-glass of clear liquid.

Aoife tried to take it at a single swallow but she grimaced most of it back into the glass. 'What is it?' she asked.

'Gin.' He shrugged. 'I didn't know what your drink was, but in my experience most women would take a wee gin.'

'Is that right?' Aoife replied, only half concentrating. She was watching her mammy approach the coffin, watching for a reaction.

Cathy stood, motionless, for four or five seconds. The room seemed to hold its breath along with Aoife. Then her mammy frowned and scratched at her chin. She looked lost and confused, like a wee girl who'd wandered further than she'd ever been before and found herself on a street she didn't know. Placing a hand on his wife's shoulder, Aoife's daddy looked over to the windowsill and gave a soft, sad, tired smile.

Swallowing the rest of the gin, Aoife held out her empty glass. Without a word, Father O'Neill took it from her. As he went to refill it, Becky came up to the windowsill, with her eyes fixed on the unstained portion of carpet and with her hands hidden behind her back. She leant against the wall. Aoife waited, but the younger girl didn't speak.

She was growing into quite a looker, was Becky. It seemed to have happened without Aoife noticing, but as she looked at her standing there in her sleeveless black dress, her hair swept back into a tidy ponytail, Aoife couldn't help but be struck by the change. It was hard to imagine that the fresh-faced young woman to the side of her – with three glistening freckles on her cheek from the soldering iron – was the same person as the girl who used to follow Aoife from place to place.

For a moment Aoife lost herself in a daydream: maybe if Damien had looked to Becky for support, maybe if the two of them had possessed that wee bit more confidence – or if they'd been brought together by Aoife – then a romance might have developed. She'd have made a good girlfriend for Damien, patient and understanding through his long silences. That was what he'd needed: someone who was mindful of what had happened to him but who wasn't capable of holding any bitterness.

Becky broke the spell. Looking up at Aoife, she bit at her lip nervously and plucked at the hem of her dress like a wee girl.

'What is it you're wanting, Becky?' Aoife asked. The words tasted as acidic as they sounded. Swallowing, Aoife tried again. 'What is it, love?'

'Aoife?'

'Yes?'

'Do you think I could put something into the coffin for Damien?'

Aoife frowned down at her. 'I'm not sure he'll be needing anything, Becky.'

'It's just…'

Becky left her sentence unfinished, bringing her hand out from behind her back instead. She held a silver cross, no bigger than the palm of her hand, formed of spiralling wires tightly wound around one another.

'Give it here,' Aoife said, taking the cross and turning it over in her hand. 'What's it made of?' she asked.

'Guitar strings,' Becky replied, softly.

'Is that right? It's a thing of beauty, Becky, really it is. Thank you.'

Becky nodded, a blush flushing her cheeks.

'Let's put it in with him, then,' Aoife said, briskly, pushing herself down from the windowsill. With Becky in tow, she stepped over to the coffin and reached out to touch the hand of her brother. She stopped an inch or so short – faltered. His nails – normally bitten down to the quick – had been smoothed and carefully rounded by the undertaker. Aoife had heard it told that fingernails kept growing after death – although it might have been her daddy who'd told her that, and she'd long since grown out of believing his stories. All the same, there was something manicured and pampered about his hands that was entirely disconnected from the ink-smudged, half-chewed, dirt-streaked hands of her brother.

All eyes in the room were on the two girls at the coffin. Squinting to the side, Aoife saw Father O'Neill standing watching – gin in one hand, whiskey in the other – alongside Big Gerry and several of the neighbours. They were all waiting to see what she would do next.

Taking a deep breath, Aoife stretched out her fingertips and touched her brother's skin. She could feel every ridge of bone, every sinew, as she gently lifted his right hand and placed the guitar-string cross underneath, against his motionless chest. Swallowing, screwing her eyes shut, she let go of his cold hand and turned back to Becky.

'He'd have liked that,' she said, quietly. The words sounded hollow. They both knew rightly that he'd have had no use for it. It was something for clutching in a coffin – something funereal – nothing more. 'It was a lovely thought,' she added.

Becky nodded and looked at the blue sheet on the floor beneath the coffin.

Father O'Neill held out the glass of gin. Aoife took it and drank it in a single swallow. 'Listen, Aoife,' the priest said, 'you should go over and have a word with your mother, maybe.'

Aoife opened her mouth, closed it, then nodded. 'Maybe.'

Cathy sat on a chair by the door to the kitchen, watching events through startled eyes and maintaining a hold on both her husband's suit jacket and her nurse's hand. In order to get to her, Aoife had to run the gauntlet of children who moved to and fro across the living room, clutching fistfuls of sandwiches and overflowing paper cups of fizzy juice. As she reached her parents, a wee boy and girl came careering out of the kitchen, curving their runs around the bodies of the adults. As she passed Aoife, the girl turned and pointed a finger at the boy. 'Bang!' she said. He kept running for a moment, before remembering his role and taking a step backwards. Clutching at his chest, he let out a groan – a single syllable – before lifting his hand and resuming the chase.

'Paul! Frances!' a voice called from the other side of the room. 'Don't be doing that. Show some respect!'

A second later – a second too late – the thinner voice of Aoife's mammy could be heard, like an echo, by those close at hand.

'Aoife! Damien!' it said. 'Don't – '

'This here is Donal,' Baldy says.

I'm lying on the bare mattress, the twisted and sweat-soaked single sheet in a bundle at my feet. I squint up at the newcomer. His hand raises itself in greeting, then flicks nervously around his body as if in an attempt to bless himself. He doesn't look old enough for Sunday School. My throat burns, so I speak bluntly.

'Who the fuck – ?' I ask.

'He's a medical student,' Baldy replies.

'Not a doctor?'

'I have a textbook,' Donal says, holding it out.

'He'll have to do.' Baldy sniffs, not looking at me. 'Just show him.'

It's either the anger or the fever – I'm not sure which – that causes my hands to shake as I raise my T-shirt and lower my pants. Donal stands above me, peering down over his shoulder, with his body half turned away.

'It looks like syphilis,' he says, uncertainly.

'Have you ever seen this before?' I say. 'Or are you just guessing?'

'Have a closer look,' Baldy says.

Donal leans down. 'Syphilis with maybe a bacterial or yeast infection as well.'

He leafs through the pages. He's panicking now, his whimpers coming faster and faster as he struggles to find the page.

'Can't you see you're scaring her?' Baldy says.

At that, I realise that I've probably as much fear drawn across my face as he does. I try to turn it into a snarl. 'You're the one who went out for a doctor and came back with a student,' I hiss.

'Penicillin,' Donal says, although he hasn't found the page. 'I think you need Penicillin G, with maybe something else for the secondary infection.'

'Are you sure?' Baldy asks.

'It would really need a doctor, y'know, to be sure...'

'Can you sort it?'

'I'd need to get a prescription, I suppose – '

'No prescription. Can you sort it?'

Donal nods, swallows, and follows Baldy out of the room and into the hallway. I'm left lying there, straining to hear, wanting to shout out that I need a real doctor and a hospital. I need a diagnosis written on a chart at the end of a clean bed.

'He'll sort it,' Baldy says, as he comes back in.

'Will he?' I ask, doubtfully. The rest of it sticks, unsaid, in my throat.

'He will,' Baldy replies, kneeling down and smoothing the hair away from my forehead. 'And once we get you better we'll make the scum that did this to you pay.'

I peer up at him, wanting to ask him who he's meaning. The man who gave me this is dead already. Either number five or number six. So it'll have to be number seven who pays for it, and number eight, and number nine, and –

'They did this to you,' Baldy says.

Feverish, I squirm away from him.

The last of the water drained from the bath. Moving to her bedroom and seating herself cross-legged on the bed, Aoife pulled the wood-framed mirror across to the edge of the bedside table and tilted it up to meet her reflection. Behind her, the television showed a montage of violence – bombed buildings, bullet-pocked cars, bodies beneath sheets, bloodied streets with chalk outlines and numbered cards. She could see the inverted images in the upper right corner of the mirror, but she had no wish to turn the volume up. Even without the sound on, she knew rightly that they would only be talking about whether the peace would hold, if the ceasefire was permanent or just a lull. They'd not be going into whether one side or the other would be called to account, or what a negotiated settlement might look like. It was all just speculation.

There would be no questioning why a policeman had fired a plastic bullet at an unarmed eleven-year-old child, or why the politicians had rejected a call for an inquiry and instead accepted the account given by the other peelers stationed in Lower Ormeau that day. No chance of them doing a follow-up report on the boy with the damaged eye who'd committed suicide nine months ago as a result of his injuries. No one would seek out those responsible, or ask if state aggression in policing the protest that day amounted to murder. They'd not be going into the specifics of the case, laying blame and passing sentence. That was all well and good, though. Aoife was prepared to hold court herself – to declare herself judge, jury, and –

As she flicked her hair free from the towel, a steamed streak formed across the surface of the mirror, clouding the reflection of the telly. Lifting the hairdryer, she set to work.

The Lucozade-ginger curls of her hair were her trademark, coiling up and around her ears like a lion's mane. It made her instantly recognisable, as the owner of the only ginger afro in Belfast. She kept it short, because she'd found that it was near-enough impossible to tug a brush through it when it was long. Although even with it shorter she could rarely be troubled to brush at it, preferring to let it knot and twist as it pleased, then fix it in place with cans – plural – of hairspray. A special event was needed for her to go through the hassle of it: an event that needed her to get all dolled up, that needed her to be as thick with the make-up and as thin with the clothing as any other millie out on the lash in the city centre. Something like the evenings – plural – that she was planning.

She'd even braved the quizzical look of the sales assistant in the pharmacy and bought herself hair straighteners, though, as she dragged her curls through the heated plates, she saw why the girl had been doubtful as to the wisdom of using straighteners against the coiled springs of her hair. The tightly wound curls sprang back, again and again, as if untouched. A bitter smell of singed hair hung in the air.

After a spell that left her arm heavy and tired, she decided that enough was enough. Leaning forward to inspect herself in the mirror, she saw that most of her hair was as it had always been – curled and close-cut – but that there was a section of snarled hair to one side that was beginning to flatten. It was enough for Aoife to take heart, to be convinced that with enough effort she could arrive at the shimmering, straightened hair that others had. What she was wanting was the long, feminine hair that used to cause a wee stab of jealousy within her whenever the girls at the Convent – especially Joanne – had casually tucked it in behind their ear or flicked it over their shoulder. All she needed to do was persevere. So, humming to herself, she lifted the straighteners again.

It took a good half-hour or so before Aoife was ready for the next stage. It was the fiddly bit. The week before, she'd been in to see Cliona and begged some hair extensions – sleek red hair, of course – and some of the wash-out glue and clip-ins that were needed. It was a simple enough lie to say that she was doing the hair extensions for a mate before a night out – one that wouldn't have caused her any guilt if only Cliona hadn't started on about how glad she was to see Aoife getting out of the house for a night, how worried she'd been these past months, with Aoife not doing things girls of her age did – not taking a drink or meeting up with friends, not going to the dancing or sitting in the bar eyeing up the talent, not getting all dressed up and going out to chase after boys – not since –

The wake had ended in a conventional enough way, with people fading off into the chill Belfast night in dribs and drabs, murmuring final condolences and making their way either back to their own houses or on to the pub to continue toasting the dead. Aoife's mammy had left after an hour or so, led out by her shattered-looking husband and the still-smiling nurse. Father O'Neill had followed shortly after, but not before he'd taken Aoife to the side and imparted a few soft words of wisdom. If she hadn't been half-cut, Aoife might have heeded his advice. As it was, though, she soon joined the dregs of the mourners who stood around the card table draining the last drop of alcohol from the evening.

The gin churned in her stomach and set her head to swirling. The taste of it lingered at the back of her throat, so as she felt the need to try and rinse it away with a vodka or two. She had heard it told that gin led to depression. Sure, it had been gin that Caoimhe McGreevy – Big Gerry's sister – had been drinking before she put her head in the oven.

It wasn't having that effect on Aoife, though, not a bit of it. Instead, there was a deep and gnawing anger in the depths of her stomach – like hunger – that set her teeth to grinding and caused her to dig her fingernails into the palms of her hands until the skin broke into tiny crescents of blood.

She scanned the room. She had to squint to cure herself of double vision – had to blink several times – before she found Ciáran, seated on his own by the fireplace.

'Ciáran-an,' she called, adding an extra syllable to the end of his name.

Everyone in the room looked over to her, except Ciáran. He looked down at the hearth. Everyone in the room, including Ciáran, took a sip from their drink and waited on developments.

'Come here, for fuck sake,' Aoife called. 'For fuck sake, be a man about it, will you?'

Ciáran swallowed the rest of the whiskey in his glass, set it down and then rose from his chair. He still hadn't looked across at Aoife, still hadn't met her eye. He was like a misbehaving schoolchild called to the front of the class.

'What are you frightened of?' Aoife taunted him.

'You were right, OK?' Ciáran said, as he drew close. 'You were right about Damien and I'm sorry. If there's anything I can do...' He faltered.

They both avoided looking over to the coffin on the far side of the room.

'Listen,' Aoife said, looking him up and down. The anger within her hadn't died, but there was a focus to it now. She held a hand out to Ciáran. 'Come with me.'

'Where are we going?' he asked.

'Are you feared?'

He shook his head and took her hand. Then, with Aoife leading the way, they walked quickly from the room. All eyes were on them, but everyone seemed to be talking of something else. They stepped out by the front door.

Aoife could feel the shiver to Ciáran's hand as she dragged him across to the concrete playground, could feel it turning to a tremor that travelled along her fingers and up her arm. It was the cold rather than fright that caused it – she was near certain of that.

'Listen, Aoife –' Ciáran began.

She stopped his words with a finger pushed against his bottom lip. Then, with her other hand around the back of his neck, she pulled him down – far from gently – until his lips met her own. The kiss was urgent and dry, cracked lips against cracked lips. Aoife pressed against him, pushed and probed with her tongue, searching for something other than the stale taste of whiskey and cigarette-smoke.

His breathing was heavier now. Aoife broke away and looked into his eyes. He was looking down at her in confusion, his face flickering with unasked – unanswerable – questions. Leading him in behind the swings, Aoife stretched up and kissed him again, reaching down this time to unbuckle his belt, to unzip his fly and to pull his dick out from his trousers.

245

'Aoife, what're you – ?' he tried to ask.

This time she stopped him by grasping him in her fist and beginning to pump – ferociously – by mashing her lips up against his – as he winced – and pressing forward as he tried to edge away.

'Aoife – ' he tried again.

'Shut the fuck up, will you?' Aoife replied, gasping, with the slur of something other than drink to her voice now. She wasn't wanting him to ask questions, to have to explain, to tell him that her virginity, her wholesomeness – all that bullshit that had been preached to her up at the Convent – all of that there wasn't something to be savoured, treasured, kept for her soul-fucking-mate, but was instead something to get rid of, something that needed to be cast aside. She had no need for chastity.

She guided him to the ground. Then she hitched up her skirt and tugged her knickers to the side. She needed to lick at her fingers and fumble the moisture over herself before she was able to push him inside. He let out a moan as he penetrated. Lying there on the cold hard concrete, shielded from the road, Aoife felt the pain cut through the alcohol, through the grief and the anger. Something loosened then, within her – and something else tightened – as he tensed and took over the thrusting.

It's bitter cold, so it is. Bitter cold, and the second bar on the fire's gone. Baldy's gone half the time too, though that's maybe no bad thing because all he does in any case is make mugs of tea and fry rashers of bacon. Tea and sandwiches, that's all he's good for.

The medicine seems to be working. Red pills, purple pills, some wee white pills. As Donal hands them over, his hand shakes them like a rattle, and he gives a shrug as if to admit that he's not a notion as to whether they're the right ones or the wrong ones, whether they'll ease the pain or cause pain, whether they're kill or cure. They seem to be working, though. There's no dampness to my forehead when I wake, and no pain when I piss.

Baldy is planning something. Whenever I ask him about it, though, all he does is wink and put the saucepan on to boil water for tea, or the frying pan on for the rashers.

'I'll tell you once you're better,' he says.

'You've no call to be keeping it from me,' I say, once I'm up and about. I'm cooking scrambled eggs on fried bread for dinner (anything but bacon) and there's a bottle of whiskey lying to the side of the mattress (anything but tea).

Baldy looks up. 'You're right,' he says. No more than that. He grins, starts to roll a cigarette. Then he lifts a sheet of paper and hands it to me.

It's a list of names, handwritten in black ink.

'Who are these folk?' I ask, frowning.

He licks the cigarette paper and folds it closed.

'They're legitimate targets,' Baldy replies. 'Members of the security services, ex-paramilitaries, people with blood on their hands. We start from the top of the list and we work our way down.'

There are ten names on the list. The first is called James Bew.

I lift the blackened bread from the pan and set it on a plate.

'It sends a message, Aoife,' Baldy says.

'You know not to call me that,' I say, under my breath, lifting an egg and cracking it into the smoking pan.

Lifting her make-up bag, Aoife rooted around until her fingers plucked out the greasy plastic tube of concealer from the midst of all the soft sponge and fine powder. She'd finished with her hair extensions, got them fixed in so as – in dim light, at least – nobody would notice that the long, straight red hair wasn't her own. Not that she was expecting the men she was targeting to be looking at her hair. By the time she was finished she was intending on having enough cleavage and thigh on show to draw even a seminarian's eye.

Usually she just settled for dabbing concealer here and there, wherever she had a spot or a blemish or something like that. Rarely more than a wee touch on her chin, or a careful dot down at the side of her nose. She knew she'd need more for what she had in mind, though. Swirling the applicator around the inside of the tube, she gathered a clump and set to smearing it up and over the bridge of her nose in a thick band, like warpaint. Her smattering of freckles near disappeared beneath it, with only the outline of one or two showing around the edges. Lifting her foundation then, Aoife set to spreading and smoothing it across her cheeks until all traces of the freckles were covered.

Peering into the mirror, she inspected the result. Her face was two-tone: pale Irish skin on her forehead and down across her chin, with a strip of solid unnatural-looking peach through the middle. She'd need to use near enough all the foundation she had, she realised, so as she could even it out. After all, she wasn't wanting to look as though she had some wick skin disease. That would send them scuttling off before she'd even had a chance to lay a gentle hand on the arm and flash a smile at them. Before they'd had the opportunity to buy her a drink and admire the view from behind as she walked over to the table. Before she was able to slip her foot out from her shoe and trail it up the inside of a trouser leg, then lean over and suggest in a low voice that they get out of whatever Godforsaken dive of a bar they were in and find somewhere they could be alone.

Once she'd caked on all of the hardened remnants from all of the near-finished powder compacts in her bag of tricks, Aoife examined the result in the mirror again. It surprised her how different she looked. Her normally pale, freckled face had a tint to it that made it seem as if it had seen sunlight at some point in its nineteen-year-stay in Belfast. Her normally short, tightly curled hair now stretched down to her shoulders in a – relatively – smooth and straight sweep. She looked like a cartoon image of herself, all clean lines and blocks of colour.

Considering her new look from all angles, Aoife was fairly satisfied. It wasn't perfect as yet, but it was a good start. This was only a practice run, anyway. By the time she made use of it she'd look just like any other slapper out on the tear, trying to pick up a man in uniform. The olive-green towel wasn't what she'd be wearing when the time came, right enough, but it showed about the right amount of flesh – leg to the upper reaches of her thigh, a glimpse of bare shoulder, and cleavage so deep that a man could lose his gaze in the depths of it. She'd need to go out shopping at some stage, to get herself skimpy clothes that had the same effect.

Aoife would have liked a second opinion, someone to cast an eye over it and tell her that she looked a new woman. That would have defeated the purpose of the disguise, though. Even her daddy couldn't be told. Aoife wasn't wanting to give those closest to her the opportunity for talking her out of it. This was something she had to do alone.

The thought had crossed her mind that Ciáran was the one most likely to understand her plan, but she wasn't wanting him and his gangster friends getting involved, wasn't for giving them the opportunity to hijack it.

Becky would have listened readily enough and she'd not breathe a word to anyone about it, but Aoife was reluctant to deepen the worried frown that had creased its way across the wee girl's forehead. The less Becky knew about it, the better. She could just continue innocently making the jewellery, and Aoife would continue using the sales route and the money for her own purposes. There was no need to involve Becky beyond that.

Reaching into the top drawer of her bedside table, Aoife drew out a pair of earrings that Becky had made a couple of years before. Aoife had decided to keep them for herself because she liked them so much. It was one of the perks of being her own boss. They were formed from off-cuts of barbed wire – easy enough to find in West Belfast – which spiralled down from the ear-hooks, with tiny fake gemstones set between the two strands of wire. Only an inch or so long, they were, with three glass beads in each. They reminded Aoife of the coiled double helix of DNA that was pictured in the biology textbook that she'd used to home-school Damien. The same textbook that she'd torn an entire section from one morning – from page forty-eight to page sixty-four – so as she could avoid having to teach her wee brother about the facts of life.

It wasn't until Aoife had hooked one of the earrings into her right earlobe, tucked her newly straightened and lengthened red hair in behind and was reaching up to attach the other one that she caught herself on. There she was trying to make herself look like any other bit of skirt out and about town and yet she was thinking about wearing customised jewellery that didn't have a matching pair in all the world. If someone recognised the jewellery then she'd be sunk, simple as that.

Shaking her head at her own stupidity, Aoife set the earrings back in the drawer. If she was wanting to do this properly then she'd need to go out and get herself some cheap store-bought jewellery, the type of thing which sparkled so brightly that it couldn't be anything other than fake.

Reaching for the remote, Aoife turned up the volume on the telly in the corner. The reporter was on about graffiti and how the intricate artistic detail of the murals was being lost to scrawled words of sectarian hatred. Aoife would have put money on it, though, that the worry wasn't about the hate – they were more worried about losing those American tourists who had started going on bus tours around the murals. They'd sprouted up since the ceasefire, the so-called 'terror tours'. And the Americans weren't wanting to see misspelt declarations from dissident Republicans that related to what was happening in the here and now; they were wanting to see lovingly painted gunmen and shrines to martyrs who'd died back in the days when their parents had first left the old country.

The picture on the telly cut to a picture of a shuttered shop that had 'The war is not over' spray-painted across the front of it in awkward, disjointed letters. Probably written by the Continuity IRA or a lone vandal rather than anyone associated with the Provisional IRA, the reporter speculated. Aoife smiled to herself at that. It did her head in how the media had this attitude that the murals were somehow the only representation of community feeling, while some wee spide daubing 'Brits out' on a garden wall was just to be ignored. Surely graffiti was more representative, in any case, seeing as you would only need a tin of paint. If you were wanting to repaint a mural, you'd most likely need the say-so of the politicians, the community leaders, the residents and – especially – the boys in balaclavas. The difference between the murals and the graffiti wasn't that one was a collective expression of feeling and the other was just some hallion acting out – it was that people would pay to see the murals but if they wanted graffiti then they could see it in whichever town or city they'd sprung from. Belfast was the same as anywhere else: people wrote on the walls because that was where they knew it'd be seen.

Aoife lifted a red lipstick from her make-up bag and started to apply it, thickly but neatly. Pressing a tissue to her lips, she considered the effect in the mirror. It was perfect, so it was: garish and brash. Then she set to work with the mascara, eyeliner and eyeshadow.

By the time she'd finished she was a sight for sore eyes, liable to catch the eye of any lonely soldier or cocky policeman who'd stopped off for a quick pint. As carefully painted as any mural, but with a short, simple, brutal message – *fuck you and yours, for all you've done*.

Smiling into the mirror, Aoife modulated her accent into the polite and polished voice she used whenever she was going door to door around the houses on the other side of the River Lagan, the voice she used for those houses with the Union Jacks hanging from the flagpoles outside, with the commemorative royal plates and portraits of the Queen. She slipped into her saleswoman voice easily; it came naturally enough to her. And the name – a name that she could hate, a name that had a wee nasal sneer to it – came easily enough as well.

'Hello, I'm Cassandra,' she said. 'But call me Cassie.'

Book Two

James Bew

Roger Armstrong

Eddie Ross

Keith Sinclair

John Fyfield Senior

John Fyfield Junior

David Meters

Aaron Morrow

Raymond Patterson

Robert Marchetti.

I get the particulars of Jim Bew from a videotape taken out from the local library. From a documentary series about the peace process which talks about it all as if it's been consigned to history. Even though Peter Mandelson – the Northern Irish Secretary – had to reintroduce direct rule before there'd even been an 'i' dotted or a 't' crossed up at Stormont. Despite the fact that the Unionists haven't let up muttering about decommissioning for going on two years since the Belfast Agreement. There's precious little movement, so there is, precious little action. The politicians are sitting on their hands and claiming that they're all about the handshakes.

I've to wait until about an hour into the tape before they speak about Bew and even then I've to rewind and replay the twenty-second snippet until I get all the details straight. It isn't a physical description of Bew I'm after, but the details of what he did to get himself on Baldy's list, what he did to get himself in a documentary about the Troubles, to land himself with a life sentence. A grainy image of the old Bakery up on Ormeau Road with a voiceover on top: '*UVF gunman James Bew stepped out from the doorway and shot the lawyer Patrick Sheridan at close range, in spite of the presence of Sheridan's five-year-old daughter Fiona, who was eating an ice-cream at the time. Sheridan was working on the case of five suspected Provisional IRA bombers...*' Pause. Rewind. I've a picture of it in my head: the wee girl screaming as the ice-cream drips then drops down, maybe with the chocolate flake following – *leaving a deep crater in the remaining ice-cream* – the whole melting mess of it floating there on top of her daddy's blood.

The sixth of March, 1983. I'd have only been eight years old myself, only three years older than Fiona Sheridan. How do you recover from something like that at that age?

I decide that I'll scout Fiona as well as Jim Bew, see if he's left a victim or not. Maybe she's recovered, made her peace, and all I'd be doing would be peeling the scabs from old wounds. Truth be told, it's a safety valve for me as much as anything, because I've my doubts about the turn events have been taking and I know rightly that if I get this Bew into the bedroom of whichever house Benny has lined up then he'll not only be getting the broken glass from me but the bullet from Baldy as well. I'm wanting to make sure that he deserves it, so I am, because I know that he's served sixteen years for his crime and I'm not wanting to end his life unless I know it'll help Fiona out.

There's only one question I need to ask. *Should I?* I'll ask her, with my eyes. Look like you've never recovered for yes; show yourself as a confident, well-adjusted young woman for no.

She's not hard to find. She sells charcoal sketches at the weekly St George's Market down next to the Law Courts. As soon as I find that out, I take the opportunity to phone up and get myself and Becky a stall for the coming weekend. A captive audience of locals and tourists to sell our jewellery to. Becky seems lured by the prospect, telling me in her whispering voice that she's always dreamt of opening a shop and that a market stall, whilst not having the necessary four walls, is at least a step up from working from home – *a corner of the table by the window in the Gildays' kitchen spread with thread, wire, beads and assorted scraps* – and trudging round to sell the jewellery door-to-door from a battered attaché case.

Fiona Sheridan sits on a stool by the side of her stall and sketches from memory. She sketches the City Hall and the Botanic Gardens and two graduates, with their mortarboard hats on, standing outside Queen's University. She draws the landmarks, with clean and even lines, but all the while she's thinking of that one scene from her childhood. I can tell from the eyes. Rheumy and vacant, looking like they'd overspill if she were to hear the tinkling bell of an ice-cream van, or smell freshly baked bread. She's never recovered; she's woken screaming in the night and sobbed uncontrollably in the day – it's there in the tangled knots of her brown hair and the cigarette burns that pock-mark her crumpled patchwork skirt, the nervous way she fumbles change to those who buy her work and the tremble to her fingers that only settles when she lifts her charcoal again.

It's all the answer I need. Turning from her, I go back to my own stall and tell Becky that I'm needed elsewhere. She's barely time to look up at me and nod – *with eyes widened to the size of shiny ten-pence pieces* – because there's people crowded around the stall, lifting bangles, bracelets and necklaces. Bless her, she doesn't even raise a word of protest – *good old dependable Becky* – just smiles up at me and lets me wander off, no questions asked.

I go to the bar right beside the Market and make for the payphone. I think of the shake to Fiona Sheridan's hand as I clink the coins into the slot. I think of Jim Bew as I look around the men gathered at the bar. One or two of them have that same guarded air of men who've been locked away; one or two have that translucent skin that looks as though it would curl and blister if it were ever to see the sun. One or two have the same greying strands above the temples that Bew has. But none of them will die tonight.

I dial. The phone rings and is quickly answered.

'Yes?' The voice is Baldy's.

'OK,' I say.

'He'll be at Windsor Park tonight, for the football.'

'And the address I'm to take him to?'

I note down the address in the corner of a beer mat. There's no more to our conversation than that; it is short and terse and functional. There's nothing more to be said. I put the phone down.

Over the course of the week I've tailed Jim Bew as he's gone about his business – following him from his mother's house to the local shop as he buys a pint of milk, then back again. He's not a live-wire. There's nothing of the celebrity gunman to him: he's not one for hanging out in Loyalist holes and waiting for the regulars to buy him pints, or for visiting the social clubs and looking down the length of a pool cue like a sniper's rifle while he tells his story. He's a quiet one, so he is. Stays with his mother and ventures out only for the messages or the football. That's his Achilles' heel: the football. Linfield FC. The Blues.

I wait for him by the steps to the bridge across Tate's Avenue, scanning the grim-set faces of the fans. I've a bit of nervousness about me, because I've only ever trailed him at a distance or seen his photograph on the skip-static of the paused videotape. As it turns out, though, I've no problem in picking him out. The stiffness to his shoulders marks him out from the rest. He's tense, so he is, and in need of the looseness of drink.

'Good match the night?' I ask, falling into step alongside him.

He looks at me in silence. I realise I should have done some homework, looked up the score, or at least who they were playing. Still, in for a penny, in for a pound.

'I only ask,' I say, quickly, 'because my son's a fan and I said I'd find out the score for him on the way home.'

'Two-nil,' he replies.

'Good.' I smile. 'Who were they playing?'

'Lisburn Distillery.'

'Good.'

He lengthens his stride. I'm panicked now, thinking that I've no reason to stop him, nothing that I can say that'll convince him to come for a drink. He's not even looked at my legs beneath my knee-length skirt, or the glimpse of cleavage beneath my jacket. He's not given me the once-over. I'm angry with myself, if truth be told, for not thinking it through, for blindly stumbling forward – *fuck you and yours, for all you've done* – and letting the emotion of it take over from the planning. And once he pulls away from me, once he puts a bit of distance between us, I'll not be able to approach him again without raising his suspicion.

'Bew,' I shout. 'I'm Fiona Sheridan.'

He stops. He stops and he turns. He stops and he turns and he stares.

'I'm Fiona,' I repeat. It's a risk. I've not a notion as to whether he's seen Fiona before, maybe, or followed her childhood from his jail cell. It's a risk.

'What do you want?'

'Will you come for a drink?'

He takes a step towards me, studies me with his eyes. 'Of course,' he says softly, as if he's been expecting this moment for seventeen years.

Once we get to the bar, out on the Lisburn Road, I let him buy me a vodka-tonic and then I sit and watch as he nurses his pint between cupped hands. He takes a sip every minute or so, but he seems to have no taste for it. There's no small talk; we both know there's only one thing to be discussed.

'What do you want to know?' he asks, after a spell of silence.

I shrug. I struggle to form a question. I must be quite convincing as the overwhelmed, speechless daughter coming face to face with her father's killer.

'I'm sorry for the hurt I caused,' he says, addressing his apology to his drink. 'It's of little consolation to you, I'm sure.'

I nod. I look at him over the top of his glass, wanting him to continue.

'It wasn't personal.' He looks me in the eye, then looks away. 'Your father was a target given to me. I was given instructions. It was a job, no more.'

'Did you regret it, afterwards?' I ask.

'Of course. I regret it now. Of course.' He takes a breath. 'But it was a different time back then, Fiona. That's no excuse,

260

but it was. There were killings on a day-to-day basis. I probably wouldn't have even been caught, if...' He trails off, choosing his words carefully. 'If I'd got away from the area, if I'd got rid of the gun, then I'd never have been jailed for it. They might have known it was me, but no one would have talked out of turn.'

'But, if you'd got away with it – ' I begin.

'Don't be getting me wrong, I'm glad I never did. If I'd gotten away with it then I might not have thought about it as long and hard as I have. It does a body good to think on your misdeeds; it's a form of punishment in itself.'

I take a drink. It's not punishment enough, I'm thinking. It doesn't bring Fiona Sheridan's daddy back. There's no justice in sixteen years in jail – *an eye for an eye, a tooth for a tooth* – when Fiona Sheridan has to live with it for the rest of her days.

'How did you get caught?' I ask, evenly.

He smiles, just a twitch at the corner of his mouth. 'My own fucking stupidity,' he answers. 'I had a bicycle stashed in one of the back lanes. I ran to it and then pedalled away down the Ormeau Road, going the opposite direction to the police and the ambulance that were all coming up towards – ' He stops, clears his throat. 'There was a safe house at the Annadale Flats I was to go to. I had to make a left turn along the embankment. I held out my left arm to make the turn, and I still had the fucking gun in my hand.'

He tries to share a laugh. It hangs in the air between us.

'Would you have turned yourself in?' I ask.

He looks at me. He shakes his head.

Rising then, I excuse myself to go to the bathroom. I ask him to wait there, although I've my doubts as to whether he will. Lifting the empty tonic bottle and my empty glass, I walk away from the table. On the way to the bar, I tuck the tonic bottle into my handbag. Then I walk past the toilets to the payphone at the back.

I dial. The phone rings and is quickly answered.

'Yes?' The voice is Baldy's.

'Change of plan. He'll not come to the house.'

'I see.'

'He isn't one I can lead by his prick.'

Silence.

'So – ' I tap my fingernails against the tonic bottle in my bag ' – can you wait outside in your taxi?'

'Give me fifteen minutes,' he replies.

I give him the name of the bar and hang up.

On the way back to the table, I get Bew another pint and myself another vodka-tonic. He's still there, but he's barely drunk the head off his first pint. He eyes the second one I set in front of him, knowing that it'd be rude to get up and leave whilst there's still drink on the table. He's counting the seconds in sips, so he is, and I've an eye on the clock as well, waiting for the fifteen minutes to be up. There's precious little conversation between us. He tries to ask about me, about Fiona, and whether there is a husband or kids in my – her – life. I don't know, so I don't answer.

By the time the fifteen minutes has passed, the silence is near ringing in my ears. It's painful to speak, because each word seems weighted with someone else's hurt, someone else's loss, someone else's grief.

'Where do you live?' I ask.

He looks at me, surprised by the question.

'Maybe we could share a taxi,' I say.

He nods. 'Down near Sandy Row.'

'I'm in Botanic,' I say, and hold my breath. This is the biting point: he's either getting into the taxi with me and I'm in control, or he's walking home through the streets of Belfast and then there's a danger to even think of lifting him. 'Going in the same direction,' I say, nudging him along.

'I wouldn't…' he says. 'I couldn't…'

'It's been seventeen years,' I say. 'I wanted to meet you, I wanted to hear what you had to say for yourself. No more. I'll not darken your doorstep again or – '

'If I'd known you would be with him that day…' he says, his voice cracking.

I watch him, catching my bottom lip between my teeth. I'm not wanting him to show his emotion, not wanting there to be a redeeming feature or a display of genuine regret.

'You were only a wee girl,' he says.

'I was only five,' I reply, rising from my seat and gesturing towards the door with my hand. I know, now, that he'll follow. I know that he'll climb into the taxi and that he'll listen while I tell him that I'm not Fiona Sheridan but her proxy, and that I'm not seeking understanding, but revenge. He'll listen rightly.

'Evening,' Baldy says softly as I climb into the back of the taxi.

'Evening,' I reply.

'Evening, sir,' Baldy says to Bew, waiting until the back doors are shut before he pulls away from the kerb and flicks the locks shut, doing a U-turn out onto the Lisburn Road and heading down towards Sandy Row. He'll not be stopping there, though. Two of us in the taxi know that, and the third is about to find out.

Bew leans forward in his seat, to tell the driver his address.

'He knows where he's going,' I say. There's an edge to my voice, I can hear it myself and it surprises me. I deliver the line like dialogue in a gangster film, flat and terse, without emotion. The adrenalin rises and I tap my fingernails against the tonic bottle in my bag, reassuring myself of its presence.

There's little reaction from Bew, though. He looks across at me and then catches Baldy's eye in the rear-view mirror. With a nod, then, he settles back against the seat. As if he's been expecting this moment.

~~James Bew~~

Roger Armstrong

Eddie Ross

Keith Sinclair

John Fyfield Senior

John Fyfield Junior

David Meters

Aaron Morrow

Raymond Patterson

Robert Marchetti.

I take the decision to travel down to Portadown, after the first round of Drumcree protests, to see Roger Armstrong in action amongst his brethren. I'm wanting to see him in with the LVF and UFF men who're throwing petrol bombs and fireworks at the police barricades. The first Drumcree march of the new millennium, the week before the Twelfth, and they're all carrying on as if they're back at the beginning of the last century, or the century before even. Spitting the dummy because they're being stopped by the RUC from walking down the Nationalist Garvaghy Road – *lined up like Lego men, they were, none of them moving, all of them helmeted, bullet-proof-vested and plastic-shielded.*

I'm an observer, no more. Arriving after the parade itself to find the field up by Drumcree Church filled with Orangemen. Not only Orangemen, though, with their suits and sashes, but also thugs in tracksuits, some of them Scottish, some of them even with German accents. Alongside them, there's housewives seated on the grass giving out tinfoil-wrapped sandwiches to the youngsters, and the youngsters sitting with their picnic to watch the men make their speeches. Listening to the declarations of war, the call to arms, and then setting down their lemonade so as they can clap their hands, pure lured by the whole game – *the wee ones were being treated to some show.*

It's been five months since Bew. Five months since the report in the paper about how he'd been seen talking to a red-haired woman on the night of his death, the peelers appealing for information as they tried to piece together events in the hours before he was found down a back alley, in South Belfast, with a bullet in his head. But I've still taken precautions before venturing out again. I've dyed my hair chestnut-brown and cut it short and choppy. Even with the precautions, though, I've still a fair few nerves about me, because I've had nightmares of someone catching on to who I am and what I'm doing here and then everyone in the field turning on me, turning on me and chasing me – *steadily tramping feet behind… footfalls that keep time to the marching beat of the Lambeg drum.*

Roger Armstrong is the inventor of 'dial-a-taig'. That's what got him onto Baldy's list; that's what led me down to this Loyalist mecca to sniff him out. A simple but brutal invention – him and a couple of his mates would order a taxi from a company known to employ Catholics, ask for it to come to such-and-such an address, then lie in wait to ambush the driver. Sectarian murder, it was. There'd been two or three of them carried out since the Loyalist ceasefire, but the police couldn't touch him for it because when they made enquiries, up and around Corcrain, they were met by a stony and defiant silence.

I've to wander around the crowds for a while before I spot Armstrong. He's a fair bit older than he was in the photograph Baldy's given me, as well, so I've to skirt about the fringes of his group until I hear someone address him by name. By nickname, that is. Strongarm. They're clever bastards, so they are, these Loyalist killers. If you need a nickname just switch around the surname, and if you need a victim just order in a member of the opposite religion like he's a takeaway pizza – anyone will do.

I've no intention, like I say, of going up to Armstrong or of trying to catch his eye. There's too many folk about, and I'm only wearing jeans and a T-shirt. I'm trying to blend into the crowd, trying to hide in plain sight. I've no wish to draw attention to myself when I'm surrounded by jaffas. But then I catch sight of a stray length of tinfoil and I see that Armstrong's eating his burger on his own – Billy No-mates – and I see an opportunity that I need to take. I'll just introduce myself, just get under his skin so as I can approach him at a quieter moment and lead him away. After all, I'm not wanting a repeat of the Bew incident where I'd to brassneck it just to get him to have a drink with me. No harm in making a first impression. So I lift the foil, I roll it quickly into a long cylinder and I step forward. Smiling at him, I raise the foil to my lips and begin to mime playing it like a flute. He's noticed me now. He smiles, he turns.

It's not only him who's noticed me, though. There's another pair of eyes on me from the other end of the field, squinting across as their owner tries to place me, tries to work out where he knows me from. I catch on before he does. *He wears a twisting vine shirt, in blue and white, with the sleeves cut shorter than they should be.* I drop the foil flute and begin to walk quickly in the opposite direction. I ignore the call from Armstrong, ignore the hurt and anger of a man who's felt his prick stiffen then soften in the space of a few seconds. I'm not for caring about him, not at the moment. I work my way through the crowd – *squeeze between, edge around, and push past* – and then look back over my shoulder. He begins to run – *the Red Hand tattoo on his bicep. A blood-coloured hand, framed in black* – his mouth opening to shout something that I can't hear. *Nigel.* I begin to run too, not looking back now, my heart pounding to the beat of the Lambeg drums and my thoughts flittering like a flute. I'll outrun him, I'm certain of that, because I've a good head-start and I'm wearing my runners instead of high heels. But he's seen me. In spite of the change in hairstyle, in spite of the years that have passed since that night – *my heartbeat quickens to the sound of his breathing on the other side of the door. As it opens, I swing* – he's seen me and he recognises me. He knows who I am.

I'm fair shook after that, I can tell you. I lie low for a week or two before I come back to Portadown, so as all the parading is done and the aggro out on the streets is back to gesturing and the occasional flung stone rather than petrol bombs and the occasional snap and crackle of gunfire. If you hear the 'pop' then it's too late, my daddy used to say – you can listen out for the snap and the crackle, but if you hear the pop then you've been hit. In any case, it's not fear of the riots that keeps me away, I'm feared of being spotted by Nigel again and having a whole rack of folk baying for my blood, pulling me to pieces right there in the streets of Portadown. It keeps me from my sleep at night, so it does, and it keeps me from getting up and out of bed in the mornings.

I tell Baldy about it. He sits down on the edge of the bed as I start in about how Nigel was my second, back in the days before I knew I'd need help. He reaches out a hand to smooth the dark fringe from my forehead, draws me into a hug as I whisper that it's Nigel who haunts my dreams.

Still, only fifteen days after Drumcree, I'm back down there and back on the hunt. Fair enough, I'm for checking each and every shadow in each and every corner of each and every pub I go into, and Baldy's never far away, with instructions to come in and check on me every half-hour or so. Even with that, it's a risk, I know, because Nigel could have got to Armstrong in the meantime and told him the whole story. Sure, the whole of Protestantism could know about the girl called Cassie and I'd be none the wiser. But I've known the risks from the beginning and I've got a little list to be getting through.

'My ex-boyfriend,' I say to Armstrong, by way of explanation for running off on the day of the parade. 'He's the jealous type.'

Armstrong just nods and leers at me over the rim of his glass. There's no suspicion to him, no doubts that can't be swallowed down with a pint. It's him that came up to me, at the bar. He offered to buy me a drink and I held a hand to my chest like he'd frightened me, then squinted up at him as if I'm trying to place him, as if I was trying to work out where I knew him from – the same look Nigel gave me from across the field, except that mine didn't send Armstrong running.

'I'll protect you, love,' he says. 'I'll look after you.'

'Is that right?' I say, then I look him up and down. I've a tease of a smile on me, and my hand trails up and down his arm. 'You look like a pussycat to me.'

'I've some growl on me, though,' he grins.

'Let's be hearing you, then.'

Instead of growling, he pulls me in towards him, kisses me ferociously on the mouth and snags my bottom lip between his teeth. I taste beer, I taste blood. He's never had to learn to kiss gently; there's not a girl in Portadown that would tell him that he kisses like a thresher. I'm willing to bet that all the girls he's kissed before this have done exactly as I do – step back, shudder, and then smile.

'Alright,' I say. 'I'm convinced.'

'How convinced?' he asks. He's cocksure now, so he is. He thinks he's courted me, thinks he's charmed me into submission. Not a bit of it, of course – it's me that's snared him. I've known how it's going to play out from the beginning. There was a period of uncertainty, with Nigel making a reappearance, but I was always in control. I've always been in control.

'Taxi back to mine?' I ask.

'If I had a coat with me,' he says, 'I'd fetch it.'

Baldy drives silently out of town, towards Craigavon. We've performed this wee play for Armstrong in the meantime, with Baldy driving round the corner towards the pub and me stepping out into the street to flag down the taxi. I hold my breath as I do it, if I'm honest, because it's a legacy of the Troubles that there's still folk who are feared of hailing a taxi rather than phoning a company you trust – where you know what community the driver's from – and I'm thinking that Armstrong, with his past experience, might be one of those folk. Not to worry, though: he climbs into the back without a care in the world and, ignoring Baldy, leans close to me.

'Where is it you live, then?' he asks me.

'A wee farmhouse, used to belong to my grandparents,' I say. 'Been in the family for years, so it has. It's about ten minutes outside town.'

'Secluded,' he says, smiling.

'Very,' I reply, returning his smile with interest.

The house that Benny set us up with is near derelict. He wasn't wanting to give us a house on an estate or that because we know next to no one around these parts and you can't guarantee that people will turn a deaf ear to screaming or gunshots. Maybe back in the day they would have, right enough, but since the peace process a fair few people seem to have found their conscience.

There's a room set out for us up the stairs: a wrought-iron bed with a sheet on the mattress and pillows, with pillowcases and everything, at the head of it. It's the height of luxury as far as I'm concerned, but Armstrong looks about himself with this wee sneer to him. He's not for letting it worry him, though; he's taken it as his due that he'll be getting his hole, so he divides his attention between getting himself undressed and cutting himself a line from a wee bag of white powder that he pulls out of his jeans pocket. I sit myself down on the bed and set to taking off my shoes and peeling off my tights.

'You want a line, love?' he asks, leaning over to the bedside table to snort it up.

'Not for me,' I reply.

'Fair enough.' He gathers up the remainder of the coke on his thumb and his cock swings as he rubs the powder on his gums. 'It makes it all that bit more enjoyable,' he says.

I bite my tongue and beckon him over to the bed. I'll enjoy it rightly, I want to say. Truth be told, I'm wanting him to say that it'll make the sex 'brutal' or that I'll remember it for the rest of my days. I'm wanting him to set me up for a film-star line: 'It'll be the best ride of my life, you say? Well it'll be the last ride of yours.' It never works out like that, though. Instead there's always this hollow intake of breath – from me – as Baldy steps into the room, and I always feel as if I could never speak again, as if there are no words worth saying.

'Lie down,' I say, settling for functional language. Then I set about tying his wrists to the bedframe with my tights. I've to tear the tights down the middle to make the two shackles. 'You ready?' I ask, once I'm sure that he's secured.

He nods; he closes his eyes. I clamber on top of him and sit myself – fully clothed, save for shoes and tights – across his midriff. He's pinned down; no matter how much he strains, he won't be able to raise himself towards me. Satisfied, I reach into my handbag for the miniature tonic bottle. I pause and consider. I'm thinking about breaking it over his head – *you'd expect the bottle to shatter against his skull* – but I settle instead for bringing it down against the iron frame of the bedstead. His eyes snap open. Broken glass litters the ground around the bed. Selecting the largest shard, I hold it – poised – over his bare stomach.

'What're you doing, Cassie?' he asks. There's no panic to him, only confusion.

'Zero,' I say, and slice at the flesh just above his pubic hair. It folds open and then blood begins to rise up and over the lip of the wound. Blood begins to rise up and over the lip of the wound and his mouth stretches open into a scream.

There's panic now. He tries to lift himself from the mattress, but only manages to shake the bedframe, shifting it across so that the broken glass crackles beneath its legs.

'Two,' I call, over the noise of his cries. 'Eight,' I shout.

He screams, he tries to kick out; he even tries to spit at me. I'm not for letting that worry me, though. A bit of spittle never harmed anyone.

'Three,' I hiss. I'm getting into the rhythm of it, getting into my stride. I'm wanting to give him a cut, give him a slice, for each digit of the number he dialled to order those taxis, for each button he pressed knowing that the driver who arrived would never be leaving again. 'Eight,' I call.

It's Baldy who stops me. I don't hear him come in – I don't know how far through the phone number I've got – maybe I've misdialled and started again, maybe I've gotten through it all but kept on going anyway. It's Baldy who stops me. He puts his hand on my shoulder and leans in close. I have to blink the tears away from my eyes so as I can focus. 'That's enough now,' he says. 'Let's put an end to it.'

'You know what he did, though,' I say. It's not a question.

'He's had enough,' Baldy replies.

Without another word, I raise myself from Armstrong and climb off the side of the bed, stepping into my shoes. As I lift my weight from him, Armstrong lands a kick on me that sends me sprawling. My head glances off the bedside table on my way to the ground. Credit to him for that – he isn't for giving in – but his time is coming in any case. Baldy will see to that.

For the time being, Baldy ignores Armstrong and kneels by me. 'You've had a difficult couple of weeks,' he says, cradling my cheek in his hand. I imagine I can feel a hardened callus on the index finger, the trigger finger. It comforts me. The tears have started again. So has the screeching from Armstrong. He's like a toddler having a tantrum. Baldy holds out a hand to him, as if telling him that he has to be patient. His time will come.

'We'll get this Nigel one,' Baldy says to me. 'Don't you worry.'

'What if he's not done anything to deserve it, though?' I ask. I'm thinking of the list, those carefully selected names, each one written for a reason, each one chosen as a result of their actions during the Troubles.

'He's done enough,' Baldy replies. Then he turns from me and leans over the bed. Lifting a pillow, he places it over Armstrong's opened mouth, stifling the screams. Then he rests the muzzle of the gun against the pillow. Screwing my eyes shut, I wait for the shot. It will not be a 'pop'. It will ring in my ears. It will echo and reverberate in my head. I will hear it for months. Right through until the next time.

~~James Bew~~

~~Roger Armstrong~~

Eddie Ross

Keith Sinclair

John Fyfield Senior

John Fyfield Junior

David Meters

Aaron Morrow

Raymond Patterson

Robert Marchetti.

Nigel.

Auntie Eileen says it's the stagnation of politics that made her want to get herself involved. The lack of movement, she says, makes all the hatred of it settle in a slick and then we're all just stood about waiting for the marching season to churn it up again. She has a turn of phrase about her, does Auntie Eileen. The only time anyone ever seems to do anything, she says, is when Bill and Hillary Clinton visit. Then everyone's on about 'political agreement' and 'disarmament' like they're needing to dust the place before the in-laws arrive, but between times they're all happy enough to live in their own filth, with the politicians only meeting to discuss wee passive-aggressive disputes like when the Shinners tried to put Easter lilies in the lobby at Stormont and the DUP called an emergency session because the lily was seen as being a Republican symbol.

So when the local council elections come about in June 2001, Eileen puts herself forward as the only female candidate in the Short Strand area. Wanting to make the voices of the housewives heard – *chained to the sink and tuned to the moon* – wanting to bring the day-to-day struggles to the attention of the politicians – *rooting through her mammy's purse, her fingers searching right down into the lining and coming up with lint and brown coins.* Door-to-door Eileen goes, week after week, like a jewellery saleswoman, and at the end of it all, when the results come in, she finds that she's got herself elected. A councillor for Sinn Féin, the progressive party with no links to armed Republicanism – *thieves and murderers, they were* – a woman at the frontline of politics, improving conditions on

276

the ground – *she knew all the arguments, she'd heard the spiel* – but with no power to stop the Loyalist pipe-bomb attacks, with no ability to move the process forward by anything more than millimetres and with no mandate to address the injustices of the past.

That's my job. I've no gift for words, no ability to organise in the community, but I've a means to see that justice is done. My own lack of movement, though, is down to the fact that I've had a stressful year since Armstrong. If truth be told, the fright of seeing Nigel in that field at Drumcree and the fear of seeing him again has set my nerves on edge and left me without comfort. I've moved onto autopilot, over the winter months and into the new year, without troubling myself with Baldy's list. The fear of being found out has left me dying my brittle hair brown every couple of days so as I can be sure that there's no ginger showing through at the roots. I split my time between the two-up, two-down bunker I share with Baldy and the memory trap I share with my daddy. Neither feels like home. I can't settle in one or the other, can't convince myself to stay for any length of time in the one place.

It comes as a relief, then, that as we approach marching season again we decide to set the wheels in motion for stiffing this former UVF bomb-maker we've been scouting – Eddie Ross. He's responsible for countless deaths, mainly as a result of pipe-bombs but with one or two larger devices to his name as well. 'Steady Eddie', as he was known back in the day, has retired from all but consultancy work on account of the anxiety attacks – *a tremble to his fingers* – he's suffered from since he narrowly escaped from the premature explosion of one of his own bombs back in the late Nineties. He's never been the same since, rumour has it, and the burns from the bomb have left it so that on the odd occasion that there's sunshine his face tans only in patches, and so that his beard grows in tufts like coarse grass. More than that, though, there was psychological damage done by the explosion. He won't set foot inside a bar, so the story goes, without carrying a bomb in a satchel with him. No trigger mechanism, timer or tilt switch to it, just the explosive itself. He's not wanting to use it, you see; he just wants to lengthen the odds – the idea being that statistically there's precious little likelihood of a bomber choosing that bar, but the likelihood of two bombers choosing the same bar on the same day is next to non-existent.

There's no problem with following Eddie into the bar. There's no issue, either, with catching his eye, or with offering to buy him a drink. He's eager for anything that's going. But I still hold off from approaching him, because I'm wanting to be sure about this bomb of his – wanting to be certain that there's no satchel of Semtex under his table, no bagstuff in underneath his jacket or pipe-bomb in his pocket. It's into July before I've seen him arrive and leave empty-handed at enough bars, into July before I'm convinced of the fact that the bomb in a satchel is just an urban legend, just a tale to keep the Loyalist women hanging off his arm and the Republican dissidents at arm's length.

'Mind if I join you there,' I ask, sauntering up to his table with a vodka-tonic in hand.

He looks up, smiles crookedly, then gestures to the seat opposite. His hair hangs lank and greasy down over his ears, his morning shave has missed a tuft of beard in underneath his chin and he's got a stain – looks like egg yolk – down the front of his shirt. You'd not take him home to meet your mother, but I'm not for fixating on those things.

'I've seen you before,' he says. 'You been following me?'

I take this in my stride. 'I've heard a fair bit about you.'

He nods, never thinking to question what it is that I've heard. He's a hero, so he is, in his own eyes and in the eyes of those he meets day to day. A defender of the community, loyal to the Crown and to Ulster. No longer a UVF man because of his nerves and because of the peace, but still enjoying all the benefits of the paramilitary lifestyle. All of the benefits and none of the risk.

He notices me watching his hand as he lifts his pint again; we're both aware of the tremor as he quickly puts the pint down and sets his hands on his lap, out of sight.

'I wanted to meet you and *shake* you by the hand,' I say, holding my hand out across the table and hoping that I've not put too much emphasis on the word shake. 'I'm Cassie, by the way.'

He takes my hand and then sets to grinning as I caress away at his wrist with the tips of my fingers. It's all it takes, that wee touch. With just that I've got him snared. There's not much needed to lead a man astray, whether they're the great and the good – Bill Clinton, for example – or just some small-time sectarian murderer like Eddie Ross here. All it takes is a gentle touch.

'Pleased to meet you, Cassie,' he says. 'Can I get you a fresh drink there?'

I smile, I nod. 'Vodka-tonic, please.'

'Slimline tonic?'

'It makes no odds.'

We sit there for the next hour or so, drinking and nattering away like we've the excitement of young love about us. Not a bit of it. He's excited because he thinks he'll be blowing his scoot shortly and I'm excited because I know how he'll actually end the night. It's all in the anticipation, so it is.

For the most part, I keep him to the sort of mindless chatter you'd expect from a drunken Prod: he goes on about this Ford Cortina he used to have back in the day – which he called Courtney, if you can believe that – he tells me about the summers he used to spend in Portrush, and he has a brief rant about the Polish immigrants arriving in Belfast and taking jobs from good Ulster folk. All the while he's sinking the pints and getting closer to the point when I can lead him away. Only once does he veer off course – only once. After his fourth pint, it is.

'We should have the right to protest too,' he says, pausing from his drinking and looking me direct in the eye. 'Our community has as much right to make our voices heard as them others do.'

I quickly nod. We've strayed into dangerous territory.

'They try to stop our parading,' he says, 'with their residents' associations and their consultation groups, but if we try to stop them – '

'You're right enough,' I interrupt. I know rightly that he's not talking about parading, but about primary school children walking to school in the mornings. He's talking about the Nationalist schoolgirls up at Holy Cross Primary in the Ardoyne who've to walk through a Unionist area to get to school, about the protests from the Unionist community over the past couple of months, with the Unionists blockading the road and stopping the wee girls from getting to school. More than that, he's defending the Unionists blockading the roads and stopping the schoolgirls.

'It's time our community stood up for itself,' he says.

'Is right,' I reply, although I've to grit my teeth. 'That's why it's as well that Trimble resigned as First Minister. He doesn't represent Unionism, that man, not true Unionism.'

He nods. 'Too cosy with those IRA murderers, so he is.'

'Is right.'

I draw breath. Reaching across the table, I try to steer the conversation back to where I want it to be. Back to the mundane. Back to the calm before the storm. 'Did you say you had leather seats in that Cortina? In Courtney?'

'Too fucking cosy with the IRA, the whole lot of them up at Stormont,' he mutters. As he says it, he catches on to what I've just asked. 'I did indeed,' he says. 'I stripped out and customised the whole of the interior, so I did.'

'I'd like to have seen that,' I say.

'It was a beautiful sight, I tell you.'

'How would you feel about seeing the interior of a taxi on the way back to mine?' I ask.

'I'd like to see that, most definitely.' He grins. As he drains his pint and sets the empty glass onto the table I notice that the shake to his hand has disappeared. It'll not take me long to get him nervous again, though. In next to no time he'll be so nervous he'll have even forgotten the name of his precious Ford Cortina.

The house Benny set aside for me is on Madrid Street, on the Nationalist side of the peaceline, in a row of terraced houses that Auntie Eileen probably called at in the run-up to the election. She'd not have got much joy from knocking at the door to this house, right enough: it both looks and smells as if it was abandoned long ago, but it's perfect for what I have in mind. There's even a scrawled piece of graffiti on the peaceline wall around the corner on Bryson Street that reads 'Courtney'. It must be meant: seren-fucking-dipity.

Eddie puts up no struggle as I tie his hands to the bedstead with his belt. He's happy enough to let me do it, so long as I keep fiddling with his cock between the tying of the knots. His eyes bulge when I tear at his egg-stained shirt and stuff a strip of the fabric into his mouth, but he's still up for going along with it because I've taken a firmer grip of him and I've pulled him on towards the vinegar strokes. It's only once I let him go, lift the tonic bottle and bring it down against the edge of the metal bed frame that he lets out a choked shout, but by that stage I've got him pinned down and secured so as he can only buck, kick, snort, gag and shake his head in protest.

'Eeeee – uuughh – hhh?' he asks.

Maybe he's not caught on, not fully, to what's expected of him. He's still got half an erection, his body still in that confused state where it knows something isn't right but it's been told to expect a ride. A rough ride, certainly, but a ride none the less. I answer the question, I clear up the confusion, by selecting a shard and dragging it down the length of his foreskin until the pink of it shows through.

'Arrhh – fff – arrhh!' he screams, as best he can.

'What's that?' I ask.

'Fff – ckck!'

'Nope,' I say. 'I can't understand you, love.'

281

Straddling his chest, I turn my attention to the tuft of bristled hair in underneath his chin. It's been annoying me the whole night, so it has. The sweat running down him is now collecting in it. With a flick of my wrist, I gouge it out of him so that he's clean-shaven and spurting blood. 'Eeeee – arrhh!' he says. Then another noise, a higher noise. In it I can make out a single word. It's muffled, but I can make it out.

'Are you asking me why?' I say.

He nods.

'Why…' I sit up, consider. I could tell him that it's because of all the people he's helped to kill over the years with his bombs, or it's because of all the hurt I've suffered, all the pain I've endured, or that it's because him and his kind think that it's OK to throw stones at schoolgirls as they walk to school. It's that they've not changed since back in the day, they still think they're a cut above, that they're the superior ones, that they're the ones in charge. I could tell him all of that, I could tell him more – *it wasn't the anger of being the hunted* – I'm not wanting to examine it too deeply, though – *but the thrill of being the hunter* – because I don't owe any explanation. I don't need to go explaining myself to a man who's never given a second thought to –

'Are you ready for me?' Baldy asks, stepping in at the doorway.

I nod, then push myself off Eddie. The struggling's gotten worse at the sight of Baldy. It always does. They always seem to think that I'll have a change of heart, that I'll let some deep-seated maternal instinct take over, that I'll tend to the bleeding, nurse their wounds. They've always some hope about them whenever it's just me. But at the sight of a man they go into their death throes. Their vinegar strokes. At the sight of Baldy, they know it's over.

'Tommy Mooney. Frankie McGahern. Jimmy Morse…' Baldy moves towards the bed, reading from a handwritten list. 'Angela McIlmurray. Stevey Kelly…' A list of the victims of Eddie Ross. 'Paddy McGinn.'

'Mnmmm – aeeee – mmm.' Eddie's questions become moans, become whimpers. He's certainly shaking now. He's convulsing, from top to toe, from the bloody flesh at his chin down to the bloody flesh of his cock.

'Because of the list,' I answer him, stepping away, although I'm not too sure which list it is I'm meaning, which list it is I'm thinking of. 'Because of the fucking list.'

~~James Bew~~

~~Roger Armstrong~~

~~Eddie Ross~~

Keith Sinclair

John Fyfield Senior

John Fyfield Junior

David Meters

Aaron Morrow

Raymond Patterson

Robert Marchetti.

Nigel.

As it's the height of summer, it only takes a matter of days for Eddie to be sniffed out. The neighbours, as they did with Armstrong, get over their dislike of the police for long enough to phone through and complain about the fearful stench and, as they did down in Portadown, the peelers land up and do the whole bit with the fingerprinting and working out the trajectory of the bullets and all of that there. A brief statement is released to the press, saying that the death appears to be the result of a Loyalist dispute but that no group is claiming responsibility and, as in Portadown, there's precious few column inches devoted to it in the papers. Someone who deserved a bullet got a bullet, they say, or as good as. It's quickly yesterday's news – used to wrap the fish and chips.

And they're right. There's nothing unique about the killing of Eddie or of Armstrong; they're just two deaths to add to the toll of the strained peace. Whether they were shot by Loyalist or Republican dissidents doesn't really signify, nor does the reasoning behind it – so long as it doesn't threaten the series of uneasy truces that has the province balanced on a knife edge. No one's for caring about them; there's precious few tears to be shed. And that's what we're looking for – *no loose ends* – it's what we're wanting.

All the same, I can't help feeling a bit let down. After all, nobody's talking about the brunette seen out drinking with both men; not one of them has seen the trend – *the broken and jagged neck of a miniature tonic bottle* – that stretches back to 1994 and Billy. Fair enough, the peelers are busy with the changing of the guard, from the Royal Ulster Constabulary to the more neutral-sounding Police Service of Northern Ireland, and the journalists spend that much of the day trying to figure out what in fuck the politicians up at Stormont are at that they can't be expected to piece it all together. But, all the same –

Still, as I say, it suits us down to the ground. And I've got enough to be getting on with in any case, because myself and Becky manage to get ourselves a lease on a wee shop just off the Lisburn Road. It's not much, just a room between a clothes boutique and a coffee shop that's so narrow that I can stand in the centre of it, stretch out and touch both side walls with the tips of my fingers – but it's good enough for what we need. Within a couple of weeks we've got a new coat of paint on the walls, and we've set up a work table for Becky in the back and a window display for to catch the eye of the passing trade. Then, on a bright winter's morning, we open our doors for the first time. Gilt Edge Jewellery, we call it. Gilt Edge.

I've not a lot of time to enjoy the feeling of being a small-business owner, though, because Baldy's wanting to strike while the iron's hot and move on to the next name on the list: Keith Sinclair. There's not much scouting needed: he stands out from the crowd rightly, on account of the brass-topped cane he uses and the tattoos that cover every available inch of skin. There's ink spiralled up his neck and curving up onto his bald head and he's got sleeve tattoos showing beneath the rolled-up cuffs of his tracksuit jacket. I follow him half-heartedly from place to place, between visits to the bank and to the tax man and the like, on Gilt Edge business, noting that he drags his right leg behind him slightly as he leans on his cane. I lose him at one point, as I trail him from the supermarket back to his house off the Crumlin Road, and then near run into him as he comes unexpectedly out of a newsagent. We do that awkward dance that people do when you both step one way, then both step the other – a businesswoman and a tattooed paramilitary doing a two-step on the street – and then we share a smile and walk in opposite directions.

'Did he see you?' Baldy asks.

'Of course he saw me.'

'But you didn't talk to him.'

I shake my head.

'So…' Baldy pauses. 'Would he recognise you if he saw you again?'

I shrug. 'He might do.'

'We'll need to change it up a bit, then.'

By the end of November we're ready for him. We send him a letter, on headed notepaper, that says that we're researchers from a television production company looking to put together a documentary on forgiveness and reconciliation in Northern Ireland. You know the type of programme, where the killer sits on one side of the table and the relative of the victim sits on the other and they're asked to talk through their feelings – they did a rack of them in South Africa after apartheid. Except, with us, there's no programme and no hope of forgiveness for Keith Sinclair. He's being summoned for execution.

I give him a call about a week after the letter's sent, all businesslike – *the polite and polished voice* – and ask if he's had a chance to consider our proposal. Would there be payment, he wants to know. I consider – *she slipped into her saleswoman voice easily; it came naturally enough* – and name a figure that's just slightly more than the amount we pay, per month, for the lease on the shop. In the pause that follows I wonder whether I shouldn't have offered more. After all, he isn't going to be seeing a penny of it in any case.

'Add an extra hundred and I'll do it,' he says, thinking he's got a hand to play.

'Fifty,' I say. 'And we'll send a taxi to collect you on the day itself.'

'OK,' he says. 'Deal.'

'Excellent – see you then,' I say, before setting down the payphone and smiling across at Baldy. Not only have I saved us fifty (fictional) quid, but I've also worked out a way of convincing him to get into Baldy's taxi voluntarily.

Benny outdoes himself in setting up for this one. I'm thinking that he must've been in the theatrical way in a past life, because he finds this isolated country house out near Lough Neagh and he sets the stage perfectly by taking the overgrown estate agent's signs from the garden and the plywood from the windows, by furnishing one of the downstairs rooms with a plain wooden table, two chairs and a spotlight and by adding this tray of tea and coffee off to the side. The devil's in the detail and the room certainly looks the part, only without the cameras or any of that there television equipment.

With everything in place, we drive up in the taxi and park round at the back of the house. I look every inch the television researcher, dressed in a pleated black blouse and grey pinstripe miniskirt. Sinclair doesn't recognise me from the day outside the newsagent, but that might be because his eyes, on the drive over, never seem to leave my legs. I tell him that we'll have an off-camera production meeting first, then a break for lunch while the camera crew set up, before we move on to the actual filming in the afternoon. He'll not be meeting the relative of one of his victims, I say, but a 'community representative' who wants to express 'the current hue and timbre of community feeling'. I'm thinking that I may have missed my calling in never getting into acting.

'How many people would you say you killed during the conflict, Mr Sinclair?' I ask him, once we're seated on either side of the table. The spotlight, running off a generator, shines down on us and we both have a cup of tea set in front of us by Baldy.

'Directly?' Sinclair asks.

'What do you mean by that?'

'Well…' He looks down at his hands, clasped on the table in front of himself. The tattoos stretch down over his wrists. On his right hand there's even writing inked across the knuckles.

I can't make it out from where I'm sitting, though. 'I've been involved in the planning of quite a few operations, you know, or been there without actually taking part.'

'OK,' I say. 'How many killings have you directly been involved with?'

'Three,' he says. 'There's three that I've actually pulled the trigger on.'

'Three,' I say, pausing to shuffle my notes on the table in front of me. There's fuck-all written on them; it's all scrap paper from Gilt Edge, with the exception of a handwritten list from Baldy, on the top. 'Would Gerard McCracken be one of those? Does the name mean anything to you?'

'It does.' He looks down at his knuckles, as if consulting his own notes. 'He was a young IRA man I shot and killed back in '88.'

'Actually,' I say, 'there's no evidence that he was an IRA man, Mr Sinclair. He was a bricklayer and a GAA coach, but nothing else.'

I pause, gather myself. Gerard McCracken was shot at a roundabout on the outskirts of Belfast as he waited for a lift in to work.

'There's nothing to indicate that he was involved, in any way, with the IRA.'

'I was told he was, love.'

'Is that right?' I say, a bit of anger creeping into my voice. 'And who told you that, then?'

He looks up. 'I forget,' he says. 'But I was told that.'

'And do you have any regrets about killing him?'

He stays silent, but his stare has turned hostile. So has mine.

'Please answer the question,' I say. 'Given that there's no evidence that he was an IRA man, do you regret shooting and killing Gerard McCracken?'

'He was an IRA man,' he replies, softly.

'And what about Aidan Judge?' I ask him. 'Was he in the IRA as well?'

Aidan Judge was a seventeen-year-old from the Ardoyne who'd crossed over into Unionist territory one night to paint over a mural of King Billy and never made it back. This was in the mid-Eighties. His mother killed herself the year after, unable to live with the grief of it.

'He wasn't one of mine,' Sinclair says. 'Although I knew about it.'

'And Francesca Burns?'

'That was a crying shame, right enough,' he says, looking down at the table. There's no admission of guilt, though, no word on how a nine-year-old out walking her doll in its pram was caught in the crossfire.

I decide to try a different line of questioning. 'Is there hatred in you?' I ask. 'Is that it?'

He looks up. 'What sort of a question is that?'

'I'm only trying to understand,' I say.

There's a wee shake of the head from Sinclair and he takes a slurp of his tea. As he does, Baldy steps across to me and whispers in my ear. 'What's the point of all this?' he asks. I look up at him: his grey-streaked hair is slicked back from his drawn face. He looks old, so he does. He's wanting to do it as he's always done it, as we've always done it. Force of habit. For some reason, though, I'm not wanting that. I'm wanting actual answers.

'Why did you join the UVF, Mr Sinclair?' I ask.

Before we arrived here – during the months of planning, the weeks of preparation, the days of nervous anticipation, the polite conversation with Sinclair on the phone, even on the drive over itself – I'd been thinking that this job would follow the same course as the others. I'd even a notion, at the start of the day, that I'd like to trace the lines of his sleeve tattoos with a shard of glass – *inch-wide gashes on his wrists*.

'It was a case of protecting my community,' Sinclair says. 'It was a case of creating a sense of law and order, of right and wrong. Of saying to those IRA men that they couldn't come into our areas and – '

'So you killed to stop the killing, is that it?' I interrupt.

'You could say that,' he says. 'You could say that we terrorised the terrorists. We made the wee grannies up the Falls realise that all the IRA were doing was bringing violence to their own streets.'

'But you've not answered the original question. Is there hatred in you?'

'Not hatred,' he says, considering. 'Are you asking what it is that makes a paramilitary, is that it?'

I shrug. I nod. The intention had been to move from the sleeve tattoos to the tattoo that curved up his neck and onto his head, just grazing the outline of it so as to open it to the air, so that he could watch the blood dripping to the floor – *staring eyes following the flow.*

'I think…' he says, 'I think you need to see no other alternative. I think you need to view the person you're targeting as less than human. I think you need others along with you for the ride, others who won't let you back out.'

'You mean, people who'd kill you if you didn't go through with it?'

'Others who'd think less of you, at least.' He leans forward, suddenly intent on getting his point across, intent on shifting the blame, shifting the responsibility. 'Peer pressure. Law of the playground. It's all about cliques. The whole thing. The young bucks are always brought along on the kills, so as they get initiated. You're not going to tell teacher if there's blood on your hands too, you know.'

'But still,' I say. 'In the moment of killing, at least, you're alone, aren't you?'

'Maybe so.' He drains his tea and the cup rattles on the saucer as he sets it down. 'But by the time it's got to the stage of pulling the trigger it's usually an act of mercy. It's usually just a case of letting the poor bastard die. It's a mercy.'

Once all the tattoos had been fringed in red, once his body was carved open and exposed to the spotlight, it was then that I was going to read to him from the list of victims. Letting him

292

bleed out – *reaching out to touch his cold skin* – to the sound of the names of those he'd killed.

'Do you think the conflict is over?' I ask. It sounds abrupt in the echoing room.

'I think it's complicated,' he says, shaking his head. 'I think it's changed. It's become more underground, more sly. Have you heard what Seamus Heaney said after the '94 IRA ceasefire?'

'No,' I say, trying to hide my surprise. Maybe he's done a degree in jail, or taken to reading poetry to take the edge off his instincts. At least he's not quoting the Bible, I'd slit his throat for him here and now if he took to quoting the Bible. 'What did he say?' I ask.

'He says that we've passed from the atrocious to the messy.' He pauses for effect. 'But that the messy is a perfectly OK place to live.'

'Can you move on from the atrocious, but?' I ask. 'Is there not a need to address it?'

Sinclair shrugs. 'Maybe we are addressing it. Folk are making an effort to understand, an effort to reconcile. I mean look at this here, today – '

'Let me stop you there,' I say.

I'd decided that, for this one, there'd be no bullet. I wanted the peelers to see the slash wounds so as they wouldn't dismiss it as another Loyalist feud; I wanted the journalists to write about the fragments of glass found in the congealed blood, so as they would speculate about whether this death, among all the others, was personal. I wanted there to be enough blood on the uneven concrete floor that they'd go searching through the rest of the house, the grounds even, looking for other bodies.

It's not about that, though. It's about redressing the balance.

'It's simple,' I say to Sinclair. 'It's always been simple.'

'What do you mean by that?' he asks.

'Baldy,' I say, rising from my seat. 'Do it your way.'

The chair across from me clatters to the ground as Sinclair catches on, too late, to what's about to happen. There's nowhere for him to run, though. Nowhere. I close my eyes. *It's simple.* The shot is fired. *It's always been simple.* A second shot follows in the echoes of the first. *It's a mercy.*

'Nice talking with you,' I say to Sinclair, to no one.

~~James Bew~~

~~Roger Armstrong~~

~~Eddie Ross~~

~~Keith Sinclair~~

John Fyfield Senior

John Fyfield Junior

David Meters

Aaron Morrow

Raymond Patterson

Robert Marchetti.

Nigel.

In May 2002 I come close to losing another member of my family. My mammy tries to hang herself with the cord from her dressing gown. It snaps under her weight and she lies on the floor of the nursing home, trying to throttle herself with the frayed ends of it, until a nurse comes along and quietens her. My daddy is called, but he arrives with that much of a skinful that he can't even sign the forms to re-admit her to the hospital. I'm the second emergency contact. I get a lift to the hospital in Ciáran's white van. He's an electrician's apprentice these days, working during the day and attending the college at night.

'Makes you think, doesn't it?' he asks me, eyes on the road, as we drive down Great Victoria Street. I've not a notion what it is he's referring to – for all I know he could be talking about the drunken millie in the short-skirt spilling her guts into a bin by the side of Robinson's Bar, or the open-top bus that's stopped outside the Europa Hotel so as the tour guide can give out that tired old line about it being the most-bombed hotel in Europe.

'What does?' I ask.

'Your mammy…' He swallows. 'Like, it must bring back memories…'

I nod. I stare at him.

'This sort of thing can make you re-evaluate,' he says. 'Can make you see what's important.'

'Re-eval-u-ate,' I say, spacing out the syllables.

'I know about you and Baldy,' he stumbles on. 'I know about what you do together.'

'Is that right?'

He darts a glance across at me. 'Well?'

'Well, what?'

'Have you nothing to say about it? Are you not going to deny it, even?'

'No point, is there? If you know, then you know,' I say, shrugging. If truth be told, I'm not sure if he's talking about us fucking each other, or if this is about us working our way through our list. 'After all,' I say, 'you introduced us to one another, so – '

'Not to do this, though,' he says.

'To do what, then?' I turn on him, my eyes burning. 'What were you expecting? Were you thinking I'd sew name-tags onto his camouflage jacket for him, that I'd knit him and his friends balaclavas, is that it?'

He goes quiet.

'Well?' I demand.

'At the time,' he says, his words near scraping the enamel from his clenched teeth, 'at the time I knew you'd be involved. Back then. But times have changed. The Provos are decommissioning.'

'Your point being?' I say.

'That you're out there on your own now, just you.'

'I'll not be lonely, Ciáran, don't you worry.'

He shakes his head, steals another glance at me. 'I'll never know what happened to the nice wee girl that used to live along the street.'

'She grew up, love. You should do the same.'

After that, we don't speak. If I'd to guess, I'd say that he's thinking of something more to say, something that'll break both tension and silence. For my part, I've more important things to be thinking of than Ciáran Gilday and his new-found conscience. I've the Fyfield family to be planning for – father and son.

John Senior was in the B-Specials back in the Sixties, one of those volunteer policemen who stood back for the worst of

297

the violence against the Catholics and then stepped forward to beat down the reaction to it. On its own, his membership of the B men wouldn't have been enough to get him on the list. Even talk of his links with the burning of Bombay Street wouldn't have done for him, if only he'd left it there. As it was, though, he went on to join the Ulster Defence Regiment in the Seventies and then he had a son, John Junior. His only child. It's the son that gets them both on the list, because it's the son who arranged, in the late Eighties, for the keys to the UDR barracks to fall into the hands of the paramilitaries. The Loyalists had themselves a fine old time in the armoury, kitting themselves out with enough rifles and ammunition to take the first steps towards ethnic cleansing. Then they locked the door behind themselves, using John Senior's key. Collusion, pure and simple. One red hand washes the other and they both come up clean.

It only takes us a week or so to scout the two of them out, although I manage to get pigeon shit over my hands in the process. The shit is the result of staking out the father's house up in Cregagh. He's a retired widower and a pigeon fancier, keeps a coop of them in his front garden and spends his days tending to them and singing to them in a voice – *he hadn't a note* – that sets the lot of them to beating their wings and letting out these wee moaning coos that sound like they're building up to a full-blooded scream. Because he never really leaves the house, we'll need to work out a way of getting to him without him sending an SOS off by carrier pigeon, but we decide to leave that until the day itself. It's safer to sort the son out first, since he's the one that's more likely to cause us a problem.

John Junior's a mountain of a man, so he is, a bouncer at a pub up in Ballysillan with a neck near as wide as his shoulders and with thick, knotted muscles in his arms. He's one to be wary of, definitely. I've no intention of letting him get further than a fumbling with me, because I know rightly that he'd snap me in two if we tried anything more. I'll have a fair task on my hands, though, because he seems to fancy himself as a bit of a gangster. You know the sort: hair shaved up the sides but spiked on the top, thick neck made even thicker by the kind of cheap gold that gives a rash, ear studded with a fake diamond that cost even less than the necklace, and pockets filled with wee white pills that he sells – on a 'buy one or you're not getting in' basis – to the punters as they queue up outside the pub.

'What time do you get off, then, love?' I ask him, as I leave the pub at the end of the night. I'm wearing a fake leopardskin blouse and black mini-skirt combination, which passes for classy in these parts, and I've a zebra-print scarf tied around my neck to clash with the blouse.

'Just waiting for everyone to go home, then I'll do the same,' he says.

'I wanted to thank you for the pill earlier,' I say, trailing a hand up onto his arm.

I never took the pill. I'm not sold on the idea of drugs of any sort, recreational or otherwise – *hold onto her nose and wait for her mouth to open so as the pills could be popped in* – so I flushed the white one John Junior gave me down the toilet when I went into the ladies', with a miniature tonic bottle, to arm myself.

'You're more than welcome, love.' He grins.

'The name's Cassie.'

'I'm John,' he says, reaching out a hand. His grip is as firm as you'd expect, but with a slip of sweat to it as well. 'Would you like to go on somewhere else, maybe, and have a drink?' he asks.

'That would be nice, John,' I say. 'Although I'm not much of a one for clubs, if I'm honest, so could we maybe just go for a drink up at mine instead?'

He mumbles something about seeing if he can get away early, asks me to stay where I am, and retreats into the pub to beg the other doorman to cover for him so as he can go ahead and get his hole. Then he's back out with me.

'Is it far?' he asks. 'Your place.'

'Not too far,' I say, smiling. 'But let's take a taxi in any case.'

When we get to the house up in Cliftonville, set aside for the Fyfield family, I go inside with John Junior and Baldy sits outside in the idling taxi. Taking off the scarf, I look around for something to secure him to, a fixture or a fitting, but there's nothing, so I settle for using it as a blindfold instead. After five minutes of stubby-fingered groping from Fyfield, Baldy and I switch places and I sit in the driver's seat of the cab whilst Baldy sees to Junior. He takes a knife and a nailgun in with him, as well as his usual shooter, because he's wanting to do it as silently as possible tonight so as we can return to the same house tomorrow with the father.

There's a danger to it, in that Fyfield Junior, realising what's happening, could easily take exception to Baldy securing his wrists with a cable tie or to the fitting of the home-made gag – formed of a ballcock from a toilet cistern and some medical tape – and, if he were to take the view that it was worth the risk of getting a bullet, he could blindly overpower Baldy and we could all find ourselves in a shitstorm of a predicament. I've faith that it won't happen that way, though, because Baldy knows how to handle himself, knows how to use the other man's fear to his advantage. Rumour has it that he was in the INLA nutting squad, with responsibility for interrogating touts, before we struck out on our own. He's an experienced man, so he is, so I can't be worrying about it. Besides, I've got the engine running so that if the worst comes to the worst I can still make a getaway.

In the meantime, I get myself a scrap of paper and a pen from my handbag and set to working out whether I can afford to go ahead and hire a private nurse for Cathy. The shop is doing well enough and is turning a tidy profit, but it still seems that I've barely enough to be getting a nurse's uniform let alone the nurse to put inside it. I do the maths again, knowing it was never my strong suit, knowing that I've not so much as looked at a maths problem for years – *the syllabus was formed from the pages where she'd been given a neat line of ticks –* trying to find a way to make it work, desperately wanting to make it work.

That's surely the solution: to get Cathy back into her own house and to have her looked after. That's the solution right enough, but I can't see a way of affording it without accepting some help – *lifted a corner of the bag and saw a thick roll of notes –* or letting social services come around the house – *she's a Prod and she works for the Brits and she's from East Belfast –* to pry into every aspect of our life. Every aspect of my life.

'You drive,' Baldy says, as he opens the door and slides into the passenger seat.

'I can't,' I say. 'I never got my licence.'

'How were you going to get away if it all went tits-up, then?' he asks, staring at me.

'I know where the accelerator is. And I know what a steering wheel looks like, but I'm not legally allowed to drive.' I stare back at him. 'And, in the state you're in, I wouldn't think you'd want us to be stopped by the peelers.'

He has a spatter of blood up and over his glasses and a long streak of it over his forehead. His left eye is beginning to close over and he has deep-red fingermarks along the side of his neck that are already turning to bruising. He sees me examining him.

'I tried to slit his throat,' he says. 'But he put up a struggle. In the end I had to put a nail or two in him as well.'

'He's dead, though?'

He nods. 'Get in the back,' he says. 'And I'll drive.'

'Baldy?' I say.

He looks up at me. 'What?'

'Are you alright?'

'I'll be grand,' he says, sliding across to the driver's side.

By the next day, though, Baldy's eye has completely closed over and he's a series of bruises, like vampire bites, all along his neck. It's hard to believe that he won the fight, hard to believe that the other guy looks worse than he does. He stays in the taxi while I go up to the door of Fyfield Senior's house. I'm wearing a pinstripe trouser suit and carrying a clipboard.

'Can I help you?' Fyfield says, opening the door. He's not a small man, but age has bowed his back so as he appears shrivelled. He has yellowing fingertips, stained teeth and, up close, his eyes seem to have a nicotine tint to them as well. A cigarette dangles from his bottom lip, moving as he talks.

'Morning, love. I'm from the council,' I say, flashing Baldy's taxi licence at him. 'I'm here about your pigeons.'

'What about them?'

'We've had complaints, I'm afraid, and…' I pause. 'Have you a permit for them, no?'

'I never knew you needed one.'

'You do.' I smile sympathetically, I look down at my clipboard. 'If you don't get one in the next five working days then we'll need to remove the birds.'

'Are you serious?'

He looks panicked at that, wide-eyed.

'I'll tell you what I'll do, though.' I look back at the taxi. 'I'm going back to the office just now, and I've some forms there. So, if you're not busy, then you can come along and I'll help you fill in the forms so as we can get it all sorted this morning.'

'That'd be good now, thanks,' he says, throwing his cigarette down to smoulder in the flowerbed and lifting a flat cap from a peg behind the door. As he leaves the house and follows me down the drive I note that he doesn't even take the trouble to lock up. Some folk are just too trusting.

The drive to Cliftonville is taken up by Fyfield fidgeting his fingers over one another and me quietly fretting about whether he'll come inside once we get there. As it is, though, he unquestioningly follows me up to the door and through to the living room. He's thinking about his pigeons and nothing else. It's only when he catches sight of what's lying in the living room that he lets out a wee cooing moan of protest; it's only when he sees his son splayed out across the carpet that he looks about himself. I should be moving in to quieten him, I know that, I should be stepping across and putting a hand over his mouth, but it's the first time I've seen Junior as well. In this state, I mean.

He seems to be floating in a lake of his own blood, blood which has worked its way into the grain of the wooden floorboards, blood which has saturated the scarf so as the pattern of it is no longer visible, blood which is starting to harden at the edges, but which still has a sheen to it. Most of it will have come from the gash across his throat, spilt out when the ragged cartilage of it yawned away from his lolling head, when the neck twisted away from the body so as the wound opened further. But there's also a fair amount crusted around the nails – the flathead nails – that bristle from his face. They've all gone in to different depths: there's one above the eyebrow that's barely in beyond the tip and another at the bridge of the nose that's gone in at an angle, but there's also a cluster of them beneath his cheekbone and around his mouth that have gone all the way in. And his eye. There's one that's embedded itself in his right eye, through the fabric of the scarf. The head of it sticks out where the pupil should be, staring sightlessly across at the far wall.

It's too much for the boy's father. He sinks to the ground and sets to keening and pulling at his clothes, shutting his eyes against the sight of his son lying there brutally murdered, his eyes reddening and his skin greying from the effort of not looking. He lets out a thin, inhuman scream that has no breath behind it but which keeps rising in any case, cracking and breaking at its highest pitch.

I can't watch. This was what we wanted, what we imagined would happen when we decided to take care of the son first and then show the remains to the father. This was the punishment. But it's pitiful to see someone fall to pieces in front of your eyes, to see the raw pain of it. He's an old man, is all I can think. He's an old man.

Without a word of comfort, of explanation, I turn and leave the room. I leave the house. I meet Baldy coming up the path, with his gun held loose and swinging by his side. I wrench it from him, turn, and come back inside. I stand over Fyfield Senior then, waiting for him to open his eyes, wanting him to focus on me, not on his son, wanting him to know that the pain is ending – wanting him to have that last thought. He opens his eyes at the sound of the gun being cocked. I pull the trigger, stumbling backwards from the kick of it. Trembling, I regain my balance, and then I fire again. To make sure.

~~James Bew~~

~~Roger Armstrong~~

~~Eddie Ross~~

~~Keith Sinclair~~

~~John Fyfield Senior~~

~~John Fyfield Junior~~

David Meters

Aaron Morrow

Raymond Patterson

Robert Marchetti.

Nigel.

'You're getting older now; it's time to be thinking of the future,' he says.

'Jesus, but you're a charmer, Ciárán Gilday,' I say, trying to be breezy about it, trying not to let the events of the night show, trying to keep the crack from my voice and the shudder from my shoulders.

'Come on, now, you know what I'm saying.' We're in the concrete playground, seated side by side on the swings, just like old times. 'You've sowed your wild oats,' he says. 'You've gotten it out of your system – time to leave it be and move on.'

'Wild oats?' I say, rocking the swing back with my heels. 'I'm fairly certain that it's only a man can be doing that, love. I've no oats to be sowing.' I rock forward again, serious now. 'But it's not a case of getting it out of my system. I'm not one of those ones who riots on their school holidays, or on the weekends if the sun's shining and the boys give me the nod.'

Like you, I want to say. *As the crowd ebbed and flowed, she caught sight of Ciárán beside her. He was clinging grimly to her hand, his jaw clenched and his wiry frame set against the crushing crowd. As their eyes met, he winked at her, slowly.*

'Remember you used to say to me that without any reasoning behind it, without it being part of a wider struggle, it's all just sectarian,' he says. 'And it's not about a united Ireland, for you, is it? It's not about civil rights or prisoners' rights or – '

'Right enough,' I say. 'It's not. It's about right and wrong.' I don't want to talk to him about it. I don't want to talk about it, full stop. There's nothing to be said. Not after tonight.

Ciáran had shouted out to me from the swings when Baldy dropped me off in the taxi, calling out for me to come across and join him, wanting to talk it through. He'd been sitting there waiting for me, I was certain – *bleakly wondering when it was that a chill turned into frostbite* – for all the time that I was off up in Glengormley. When he called out, I thought about ignoring him, carrying on into the house without taking heed of him. Maybe in the normal course of things I'd have ignored him, maybe I'd not have wandered over to where he sat, but I've Andrea to be thinking of. Andrea – the home help the social are paying for – is in the house with my mammy and daddy and I'm not wanting to speak with her with the smell of Meters still on me, wearing borrowed clothes and fretting about there being blood under my fingernails. With Ciáran it doesn't matter so much, he'd never tout. But Andrea, that's a different matter – *you know that if you tell them the time of day they're liable to take the watch from your wrist* – you can never be too careful with the likes of Andrea.

'You're in your late twenties,' Ciáran says.

'I am indeed,' I say. I pause, I think. The rusted chains of the swing creak as I sway backwards and forwards. Damien would be twenty-three. I mark his birthdays as they pass – I keep count – but I never mark my own. 'What of it?' I say.

'Is it not time you were leaving all this behind?'

'It's what everyone says, isn't it?' I turn on Ciáran. 'That you should move on, that it's in the past. Trimble's throwing his toys out of the pram up at Stormont because he thinks the IRA are spying on him, but he should set that aside for the greater good, forget about all those times that the 'RA were watching others so as they could stiff them. And McGuinness thinks the Brits are setting them up, that they'll turn on Sinn Féin as soon as the guns are gone, but he should forget about all the times that the Brits have sold them down the river before, all the times they made agreements then changed the terms – '

'Everyone has to make compromises for it to work,' Ciáran says.

'Everyone has to forget, you mean.'

'Maybe, aye.'

'I don't, though,' I say. 'I don't have to make compromises. I don't have to take part in this collective forgetting. Because that's what it is, Ciáran. It's not a peace process, it's a collective forgetting. If you forget about those three people killed in that bomb, then we'll forget about those five you shot in cold blood. And, just to sweeten the deal, we'll let the man who set the bomb out of the jail early so as he can talk to the rest of the community about setting aside arms and learning to forget. Maybe we can all read the Bible together, or some poetry – '

'There's bitterness on all sides, but – '

'I don't need to forget.'

'No one's saying you need to forget. It's just that you don't need to keep it going.'

'I'm doing nothing other than calling folk to account.'

'Is that right?'

'It's justice, so it is.'

He shakes his head. 'Baldy – Sean – was always a bit of a head case, was always one of those boys that was kept on a tight leash because you never knew when he'd bark and when he'd bite. But you – '

'Is that so, Ciáran? Is Baldy an animal now, is he? Not so long ago he was your hero; now he's not even human.'

He shrugs. 'Look what he's made you do.'

'He's not made me do anything I've not wanted to.'

Ciáran looks away.

'And what about me?' I ask. 'Am I human?'

Earlier that night, me and Baldy drove slowly through Glengormley. I'd never been there before. It's a quiet wee town, but with enough in the way of Loyalist murals and flags so as you know the flavour of the place. David Meters is a mechanic, self-employed. Goes by the nickname of Yards – the idea being that he's not advanced enough, in the head, to be thought of by his metric surname. He works late in his garage, night after night. Back in the day, he let others work late in his garage too.

Night after night. They used tyre-irons, they used drills, they used compressed air. They had their victims in the garage for hours at a time. They kept the radio on loud to drown out the screams, and they kept the pressure washer running so as they could wash away the blood.

We lift Yards as he's locking up. A single blow to the back of his head with a hammer. It's Baldy that does it; I don't trust myself to hit him hard enough to crumple him to his knees, to leave him splayed across the concrete so as he twitches only for a second before he lies still.

There's the tackiness of blood to my fingers after we carry him to the taxi, but the hammer's only split his head open enough to matt his greying hair, only enough to leave a wee slick on the concrete by the garage door – *darker and with a swirl of colour at its centre* – that will, at a glance, pass for oil.

We drive down the Antrim Road towards Belfast, with me and the unconscious Meters in the back and Baldy driving. I'm feared that Yards'll waken before we get to the address we're taking him to, that he'll jolt himself up and grasp hold of me, that the two of us will be wrestling away in the back and that he'll have me overpowered before Baldy can pull over and help me. As insurance, I've the gun held out in front of me – at arm's length – pointed at Yards lying there on the floor, but Baldy's loath to let me pull the trigger. He's not wanting to leave a bullet-hole in the underneath of his taxi, not wanting the risk of it hitting the engine or bouncing up and off something and pinging around the inside like pinball. He's not wanting the risk of the shot being heard when we're travelling down a main artery road back into the city, with his licence plate on full show and CCTV pictures to be trawled through. If the worst comes to the worst and Yards wakens, he's wanting me to use a shard of broken glass. He's saying that I've used it before, that this is no different, that it's just a case of setting the edge against the throat and dragging it across. And I hear him. I know what it is he's saying, I can see the sense in it, but I'm still shaking my head. 'No,' I'm saying. 'I can't.'

I put the gun down, pick up the hammer from the seat and spin the handle of it against the palm of my hand – head, claw, head, claw – then lean down over Meters, anxiously inspecting the flare to his nostrils. His eyes open. I shut mine, scream out, and bring my arm down. I let out another yelp as the hammer hits. Then I lift my arm again. And again. The taxi swerves as Baldy calls out, but I can't hear him. Not really. I raise my arm again. Meters is screaming fit to tear my eardrums, so I bring my arm down again, and again, wanting the screech of it to stop. Again. There's a fearful stench coming up off him – shit and piss and the still-sharp smell of oil and then, beneath all that, a metallic smell that catches at the back of my throat. Again. The hammer connects with something each time, there's always a crunch or a crack to it, but I'm not able to open my eyes to see which part of him it is that I'm hitting. All I know is that I'm hitting something, I'm hitting something and I need to keep hitting something if the noise is to stop. Hot tears bubble and burn at my closed eyelids and – suddenly, mercifully – I'm aware that I'm the only one making noise. A throaty cry is coming out of me, a guttural battle-call from somewhere deep inside, but apart from that it's all silence. The engine has stopped; the screams of Meters have stopped. Everything has stopped.

I open my eyes as Baldy lifts the hammer from my hand. He places a hand over my mouth, tightening his grip until I quieten. I try not to notice that the head of the hammer is clean, that it's the claw that's dripping with blood. With blood and more.

'Let's get you cleaned up,' Baldy says. His voice comes from miles away – *somewhere near-distant* – it seems to echo and fade. He draws me to him, keeping my face averted from what lies on the floor of the taxi. My body heaves, convulses. He sets his weight against me, pins me back against the seat of the taxi. He needs to call out to me, to shout to make himself heard. He's telling me that it's over, that I've not to think about it, that it's done.

'There's a safe house we can go to down near New Lodge,' he says to me. 'I'll take you there and you can get a bath and a change of clothes, then I'll take you home, OK?'

I nod. 'Sean?'

'What?'

'Can you smell that?' I ask, sniffing at the air.

'We'll get that cleaned away and all,' he says.

'Good,' I say, keeping my gaze on the darkness outside.

Baldy doesn't drive much further before we stop again. He doesn't go far. He pulls in near the zoo, down a side-street near Drumnadrough. I stare out of the rain-spattered back window as he drags the body out from the back of the taxi, feet first, and leaves it in the weeds by the side of the road. Fly-tipping.

As we move off down the road, there seems to be one set of headlights behind us that speeds up when we speed up, that slows down when we slow down, that turns when we turn. All the way to New Lodge it stays close behind. I open my mouth to ask Baldy if he's noticed. After what's just happened, though, and with the smell of it still in my nostrils, I can't be thinking about whether the car behind is tailing us. And Baldy hasn't noticed; he's focused on the road in front. So I sit there and I gulp in the foetid air and I stop myself from speculating about who could be in the car behind, about why they've not stopped to see to Yards, about why they've not pulled us over or drawn level so as they can fire shots at us from alongside. I'm not for caring who it is or what they'll do – *she knew what happened*. There's no sense in panicking – *legs broken, bones jutting and blood pooling* – in losing my head with worrying about where this'll all end – *lying in a ditch somewhere* – with being feared of pain or of death – *in some back alley*. No sense in that at all. Instead I sit back in the seat, close my eyes, and wait for the taxi to take me home. To my childhood home – not the two-up, two-down bunker – so as I can rest.

'Ciáran,' I say now, rising from the swing. 'It's best – it's always been best – if you just don't concern yourself with it.

Things happen, things don't happen. It all just happens. Don't think on it.'

'What does that mean?' he asks.

'It means…' the stress of the evening is starting to slow my thoughts '…it means that there are things, that there have always been things, that you need to turn a blind eye to.'

'Is that not forgetting, but?' he asks. 'Is that not the very opposite of what you were only just now saying?'

'There are things to remember and things to forget,' I say.

'Who decides which is which, though?'

I turn from the playground, I fumble my keys from my handbag. Andrea might not have left yet, but she'll leave soon enough. She'll leave soon enough and then I can draw a bath – *opening her eyes, then, she let out her breath in one stretched, distorted, bubbling scream* – can seat myself on the sofa, close my eyes, and decide what to remember and what to forget.

'Aoife?' Ciáran calls after me.

'No,' I reply, softly, and keep on walking.

~~James Bew~~

~~Roger Armstrong~~

~~Eddie Ross~~

~~Keith Sinclair~~

~~John Fyfield Senior~~

~~John Fyfield Junior~~

~~David Meters~~

Aaron Morrow

Raymond Patterson

Robert Marchetti.

Nigel.

I'm out in a pub on the edge of the Rathcoole estate in Newtonabbey, sipping at my vodka-tonic and trying not to reciprocate whenever Aaron sets to giggling. He's a wile infectious laugh and this smile-dimple on his left cheek that has no match on the right. A crooked smile and a crooked sense of humour, he has. We've been sitting here for the best part of an hour, and he's been slegging the rest of the punters for the duration: 'Jesus,' he says, 'with the nose on her you'd be able to smell if Mrs Singh in Mumbai had put the curry on,' and, 'If that lad was wanting to steal my curtains for his shirt I only wish he'd have asked first.' He's barely looked at me, but he's got me so as my sides are hurting from laughing and so as more tonic bubbles seem to have fizzed up my nose than down my throat. It's a shame I'm needing to kill him, really, because he's good craic. In spite of all he's done, he's good craic.

'Are you serious?' he says, looking at me now, one of my own imperfections on display. 'Never once in your life?'

'Not once.'

'That's like living in Paris and never being up the Eiffel Tower, or – '

'I've never been to Paris either, now you mention it.'

'We'll leave that for another day.' He winks. 'Let's start with this one.'

The wink leaves me confused for a moment – *face reddening* – and he continues by shaking his head until his dark curls dislodge from their neat side-parting – *a flush and flutter came over her* – and then he stares at me, not unkindly, with those

314

grey eyes of his, until I nearly forget what it is he's done to get himself on Baldy's list, until I nearly forget why it is I'm here and what it is I've to do.

'You've never been up Cave Hill?' he says again. 'Never once?'

'You say it as if I've missed out on a rite of passage.'

'But you have, Cassie – that's exactly it.' He looks about himself, checks his watch, feels for his wallet, all with the impatient energy of someone twenty years younger. 'We're going to sort it, that's what we'll do. Right now. We're going to get ourselves a carryout and walk up Cave Hill.'

'Actually,' I try to slip into seductress mode, 'I was thinking we could – '

'I'll not take no for an answer,' he says, smiling. 'You might as well save your breath. We're taking a walk up Cave Hill. Not far up, like, just so as you can see the city from above.'

I can't help but smile back. 'OK,' I say. 'Just let me get freshened up first.' I rise and lift the miniature tonic bottle from the table. 'I'll only be a minute.'

'I'll get us a bottle of vino to take with us,' he says, leaping to his feet and near sprinting ahead of me to the bar.

'I'll meet you outside, then,' I call, suddenly aware that I'll be needing to warn Baldy of this change of plan, to explain that I'm not wanting to stiff this one in the back of the taxi – *I lift my arm again. And again. The taxi swerves as Baldy calls out* – or out in the house in Whiteabbey that Benny's prepared – *single mattress by the radiator in the upstairs bedroom. Bare. With a bottle of whiskey beside it.* With this one, I'll tell him, I want to do it out in the middle of nowhere, on the top of Cave Hill. Where no one will hear his screams for mercy. He deserves it, I'll say, after what he's done.

'Where's Morrow?' Baldy asks, as soon as I open the door of the taxi.

'Wee change of plan...' I say. I've a shard of glass tucked into the top of my tights, but in my hurry to get out to the taxi before Morrow I've not positioned it well and it's grazing against my stomach. 'I'm going to take him up Cave Hill and do it there – '

I've no time to explain it further, to expand on the details. Aaron opens the door, flourishes the bottle of wine and climbs in. 'Good work finding a taxi,' he says. 'I've got all the other necessaries.'

I nod. 'Driver,' I say to Baldy. 'We're going to take a wee walk up Cave Hill – will you drive us there, please?'

'You're sure?' he says, his eyes searching out mine in the rear-view mirror. 'No other stops along the way?'

'Just the car park near the adventure playground,' Aaron says, leaning forward. 'Can you believe that this one has never been up there?'

'Is that right?' Baldy replies. 'And do I want to know what it is that you two'll be doing up there, or is it X-rated?'

I laugh, but it's uneasy. I'm needing to find a way of letting him know that I'll go through with it, that I'll go through with it rightly, but that I want to do it this way, to do it on my own terms.

'This one,' I nod across at Aaron, 'might be getting ideas, but don't you worry, I'm the one in charge.'

'As it should be,' Baldy replies, as Aaron chuckles away. Then he starts the engine and we're off on a journey out into streets and countryside that I don't know, that I've never seen before. Even from the road Belfast is spread out beneath us, an intricately woven blanket of lights.

Once we're out of the taxi and walking, we only make it a short distance up the path before I'm out of breath and craving a rest. Aaron teases me about it, but does so gently, leaning towards me in the dusky half-light and offering me first a piggy-back and then a Zimmer frame. I settle for a seat in amongst the heather and a drink from the bottle of red wine, with the cork pushed down into it, that Aaron hands across.

'Beautiful from up here, isn't it?' he says.

I look down on Belfast. The stitched lines of lights, the crocheted circles, fade off into countryside on one side and reflect out into the water of the harbour on the other. They unravel and fray as they stretch along the coast towards Whiteabbey, where we're meant to be. From this distance, at this height, it looks like any other city.

'It is,' I say, passing him the wine. 'Save for the Eiffel Tower, it could be Paris.'

'You can't see the murals from up here, can't feel the claustrophobic streets. From up here you'd never know that one area is UVF and the housing estate beside is IRA. You'd never know. They all just look like streets and houses.'

There's silence for a moment. I listen to it, and realise that it's only on the rare occasion that I'd hear silence. Actual and absolute. No murmur of telly, no distant shout, no beat of music. None of that. No sirens, no gunfire. None of that either. No screams in the night.

'You were in the UDA,' I say. It's not a question.

'I was,' he replies, handing me the bottle again. I can tell that he's looking across at me, but I can't see his features in the near-darkness. 'How do you know that?'

I shrug. He probably can't see it, but he'll have sensed the movement.

'Does that trouble you?' he asks.

'Are you still in it?'

'No,' he says. 'I left after my wife died.'

I pause, I bring the bottle to my lips again. There was no mention of a dead wife in Baldy's notes, no indication that he's a widower. Baldy just neatly noted Morrow's crimes, filled an A4 sheet with them.

'How did she die?' I ask. Thinking of Baldy leads me to wonder whether he's followed us up the path, whether he's lurking somewhere in the night, with his safety off, listening to our conversation.

'Cancer,' Aaron says. 'In the early Nineties. '92.'

If Baldy is close by he'll be cursing me for all of this, for engaging in conversation when I should be seeing to Morrow and then putting a bit of distance between myself and the body.

For filling the silence with whispers instead of cries of pain.

'I was in prison when she died,' Aaron continues. 'That's the greatest regret of my life. To think of her in agony, at death's door, and not to be with her. And it was my fault, as well, that I wasn't with her. Because of what I'd done, I couldn't care for her.'

'She was the reason you walked away, then?'

I pass him the bottle. Our fingers touch, briefly.

'I started thinking,' he continues. 'In prison. About all the grief that I'd caused. And the most of it I could see the reasoning for; the most of it I could justify, for right or wrong, in one way or another. But the pain I put my wife through – it was too close, too personal.'

I look down at Belfast, with the artificial stars of its streets and cul-de-sacs, its terraced houses and its huddled estates, then up at the night sky with its stars near-obscured by the bleed of light from below. Except for out here, directly above us, where the stars form into seemingly random shapes that – if I'd ever learnt – I could trace, that I could make sense of.

'Can I ask you to do something, Cassie?' Aaron asks.

I nod, but I am silent. I stretch out on my back, look up at the night sky and ignore Belfast beneath me.

'Think of one person,' he says. 'One person down there who's carried on regardless. Through all the violence, all the pain of it. One person who never complains or bears a grudge. Is there someone like that you can think of?'

I think. I struggle with it. But there's always Becky, who's always kept herself to herself, who only lets her grief out in the simplest of gestures, in spite of all she's seen and heard. In spite of all she might suspect, all she might know without fully knowing.

'Right,' Aaron says. 'Now think of one person down there who's bitter to the bone, one person who lets it eat away at them and who infects everyone else with their hatred.'

There's no struggle to this one, no contest. It's me. It's myself. I'm the one who comes to mind – *fuck you and yours, for all you've done* – all the other worthy candidates pale in comparison.

'Now tell me, Cassie,' Aaron says. 'Which of those two people would you rather be?'

I don't answer. I can't answer. The quiet on the hillside seems oppressive now – it chokes me.

'My wife was the first of those two people,' Aaron says. 'And I was the second. Yet she got cancer and I live on. Where's the fairness to that? So, after she died, I decided to at least try to act as she did, to think as she had.'

I sit up, quickly. Nausea. I lean back on my elbows, I peer into the darkness, over to where Aaron Morrow is. At the angle I'm sitting, I can feel the shard of glass jutting into my skin just below my hipbone. It's broken the skin: I can feel the wetness of blood.

I wonder if Aaron regrets what he's done. I wonder if he'd welcome the prospect of death – if it would be a release to have someone decide his punishment for him. He's said nothing about his victims, save for his wife... nothing about what he's done in the past.

'Can I ask you to do something in return, Aaron?' I say.

'Of course.'

'I need to leave – '

He begins to protest, but I reach across and stop him with a hand that rests first on his elbow and then on his arm.

'I need to leave,' I repeat. 'And I want you to sit there and finish that bottle of wine without following me. OK?'

'But why?'

'I have a reason, trust me.'

'Can I see you again?'

He reaches out to me, thinking he can get the consolation of a kiss or, at the very least, a quick embrace. But I've risen and I'm already away, stumbling back down the uneven path, tripping on stones and tufts of coarse grass, with only momentum keeping me steady on my feet. I hum as I walk, a tuneless murmur that might come from some half-remembered song from the radio but which has no melody and no words. I hum it so as I don't have to listen to the silence, so as I don't have to hear his footsteps running down the path behind me, or the firing of a shot, then maybe a second following it – *to make sure*. So as I don't have to hear whether my gesture – my gesture of mercy, of clemency – has been taken up.

'I thought you'd have followed us up?' I say to Baldy as I climb into the back of the taxi. It's in the car park, where I left it, and Baldy's in the driver's seat, where I left him, shrouded in cigarette smoke. 'Did you not follow us up?' I ask.

'Is it done?' he asks, starting the engine.

'It's done,' I reply, avoiding his gaze. 'It's done.'

~~James Bew~~

~~Roger Armstrong~~

~~Eddie Ross~~

~~Keith Sinclair~~

~~John Fyfield Senior~~

~~John Fyfield Junior~~

~~David Meters~~

Aaron Morrow

Raymond Patterson

Robert Marchetti.

Nigel.

They suspend the Northern Irish Assembly elections, not for the first time, in the spring of 2003, leaving Auntie Eileen so raging that she tells all within hearing distance that she's half a mind to hike up to the hills herself so as she can personally put the rest of the Provos' guns 'beyond use'. If need be, she's willing to take Dr Paisley along with her, as well, so as he can't gripe about there being no proof of it and then go on to preach about the deceitful nature of the Catholic folk.

She seems to take all the delays and objections personally, does Eileen, as if she's thinking that Blair is sitting there in Downing Street thinking up inventive ways of keeping her from becoming an MLA. It's probably not far wrong, in all honesty, in that there's probably cabinet meetings where they discuss how to keep Sinn Féin from power without fucking up their precious Agreement – how to keep this new government free from the undesirables – gunmen and women – who'll be voted into the Assembly even if the blood still stains their hands.

I'm not concerning myself with any of that there political shite, in any case; I'm not for worrying as to whether devolution will ever take hold. That's beyond my pay grade. For me, it's fretting about whether Baldy will find out that Morrow is still living and breathing, still able to stand as a viable candidate for election. It's trying to keep Baldy from his desire to move on to the next name on the list – Raymond Patterson – and trying to explain away the fact that I've been avoiding Baldy, steering clear of the bunker we share, and spending all of my nights at my childhood home with my vacant mammy and my vagrant daddy.

All the rest of my time is taken up by Gilt Edge. I've put a brave bit of effort into the business these last months, working on commissioning a wee website so as we can move into the twenty-first century and advertising for an apprentice to come and work with us, someone who can spend a few days a week in the shop and a couple of days up at the college learning jewellery-making. Becky seems bemused by all the attention I'm giving the business, by all the plans I'm putting in place and all the hours I'm spending in the shop, chatting to the customers, keeping her company while she toils away at her workbench and doing a passable impression of running the place.

'There was a fella in here asking after you this morning,' she says to me, one day in early June. I'm only just back from sorting out the ownership documents for Gilt Edge, from making sure that Becky would be sole proprietor if anything were to happen to me – *at some point, you'll either get caught or killed* – so I'm preoccupied and I don't take her up on it at first. 'Nice-looking,' she adds softly, her eyes never leaving her work.

'Who is?' I ask, catching on.

'The fella asking after you.'

'In here?'

She nods. My mind races over the possibilities – peeler, MI5, Provo, Loyalist – before narrowing to individuals – Baldy, Aaron, Nigel.

'Looked young,' she says. Not Baldy, then. Maybe Aaron, maybe Nigel. Maybe an unknown.

'Belfast accent?'

'Aye.' Probably not MI5. Maybe Provo, maybe Loyalist, maybe peeler.

'Dark hair?'

A quiet nod.

'Muscles?'

323

A shrug.

'Tattoos?'

'I think so, maybe.' She pauses, considers. 'On the arm, maybe.'

Nigel has tattoos. I've never seen Aaron's arms; he had them covered with a long-sleeved shirt that night at the bar and he put on his coat when we started up Cave Hill. He's bound to have tattoos, though, if he's ex-UDA.

I send up a silent prayer that it was Aaron who came calling. Aaron rather than Nigel. Of the two, I hope to God it's him.

'What did you tell him, Becky?' I ask.

She looks up sharply, surprised by the tone of my voice. Abrupt, it is, harsh and accusatory. Here's me trying to be nice to her these past weeks, as well, and then I near bite her head off of her at the first opportunity.

'I told him nothing,' she says, in a hurt voice. 'And he never said what it was he was wanting, or left a card or anything.'

'Right.' I wait, I watch her fiddling with her soldering-iron. 'Becky?'

'Yes?'

'Has Ciáran said anything to you about me? Recently.'

'Like what?'

I study her, but she's only showing me the top of her head. She works on through the silence – *tension to all of her movements* – without saying another word. If she knows about the list, if she knows what I do of an evening, then she's not for letting on, she's not for acknowledging it.

'Nothing,' I say. 'Never mind.'

I'm on the verge of saying something more, of reaching out to her. I'm wanting at the very least to tell her that it'll all be alright, that – no matter what – she'll be provided for. Even in my head it sounds wick. So I just leave her be. I leave her to her work and I retreat to the back shop to consider who it was that paid me a visit: unknown peeler, unknown Provo, known Loyalist.

My first instinct is to make myself scarce – *pack a bag, then. A light one* – take myself off to somewhere quiet and remote – *nothing for miles but sheep, sagging telephone wires and a solitary farmhouse*. After I've sat for a moment, though, and collected myself, I realise that I've no need to go reacting like that when I'm not even certain who it was that was asking after me. After all, I don't want to be running from shadows. It might have been the tax man or someone like that there – might have been nothing whatsoever to do with the list. It's worth looking into, at least, worth doing a wee bit of investigating before I go on the run over a visit from the gas man or take myself off into hiding because a salesman happened to call that morning.

'I'll be back shortly,' I say to Becky, in passing, as I leave the shop.

She seems to give the faintest of smiles at that – as if everything's back to normal. I let it pass without comment and hurry on to catch the bus out to the Shore Road.

'Cassie?' Aaron says, coming out from the back of the off-licence with a case of imported German beer. I've been busy browsing the whiskey selection for the best part of ten minutes, with his co-worker eyeing me from behind the counter. 'How are you?'

I nod, I smile. 'I'm good, yes. You?'

He ignores the question.

'What are you doing here?'

'Well…' I pause. 'Looking for a bottle of whiskey for my dad. It's his birthday coming up.'

'Right.' He looks disappointed by that. 'Let's see what we can find for you, then.'

For the next few minutes he lifts bottles from the shelf, passes them to me so as I can examine the label and then sets them back. It's like when we sat on the hillside and shared the wine, except that the alcohol never leaves the bottle. The conversation suffers for it.

'Listen,' I say, eventually, 'have you been asking after me?'

He grins, but it's uncertain. 'How d'you mean?'

'Have you been making enquiries about me?'

'Jesus!' He laughs. '"Making enquiries" sounds a bit grand. I've asked a couple of friends about you, is all.'

'This is important.' I've a firm grip on a bottle of Bowmore. 'I need to know. Did you visit my shop this morning?'

'Your shop?'

'Did you? It's important.' It's fucking vital.

If it wasn't you –

If it wasn't –

If it was –

He shakes his head. 'I never even knew you had a shop.'

It was Nigel. It was an unknown. It was a peeler, or a Provo, or a Loyalist. It was someone who knows about the list, someone who sees me for what I am. If it wasn't you, Aaron, then it was someone worse. Not the gas man, or the tax inspector. It was someone about the list. Someone who'd not give Becky their card, who'd not tell her what it was they wanted. Someone who was wanting to find out about me, searching me out because of who I am and what I do.

And, in spite of all you've done, Aaron, I was hoping it was you.

'Right,' I say, doing my best to share a smile with him. 'Never mind, then. Listen, I'll take a bottle of the Highland Park, OK?'

'Can I ask you,' he says. 'About that night...' His voice drops to a whisper. 'Is it because of my past? Is that why you left?'

'In a way,' I reply.

'I thought so.'

He holds the bottle out to me, but he keeps a hold on it himself as well, so as our fingers are near touching at the neck of it.

'Can I buy you a drink, maybe, and explain?'

'You've nothing to explain.'

'Can I buy you a drink anyway?'

I think. I nod.

'What harm can it do?' I say.

He mitches off work the rest of the afternoon and we go into the city centre and find ourselves a quiet bar to get drunk in. I'm drinking to forget, to keep from thinking about my mystery visitor. Aaron, for his part, is drinking to keep up with me. He's a fair task on his hands. I drink straight whiskey, sampling each of the single malts on the menu and then returning to the top of the list once I reach the bottom. No expense spared. No tonic bottles in sight. This is a drinking session designed to obliterate memories, to kill as many brain cells as possible and to leave those that remain teetering on the edge of a black hole.

By closing time, we're both stocious. I hang onto Aaron's arm as we stumble out into the night air, and he holds the two of us upright against the outside wall of the pub. We hail a taxi and he tries to package me off into it, tries to kiss me goodnight and leave it at that. I'm not for letting him go, though. I've dug my nails into the cloth of his jacket and I'm for clinging on until the last thread. There's a safety to being with him, certainly. There's a sense in me that whoever it is who's looking for me won't step out of the shadows when I've Aaron on my arm. There's this idea in my head that as long as I'm not alone then I can't be targeted, that there's safety in numbers. But there's more to it than that and all.

It's not a fear of the shadows that leads me to give my real address to the taxi driver; it's not because I'm shit-scared that I bribe my daddy with the bottle of Highland Park and quieten my mammy with an extra pill or two. It's not for security that I take Aaron Morrow upstairs, to my childhood bed, and tear at his clothes until there's enough of him showing for me to fuck – *urgent and unpunctuated by caressing or whispering* – until there's enough of him inside me to cause me to gasp and to moan and to cry out and to bite at his lip until I draw blood. It's not a need for security that draws me to him afterwards, that leaves me lying in his arms. It's not worry that leads me to think of all the unspeakable things that he's done and compare them with all the unspeakable things that I've done. It's not fear that leaves me lying awake in the darkness, listening to his shallow breathing as he slides towards sleep –

It's the beginning of tenderness.

~~James Bew~~

~~Roger Armstrong~~

~~Eddie Ross~~

~~Keith Sinclair~~

~~John Fyfield Senior~~

~~John Fyfield Junior~~

~~David Meters~~

Aaron Morrow

Raymond Patterson

Robert Marchetti.

Nigel.

It's several months before Baldy pulls me up on it. He was bound to find out. Truth be told, I'm surprised it's taken him this long. The elections are back on by the time he marches into the back office of Gilt Edge. The question of decommissioning has been sorted – to everyone's dissatisfaction – before he gets around to seating himself on my chair, swinging his legs up onto the desk and lighting himself a cigarette. He takes off his tinted glasses and sets them on the keyboard of the computer.

'Make yourself at home, why don't you?' I say sarcastically, standing on the other side of the desk and feeling at a disadvantage even though I'm technically looking down on him. I've not seen him for a couple of weeks, not since he arrived with a document detailing the movements of Raymond Patterson, and I'm not looking forward to hearing what he has to say for himself now.

'You've been on some dates,' he says, pausing to blow smoke at me. 'With a dead man.'

Fuck. I knew it was coming at some stage, but I still find myself at a loss as to how to answer. Confirm, deny, throw the (accounts) book at him? When has he even seen us? I've been so careful to make sure that we've not been watched, that we've not been followed. That dinner we had down in the Cathedral Quarter. That trip we took to Ballycastle to visit the seaside. Those drinks we had in the new cocktail bar in the old newspaper office. I was so careful, so watchful. Then again, there were also those nights when Aaron came over to the house. Those evenings when we wandered down the street, arm in arm, to get ourselves fish and chips, or to visit the video store. At times, I near forgot that we weren't meant to be seen together. At times, it slipped my mind that I was meant to have killed him that night up on Cave Hill. And Aaron, to be fair to him, had an excuse for not acting the part – he'd never been informed of his own death.

'Have you forgotten what he's done?' Baldy asks.

I shake my head. I haven't.

'Kidnap, torture, murder, rape, mutilation of a corpse.' He counts them off on his fingers and makes a fist of them. He brings it down against the wooden table. Then he starts on the other hand. 'Possession of a Class A drug, possession of an unlicensed firearm, armed robbery, assault with a deadly weapon, money laundering.' He runs out of fingers. 'Desecration of a grave.'

'I know,' I say. 'It's just – '

'There's a reason he's on the list.'

'I know. It's just – '

'What?'

'None of it shocks me any more, Sean. You list off his crimes like that, and you could list his victims as well, but it's all just words. I'm numb to it.'

'Is that right?' He rises from the chair, comes around the desk and stands just inches from me. 'How about specific details, then? How about the house up in Turf Lodge he broke into in 1990. Eileen McCormack. A Catholic grandmother in her sixties caring for her twelve-year-old grandson. Three of them gang-rape her, make the grandson watch and then shoot the two of them, leaving them for dead. Only the young lad isn't killed. He's left paralysed. Bed-bound for the rest of his life, shitting himself and screaming while the image of his grandmother being raped replays on a constant loop in his head. Is that real enough for you?'

'It's brutal,' I say. 'It's horrific.'

'And?' Baldy cups my chin with his hand and looks into my eyes. Once it would have been a gentle gesture. I've felt his touch before – his body pressing against mine, his breathing heavy. I've known this man as a lover, I know near every centimetre of his body – *trace the scar up near his collarbone with the tip of my finger* – yet I don't know him. I know what he's capable of, I know what he's done, I know he's to be feared – but I don't know him.

'He's a changed man,' I say, trying to keep the tremor from my voice. 'I'm not saying what he did should be forgotten, only that we need to understand what led him to it – '

He lets me go with this flick of the wrist that snaps my neck back and sends me stumbling backwards. I fall against the filing cabinet. Leaning against it, I face him, determined to stay upright, determined to look him in the eye.

'I should have known,' he says. 'I should have fucking known – '

I stay silent, watch him pacing. I know that he's a gun tucked in at the waistband of his jeans and I keep an eye on his hands – clenching and unclenching by his sides – to see if he makes a move for it.

'Stupid fucking cunt,' he hisses. 'Stupid fucking sentimental cunt. Can't keep your fucking biological clock out of it. Can't listen to sense, only your fucking ovaries.'

'It's not – ' I begin. I want to tell him that this isn't because I'm a woman, that it's not some innate motherly instinct coming out in me. I've been front-and-centre for the violence, I want to say; I've done things that no one with any shred of humanity should be doing. It's the fact that I'm a human that makes it all so shocking. Leave my gender out of it.

'You're doing it,' Baldy says, coming close again. He looms over me, the spittle of his words landing on my forehead. 'This very week. I've set it all up for this Wednesday, for the day of the election. And you'll go through with it.'

I shake my head. The tears are coming now, I can feel them.

'No, Sean,' I say. 'We've seen to most of the list; can we not just – '

'It's not about the list any more,' he hisses.

'I've done my part, I've – '

'No loose ends, remember.' He puts his forehead against mine, so as we're near enough eyeball to eyeball. Once it would have been intimate. I can see every shading of his green irises, every burst blood vessel in his eyes.

'He's not a loose end, Sean,' I say. 'He's never known what it was that I was planning that night, and he never will. I promise you.'

'Not him,' he says. 'You.'

The tobacco-scented word transfers itself from his lips to mine. It travels down through me as a chill, as a shiver that seems to follow the line of my spine.

'And you've only broken glass to protect yourself, don't forget,' he says. 'I wouldn't fancy your chances if I was to come after you.'

I swallow. 'You wouldn't.'

He nods. 'You're a liability, love. And this is a war. You can't have liabilities in a war.'

'It's not a war – the war's over. You're the only one still fighting.'

He doesn't answer, but his gaze never wavers, never falters, never softens. I close my eyes, but when I open them again he's still there and his face remains, unchanged and unchanging, just inches from my own.

'There's no room for compromise here?' I ask. 'No room for – '

He shakes his head. 'This very week, you're doing it,' he says. 'This Wednesday.'

I nod.

As he leaves, I slide down the filing cabinet until I'm sat on the ground at the base of it. I raise my hands to my head and begin parting the hair with my fingernails – *her hands went up and she began clutching and clawing at her hair, lifting fistfuls of it out by the roots* – until I can feel the scalp showing through. A thin wailing cry comes from my throat – *a pitiful wee whine* – building to a full-throated scream. And through the blurred vision of my tears I see Becky coming into the room and kneeling before me. Through the numbness I feel her fold me into an embrace.

'It's OK,' she whispers to me. 'It'll all be alright.'

~~James Bew~~

~~Roger Armstrong~~

~~Eddie Ross~~

~~Keith Sinclair~~

~~John Fyfield Senior~~

~~John Fyfield Junior~~

~~David Meters~~

Aaron Morrow

Raymond Patterson

Robert Marchetti.

Nigel.

The house is in Stranmillis, at the end of a quiet street called St Albans Gardens. I tell Aaron that I'm buying it, that I've had an offer accepted for it. That's my cover story. I want to show him around, I say, to get his seal of approval. We'll go for food afterwards, I tell him, and make a day of it. We'll celebrate with a steak and a nice bottle of wine. I've visited the boutique next to Gilt Edge earlier in the week and bought myself a red dress and a white fabric belt. For the occasion.

We walk, hand in hand, from room to room. *Nice wainscoting*, he says… *you've a banister loose there… you could think about an extension out the back beyond the kitchen. The bathroom needs tiling*, he says – *I could do that for you.* I nod; I return his grin as best I can. But we're getting ever closer to the front bedroom and the brand new mattress that's been laid out, close to the radiator, in preparation for our visit.

'This is my only piece of furniture, so far,' I say, pointing to it.

He smiles, he circles an arm around my waist.

'I thought we could celebrate, that we could christen – '

I don't need to finish my sentence, though. He doesn't need convincing. He's leading me, he's kissing me and unbuckling my belt. He's not realising the danger he's in, not realising what the mattress signifies.

I take control. Pushing him, gently, down onto the mattress, I straddle him and stretch his arms back until the wrists are next to the radiator pipes. Then I cradle his cheek with my hand and look down at his face – his gaze is open and trusting, loving even. With quick movements I tie him to the radiator

336

with my belt. He lets out a wee chuckle at that, his eyes glinting and his breaths sharpening in anticipation.

'This is the best I can do,' I say to him, leaning over to kiss him on the lips. I rise and readjust my dress. Then I turn from him and leave the room. He calls after me, but I keep walking, down the stairs and out of the front door. I've given him a fighting chance, I tell myself – *mercy, clemency* – he might not work himself free, his cries might not be heard – *mercy, clemency* – but I've come as close to sparing him as I can manage.

My footsteps quicken as I step outside. There's a phone box on the other side of Stranmillis Road and I make my way towards it. Once there, I lift change from my purse – *clink the coins into the slot* – and dial. My fingers shake, but I've only three numbers to press – only the same button three times. I tell the operator the address of the house, I tell them that a man's being held there against his will. I hang up when they start asking questions.

I pause, I hesitate, I listen to the disconnected tone.

My finger hovers over the 'follow-on call' button. These few seconds could be vital, could be life and death. The peelers might well think it's a hoax, might take their time in making sure that it's not a trap, might be busy on the night of the election with ferrying the politicians from place to place, with making sure that there's not riots as the two sides – so long at each other's throats – line up to place their votes in the same ballot box.

I breathe deeply, then press the button. This call is short, even shorter than the first. 'I've left him at the house,' is all I say. 'You do it.'

After hanging up, I lean my head against the side of the phone box. It's not what I was expecting, though; it doesn't have the cold resistance of glass. The plastic gives slightly and warms to the heat from my forehead.

It'll work itself out, I think. Aaron might free himself... the peelers might get there first... the peelers might get there after Baldy, even, and still be in time to save him. There's nothing concrete yet, nothing set in stone. There's any number of possibilities, any number of combinations, and they'll sort themselves out without me. Without Cassie. Without Aoife.

As I step outside the phone box, I feel a hand on my shoulder. An arm wraps itself around my neck, pulling me back into a headlock. I squint down – *Red Hand tattoo on his bicep* – and then feel myself being half lifted, half pulled back into a doorway. He presses me against the wood, raises the gun from his side and sets it against my forehead. The metal bites into the skin, but I'm grateful that it's not a knife, or a shard of broken glass. It'll be over quickly.

'Cassie,' Nigel says. 'I've been watching you. I've been waiting.'

I watch him. I wait.

'Bet you never expected me to catch up with you, eh?' he snarls. 'Bet you thought this day would never come.'

No, I say to myself. I expected it. I knew this day would come. It's just been a long time coming, that's all –

I stay silent; I close my eyes. I think of Aaron in the house not far from me – as trapped as I am, as certain that this is the end. Except there's just a possibility, just the slightest hope, just the smallest chink of light –

I clear my head and make my peace. It will soon be over. This is how it ends.

Acknowledgements

This novel was written during my time at the University of Surrey and I owe a debt of gratitude to the staff and students for making the experience of researching and teaching on the English Literature programme such a pleasure. In particular, thanks to Dr Paul Vlitos, Dr Churnjeet Mahn, Dr Fiona Doloughan, Gavin Goodwin, Amanda Finelli, Claire Turner and Scott Collier.

I would also like to extend my thanks and appreciation to the wonderful team at Myriad Editions: Candida Lacey, Corinne Pearlman, Adrian Weston, Emma Dowson, Anthony Grech-Cumbo, Linda McQueen, Dawn Sackett and, especially, my marvellous editor Vicky Blunden.

Through the years I have been fortunate to have studied with some excellent writing groups, on my BA at Queen's Belfast and during my M.Litt at Glasgow University. Thanks to all those fantastic writers and to the tutors, including Glenn Patterson, Daragh Carville, Alan Bissett, Michael Schmidt and Zoe Strachan. Thanks also to Valerie Thornton, for first publishing my work, and to John Fulton for encouraging my early efforts.

Finally, I have a superb group of friends from both Glasgow and Belfast, too numerous to mention, and I would like to thank each and every one of them, as well as my parents, Ann and Charles, who have always supported my creative endeavours, and my sister, Katy, whose hard work and dedication has always been an inspiration.

Most of all, my love and gratitude to my beautiful bride, Orla.

MORE FROM MYRIAD EDITIONS

MORE FROM MYRIAD EDITIONS

MORE FROM MYRIAD EDITIONS

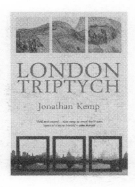

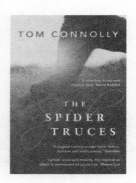